An
Onshore
Storm

Also by Dewey Lambdin

The King's Coat

The French Admiral

The King's Commission

The King's Privateer

The Gun Ketch

H.M.S. Cockerel

A King's Commander

Jester's Fortune

King's Captain

Sea of Grey

Havoc's Sword

The Captain's Vengeance

A King's Trade

Troubled Waters

The Baltic Gambit

King, Ship, and Sword

The Invasion Year

Reefs and Shoals

Hostile Shores

The King's Marauder

Kings and Emperors

A Hard, Cruel Shore

A Fine Retribution

An Onshore Storm

An Alan Lewrie Naval Adventure

Dewey Lambdin

ST. MARTIN'S PRESS
NEW YORK

AN ONSHORE STORM. Copyright © 2018 by Dewey Lambdin. All rights reserved. Printed in the United States of America. For information, address St. Martin's Press, 175 Fifth Avenue, New York, N.Y. 10010.

www.stmartins.com

Maps by Cameron MacLeod Jones

Library of Congress Cataloging-in-Publication Data

Names: Lambdin, Dewey, author.
Title: An onshore storm : an Alan Lewrie naval adventure / Dewey Lambdin.
Description: First edition. | New York : St. Martin's Press, 2018. | Series:
    Alan Lewrie naval adventures ; [24]
Identifiers: LCCN 2017060756 | ISBN 9781250103642 (hardcover) |
    ISBN 9781250103659 (ebook)
Subjects: LCSH: Lewrie, Alan (Fictitious character)—Fiction. | Ship
    captains—Great Britain—Fiction. | Great Britain—History, Naval—19th
    century—Fiction. | GSAFD: Adventure fiction. | Historical fiction. | Sea stories.
Classification: LCC PS3562.A435 O57 2018 | DDC 813/.54—dc23
LC record available at https://lccn.loc.gov/2017060756

Our books may be purchased in bulk for promotional, educational, or business use. Please contact your local bookseller or the Macmillan Corporate and Premium Sales Department at 1-800-221-7945, extension 5442, or by email at MacmillanSpecialMarkets@macmillan.com.

First Edition: May 2018

10 9 8 7 6 5 4 3 2 1

This one is for Harry, even if he still won't answer to his name, a yearling ex-tom who is not familiar with the word "No!" either. He can get into *everything*, and be a pest when I'm shaving or brushing my teeth, but a lover and a lap fixture when he's done with his adventures. That black and white face with a grey nose, and those jade green eyes just may let him get away with murder!

Full-Rigged Ship: Starboard (right) side view

1. Mizen Topgallant
2. Mizen Topsail
3. Spanker
4. Main Royal
5. Main Topgallant
6. Mizen T'gallant Staysail
7. Main Topsail
8. Main Course
9. Main T'gallant Staysail
10. Middle Staysail
11. Main Topmast Staysail
12. Fore Royal
13. Fore Topgallant
14. Fore Topsail
15. Fore Course
16. Fore Topmast Staysail
17. Inner Jib
18. Outer Flying Jib
19. Spritsail

A. Taffrail & Lanterns
B. Stern & Quarter-galleries
C. Poop Deck/Great Cabins Under
D. Rudder & Transom Post
E. Quarterdeck
F. Mizen Chains & Stays
G. Main Chains & Stays
H. Boarding Battens/Entry Port
I. Cargo Loading Skids
J. Shrouds & Ratlines
K. Fore Chains & Stays
L. Waist
M. Gripe & Cutwater
N. Figurehead & Beakhead Rails
O. Bow Sprit
P. Jib Boom
Q. Foc's'le & Anchor Cat-heads
R. Cro'jack Yard (no sail fitted)
S. Top Platforms
T. Cross-Trees
U. Spanker Gaff

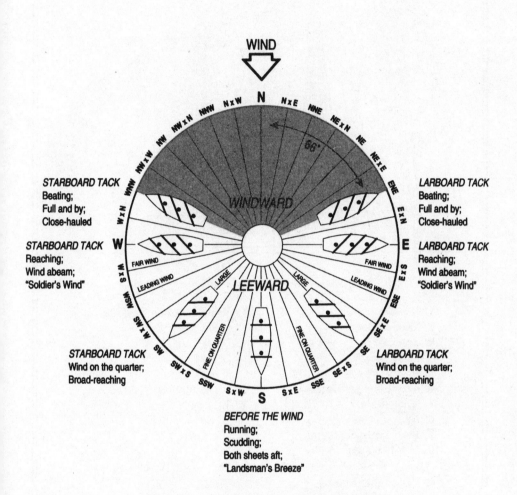

POINTS OF SAIL AND 32-POINT WIND-ROSE

ADRIATIC
SEA

Gaeta

Naples

Procida

Ischia

Nisida

Mt. Vesuvius

Capri

ITALY

BASILICATA
CAMPAGNIA

CALABRIA

Taranto

Gallipoli

*Golfo di
Taranto*

TYRRHENIAN SEA

Crotone

Catanzaro

Maida

Catanzaro
Lido

Golfo di Squillace

Aeolian
Islands

Tropea

*Vibo
Valentina*

Monasterace
Marina

Roccella
Ionica

Scylla

Siderno

Marina di
Gioiosa Ionica

Milazzo

Locri

Palermo

Messina

Reggio di
Calabria

Bovalino
Marina

Brancaleone
Marina

*Aspromonte
Mountains*

Cape Spartivento

SICILY

Mt. Etna

Catania

Syracuse

IONIAN SEA

*Mellieha
Bay*

MALTA

Valletta

Mi.   30   60

N

CALABRIA

N   Mi.   10   20

TYRRHENIAN SEA

IONIAN SEA

Cosenza

Appennino Meridionale

Crotone

St. Eufemia
Lamezia

Maida

Catanzaro

Filadelfia

Roman Bridge

Catanzaro Lido

Pizzo

Tropea

Vibo Valentia

Soverato

Golfo di Squillace

Rosarno

Aspromonte Mountains

Roccella
Ionica

Monasterace
Marina

Palmi

Marina di Gioiosa Ionica

Bagnara
Calabra

Aspromonte Mountains

Siderno

Locri

Messina

Scylla

Bovalino Marina

Bovalino

ITALY

Reggio di
Calabria

Brancaleone Marina

Brancaleone

Bova Marina

Melito di
Porto Salvo

*Cape
Spartivento*

Nec ista ratibus tanta construiturelucs;
terris minatur. Fluctus haud curso levi provolvitur;
nescio quid onerato sinu gravis unda portat. Quae
novum tellus caput ostendit estris?

Nor is that vast destruction piled up for ships; 'tis the
land it threatens. With no light sweep the flood rolls
forward; what new land shows its head to the stars?

—LUCIUS ANNAEAS SENECA,
HIPPOLYTUS, LINES 1017-21

BOOK ONE

Etsi me, verio iactatum laudis amore irritaque
expertum fallacis praemie vulgi—

Tossed though I am, this way and that by love of
renown, and knowing full well that the fickle
throng's awards are vain—

—PUBLIUS VERGILIUS MARO
CIRIS, LINES 1–2

CHAPTER ONE

*H*oly shi-i-i-t!" came a sudden wail.

"Clumsy bugger!" quickly followed, just before a thump.

"Arr!" from another startled throat, preceding a loud splash, which drew HMS *Vigilance*'s Captain from the forward edge of the quarterdeck to the larboard bulwarks so he could peer overside to find a cause for the commotion.

"Think we might've killed somebody, sir," Lt. Greenleaf, the ship's Third Officer exclaimed, standing on the slide of one of the 18-pounder carronades to look straight down the ship's side.

Vigilance's four 29-foot barges had been drawn up alongside, manned with oarsmen, tillermen, and a Midshipman each so the Marines could practice debarkation down boarding nets, then be rowed ashore.

"Oh, God's balls," Captain Sir Alan Lewrie, Baronet, groaned as he beheld the near-disaster. "Fetch that man out of the water before he drowns!" he shouted down.

One Marine had lost his grip and footing on the nets and had fallen straight into a barge. Fortunately for him, his shout had forewarned the boat crew, and his mates already in the boat, to catch him before he bashed his brains out on a gunn'l, sprawling everyone into a mound of arms, legs, and muskets. The other Marine who had fallen had just missed the same fate, and had plunged into the sea between two barges, had surfaced sputtering and coughing, and was being drawn to a barge's side and waiting hands to haul him up and drag him in. If he'd been carrying a rucksack full of rations, and eighty rounds of cartridge, as he would in a real landing, he might not have surfaced at all! As it was, his full service dress uniform, pipe-clayed cross-belts, and hat, rarely worn aboard ship except for sentry duty, got the worst of it.

"Alright, Private Quick?" Lewrie shouted down.

"Bathed, Captain sir!" Quick chirped back, which made everyone roar in relieved laughter. "Mother'd be happy!"

"Drill's cancelled," Lewrie snapped to Lt. Greenleaf. "Get 'em back inboard . . . if they can manage that without *more* casualties, that is. Christ, those damned nets!"

In 1807, off the southern Spanish Andalusian coast, boarding nets for the few troops that Lewrie had been allocated in one transport ship, re-enforced with the fifty Marines of his 50-gun ship, HMS *Sapphire*, had worked reasonably well in the raids they had undertaken, the quickest way that Lewrie could devise to get soldiers, sailors, and Marines ashore.

He returned to the middle of the quarterdeck and looked over at the three transports now under his command that lay at anchor in the sheltered bay below the Sicilian fishing port of Milazzo. Nets hung down their sides, too, but the troops of the under-strength 94th Regiment of Foot were ashore at their encampment for a day or two.

"Ahem, sir?" Lt. Greenleaf said, clearing his throat.

"Aye, Mister Greenleaf?" Lewrie said, allowing him to speak.

"It's the tumblehome, sir," Greenleaf said, "the transports are straight sided, for more cargo space, but *this* barge . . ." he ended in a hapless shrug.

"Aye, I know," Lewrie growled, recalling his own experience on the boarding nets a few weeks earlier.

Rear-Admiral Thomas Charlton's squadron, the troops and ships under Lewrie's command, and even more ships amassed to land Brigadier Caruthers's three full regiments had staged a massive raid all along the Italian shore, from the toe of the "boot" halfway up the insole, to take, sink, or burn the many large fishing vessels and coastal trader ships the French would use to make one more try to invade Sicily, and destroy the huge arms and supply depots assembled at the many small ports.

Lewrie had managed to get all of his soldiers, Marines, and armed sailors ashore in short order, whilst Brigadier Caruthers's troops had struggled, only managing to get two of his three regiments ashore and that after two *hours*. And, he *should* have withdrawn them once the Navy had accomplished its part in the mission, fired the depots, and gotten away cleanly. But, the stubborn sod wanted a battle just *so* perishing bad that he had stayed, sent out scouts who'd found him a column of French—foot, cavalry, and artillery—on its way to see what they could salvage. With no artillery of his own, the fool had signalled to *Vigilance* for gunners to man the heavy howitzers that he'd turned up in one of the depots.

Howitzers! Who knew the first thing about them, their fuses, and their use? Lewrie, for one; the *only* one! Against his better judgment, Lewrie had scrambled down a boarding net to board one of the ship's barges, which were just returning, and a proper disaster that had been!

Warships, proper warships built for the purpose and not taken into Navy service as converted and armed merchantmen, were the widest at their waterlines and lower gunwales. From there up they tapered in a sweet curve inwards, to reduce topweight and bring the guns of the upper gun-deck closer to the centreline to reduce the tendency to roll too much, and keep the heaviest weight as low as possible.

The effect of that laid the boarding nets so close to the hull that it was very difficult to get a toe-hold or hand-hold, even with no one else below him on the nets dragging them flush against wood.

Mind now, Lewrie had envisioned the boarding nets, but, being a Post-Captain of more than Three Years' Seniority in the Royal Navy, which *should* have given him some august dignity, he had never really *used* one 'til then.

Barely clinging by his fingernails, assaulted by his own rucksack, sword, canteen, pocketed pistols, and a rifled Ferguson musket, and cartridge boxes for the aforesaid weaponry, it had been a wonder that he hadn't fallen to his death into the barge, or gone into the sea like a loosed bower anchor. Even un-encumbered, he surely would have drowned, for Alan Lewrie was like many of his sailors—he'd never learned to swim! By the time one booted foot found purchase on the barge's gunn'l, he would have not trusted his arse with a fart!

"Maybe we need jacob's ladders, sir," Greenleaf suggested.

That made Lewrie scowl. In his early days in the Navy, and in smaller ships that did not have wooden boarding battens built onto the ships' sides, with man-ropes strung down each side for a grip, he'd had to use a jacob's ladder, a set of narrow wooden steps with stout ropes threaded through each end, prone to swinging free of the hull when the ship rolled, slamming back as it rolled to the other beam, and with a sickening ability to sway fore and aft as the ship hobby-horsed over the waves. The very idea made him shiver in dread!

"What we need is some way to fend the nets off the hull 'til our people get down to the lower gunwale," Lewrie said, instead, "so one can get firm hand-holds and several inches of free space for the soles of their shoes, so they can't slip off."

"Hmm," Greenleaf pondered, scratching idly on the side of his head. "Perhaps some baulks of timber to hold the nets well off, like the catheads that hold the anchors, sir? Gad, we'd look like a porcupine. They'd have to be permanent, else there's no way to secure 'em firm enough to take the weight of seventy Marines using them at the same time."

"Well, it's beyond me at the moment," Lewrie confessed, taking off his old cocked hat to swipe at his hair. "I haven't a clue as to how it could be done. Perhaps you and the other officers in the wardroom might mull it over."

"Ask of the Bosun and the Carpenter first, I'd imagine, sir," Greenleaf said. "Any way we accomplish it, it's certain to involve lumber."

"Aye, carry on, Mister Greenleaf," Lewrie agreed. "I'll be aft."

"Aye aye, sir," Greenleaf said, doffing his hat in salute as Lewrie made his way to the door to his great-cabins, but was halted by a cry from aloft of "Deck there! Some'un's wig-waggin' ashore at the Army camp!"

"Who's signals Midshipman of the Watch?" Lewrie barked.

"Me, sir," Midshipman Page, a lad of fourteen years, piped up.

"Well, read the signal, lad," Lewrie prompted.

"Should have seen it first, young sir," Greenleaf huffed.

"Aye aye, sir," Page said, reddening.

The 94th's encampment lay along the beach and stretched back inland for several hundred yards, into the fruit and olive groves. A signal mast had been erected right by the beach to speed communication 'twixt ships and shore without the need of shuttling boats. The Army had been loaned a rudimentary book of signals, and seamstresses in Milazzo had made up a flag locker full of the basics for the 94th to use.

"Ehm, ah . . . it is Send Boat, sir," Midshipman Page stammered. "And . . . Mail!"

"Must have sent a rider from Messina," Lt. Greenleaf supposed.

"Mail, well well!" Lewrie enthused. "See to it, Mister Greenleaf, and Mister Severance and I will sort it out. Carry on."

"Aye, sir!" Greenleaf replied, eager to have news from home as dearly as any man aboard.

CHAPTER TWO

*O*ne of the most frustrating things about being deployed on a foreign station was the irregular arrival of news from home, which had to be gathered and sorted at one of the naval dockyards before being loaded aboard a Post Packet, an outbound warship or transport going to a general area, or an overseas naval base where letters and newspapers could languish for weeks before being sent on.

If Lewrie's wee squadron had been at sea in company with a large portion of a fleet, they *might* have been able to count upon *somewhat* regular delivery, once a month or every two months.

Sailing and operating independently from Rear-Admiral Thomas Charlton's squadron, though, with only rare orders coming from that worthy, *Vigilance*'s mail normally came from Portsmouth to Gibraltar, thence to Malta where the larger squadron called and re-provisioned. It was only after that that someone thought to forward orders, bills, letters, and newspapers to the Army establishment at Messina and Sicily, and what was due the warship and her transports "piggy-backed" as an afterthought with the mail for the 94th Regiment of Foot, and that under-strength orphan unit was, as the General Commanding at Messina had made clear, definitely *not* on the ration strength of the British Army on Sicily. The 94th's provisions, replacement ammunition, and necessary supplies had to come from Malta, where they had been borrowed for Lewrie's "experiment"!

Indeed, whatever HMS *Vigilance* and her consorts required to keep the sea, feed their people, and continue operations forced them to leave Sicily and sail down to Malta to replenish at Valletta Harbour, leaving the 94th Foot twiddling their thumbs and "square-bashing" 'til the ships could return!

"Mail is forthcoming," Lewrie announced as he sat down behind his desk in the day-cabin, making temporary Sub-Lieutenant Severance, his cabin steward Deavers, and his cabin servants, Tom Dasher and George Turnbow, perk up with interest. Well, nothing would come for Dasher, an orphaned street waif in his mid-teens, but he could read, after a fashion, and could slowly devour the newspapers after everyone else was done with them.

Lewrie looked up from the correspondence that Severance had set into a neat pile for his approval, and fixed his gaze upon the portrait of his wife, Jessica, that hung on a forward bulkhead.

God, how I miss you! Lewrie thought, feeling a real pang of longing; *And how much I crave word from you! I'm a hopeless old colt's tooth, but . . .*

From the brief half-hour of their first meeting, Lewrie had been bemused by her, a young lady twenty years his junior, then, as they had exchanged letters over a year or so, he'd become intrigued, besotted, and hopeful, even though he knew how much a fool he'd look to even consider courting her. He'd been a widower too long, and too much at sea, with only one off-and-on mistress at Gibraltar, then at Lisbon.

Had it not been for his previous ship, HMS *Sapphire* losing her lower mainmast a second time in an epic fight with a big 40-gunned French frigate, he might still be at sea in her, but HM Dockyards at Portsmouth had stricken her and thrown him ashore on half-pay for what seemed an age, even if it was only a few months. During that time Jessica, a very talented artist (even if her Reverend father did not approve in the slightest!) had done his portrait, as she had offered early on in their letters, throwing them together daily, and he had slowly found the courage to admit to himself that he was, for good and all, in love with her as giddily as a schoolboy, and then the further courage to declare himself, and be both astonished and relieved that she had said yes, enthusiastically.

Seven months we had together, he mused to himself; *A joyous but short time, and then . . . damn yer blood, fool, you just* had *to bite at the bait of a new commission!*

But, it had been his plan, his scheme, to land troops, Marines, and armed sailors in quick in-and-out raids, and when given the chance to put it into operation, Lewrie simply *couldn't* refuse Admiralty . . . even though he'd regretted his decision as soon as *Vigilance* and her transports had pounded out into the open Atlantic.

Along with his pang of longing to be with her, Lewrie felt an equal twinge of guilt that his letters to her would be just as slow to arrive as hers would be, and that he could not write at least three letters a week to reassure her. The best he could do were very long "sea letters," page after page done a bit each day in the tiniest penmanship he could manage, the lines as close together as he could scribble, 'til they were not so much letters as hefty bundles, and sure to cost her dear when the Post Office in London sent them to their house in Dover Street, for it was the recipients that paid the post, not the senders.

"Will there be papers, d'ye think, sir?" Dasher asked.

"I hope so, Dasher," Lewrie told him.

"Good, 'cause I'm cur'yus 'bout wot Wellesley's doin' to th' French in Spain this Summer," Dasher said with an expectant grin.

"Enjoys the scandals, too, sir," Turnbow, an older lad, said with a wink in Dasher's direction. "You should subscribe to *The Tatler*, Tom."

"Likes t'read anything, now that I knows how better," Dasher said, ducking his head, and busying himself with tending to his pet doe rabbit, Harriet, that Lewrie allowed him to keep in the great-cabins alongside his cat, Chalky.

The mail sack was fetched aboard to cheers that Lewrie could hear in his great-cabins, cheers as enthusiastic as the appearance of the red and gilt rum keg when Clear Decks And Up Spirits was piped. It was carried aft to the quarterdeck with solemnity before the Marine sentry without the cabin door stamped boots and musket butt and cried its presence, to which Lewrie shouted "Enter!" most eagerly.

"Our mail, sir," Midshipman Fairfoot announced, hefting the sack with some difficulty with one hand, whilst doffing his hat with the other.

"And I am directed to convey word from the Third Officer that boats are coming alongside from the transports for their share of it, sir."

"Very good, Mister Fairfoot, plop it atop my desk, then carry on," Lewrie ordered.

God, it would be so tempting to undo the rope ties and delve into the contents that instant, strewing anything that was not his to the far corners of his cabins, but Lewrie nodded to his aide and clerk, Severance, to get on with it whilst he clasped greedy, eager hands in the small of his back and paced away aft to the transom and his stern gallery where he pretended to gaze shoreward.

Slowly, the mail was sorted out into piles for each ship, then *Vigilance*'s mail was divided into smaller heaps for the wardroom, the petty officers, the Midshipmen's cockpit, and the crew. Lewrie could not help peeking now and then to see if his stack was growing.

"All sorted, sir," Sub-Lieutenant Severance reported at last. "Should I summon the Mids in from the transports?"

"Aye, and let's hope they brought their own sacks," Lewrie said.

They did bring their own, and the Mids from *Bristol Lass,* the *Lady Merton,* and *Spaniel* quickly gathered their mail, doffed their hats, and departed for their boats quicker than one could say "Knife!" Severance stuck his head out the doors to summon *Vigilance*'s Mids standing Harbour Watch to carry the mail to be distributed, and only then could Lewrie pace back to his desk, sit down, and quickly sort through his own letters, looking for the official first.

"Well, damme," he muttered as he actually found one from Rear-Admiral Thomas Charlton. After a longing look at a promising pile of letters from Jessica, he broke the seal, spread it out, and leaned back in his chair to read it.

> *Gallant Capt. Lewrie,*
> *What a Feat we have wrought, sir! Our raids from Cape Spartivento*
> *East'rd all in one day was praised to the Skies by the Commanding Gen.*
> *on Sicily, as a Deed that utterly Scotched any hopes upon the part of the*
> *French to mount a seaborne invasion of the island for a long time into the*
> *future, a copy of which he has kindly sent me. Add Brigadier Caruthers's*
> *victory to that, damn fool though it was to delay and engage, and I'm*
> *told that Horse Guards, our Army, and the Secy of State for War are*

*mightily Impressed. So much so that St. James's Palace has seen fit to
make me a Knight of The Bath!*

  I vow I owe it all to you, you Rascal!

Lewrie whooped in glee, startling his cat, Dasher's rabbit, and his cabin
retinue. "The Admiral's to be knighted, lads, and we all have been called
heroes. Just damn my eyes!"

Charlton could not envision a future operation as vast as the last one,
but encouraged Lewrie and his wee squadron to strike while the iron was
hot (and supplies would be more readily forthcoming) and continue in their
endeavours to punish the French with future raids. If he needed additional
frigates or sloops to aid in that direction, Charlton would despatch what
he could spare from patrolling to aid him.

He laid that letter aside to file in his desk, and at last shuffled through
the many letters from his wife for the earliest. Oddly, he found one
addressed to Mr. Thomas Dasher.

"Dasher, you've a letter," he told him, bringing the lad's head up from
his squat in the corner where he'd been going through a London paper.

"A letter? *Me*, sir?" Dasher gawped.

"It seems Dame Lewrie has written you, lad," Lewrie said.

Dasher brushed his hands down his slop-trousers as if to clean them before hesitantly accepting the letter, eyes wide in wonder as Lewrie opened
his own.

Darling Husband,
*What a splendid Spring and Summer you are missing. I must take what
Delight I can from the Seasons to stave off my Intense Longing to see you
once more. I have never seen London so green, so many vivid floral
plantings, as if the city is one vast Botanical Show. Even despite my poor
talent at Gardening, our back garden flourishes most Vibrantly. Your
father says that it takes more than an hundred years to result in a good
English lawn, but he pronounced ours well on its way to a Semblance. He
has kindly offered to escort me on rides through Hyde Park at least twice a
week, rain permitting, and has proven to be most patient with my poor
seat and slow pace.*

That'd be t'get himself away from his house guests, Lewrie wryly thought.
Lewrie's daughter, Charlotte, was husband hunting for a second London

Season, and her presence meant that the Chiswicks were underfoot again, not only her Uncle Governour and Aunt Millicent but *their* oldest daughter, Diana, a girl Lewrie deemed as vapid as a flock of chickens; fetching enough, but silly and dumb. And with that crowd would come dressmakers, shoemakers, all sorts of tradesmen and women to make both girls as presentable as possible.

> *Thank the Lord dearest Alan, that I am not called upon to spend my days, and some nights, tending to their needs and wishes, for, at your wise Suggestion, I called upon your friend, Clotworthy Chute, seeking an "Amanuensis" (?) to fulfill the Duty, and he found a Way to approach Governour Chiswick and offer a quite Genteel older lady to be what your Father most amusingly called a "buttock broker."*

A retired whore, or brothel keeper, most-like, Lewrie thought, chuckling to himself.

> *Mrs. Boothby, the widow of an Army Colonel, has enthralled all, with her many Contacts in Polite Society, and the matches she has made in past. Even Governour did not balk at her Fee, which I am given to understand is rather steep.*

Lewrie had to stop reading and allow himself a good laugh; when given free rein, old Clotworthy Chute's skills as a "Captain Sharp," and a con man, were as keen as ever!

"Lookit, George," Dasher excitedly said to Turnbow, the other cabin servant, "she even drawed me a pitchure o' Bully, our ratter an' spit turner terrier!"

"Right kind of her, aye, Tom," Turnbow said, leaning over to look at the sketch. "Never met her, but she must be a fine lady to do that for ya. What she say, then?"

"Ehm, she ah . . . 'holds me in her mem-mem-or-y as a ch . . . cheer . . . cheerful lad, and in . . . includes me in her p . . . prayers t' be safe, an' serve th' Captain fai . . . faith-fully.' Imagine!"

Dasher turned his head to stare at Jessica's portrait on the forward bulkhead with adoration, flicking a tear from his eyes.

Returning to his own reading, Lewrie learned that Jessica had only done one portrait so far, but had earned £25 for it, and, with the proceeds from the ghastly book she'd illustrated, was doing quite nicely towards supporting herself and their household without the "pin money" set aside for her expenses.

In later letters, Jessica expressed some worry about her father, the Reverend Chenery. His brother at Oxford had been talking up an expedition to New England in America, and the Maritime Provinces in British Canada to search for proof that either the Romans, the Carthaginians, or the Phoenicians had reached the New World long before its official discovery, and that if he wanted to be a part of it, he would have to make a substantial contribution, which Jessica feared would be far beyond his means.

> *Father, poor Dear, sounds quite Beguiled by the Rumours, especially one in which a fleet of Templars left England for the New World, in emulation of Accounts of Viking voyages, and I dread his Restlessness to partake in the Adventure in Person, throw up his Position at Saint Anselm's and abandon his Flock.*
>
> *He has even hinted round importuning me for the Sum required, Alan! Does he write you asking for Money, pray Refuse him as firmly, but as gently, as possible!*

Damned right I will! Lewrie thought; *What utter rot! Pot o' gold at the end of the rainbow nonsense. They'll go grubbin' for the Holy Grail and the Ark of The Covenant, next! Relatives, and in-laws, my God! They'll be the death, or ruin, o' me.*

Jessica's latest letters were much more cheerful. She, the Chiswicks, Sir Hugo, and the two husband hunting girls, had coached down to Chatham to see the launch of the *Daedelus* frigate, in which his elder son, Sewallis, would be Third Officer, and in his first active commission as a Lieutenant, and Oh, it had been a grand outing, though Jessica found their accommodations lacking!

The weather had been perfect, with a good breeze to stir all the many bright flags and banners. Sir Hugo had worn his uniform of an Army Lieutenant-General, and Sewallis had looked spruce in a new uniform, too, proud but solemn as was his wont. The Chatham yards had been thronged with spectators of all classes, all of them neat and clean, even the workers who had built her. There had been bands and martial music, bold patriotic speeches, and a moving prayer from a bishop of the church just before the toasting.

Alan, it was so exciting to witness! An Admiral lifted a glass of brandy on high, and with a very loud voice intoned "Success to HMS Daedelus! Long may she swim." There arose such a great, sustained cheer that almost covered the sounds of the saws as the last impediments to the Launch were removed, and away the Ship went, sliding down the ways and into the river as gracefully as a swan! I found myself hopping on my tiptoes, huzzahing as loud as anyone present. Sewallis said that she must now sail down to the Nore to be fitted with her guns, upper masts and I don't know quite all, to recruit. So huge, so solid is Daedelus that it amazes me that she could be a Product of Man's Ingenuity. Sewallis insists I call her "she"!

Jessica had been even more impressed by the sight of an older Third Rate 64 that had been towed up the Medway to serve as a receiving ship for the Chatham Dockyards. She had not yet had her forecastle and poop deck roofed over and turned into sheds, and shorn of her upper masts . . . "to a gantline" Sewallis had called it . . . but the size and bulk of her had been even greater than the just-launched frigate. And her husband commands a ship like that? Impressive!

She, Sir Hugo, the Chiswicks, and Charlotte and Diana had met *Daedelus's* Captain, First and Second Officers, and the few Midshipmen her Captain had gathered, so far, and she had found them to be a fine set of serious-minded men.

Imagine my Pride, Alan, when your son informed them that I was the wife of Captain Sir Alan Lewrie, Bt., which prompted most complimentary expressions anent your courage, daring, and well-earned fame! They referred to you as the "Ram-Cat." Is that for your choice of pet?

Oh, please, please, never *learn what it means!* Lewrie thought with a cringe.

After a most pleasing hour of reading, Lewrie came to her last and latest, which almost made him blush, for she'd penned it a day or two after the mass raid was reported in the papers; Charlton's after-action report to

Admiralty, Lewrie's, Brigadier Caruthers's, and Colonel Tarrant's of the 94th had all been re-printed together, which Jessica swore had all but made her head reel in wonder at his success.

Though, do promise me, dearest Husband, do not take such risks with your precious Life in future, for it is my fervent Wish that you return to me, Alive, and complete in Body. Recall, you allowed me, at last, to view the scars of wounds honourably received in your past Career, and I could not bear the sight of more! I pray nightly for your Safety as earnestly as I pray for a sweet Re-Union.

Hmpf, Lewrie thought with a satisfied snort; *I guess I'm a hero all over again.* That'll *put my detractors' noses outta joint for a bit. And, Jessica's proud o' me. That's the important thing.*

There were letters from his father, Clotworthy Chute and Peter Rushton, Viscount Draywick, a congratulatory note from Peter's brother Harold at the War Office, and a rare teasing letter from Benjamin Rodgers, an old Navy friend of long standing. He left those aside to read later, for the most part, leaned back in his chair and gave out a yawn. Even being praised to the skies palled after a while.

Oh, stop! Lewrie thought, chiding himself; *You'll make me turn red!*

"Would you care for some cool tea with ginger beer in it, sir?" Deavers tempted.

"Aye, I would at that," Lewrie agreed, rising to cross over to the settee to have himself a lazy sprawl.

"Midshipman of the Watch, SAH!" the Marine sentry bawled.

Midshipman Page entered the cabins, hat under his arm and a letter in his hand. "A boat is come alongside, sir, from the Army camp ashore."

"Thankee, Mister Page," Lewrie said, accepting the folded-over note with a sketchy blob of sealing wax to hold its contents just a bit private. "Aha. The boat still alongside, is it?"

"Aye, sir," Page replied.

"Let me scribble a short reply, for you to deliver ashore," Lewrie told him, going back to his desk for paper, steel-nibbed pen, and a dip in the inkwell. "No need to seal it," he told Page as he blew the ink dry before folding it in half. "My best respects to Colonel Tarrant, and I shall be delighted to dine with him at seven this evening. Off you go, Mister Page."

"Aye aye, sir!" the lad piped, eager for a little boat work and a brief spell away from the ship. Besides, there were young and fetching Sicilian girls strolling the Army camp, and good things to snack on that could be had two-a-penny.

"Dasher, go forrud and hunt up Yeovill," Lewrie bade, "do you inform him that I'm dining ashore this evening."

"Aye, sir!"

We'll most-like end up congratulating ourselves, Lewrie told himself; *Hell, I'll probably have to shave!*

CHAPTER THREE

Lewrie went ashore half an hour before the appointed time of supper with the 94th's officers, savouring the delights of a warm Sicilian evening. The anchorage was almost mill-pond calm, reflecting the riding lights and taffrail lanthorns of the ships. Looking aft from his seat in the stern of his boat, he could see that all of the lower deck gun-ports were open for a breeze, already aglow with overhead lanthorns and hundreds of wee candle glims as the light of the day faded, and the crew partook of their suppers.

Off to the west of the bay and the narrow peninsula that led to the village of Milazzo, the coast was lit with an impressive gold and red sunset, and the mountainous hinterland had gone a smoky grey and dull blue to frame that sunset.

Lewrie's boat landed near the signals post above the beach, but he did not have to stumble forward to the bows to jump over into wet sand. The 94th, with help from the Navy, had erected a proper sort of wooden dock perpendicular to the shore and connected to the land with a long pier; Lt. Col. Tarrant did not care to get his polished boots wet. He did not care much for boats, either, and when forced to get in or out of one—as rarely as possible, that—he would do so in safety, which was an odd attitude for an "amphibious" soldier.

"Thankee, lads," Lewrie said to his boat crew once on the dock, "Enjoy your suppers, and we'll show a lanthorn when I need you to come fetch me."

"Aye, aye, sir," the Cox'n of the boat replied, knuckling his forehead in a rough salute.

Aha, Lewrie thought as he walked to the end of the pier, gazing at the Army camp; *It's lookin' a lot like Vauxhall Gardens!*

Indeed, in the short time since the 94th had shifted closer to the foot of the peninsula, gaining nearer access to wood, nails, and labour from Milazzo and the other villages, the camp had become more substantial, almost permanent-looking. In the company lines, tents had been replaced with waist-high framed timber walls over which the tents were now used as rooves, with the sides rolled up during the day and partially lowered at night. And those huts were floored with planks several inches above the dirt, and rough-framed bed-cots sat a foot or so above the floors, so even a flood would not soak their bedding.

There was a much larger pavillion where the battalion's officers dined, with the same sort of huts spaced round it, two men in each, except for Major Gittings, who had the luxury of sleeping alone.

Then there was Colonel Tarrant's quarters, a proper wood house with an office, a bed chamber, and a spacious dining room which could seat at least ten, and a "jakes" erected a little off to one side, of the building like a proper outhouse with waste bucket, not a cesspit.

There were lanthorns glowing in each of those huts, and cooking fires burned in front of them as soldiers cooked their own rations for supper, or had the battalion's women do it for them. There were only fourty or so of the sixty originals who had sailed away from England with their men for the disastrous Walcheren Expedition in 1809, then to Malta the year before. Some of the women had brought their children along, or had given birth since. As Lewrie got closer, he could hear that half the female voices spoke in Italian or broken English.

All in all, as the dusk gathered, the many fires, lanthorns, and candles of the camp could resemble the well-lit faery garden impression of Vauxhall, with children scampering in late play, and an host of local Sicilians still hawking their wares before being shooed off for the night. And young local girls flirted and strolled with British soldiers, as lovers would in the pleasure gardens of London.

At the entrance to Colonel Tarrant's quarters, a long canvas fly had been stretched out for daytime shade. A low wooden platform sat beneath it, with an assortment of folding camp chairs and tables. Colonel Tarrant and Major Gittings were already there, sipping wine and enjoying the sunset. Both rose as Lewrie came forth into the lanthorn light.

"Ah, you've come early, sir," Tarrant said with a wide smile on his face. "Come, have a seat and try this white wine. It's local, but it puts me in mind of a *Pinot Grigio*, unavailable unless one is far north on the Italian mainland."

"Perhaps *Don* Julio smuggled it in, sir," Lewrie japed, "and offered it at a scandalous profit."

"Heard from our 'prince of thieves' yet, Sir Alan?" Tarrant asked, tipping Lewrie a genial wink.

"No, not yet, though I hope to shortly," Lewrie said, shedding his cocked hat and sword belt for Tarrant's orderly to see to, then carefully took a seat on one of the rickety campaign chairs. "He's off to the mainland, looking for a likely target. Ah, thankee," he added as he accepted a glass of wine, took a sip, and let out a long "Aah" of appreciation.

"Any place likely?" Major Gittings asked.

"Mister Quill sent me a note saying that something along the Gulf of Saint Eufemia, could be promising, Major," Lewrie told him.

"What an odd way to make war," Tarrant commented with a wry shake of his head, "and not just the boats and the ships, hah hah. Government spies and hired-on skulkers, good Lord."

"Worked well enough so far, sir," Lewrie replied, even if he found their situation perhaps a bit too novel.

It was not as if Lewrie had never worked with agents from the Foreign Office's Secret Branch; he'd been their gun-dog, off and on, since 1784 in the Far East, but never in anything that struck him as so ramshackle.

First off, Secret Branch's man on Sicily—the only one that Lewrie could discover so far—was a Mr. Quill, a tall, skeletal fellow given to black clothing and the night and shadows, a youngish man more suited to be a librarian at some college at Cambridge, who didn't seem to have a budget to further his work. The Army did not speak to Quill, co-operate with him, give him lodging at the *Castello* headquarters, or put a pinch of faith in anything he might say, since spies, no matter their place in society, were not proper gentlemen. Instead, Quill lodged in the meanest set of rooms in the waterfront slums of Messina; perhaps to be closer to his set of informers, and lived the life of a shy, impoverished mendicant.

Quill's prime source of information was *Don* Julio, *Don* Julio Caesare to be precise, though that could not possibly be his given name. He was a charming brute, perhaps a heartless cut-throat when necessary; a smuggler, a thief, a pirate if needs must, and a man whom even Quill had cautioned was "the greatest rogue."

But, *Don* Julio, it turned out, was the chief of a vast criminal enterprise with its fingers in everything in Eastern Sicily, with its henchmen and petty thieves two-a-penny in every corner of the land, and Lewrie gathered that there were hundreds of them, which forced him to peer into the gathering darkness, and wonder if *Don* Julio had his own people here in the camp that very instant, posing as vendors, and cooks, itinerant musicians, pimps flogging whores to the soldiers who could afford a girl, even the whores themselves, all to keep an eye on his temporary allies, the *Inglese* soldiers and sailors.

With Julio Caesare, everything was possible and obtainable; lumber, firewood, nails, workers, food, wine, extra canvas, furniture, cook pots, and old women to do the cooking and washing. And the costs were lower than one might expect, he'd assured them. No one had tried to overcharge them, not more than once. Even the petty pilferers and sneak thieves that had plagued the 94th's camp in its original location had, at the snap of *Don* Julio's fingers, vanished from the Earth.

I wonder whose land he stole to let us set up here, Lewrie had to wonder; *so conveniently close to Milazzo and the other villages, which are most-like his home turf!*

Don Julio Caesare was a Devil's Bargain, but he did gather information well, for a price. In preparation for the raids that the battalion and Lewrie's ships had staged so far, *Don* Julio and his minions had scouted the targets most thoroughly, even reporting on the depths of water close inshore, even the condition of the sands on the beaches where the boats would land the troops, the layout of the towns, the size of the local French garrisons, and how far off re-enforcements might be.

It was only later, Lewrie learned to his chagrin, that their first raid on the coastal town of Tropea had been the seat of his rival smugglers and criminals, using the British to eliminate his closest competition! No wonder the seaside warehouses had been so full of luxury goods!

Well, I've co-operated with Serbian pirates in my time, and I'm still alive, Lewrie thought; *so perhaps this'll still work out.*

A group of battalion officers emerged from the dark, six of them, and

Tarrant, Gittings, and Lewrie rose to greet them, with Colonel Tarrant doing the introductions to his company commanders, and them to Lewrie.

"We're letting the subalterns have the mess to themselves, tonight," Tarrant explained, with a hint of glee, "and I'm sure that it will be a night of high cockalorum." Tarrant's orderly came out to the sitting area and announced that supper was ready, and Tarrant bade them all enter and take their seats.

Captains Wiley, Sydenham, Meacham, Fewkes, Bromhead, and Redgrave had only been strange faces, shakoes, and rank marks on their shoulders to Lewrie before, but was delighted to find that the bulk of them were genial and merry company as he strove to remember names and nuances. They even had good, sparkling, and well-informed conversation, stoked by the arrival of many used London papers.

And Tarrant set a fine table, with a chicken and pasta soup for the first course, followed by a roast goose, and lamb chops in *lieu* of roast beef, accompanied by various fresh vegetables, and an assortment of wines which complemented each course.

Finally, over Port, fruit, and a peach pie, Colonel Tarrant tapped his wine glass with his spoon to gather their attention.

"Gentlemen, I have a happy announcement to share with you all," he began, "Before I reveal it to you, I wish to propose a toast to our guest tonight, Captain Sir Alan Lewrie, whose scheme for raiding and harassing our enemies brought us out of drudgery, sentry-go, and square-bashing, and fetched us to this Garden of Eden. Gentlemen, I give you Captain Sir Alan Lewrie! Even if he did not rise for the King's Toast, hah hah."

Glasses were charged, the toast repeated in a friendly roar, and the wine drunk down to "heel taps."

"Does one stand to toast the King, gentlemen," Lewrie explained with a laugh, "One bashes his brains out on the overhead decks and beams!"

"Now . . . for the news," Tarrant went on after the polite laugh had settled. "In the mail which came today, I heard from our patrons in Peterborough. They have seen fit to agree to raise funds to offer the yeomanry militia a bonus if they volunteer for the 94th, and the Army will pay for their weapons, uniforms, kits, and see to their training. Furthermore . . ."

He could not go further for some moments 'til the officers' cheers and fists hammering the table top died down.

"Furthermore," Tarrant tried again, "the town fathers have seen fit to re-construct the old brickworks east of town and turn it into a proper barracks, so we will have a proper establishment when we go home. Now, I cannot promise that we will grow to a full ten companies, but we will be able to flesh out the Grenadier Company, fill the ranks of the existing Line Companies, and add a second Light Company, as well as an additional Line Company. And, I am so informed . . ." Tarrant said with a sly grin, "that company Captaincies will now go for an additional five hundred pounds."

"They don't expect *us* to pay five hundred more . . ." Captain Redgrave spluttered.

"No, your commissions are now *worth* three thousand pounds!" Tarrant hooted, "Our Leftenants are now worth two thousand, and our Ensigns are worth fifteen hundred. We ain't up there with the Coldstream Guards yet, but we're getting there, and our recent success, and fame, will attract enough new officers at the higher price."

His father, Leftenant-General Sir Hugo, had written Lewrie of the recent explosion of barracks cross Great Britain, hundreds of them, to house, train, and support the militias. It had started in the first invasion scare of 1798, re-occurred during the massing of huge French armies and invasion fleets in 1804–1805, and had blossomed yet again as more militias were incorporated into the Army as regulars; some even agreed to be deployed overseas.

"Now, our re-enforcements will not be forthcoming for several months," Colonel Tarrant informed them, "so for now, we will have to soldier on as we are, with what we have. But, I am certain that the Navy, and Captain Lewrie, will see to our getting the additional transports and what-all that will allow us to go from one success to the next, what?"

Oh, shit! Lewrie thought, cringing though he smiled back at the news; *Navy-manned transports, landing boats, boarding nets . . . where in* Hell *am I goin' t'get* those?

CHAPTER FOUR

Damme, I am not a Horn of Plenty! Lewrie moodily thought as he finished his breakfast the next morning; *I can't work miracles for 'em at the snap o' my fingers!*

Two more transport ships of at least 350 tons burthen, with six more 29-foot Admiralty pattern barges each; boarding nets, and most especially, about ninety more sailors for each transport to man the boats to get the promised soldiers ashore and back, and guard the landing beaches whilst the 94th made their assaults; King's Ships, rated as armed transports, though the three troop ships he already had didn't mount any guns. Where could he get all that, and what would Admiralty pay to obtain them for him? The last dealings Lewrie had had in England, such ships were leased for 30 shillings per ton per month—almost as costly as buying them into the Fleet outright!

When leasing and outfitting round Portsmouth for the few ships he had, with the able help of Captain Middleton, a Commissioner of Admiralty Without Special Functions, there had been so many impediments that Lewrie had almost despaired, and without Middleton and his magic writs from Admiralty, and a seemingly endless source of funds, the squadron might *still* be languishing, short of everything needful!

Towards the end of that struggle, even Commissioner Captain Middleton had begun to suspect that there had been some nefarious influences afoot that had tried to scotch, or at least, delay the squadron's departure. It was a given that the naval dockyards were rife with corruption and graft, and contractors and jobbers from which the Navy got its rope, sails, salt-meats, bisquit, rum, and small beer were just as "shifty." Lord St. Vincent, Admiral Sir John Jervis, had tried to root much of that out when he was named First Lord of The Admiralty, but "Old Jarvey's" term of office had been cut short by people in government who profited on the side from all that graft and corruption.

And the hoops through which Lewrie and Middleton had to jump could not be blamed entirely on the sloth-like workings of bureaucracy, either. Lewrie had told him that there were people in the Navy who despised him for being too lucky, too successful; officers he had riled professionally or personally, even one Lewrie had thought of as a dear friend who'd found him too idle, cocky, and carelessly rash. They all had powerful patrons in Parliament, in government, and in the Navy, far senior to the few patrons Lewrie might claim. Had some of the foot-dragging been a result of their spiteful machinations? Neither Lewrie nor Middleton could dismiss that idea completely.

Lewrie poured himself another cup of freshly-brewed coffee, sweetened and creamed it, then rose from his dining table and went to his desk in the day-cabin to get out pen, paper, and uncap the inkwell. He still had several un-opened letters from home to be read, and he dearly wished to re-read Jessica's latest, but he *had* to write the First Secretary, Mr. Croker, his local patron, Rear-Admiral Charlton, and Commissioner Captain Middleton about the need for two more transports, first.

At least I have two months or more before they're needed, he thought as he began the first letter.

"Marine Captain Whitehead, SAH!" his Marine sentry bellowed.

"Dammit," Lewrie muttered, then shouted "Enter!"

"Ah, good morning, Captain sir," Whitehead began as he came into the cabins, turned out in proper dress uniform. "I wonder if I could have your permission to man the barges, sir? I wish to take the Marine complement ashore this morning, as we discussed, to borrow the Army's firing range, and do some light infantry exercises alongside one of their companies."

"This morning?" Lewrie said, frowning for a moment. "Oh, right. We did discuss that. I'll come on deck to see you off, shortly. Do convey my compliments to the officer of the watch, and say that he's to have the Bosun pipe Man Boats."

"Very good, sir, and thank you," Capt. Whitehead said, bowing himself out.

Damn, damn, damn! Lewrie fumed in silence, looking at the few lines he had scribbled, little beyond the addressee. He tossed his steel-nib pen atop the desk and rose, cast a glance at his old cat, Chalky, then stowed the pen and the sheet of paper in a drawer of his desk before going to don his coat and hat.

Lewrie stepped out onto the quarterdeck, watching a stir of activity as Whitehead spoke to an older Midshipman standing Harbour Watch, who sent a junior Mid to the officers' wardroom to rouse one of the Lieutenants, since officers did not stand watch in port, and wait for Lt. Grace, the Fourth Officer, to emerge, yawning and shrugging into his coat with his hat awry. Only then was word passed for the Bosun, Mr. Gore, who had to come up from idling below to raise his silver call to his lips and pipe the required signal.

"Ah, Captain Whitehead," Lewrie said, looking down into the waist where the Marines were gathering, "do you use the entry-ports and the boarding battens, larboard and starboard. We'll not use the nets 'til we figure out how to avoid killing anyone, what?"

"What, indeed, sir!" Whitehead replied with a stern face. "Queue up by the entry-ports for debarking!" he yelled to his men.

"Boat crews, man your boats!" the Bosun was yelling.

At last, the occupants of the wardroom emerged from below drawn by the un-expected shouts; First Officer, Mr. Farley, the Second Officer, the laconic Mr. Rutland, and the irrepressible Mr. Greenleaf, the Third Officer. Behind them came the Sailing Master, Mr. Wickersham, with a hand of cards clutched in one hand, and the Ship's Surgeon, Mr. Woodbury, with shaving soap still on one half of his face.

"Ehm, shall the boats stay ashore 'til the Marines' return to the ship, sir?" Lt. Grace asked, and the gathering seamen and Mids who would man the boats perked up with interest.

"No need, Mister Grace," Lewrie told him, "we've drills to do of our own, and the hands'd miss their rum issue. When the Marines are done with target practice, they'll signal."

"Very well, sir," Grace said, as crestfallen as the sailors. Evidently the doings in the 94th Foot's camp were fine distractions. Lewrie could see some scowls and hear subdued groans. Lewrie's own long-time Cox'n, Liam Desmond, and his stroke-oar, Kitch, shared a shrug and a frown.

The boats were drawn up alongside the entry-ports from being tethered in a loose clutch astern, and the boat crews scrambled down the boarding battens and man-ropes, loosing their oars from bundles bound together, hoisted them erect, and readied to shove off. Then the Marines slowly went down into the first two boats with their muskets, canteens, cartridge pouches, and spare eighty rounds in their rucksacks. Once filled, the first two barges rowed free, and the two other boats filled. Finally, all four barges stroked for that dock alongside the beach, and Lewrie could go aft once more, and get a fresh start on his letters.

Lewrie scribbled for several hours, time punctuated by the twig-like crackle of musketry from shore, and the clash of steel on steel as the ship's crew practiced with cutlasses. As each letter was done, he passed it to Sub-Lieutenant Severance to copy.

"Ehm, sir?" Severance said as Lewrie hunched over a new sheet of paper.

"Aye?" Lewrie grunted.

"Might you send the copies, and retain your first drafts, sir?" Severance suggested.

"And what's wrong with my handwriting?" Lewrie snapped.

"Well, sir . . . in places, yours are hard to make out," his aide and clerk dared say. "Like here, sir . . . and here?"

"Damme, sir, I've a perfectly legible copperplate hand," Lewrie grumphed. "I've still sore knuckles from my tutors learning it!"

"If you'd compare my fair copy with yours, sir," Severance said, presenting the two side-by-side on the desktop.

"Oh," was Lewrie's comment after a moment of perusal. "Damme, am I going rheumatical, at last? I see what you mean. Very well, we shall send your copies, instead. Assuming you can make heads or tails of this'un," he said, tapping the letter he was working on. "Chicken scratches, illegible argey-bargey and all."

"Very good, sir," Severance said with a tight smile that Lewrie was not supposed to see.

"But I'll write my own personal letters myself!" Lewrie growled.

"Aye aye, sir," Severance said, returning to his desk area.

Lewrie flexed his fingers and watched them move, wondering if almost thirty years at sea had caught up with him. His hands didn't *feel* any different; his fingers wriggled quite well.

Meowr!

Chalky saw the wriggling and took that as an invitation to come get petted. He was not as keen on his toys as he had been when he was a young cat, but he did admire his "wubbies"—just as long as fingers did not turn into prey, and then he'd nip and grasp with his claws out, and attempting to touch his belly was a challenge to a fight to the death.

"Oh, alright," Lewrie relented, giving Chalky a stroking from nose to tail tip, a kneading along the top of his head and the nape of his neck, and some strokes along his jowls. "You've earned it, and I can use the break. Sweetness," he cooed.

Mrff was Chalky's response to such baby prattle.

At last, Chalky stepped down into Lewrie's lap, yawned, made some paddlings with his paws, and stretched out for a nap, purring to beat the band.

Seven Bells of the Forenoon was struck to mark the end of the morning's drills, and the arrival of the rum keg for the first issue of the day. Lewrie could close the inkwell and wipe his pen clean; the letters were finished, and copied. The wind brought the smoke from the galley funnel up forward, and the smell of boiled pork. Lewrie yawned and stretched himself, without waking his cat, though eager to stand and pace about before his mid-day dinner arrived, wondering what his cook, Yeovill, might come up with.

"Cap'um's cook, SAH!" the Marine sentry bawled at last, stamping boots and slamming his musket butt on the deck, and in came Yeovill with a large brass food barge. Chalky raised his head, looked about, sniffed the air, and stood in Lewrie's lap to arch his back, yawn, and then leap down to make a dash for the dining coach with eager meows of demand for food, instanter, if humans knew what was good for them.

"A good white will go down well with dinner, sir," Yeovill suggested as he opened the barge lid and laid out plates, and Deavers, the cabin steward, went to the wine-cabinet. "Yes, something toothsome for you, too, Chalky. Get down, now! Wait for it!"

Eight Bells chimed to announce the end of the Forenoon Watch, the beginning of the Day Watch, followed by Bosun's calls piping the hands to their dinner.

"What am I eating, Yeovill?" Lewrie asked, peering at his plate as it was filled.

"All fresh from shore, sir," Yeovill cheerfully told him. "A fat fillet of grilled and breaded perch, salad with onion, cucumbers, and lettuce, and a mix of pasta and rice in a nice tomato sauce."

"Sounds grand," Lewrie said, tucking his napkin under his chin.

"I had a chance to watch the Marines ashore, sir, with a glass I borrowed from Midshipman Langdon," Yeovill commented as he sliced a crusty loaf of shore bread. "Never seen the like, marching out in pairs, in fours, scouting and loading and firing as they advanced. They'll be late to their dinners, and their rum, but I'd wager it'll be more than welcome when they do come back aboard. Here you go, Chalky . . . grilled fish and rice for you!"

"Sorry I missed the show," Lewrie said after a forkful of his fresh salad. "Marines aren't called on to fight ashore all that often. I'm sure it's new to them, a challenge."

After a bite of fish, and fresh buttered bread, Lewrie took a sip of his wine, and had a thought, just as Yeovill was heading for the door. "I say, Yeovill, I'm curious enough to have Captain Whitehead and Leftenant Venables to supper tonight, so I can ask them all about it."

"Ehm, how many in all, sir?" Yeovill asked.

"Mister Rutland, Mister Greenleaf, for certain," Lewrie said, "since they go ashore with the boats, usually, hmm . . . let's have the Surgeon, Mister Woodbury, too. He's full of good tales, and one of the Mids. Langdon's eldest. He'll do."

"Seven for supper, aye, sir," Yeovill said with a nod, then departed the cabins.

"He said 'aye, sir,' not 'yes,'" Deavers marvelled.

"Took him long enough, didn't it?" Lewrie said with a wee grin. "Look at how many years it took Pettus t'sound salty."

CHAPTER FIVE

Supper was convivial, enlivened by the London papers the diners had just read, and Surgeon Woodbury and Lieutenant Greenleaf were as entertaining as usual. Midshipman Langdon, a man in his mid-twenties who had yet to become a Passed Midshipman, knew enough to follow his superior's leads, stay somewhat sobre, make innocent contributions, and laugh in the right places. Lieutenant Rutland was, of course, his usual taciturn and gloomy self, but then, he was married with two children, and lived on his Navy pay, which was an un-ending trial, and a *cause* for gloom and worry about his family.

"Now, sirs," Lewrie announced once the Port bottle, some soft cheese, and a bowl of table grapes had been set out, "Captain Whitehead, you and your officers must tell us of your day ashore, and what you were doing. I must own that, though I did not watch, I was told it looked novel."

"Oh, sir, we learned a lot from the Ninety-Fourth today, all about skirmishing," Whitehead said with enthusiasm. "The Captain of their Light Company put us through our paces."

"Indeed, sir," Lt. Venables chimed in. "Skirmishing pairs, scouting pairs, chains, firing from cover, re-loading on the move? All of it sound Army doctrine for Light Infantry, these days."

Neither Marine officer needed much prompting to expound upon what they had practiced. Skirmishing and scouting was done in twos, each man covering the other, ready to fire once the first man had fired and was re-loading. They didn't have whistles or bugles like the 94th, to signal the presence of the enemy, but a shako or hat raised on a musket's barrel held aloft signified a small force, and two hats in the air meant a large force was sighted.

Skirmishing was done in two expanded ranks, with the front rank kneel-ing to fire and re-load, whilst the rear rank advanced several paces for-ward of the first rank to kneel and fire in turn, and that could be performed in retreat as well.

Several grapes were deployed in enthusiastic demonstration on the table top.

"A Light Infantry company is broken down into sections of twelve men," Capt. Whitehead explained, laying out more grapes, "and further divided into groups of four. When they call for 'chain order,' most of a company will advance about an hundred yards in front, with four men in each 'link' of the chain, about ten yards between each link, sirs. The rest remain in close order, ready to advance to re-enforce or cover a withdrawal. The right hand man in each link steps out three paces, fires, then retires to the left end to re-load, whilst the second man steps forward to fire, and et cetera, so that a continuous fire is maintained."

"We were raw and ragged, at first, sirs," Lt. Venables admitted, "but our men caught on quickly, and seemed to enjoy it after a bit. It inspires, ehm . . . dare I say, personal initiative, and a sense of responsibility, to be out in the open instead of shoulder-to-shoulder in ranks. And each link of four men has to have a leader, whether he's a Sergeant or Corporal, or not, someone level-headed that the others naturally come to follow."

"Just what the late Lieutenant General Sir John Moore and his contem-poraries intended," Lt. Rutland spoke up, a bit of surprise to all at the table, "He wanted to instill just those qualities in a British Army, and its soldiers. He had no need for mindless cattle."

"When we landed at Locri and Siderno, that last big raid, we only put out about twenty Marines to skirmish," Whitehead admitted, "and kept most of our men in tight ranks, ready for massed volleys. Lord, we didn't even know to kneel before firing."

"But," Lt. Venables insisted, "we'll make a much better show, the next time we set foot ashore."

"Count on it!" Whitehead boasted. "Though I will insist that you allow us ashore to practice, sir," he said to Lewrie. "It's good exercise, more than we get aboard ship. If you listen close, you can hear our Marines groaning over sore muscles tonight, hah hah!"

"Did you see them when they came back aboard, sirs?" Venables chortled. "Foot-dragging, and their faces as black as so many Sambos, from firing so many rounds, much more than we fire at towed kegs and such. We went through sixty rounds each today."

"*Aimed* fire, sirs!" Whitehead added, with a thump of his fist on the table top. "They discovered that our Short India Pattern Tower muskets can actually be pointed, not just levelled in the general direction. If only we had something like the Baker rifles that the 'Green Jacket' regiments are issued, with real sights."

"In any case, a great many melons were shattered on the range, today!" Venables said with a bright laugh. "Bang! Headshots!"

"The Baker's too slow to load, though," Whitehead said with a sigh. "Leather patches, hammers to start the balls down the bore?"

"Too bad the Army did not adopt the Ferguson," Lewrie stuck in. "Breech loading, rifled. But, Major Patrick Ferguson only had about one thousand made, and he had only his when he was killed at King's Mountain. His troops were equipped with old Brown Bess. Had he and his men all had them, it might have been a different outcome."

"Do you have a Ferguson, sir?" Venables asked. "I'm told that you do."

"I do, aye," Lewrie said. "Care to see it?" he offered, and of course they all did. He could not remember if he had un-loaded it after going ashore at Siderno, so he gingerly screwed open the breech with the brass lever which formed the trigger guard, and, sure enough, there was a paper cartridge rammed into the breech, which he carefully extracted, gave it a shake to loosen the lead ball, then handed the rifled musket around.

"My Lord, sir!" Whitehead exclaimed after working the lever a couple of times. "Why, one could get off five or *six* shots a minute with this! A pity, indeed, that his weapon died with him."

"I was told that at some battle during the American Revolution, I forget which," Midshipman Langdon spoke up, "that Major Ferguson took aim at a mounted American officer out in front of his lines, and almost fired at him, but didn't. He later said that he did not have the heart to shoot a man, an officer especially, so intently involved with what he was doing . . .

and that officer was George Washington. If he had, we might have defeated the rebels."

"Do you ever have the time to come ashore to witness our practice, sir," Whitehead said, "you *must* bring this weapon along, for I dearly wish to fire it a few times. I hear it is accurate."

"I once potted a bastard of a Frenchman at over one hundred fifty yards," Lewrie told them, "back when the French routed the Austrians outside Genoa and ran 'em twenty miles in total panic."

Oh, that was sweet! Lewrie gladly recalled that moment; *Shot Guillaume Choundas off his horse, and they took off his damned arm! And good riddance t'bad rubbish!*

"But, it's been an age since I fired it," Lewrie amended, to avoid sounding boastful. "I may *need* time on the firing range."

"Then you must come ashore with us, the next time we're allowed, sir," Captain Whitehead insisted. "Try your eye, what?"

Two Bells of the Evening Watch chimed from the belfry far up forward, marking 9 P.M. and the time when the Master at Arms, Mr. Stabler, and his Ship's Corporals, Geary, Kirby, and Tunstall, made the rounds of all decks to see that all below-deck lanthorns and glim candles were doused for the night.

"Well, before the Master at Arms comes pounding on my door, let us charge glasses and take a final drink to close the evening, gentlemen," Lewrie instructed. The Port bottle made a quick larboard passage as they stood round the table. "I give you, sirs, our gallant Marines, and a good night's rest for the weary."

"The Marines! The weary!" they chorused before draining their glasses to the last drop. All said their *adieus* and departed, leaving Lewrie alone.

"Brandy or whisky before you retire, sir?" Deavers asked.

"Whisky, my good man, a full bumper!" Lewrie demanded.

CHAPTER SIX

Lewrie was writing, again, beginning a new letter to Jessica, when the Marine sentry announced the Third Officer, Mr. Greenleaf at his door seeking an audience.

"Come," Lewrie said with his head down, concentrating on his penmanship, which he *still* thought to be perfectly legible, damned what Severance said.

"Good morning, Captain sir," Greenleaf said as he bounced in with élan. "There's something you might like to see on deck, sir."

"Hmm? There is?" Lewrie said, at last looking up.

"We believe we've found a solution to our problem with the nets, sir," Greenleaf told him, all but bouncing on his toes in secret glee.

"Oh, very well," Lewrie replied, setting aside his pen and rising. "Show me, then." He left off his everyday uniform coat and his cocked hat to go out on the quarterdeck.

One of the boarding nets was slung over the larboard bulwarks, and half the Midshipmen stood by the bulwarks, notably the youngest and spryest.

"We're going to sacrifice the younkers, are we, Greenleaf?" Lewrie quipped.

"Look over the side, sir," Greenleaf cajoled, "we've drawn one of the barges alongside the main chains, and the boat crew has hold on the bottom of the net. *But,* sir! Do note the four-by-four laths worked into the net on the inner side. Small ringbolts with washers secure the wooden slats, with stout rope spliced and whipped round the undersides of the knotted squares of the net. It now stands out at least four inches from the hull, so there's no more tumblehome to deal with, right down to the lower gunwale. Lads! Over you go . . . smartly, now!"

They must have practiced first, for Midshipmen Page, Randolph, Malin, Fairfoot, Dunn, Acford, Darnell, and Lewrie's brother-in-law, Charles Chenery, hopped atop the bulwarks, swung legs over, and disappeared in a twinkling, scrambling down the boarding nets with as much alacrity as so many apes, down to the gunn'l of the barge, and into the boat. They stayed but a moment, then climbed back up just as easily, clambering up and over the bulwarks to land on the sail-tending gangway with triumphant whoops.

"A jacob's ladder, after a fashion, sir," Lt. Greenleaf boasted, "writ large, and *wide*! The slats are made of local fir, and easily replaceable when they wear out. The Bosun lacquered them to prevent rot, too."

"Let's go forrud," Lewrie insisted, intrigued, and led out to the sail-tending gangway by the mainmast shrouds among the Mids.

"Care to try it, sir?" Midshipman Chenery asked with an impish grin.

Christ, I'll have *to!* Lewrie quailed to himself; *They'll think me an old poltroon if I do not.*

"Good thing I left my hat aft," Lewrie said, trying to sound game. He seized a tarred stay, hauled himself atop the bulwark, and swung a leg out and over, bellied against the hull. A look down to find a first foothold, the boat and the ocean so *very far* below that it made his "nutmegs" shrink up, and he was lowering himself down, hand over hand, foothold by foothold, trying to count planks in the hull scantlings; upper gun-deck ports, then lower gun-deck ports, then the dark black, tarry lower wale, and there were no more slats, but the net hung vertical, held off a bit by the crew in the barge, and he was atop the white-painted gunn'l, then into the boat on a midship thwart, resting a hand on a sailor's shoulder to prevent teetering as the slight scend of the waters made the barge bob and roll a bit.

"Right, then!" Lewrie said loudly, as if he'd enjoyed it, "Do steady the net, lads. I'm off!"

Back up the nets he went, gaze fixed on the mainmast shrouds and the top of the bulwark, where many amused faces peered down at him, which was much easier than looking down at the sea and the hard wood of the barge should he slip and fall. The last few feet, with plenty of depth off the hull for hand grips and room for his boot tips, and he reached the top of the net. There was a tense second or two before he found something substantial to grasp before he could heave himself over the bulwark and swing a leg inboard, but he made it.

"Whew!" Lewrie exclaimed. "That was good exercise I must say, and much easier than the last time I tried the bloody things. Very good work, Mister Greenleaf. My compliments, and my thanks, to all involved in the making, and make sure that they get full measures of their rum issues, this morning, and in the Dog Watch."

"That I will, sir, and thank you!" Lt. Greenleaf replied, just about ready to try and pat himself on his own back.

"Much more elegantly done than last, sir," Midshipman Chenery commented tongue-in-cheek.

"You haven't been 'mast-headed' lately, have you, young sir!" Lewrie gravelled in mock threat, "Bloody fine work. Now, I go aft. Writing your sister and telling her what a scamp you are."

But, barely had Lewrie sat down at his desk, drawing deep breaths at last, the need for which he'd disguised from the crew, and called for a glass of cool tea laced with ginger beer, then he heard a shout. "Deck, there! Large fishin' boat enterin' harbour, bound for us!" which prompted Lewrie to snatch up his telescope and dash back to the quarterdeck, then up to the poop deck, to see what the commotion was about. With the tubes of his glass extended, he discovered that the approaching fishing boat was one of three that his landing parties had snatched out of the harbour during their first raid on the coastal town of Tropea, and then turned over to *Don Julio* and the needy town of Milazzo.

Well, gulled out of, not given, *exactly,* Lewrie thought with a grimace of disgust. Even if they'd be worth less than nothing at a Prize-Court, it still galled him.

The fishing boat was still too far off to determine which one it was, or to make out anyone he recognised aboard her, though there was someone aft near the helm in a white shirt with a red sash round his waist that he supposed *could* be their arch criminal spy. And, by the single mast there was a stick figure all in black, clinging like a fearful landlubber.

Mr. Quill? Lewrie asked himself; *Quill and Caesare together? Damme, we just may be back in business!*

"*Ciao, Signore Inglese!*" *Don* Julio cheerfully roared cross the water after his fishing boat came to anchor, and he and Quill, for it was indeed he, clambered down into a scrofulous rowing boat and rowed for the jury-rigged dock ashore. Mr. Quill appeared to be as leery of ships and boats as Col. Tarrant, sitting stiffly upright in the middle of a thwart, hands in a death grip. Watching him totter from his hold on the fishing boat's mast to the rails, once she'd anchored and lay still, then over the rails and groping to a single rope line to get down into the rowing boat had been almost too cruelly amusing to watch.

"We go see *Colonnello Inglese* and *Maggiore Inglese, Capitano!*" *Don* Julio added as the rowboat passed close by *Vigilance*'s starboard side. "You come join us! Having *importanti informazioni* to share!" To prove it, *Don* Julio swivelled his head to peer all about, then put a shushing finger to his lips, then laughed out loud. Quill just sat, staring straight ahead at the rowboat's stem post and the shore.

"Bosun Gore," Lewrie shouted, "summon my boat crew, and ready a side-party!" He paused, then added, "At the starboard entry-port, not that bloody net!" which drew some grins from the sailors and Marines on deck.

Minutes later, dressed in coat and cocked hat, with his everyday hanger at his hip, Lewrie stepped onto the low wooden pier along the beach, telling his Cox'n, Liam Desmond to row back to the ship and await a signal to come fetch him, though he did not know how long that would be. Then, tugging his coat cuffs and the bottom of his waist-coat into better order, he made his way to Col. Tarrant's quarters, amid the bustle of soldiers doing close-order drill on the large quadrangle, and some companies practicing some sort of manoeuvres back in the woods and groves.

Tarrant and Gittings were under the shady tent fly, with Quill now looking much more relaxed and at ease with a glass of white wine in his hand, though still prim, proper, and upright on the edge of the campaign chair. *Don* Julio Caesare, in contrast, sat slouched in his seat, booted feet and his striped "ticken" trouser legs sprawled out before him, hands in constant motion, even the one that held his wine, and doing all the talking.

"Ah, *Capitano Inglese!*" *Don* Julio rumbled in a loud *basso,* "It is good to see you, again." *Don* Julio had never bothered to try to remember their names; only *Signore* Quill got differentiated, because he was the one who held the Secret Branch's purse-strings, Lewrie imagined.

"*Signore* Caesare," Lewrie said, to be polite, as Tarrant's orderly fetched him a glass of wine, "*buongiorno*. Prosperin', I see?"

"Prosper . . . ? Ah, you mean make the *denaro*? Hah hah, *sì, molto denaro*! The business, she is good!"

Indeed, Caesare had left off his version of canvas slop-trousers and sandals for clean trousers stuffed into new-looking ox-blood brown boots, and his shirt was now a snow-white linen with lace. In that red waist sash, though, he still showed an ivory-handled dagger, and a brace of silver-chased pistols.

"I take it you and Mister Quill have brought some business to us, *Signore* Caesare?" Colonel Tarrant mildly asked. He and the *Don* had had little interaction, so far, and it seemed a little of the man went a long way.

"Ah, *sì*, a new place to fight and kill the *Francesi*," *Don* Julio hooted. "*Signore* Quill, he has the maps."

"I requested *Don* Julio to scout about the Gulf of Saint Eufemia, gentlemen," Quill began in his reedy voice, reaching inside his dark coat for a thin sheaf of papers, and a portion of a map, which he laid on the small campaign table between them. "Some place that we could raid that would do great harm to the French forces occupying Italy, and more to the point, hurting their armies massed round Reggio di Calabria in hopes of invading Sicily."

"Perhaps we should take this inside, Mister Quill," Col. Tarrant suggested, "to my office table."

"Oh, of course, Colonel," Quill replied, tossing his head back and laughing at his mistake; his own brand of laughter that sounded as if he was half-drowned or hiccuping. "Secrecy is the thing, what?"

Thank God he wasn't really *amused*, Lewrie thought, for that form of noise quite put him off.

"Here, sirs," Quill said a minute later after they had shifted inside, and the orderly had topped up all their glasses. "Near a wee coastal town called Pizzo," he said, pointing a long, thin finger at the place, then moving his finger a tad north up the coast. "There is no garrison at Pizzo, though there is a sizable one at Vibo Valentia . . . here, to the south, and there *may* be a small garrison at Filadelfia, but that's about an hour or two inland. Cavalry. Perhaps one squadron."

"So, what's at Pizzo?" Tarrant asked.

"It's what's north of Pizzo that matters, Colonel," Quill said with a sly look. "See the road along the coast? Up by Saint Eufemia Lamezia, the land is open, and the road goes inland for a spell. But then it is shouldered out right along the coast by these hills. It is the only road, poor as it is, that supplies the French in Calabria, from Naples. And right *there*, there is a bridge," he said with a grim smile of anticipated triumph.

"Wood, stone?" Major Gittings asked, with some excitement.

"Is stone," *Don* Julio supplied, "very old, since Roman times. But only one cart or waggon wide," he said, digging into a trouser pocket to produce a pencil sketch of it.

"Damn," Col. Tarrant grimaced, "the Romans built to last, *over*-built really. It might take half the gunpowder you have aboard your ship, Sir Alan."

"Where to place the charges, though," Major Gittings, added, "I see one pillar in the centre of the span. Perhaps if we laid kegs both sides of that. This defile it spans, is it dry, *Signore*?"

"Most of the time, *Signore Maggiore*," *Don* Julio replied with a shrug, and a lift of his hands. "Sometime in the heavy rains, there is a creek. In winter, mostly."

"How did you get this sketch?" Lewrie had to ask.

"I have *capo* in Reggio di Calabria, *Signore Capitano*," Caesare said with a conspiratorial wink. "He have son who is studying to be . . . how you say, builder of fine buildings?"

"An architect?" Col. Tarrant supplied.

"*Sì sì*, the . . . what you say," *Don* Julio said with a shake of his head, "soft-headed boy is hopeless at the family business, too sweet, with his head in books all the time. He go sketch the churches, old *castelli* and *palazzi*, and *i Francesi* see picture of the bridge when they stop and question him, but do not notice. He brings back, and his father give to one of my *Capitanos*."

"*Don* Julio's, ah, associate," Quill further explained, "saw the bridge and realised that its destruction would hurt the French, so I asked *Don* Julio to sail over and take a look at it."

"Ah, *sì*," *Don* Julio said with a crafty grin. "Do some fishing, go into Pizzo to drink and sell some things . . . fishing is very good off that coast. For the fish, *and* the *informazioni*, *sì*, heh heh? Right here is beach, coarse sand, and the gravel. Is word, gravel, *sì*? Good. Ten fathom water the three-quarter the *miglio* . . . mile? . . . off the beach, five, four and a half fathom a half a mile offshore. And what the bridge crosses comes right down to the sea, with *molto* bigger rocks above the beach."

Caesare had drawn a pencil sketch of his scouting of all that, too, and laid it atop the rest of the papers with a laugh at his own boldness.

"How steep are the slopes, either side of the bridge?" Tarrant asked, frowning and humming over the sketch. "How do we get up there?"

"On north end, very steep, and the dry creek bed, not so bad," *Don* Julio said with a dismissive shrug. "On south end, is easier to climb up. *Molto* boulders, can go up like goat, like step stones to the road, and the end of the bridge."

"Hmm, one company in the gorge to lay the charges, and two or three companies to scale the boulders on the south end to cover the bridge 'til it's blown," Col. Tarrant decided. "Any French who come along would be coming from Filadelfia's garrison, and the road that connects to the coast road leads into the north end.

"Our troops near the bridge, and in the rocks uphill from it could keep them busy. You say the bridge is only one waggon wide, sir? They can't charge across it, then, unless they're suicidal, so they'd have to dismount and skirmish with us in what cover they can find . . . with musketoons, not long-barrelled weapons."

"Only three or four companies, this time, sir?" Lewrie asked.

"Yayss, I believe so, Sir Alan," Col. Tarrant said after a long pause. "Do you concur, Gittings? It's a quick in-and-out, land, get up the slope, lay the charges, light the fuses, and get out."

"There's no room to manoeuvre, no room to deploy the whole battalion," Major Gittings agreed. "Getting all our troops ashore would take too long, to no good purpose."

"So, who knows how to plant charges and blow a bridge?" Tarrant asked with a perky chuckle.

"Oh, don't look at me, sirs," Lewrie said, for damned if they *didn't* turn to look at him. "I know naval guns and howitzers, and that exhausts my knowledge. I love big explosions as well as the next fellow, but . . ." he said with a shrug. "Though . . ." he added after a longer look at the sketch of the bridge.

"Yes? An idea, Sir Alan?" Tarrant prompted.

"The pillars of the bridge are quite substantial, well, the ends that seem to merge into the ground," Lewrie speculated. "The central pillar, hmm. *Don* Julio, did you get a good look at that pillar?"

"Ah, *sì*," Caesare said, "It is thick, and about ten feet long, but about eight feet thick, and it makes the two arches."

"And the road bed atop it," Lewrie pressed. "How thick is that?"

"Oh, that is only four feet thick," Don Julio said, shrugging.

"Kegs of gunpowder at either side of the central pillar, slung up in cargo nets, and fused to go off together, *could* take down the road bed, and damage the centre support," Tarrant suggested.

"Ehm, too easily replaced with wood, though," Gittings said. "And, the Romans built thick, to take the weight of traffic on the bridge *downward*. A ton or two of gunpowder might not move it."

"Downward force, sirs?" Quill stuck in after listening for a long time. "Is there a way to explode the charges upwards? Either side of the central pillar? I dare say the Romans never thought to build for *that*."

"Well, two cargo nets full of powder kegs, fuses linked to one long one that can be lit down in the gorge," Lewrie suggested. "One under each end of the central pillar, and another set of kegs lashed round the base of the pillar. We could hoist the cargo nets up snug under the road bed, with ropes dropped down from the bridge, either side. One of your companies could do the pulley-hauley whilst the other two cover their doings, and . . . I could land my Marines ashore, right up the gorge to the foot of the bridge with the powder and the nets, and an armed shore party of sailors could cover them and hold the beach."

"Your Marines, and say, two companies of the battalion, then," Tarrant said with some enthusiasm. "An hour's work, ashore, fifteen minutes to land everyone, another fifteen to get everyone off, if the French don't interfere, and . . . *bang*!"

"I like it," Major Gittings said.

"Don't get too excited, yet, though, sirs," Lewrie cautioned. "I'd have to consult my Master Gunner and Captain Whitehead, and see if anyone of them has a better idea on how to bring down a bridge that sturdy. A working supper this evening, I expect. Unless we could lay hands on an officer, or a party, from the Engineers here on Sicily. Surely, the Commanding General should see the sense of it, and might co-operate with us."

"They haven't yet," Gittings said with a sour grunt.

"Good God, do we speak with the Army staff at the *Castello*, and

Brigadier Caruthers might hear of it, and the next thing you know he will want to be a part of it," Tarrant said with a dry laugh. "Look here, sirs. The former battlefield of Maida is not too far away from the bridge, and General Stuart landed his troops in Saint Eufemia Bay to fight the French!"

"No room for his three regiments to deploy, thank God," Major Gittings chimed in. "If your sailors and Marines can do the dirty work in the gorge, Sir Alan, we could do with two companies of the battalion, and only use one transport, this time. As the Colonel says, in, boom, and out, quick as one could say 'knife'!"

"Guards, though," Mr. Quill said in a soft, speculative drawl. "You saw none, *Don* Julio? Nor did your, ah . . . *capo*'s son? Whyever not, I wonder? Surely, if we recognise it as vital, so must they. I would imagine that the French would post guards to protect it, or to charge fees, and inspect cargoes, for civilian users."

"Aha, good point, sir," Col. Tarrant said, frowning. "Whyever not? You looked the bridge over during the day, *Don* Julio, on a weekday? And what did the locals in Pizzo tell you about sentries?"

"I saw small parties of *cavalleria* cross the bridge," *Don* Julio said in a low voice, arms crossed over his deep chest in defence, "a convoy of waggons, with soldiers on foot. Local waggons, pack mules, and carts," he added with a dismissive shrug, "but no guards who sat close by, except for some who stopped to eat, then moved on. Guards? I see none," he concluded, as if to say "so there!"

"Before we launch this, I fear we must find a way to place some watchers over the bridge," Col. Tarrant decided, pulling at his nose in frustration. "If there are sentries, they may not be in strength, but there might be enough to see us land, and scale the boulders."

"Hah!" Lewrie added, "If the French *do* have sentries, the sight of our ships closing the coast off the gorge would be warning enough. If they're mounted, a rider could summon their cavalry from Filadelfia, or infantry from Vibo Valentia. Too bad we can't send off a landing party in the wee hours from far offshore, who could creep up on them and cut a few throats."

"What a ghoulish idea!" Major Gittings exclaimed, though with a laugh. "More Mister Quill's line of work, what? Pity. Going ashore round two A.M. would be far too noisy, troops stumbling over themselves, getting lost in the dark, trying to carry powder kegs and fuses, picks and shovels? I fear even the lads in our Light Company are not that stealthy."

"Picks and shovels?" Quill asked.

"We might have to dig round the foot of that central pillar to lay charges," Gittings told him. "Though, it's surely firmly bedded 'gainst solid rock. Another matter, sirs . . . we don't have any, at present. Not nearly enough, anyway."

Christ! Lewrie thought with an inaudible groan; *It started out sounding like an easy operation. A total waste of time and effort, so far. Blather, blather, blather! At least the wine's good!*

"More observation is called for before we sail off, all eager and un-informed," Col. Tarrant summed up. "We must knew if there are sentries guarding the bridge, how many, and what their hours are. And I think that we'll need to scrounge up picks and shovels to add to the ones we have. Whilst you, or some of your men, *Don* Julio, go back to Pizzo, and fish within sight of the bridge and the gorge, I will ask the Army staff at the *Castello* in Messina if they might lend us an officer of Engineers. Failing that, at least a brief tutorial on how to blow up a bridge from someone who knows how."

"*Sì*, I go back," *Don* Julio agreed, though sounding weary of the ne-cessity, "but *Signore* Quill must advance me some funds, first."

"Oh, of course, *Don* Julio," Quill responded, though Lewrie got the impression that Caesare did not come cheap, and had already asked too often.

"Hmm, I wonder . . ." Lewrie said as the conference drew to its own closure, all of them rising as if nothing more need be said at the moment, "when you go back to scout, *Don* Julio, it might be a good idea for one of my officers, or an officer from the Ninety-Fourth, go with you. A naval, or military eye might speed the scheme along."

Julio Caesare uttered a dry, sarcastic laugh at that.

"This *ufficiale* speaks Italian like a Calabrian, *Capitano Inglese?*" *Don* Julio smirked. "Wear uniform, hah? He smell of fish and have hard hands? He know how to act like a local? I tell you *no!*"

"That might be a tad too dangerous," Mr. Quill seemed to agree. "Give the game away. Unless you're thinking of going, yourself, Sir Alan?"

"God, no!" Lewrie was quick to say. "Not me! Bull in the old china shop, hey? I can barely get by in *English*. I just thought a professional appraisal of the lay of the land would be useful."

"I have man who was *soldato* before *i Francesi* defeat the Neapolitan Army," *Don* Julio assured them. "He can do what you ask. You met him in Messina, *Capitano*. 'Tonio?"

The first time that *Don* Julio and his henchmen came to Quill's water-front lodgings to meet Lewrie, he had introduced them, and more than half of them had borne the cover name of "'Tonio" . . . except for the odd Julio and one "Antonio"; his mother insisted on using the full name!

"If you say so, *Signore*," Col. Tarrant grudgingly allowed, after a long thought. "Take you some time to sail there, scout, and report back? Good. I'll ask about at the *Castello* in the meantime. Obtain sufficient powder and fuses, tools, and advice from an Engineer."

And I'll still have that working supper, Lewrie assured himself; *and pick my officers' minds*. And *finish a letter to Jessica!*

CHAPTER SEVEN

L ewrie's officers, Navy or Marine alike, had been enthused by the challenge, though none had the first clue on how to blow up the bridge; nets full of powder kegs hauled up taut against the bottom of the spans either side of the pillar *sounded* like a good idea, but there was no way of knowing. Lewrie had made a quick, slap-dash copy of the drawing to refer to, and they had all pored over the coastal charts of Saint Eufemia Bay, which did not avail them much, for any sea chart depicted no details beyond what could be seen from a ship as so much blank *terra incognita* beyond the last and tallest line of hills or mountains. Pizzo was there, the coast road was indicated, but the bridge was not, though the gorge was shown. Land maps were sent for in Messina, and Col. Tarrant produced the only one available, which they had to share. Not trusting a short trip by sea, Tarrant and a subaltern hired a farm cart for his trip there and back.

Of course, rumour and speculation about the pending operation were rife among *Vigilance*'s crew mere hours after that working supper in the great-cabins; there was no secrecy aboard a warship, and never could be, so wagers as to what day the squadron might sally forth were made, in money that most had to promise from future pay or in sippers or gulpers from the rum issues after *Vigilance* returned to its anchorage off Milazzo. British tars would bet on anything!

Lt. Creswell commanding the *Lady Merton* transport was sent off to Malta with mail in reply to what they had recently received, along with requests for the ships, and items the 94th thought necessary to fulfilling the raid, along with their usual supply requests. He returned, and still there was no word from Julio Caesare.

The *Lady Merton* also brought fresh batches of mail, into which Lewrie dove with eagerness. The official stuff, though, didn't please. Admiralty sounded as if they *might* find him two more armed transports, naval crews in the numbers requested, and pay for twelve new barges to be constructed, but . . . before they could order Captain Middleton off to repeat his previous searches and purchases, the First Secretarty, Mr. Croker, had to hear specifics from the Army's headquarters at Horse Guards, as to exactly how many recruits had been obtained for the 94th Regiment of Foot, and Horse Guards had yet to receive any confirmation from Peterborough, on the numbers, or when the new volunteers would be considered well-trained enough to be sent overseas. For the nonce, Lewrie and the 94th would have to make do with what they had!

In the meantime, *Vigilance* and the 94th continued to drill, to practice boarding ship, rowing ashore, staging mock attacks, and rowing back to re-board. The Marine complement spent long hours at the shore firing range, or skirmishing in the woods, fruit and olive groves. With the new additions to the boarding nets, the time that it took for them to scramble down into the boats greatly improved. Cutlass drill, pike drill, boat crew sailors, and others honed their musketry, from the rails, or in trips ashore to use the Army's range. And artillery drill! Lewrie had always found great satisfaction in the roar and stink of the great guns, and had enthusiastically adopted the concept of *aimed* fire at practical ranges, with crude sights notched into the muzzles and breeching rings of his ship's guns, to useful effect in HMS *Sapphire* off the north coast of Spain, and now in *Vigilance*. When dry firing drill palled, he took the ship out to sea for a few miles, and let his crews fire at towed targets behind one of the barges under sail, spending his own money on tobacco and full rum issues to reward accurate gun crews.

Seemingly a fortnight later, a signal was broken out on the flag tower on the beach, a Navy order/request hoisted by the Army; Captain Repair On Board, followed by Q Here.

About bloody time, too! Lewrie thought as he scrambled to get present-able for a call ashore.

"Our pirate didn't come, this time?" Lewrie asked once he had been wel-comed into Col. Tarrant's hut, and a bottle of cooled wine had been shared round.

"Pressing business concerns, he said," Mr. Quill explained to him. "We're not his only iron in the fire, as it were. But, he gave me everything he'd gleaned before sailing off to do God knows what."

"It's looking better and better," Major Gittings declared the new infor-mation, pointing to a map and a sketch already spread out on a table top.

"That signal we sent, Sir Alan," Tarrant enquired, "was it nautical enough, hah hah?"

"Well, actually, Captain Repair On Board is more of an order from a senior officer to a junior, Colonel," Lewrie informed him.

"Oh my word, how clumsy of me!" Tarrant exclaimed, aghast at his er-ror. "Do pardon the wording, sir. And my ignorant insult."

"Nothing of the kind, Colonel, don't worry about it," Lewrie said with a grin and a wave of one hand. "Now, what's more promisng?"

"There's a better way up to the coast road, for one thing," the Major said with a faint grin. "*Don* Julio's man, that ''Tonio,' walked from Pizzo to the bridge, and actually *crossed* it, then went another mile or so farther on, and found a much easier slope down to a wide sand and gravel beach, much wider than the one at the foot of that gorge. Wide enough, too, for all the barges to land abreast at the same time. We could put two compa-nies ashore there, out of sight of any watchers or sentries on the bridge. A quick march at the double a mile or so to the bridge, and we'd have it in our hands in a twinkling, hah!"

"Whilst I land my Marines with the explosives and fuses below the bridge?" Lewrie presumed.

"Well, not at the same time, Sir Alan," Col. Tarrant said with a wee chuckle. "That would give the game away, especially if we land in broad daylight. Is there any way to get the transport off that beach, there, in the dark, and land my men before dawn? You and your ship could lurk offshore, and only sail in after we show a light to signify that we hold the bridge."

"At night?" Lewrie gawped. "We made a couple of landings off South-ern Spain in the wee hours, but something always went wrong."

Boats had gone ashore at the wrong places, troops had swanned about, lost in the dark, and they had both been damned close-run things full of confusion, and hot fights with Spanish soldiers who should not have been there, with nought but muzzle flashes and the sparks from the pans to mark where anyone was.

"Well, we can't land during the day, sir," Tarrant objected. "There's too much military traffic cross the bridge, in daylight, and all the convoys have escort. I expect the mere sight of our ships closing the coast would bring half the French Army in Calabria down on us. Night would be best. There is only a small guard detail at the bridge after dark."

"Sentries?" Lewrie gawped again, feeling a twinge of alarm.

"A small party, *Don* Julio's man reports," Mr. Quill spoke up. "A dozen, perhaps, at most, under a Sergeant, not a mounted officer."

"And half of them will most-like be fast asleep, wrapped up in their bed-rolls," Major Gittings said dismissively. "Easily overcome."

"A night landing's a great risk, sirs," Lewrie told them. "If there's a moon, or a clear night, we could be seen for miles away, and if it's over-cast and really pitch-dark, it's good odds the transport will not be able to find the beach, and if they do spot it, the boats can still go astray. Christ, *I* might not be able to find the gorge, or the beach at its mouth. *My* boats might go astray and land in the wrong place, adding hours to the work. Two pieces of the puzzle, on their own and unable to support each other? This sounds a bit too complicated, sirs."

Must be drunk on their recent praise, Lewrie told himself.

"So, you see no way to accomplish it?" Col. Tarrant asked with a sad frown of dis-appointment.

"Ehm, what if *Don* Julio's men could light a campfire on the beach in question, Sir Alan?" Mr. Quill proposed.

"Yes, what about that?" Tarrant exclaimed, grasping at the offered straw.

"Hmm . . . well, if one of the ''Tonios' could pretend to fish off the coast there during the day," Lewrie mused aloud, "and go ashore to cook supper, or sleep for a few hours, hmm. The transport could fetch-to instead of anchoring, get your troops onto the beach quickly . . . that *could* work. And, if the night's dark enough, I could sail *Vigilance* in within a couple of miles offshore 'til I see your light on the bridge. Would *Don* Julio do it, Mister Quill?"

"With *Don* Julio, anything is possible, for an additional fee," Quill dryly agreed. "Some of his men are still loafing about in Messina. I will put the matter to them and see what they say. It all will depend on what night you intend to land."

"That'd help," Lewrie said, feeling only a tad relieved. "But . . . these sentries. Cavalry or infantry? And, where do they come from?"

"Foot soldiers, was what I was told," Mr. Quill replied. "No more than a dozen. With a Sergeant in charge, call it a 'baker's dozen,' hah hah."

There's that damned laugh, again! Lewrie thought, cringing; *Someday he'll strangle himself with it, and nobody'll know t'try and help him!*

"Yes," Major Gittings wondered aloud, "where *do* they spring from? There's that cavalry squadron at Filadelfia, and there's foot units at Vibo Valentia, but that's much too far away to march a detachment twelve miles or more each afternoon to guard that bridge. Have the French established a small garrison at Pizzo?"

"*Don* Julio's man says not, Major," Quill told him.

"It would be nice to know if there is an encampment somewhere nearby," Gittings puzzled, leaning over the land map, "perhaps only one company or so, say . . . an hundred men? If only one of the guards slips away from us . . ."

"If they're camped north of the bridge, he won't," Col. Tarrant pointed out, since that was the direction his men would land. "If they're somewhere south of the bridge, 'twixt there and Pizzo, one might, and things might get dicey about the time that we're laying the charges. We must look sharp that we round up all of them, and count all thirteen of your 'baker's dozen,' Mister Quill."

"And hope that a French supply convoy doesn't come rumbling down the road at the wrong time," Major Gittings added.

"Oh, they don't, sirs," Quill piped up. "Their convoys don't move after dark. They encamp in some town or village along the way, and don't set out 'til after their breakfasts, in daylight. You see, it turns out that there *are* partisan bands on the mainland, after all. The sentries on the bridge are there to deny any traffic at night, especially locals intent on mischief. They've only accomplished some few pinpricks, so far, but the French, and their so-called allied troops, are very cautious of late. Messengers now ride with strong escort, in company strength, and small parties of French out foraging, looting, or raping, are found most ghastly dead, with their weapons missing. Lord, how I wish I could converse with *them* to co-ordinate operations! Though, their Marshal Murat repays the partisans with mass executions, *Don* Julio's men say that it only inflames the local fighters the more."

Wish t'God *we had* them *on our side, 'stead of arch-criminals!* Lewrie wished fervently; *And I wager they wouldn't cost us barrels o' guineas in bribes, either!*

"That is most interesting to know, Mister Quill," Tarrant said with a satisfied expression. "So, Sir Alan. Does *Don* Julio light a fire on the beach to guide us, do you now deem the landing practicable?"

"In that event, Colonel, getting two of your companies ashore at the right place seems to be the most important part of the operation, so . . . *if* we get a fire to mark the beach, I'd say it can be done. Pick the day . . . or night, rather," Lewrie said, looking at the eager faces cross the table from him, and assenting, even if he still had doubts. "I'll send you off in *Bristol Lass,* under Lieutenant Fletcher, my most senior, and ablest.

"Mind," he went on, raising a hand to still their enthusiasm, "I'll insist on some practice first, to get your men used to going into the boats at night, and some practice landings somewhere up the coast towards Messina, somewhere that's darkest and least populated."

"Good fellow!" Col. Tarrant exclaimed, all but clapping his hands. "Let's be about it, then, as soon as possible. Our men are eager enough, so even the practice you suggest won't daunt them. I say, Sir Alan, might you stay for dinner?"

"Ah, thankee for the invitation, Colonel, but I must beg off, this time," Lewrie demurred, "my cook promises one of his experiments with local wines, fruits, and spices over a batch of pigeons that we bought, and I cannot let him down. He's much too talented to brush aside, d'ye see. Then, after my repast, I must have my officers in to bring them up to date. Some other time, perhaps. Better yet, I should dine you both in aboard so my man can impress *you.* With his skills."

Lewrie retrieved his hat and sword, and bowed his departure, to make his way down to the beach and the boat landing, but Mr. Quill came trotting after him, calling his name.

"Something else, Mister Quill?" Lewrie asked once brought to a halt.

"This all depends on me getting one of *Don* Julio's men to light a fire, sir?" Quill asked, sounding fretful. "Without his approval, I wonder if he'd care for any of his under-captains getting money from me that he didn't touch, first. If *Don* Julio doesn't allow it . . . !"

"But of course he will, Mister Quill," Lewrie replied, "for you will slip him ten pounds, fifty pounds, whatever he asks! He knows who butters his bread!"

"Yes, he is a man with his eye on the main chance," Quill said with a sigh to acknowledge what a cleft he was in with their piratical scoundrel. "Recall, though, sir, how the drawing of the bridge came to us? How the son of one of his *capos* in Reggio di Calabria made it, passed it to his father, who passed it to *Don* Julio when he visited the man?"

"Aye," Lewrie said, intent on strolling on.

"In Reggio di Calabria, Sir Alan," Quill pointedly said, "where the French have their headquarters. *Don* Julio's criminal activities reach *beyond* Eastern Sicily, onto the mainland. Your first raid at Tropea, we learned after the fact, eliminated his biggest competitor, and emptied his warehouses of his wealth and luxury goods. I begin to wonder how *Don* Julio flourishes on the mainland, *without* some collusion with the French?"

"Good Christ, Quill!" Lewrie spat, "mean t'say ye can't trust your own best source of information?" He said it a tad louder than necessary, forcing Quill to make shushing motions.

"I've had misgivings from the start," Mr. Quill confessed, all but wringing his hands impotently, "My late mentor, Zachariah Twigg, warned us that we might be dealing with scoundrels, rogues, and criminals in our work for Secret Branch.

"He said there are patriots, eager partisans who will work for nothing beyond expenses," Quill went on in a sorrowful voice. "There are some who will sham patriotism and demand money for their services, and there are some others who will serve the highest bidder. *All* of them will betray their countries, and if they become used to betrayal long enough, they will sell out our side as effortlessly as Judas Iscariot betrayed Jesus. I have no illusions about Julio Caesare, *if* that's his real name, I *still* can't determine, but now . . . the more I learn, the more dubious I become."

"You think he's setting us up for a trap?" Lewrie asked him.

"I don't *know*!" Quill confessed. "Two companies, a party of Marines? What would their loss avail the French? Very little, I'd imagine. No, Sir Alan. This may not be his moment. Eliminating a whole specially-trained battalion and your squadron might be reason for him to accept gold napoleons 'stead of gold guineas."

"Now you make me wonder why he was so insistent that none of my officers, or officers from the Ninety-Fourth, went with him on that last scout," Lewrie gravelled.

"Well, it would have been too risky, as he said," Quill allowed with a weak grin. "Someone who can't speak Italian in either a Sicilian or a Calabrian accent, and play the part to the hilt? So long as *Don* Julio is my only source of information, he gets all my gold, with no need to share with anyone else. I dearly wish that there was but *one* patriotic bone in his body, but *Don* Julio is a mercenary right down to his toes. And if London ever did get round to sending me a fellow who *could* pass himself off over there, who could get in touch with a band of partisans, I expect he'd die under suspicious circumstances, so Julio Caesare *remains* my only source.

"Believe me, Sir Alan," Quill added, striving to make light of his burdens, "that library at Cambridge from which I was plucked . . . beguiled, rather . . . seems a paradise now, dry and dusty though it was. So many fascinating and ancient tomes to read, or hunt up for others."

"The best of luck to you, Mister Quill," Lewrie bade him, "And do inform us instanter, soon as you make arrangements for that light on the beach. Back to Messina, are you?"

"This very hour, Sir Alan," Quill told him. "And yes, I shall let you know as soon as the arrangement is made. And the best of luck with you, too, sir."

Christ on a crutch! Lewrie thought; *If I told Tarrant about Quill's suspicions, would he just chuck it all and ask for return to garrison duty on Malta? When and where might we be betrayed to the French? Brr!*

CHAPTER EIGHT

Almost a perfect night for it," *Vigilance*'s First Officer said as he looked aloft for any sign of the commissioning pendant, and how it streamed on the winds. "No moon, no stars, everything black as a boot, and a heavy overcast."

"And the coastline's just as black," Lt. Grace, the Fourth Officer added. "Not a light to be seen anywhere."

"Just about t'say," Lt. Farley agreed with a snigger.

"Captain's on deck," Lt. Grace warned, sensing a new presence.

"How could you tell?" Lewrie quipped as he stumbled forward to the double-wheel helm, the helmsmen, and the only wee glim lit in the compass binnacle, mostly by memory, for the compass cabinet was covered with a folded-over jute bag, only peeked at now and then to see if the ship was still on course of East by North, Half East to stand into the Gulf of Saint Eufemia after a fairly short passage on East, Nor'east from their anchorage off Milazzo.

Three Bells chimed up forward at the belfry, which was below the level of the ship's bulwarks, allowing ship's boys to watch their sandglasses by the light of a small lanthorn.

Dumb habit, Lewrie chid himself as he groped for his pocket watch to confirm the striking of Three Bells; half past 1 A.M. in the Middle Watch. Instead, he raised his head to sniff the wind. It had rained in the afternoon before sailing, from a complete overcast sky, but the winds that drove the clouds had not been overly strong, so it was possible that somewhere over mainland Italy, perhaps on the bridge or beaches, the rains might have lingered, presenting problems for the soldiers who would scramble up to the coast road. It had not been a hard rain, so Lewrie could yet hope that the gorge under the bridge would mostly be dry, so his Marines could dig and plant their charges, and the kegs of powder would not get damp while they did so.

He thought of feeling about the binnacle cabinet racks for one of the night-glasses, which could gather some light, but shrugged and told himself that there could be nothing to see, even upside down and backwards; black was black, and so was Italy.

"Deck, there!" a lookout in the main top shouted down. "There's *some* sorta light ahead! Two points off th' starb'd bows!"

"That'd be somewhere Due East?" Lewrie asked. "You here, Mister Wickersham?"

"Aye, sir," the Sailing Master spoke up from somewhere over to larboard. "Perhaps a bit below Due East. Chart space, sir?"

"Aye, let's have a look," Lewrie agreed, leaving his rightful place at the weather corner of the quarterdeck to join Wickersham at the door to the chart space. The Sailing Master opened the flimsy door, swept back the dark wool blanket hung to hide the light, and they both stepped into the glow of two bulkhead candle sconces that illuminated the pertinent chart.

"Ah, roughly Due East of our track by Dead Reckoning, hmm . . ." Wickersham mused aloud, stepping off their course with a pair of brass dividers, "that would most-like be the village of Pizzo, sir. Tropea's Sou'West of us, by now."

"And with Pizzo two points off the starboard bows, that'd put us almost directly headin' for the beach by the bridge," Lewrie said. "And, with any luck, we're well clear of the coast twixt Tropea and Pizzo. Ehm . . . say ten miles to our landing place, sir?"

"Aye, about that, sir," Wickersham gruffly agreed.

"Think I'll go to the poop deck for a look-see," Lewrie told him, brushing the blanket aside and standing between it and the door before leaving the chart space.

This time, a night-telescope availed to reveal a weak and dim constellation of lights ashore, right on the horizon, and sometimes dipping out of sight as the sea scended and the ship rolled over it.

Lewrie didn't think that he was seeing lanthorns round Pizzo's small fishing harbour; like most coastal villages on that coast, what lights he could make out would be up-slope in the upper town. Lewrie paced over to the larboard side, breasted into the bulwarks to steady himself, and swung the night-glass in hopes of spotting *Bristol Lass,* but she was still invisible. The last the two ships had seen of each other had been hours before, when taffrail lanthorns had been doused. He could only imagine that Lt. Fletcher was firm on course for that beach where he would land Col. Tarrant and his two companies.

If *there's a bloody beacon,* Lewrie thought; If *the French don't bag Caesare's men. God's Balls, what a cock-up this could be, yet! Just t'be a bit safer . . . !*

"Mister Farley, a *quarter* point to larboard, if you please," Lewrie called down to the dark quarterdeck below him. "A spoke or two."

"Aye, sir," the First Officer replied, "a spoke or two to larboard, Quartermaster," he relayed to the helmsmen, and there was a brief wink of light as the compass was bared for a second to peer into the bowl.

Lewrie went down the ladderway to the quarterdeck by feel in the stygian blackness, step by careful step, then made his way to the cross-deck hammock stanchions at the forward edge, so he could look down into the waist.

During a normal night at sea, only half the crew would be up and standing watch, and all the Marines who got "all night in" privileges, but for those who stood sentry, would be asleep below, swaying, snoring, and breaking wind in their hammocks. Not tonight, no.

Everyone was astir, and Lewrie could sense their presence more than he could see them. Boat crews were already mustered, boarding nets were already slung overside, and Marines assigned to each boat were clustered by the nets, fully uniformed and armed, rucksacks, canteens, and sheathed bayonets rustling and clinking now and then. The men could not be silent, though their conversations were muted into whispers, broken here and there by bad jokes, almost gallows humour, and the groans or laughs forced from the listeners.

Somewhere, amidships of all that there were heavy cargo nets, and keg after keg of gunpowder sacrificed from the ship's magazines, along with a quarter-mile of slow-match fuse, and a Gunner's Mate and one of the Yeomen of The Powder to see to it all, go ashore with the Marines, and set and light the fuses when the time came.

"Deck, there!" the main top lookout shouted, again. "Wee lights, dead ahead! And another'un, one point off the larboard bows!"

Lights dead ahead? Lewrie thought, the sudden loud voice like to make him jump out of his skin; *One off to larboard, aye, that'd be the beacon on the beach, but . . . what the bloody Hell are lights doin' smack on the bows?*

"Mister Peagram, we will fetch the ship to," Lt. Fletcher cautiously ordered, after a long peer forward with his night-glass.

"Helm down, Quartermaster!" Sub-Lieutenant Peagram shouted to the helmsmen at the wheel aboard *Bristol Lass*. "Hands to the sheets and braces, ready to flat aback the fore course and tops'l!"

"There's your beacon, Colonel Tarrant," Fletcher said to the man standing near him. "I think I can just make out a cutter-sized boat drawn up ashore, some sort of canvas lean-to shelter, and some men pacing about."

"Very well, Lieutenant, we'll be off, then," Col. Tarrant said as he hitched at his sword belt and accoutrements hung about his waist and shoulders. "How far is it to the beach, do you think?"

"I make it about a mile, or a little less, sir," Lt. Fletcher replied. "There's very little surf, I believe, so you and your men should land without getting your legs soaked to their knees. Do you hear, there!" he shouted forward. "Draw the barges up from astern, and prepare to man them!"

"Ehm, sir," Captain Wiley of the Light Company intruded, "The lights down by the bridge . . . any idea what they signify?"

Tarrant raised his small pocket telescope for a better look.

"Looks to be a campfire, and torches, either end of the thing," Tarrant said at last. "The guard detail had to eat and keep themselves warm, and most-like needs torches to see anyone, or anything, coming along the road at night. Rejoin your company and make ready to get into the damned boats. God, I *hate* the bloody things!"

"Boats alongside, sir!" Midshipman Mabry reported.

"Boat crews, man your boats!" Fletcher snapped. "Haul taut to the nets and be ready to take the soldiers aboard!"

"The ship is fetched-to, sir," Sub-Lieutenant Peagram called out. "Only a very slight lee drift, less than one knot."

"Thank you for the yachting, sir," Col. Tarrant said, shaking hands with Fletcher for a moment, "We'll see you in the morning."

"Aye, sir. Piping hot gruel for all after we pick you up." Fletcher japed.

"Ninety-Fourth, board your boats!" Tarrant shouted, leaving *Bristol Lass*'s small quarterdeck, bound for the nearest net.

"Where we goin', then?" one of the soldiers cried.

"Inta bloody boats, ye idjits!" dozens shouted back the old saw from their first days of training. "Tarrant's Tadpoles, huzzah!"

"Aye, sir, that's a large campfire on the beach north of us, no error," Lt. Farley said as he peered hard with his night-glass. "And I can see a boat drawn up on the shore. Just one, so far. No sign of the boats from *Bristol Lass*."

"Then what the Hell are *those*, then?" Lewrie fumed, peering just as hard at the lights on or near the bridge. "Tarrant and his troops simply *can't* have taken it already! They're *s'posed* t'show a light when they do, but so many? Shit!"

Stoic, dammit, stoic! he chid himself; *Act like a proper Post-Captain, at least!* But his talk with Mr. Quill about *Don* Julio's trustworthiness, disloyalty, and betrayal had him flustered, expecting that they'd sailed into a clever ambush.

"How far offshore are we, d'ye make it, Mister Wickersham?" Lewrie asked, after taking a deep, calming breath.

"Still two or three miles seaward, sir," the Sailing Master estimated.

"Well, then, steer for the lights, Mister Farley," Lewrie said, "and, I'll have the main course drawn up in 'Spanish reefs' to get a bit of way off her, and the fore course reduced one reef."

"Aye, sir!" Farley replied, stepping forward to the hammock stanchions to shout orders forward.

Lewrie made a quick trip to the poop deck to sense the winds, swivelling his head back and forth to feel it on his cheeks, determining that the wind was out of the West by North, very fine on the larboard quarter, but light, and steady, as night winds usually were. From that higher perch, he raised his telescope, again, straining to make sense of those shore lights, just as Five Bells of the Middle chimed; half past two in the morning.

He saw four wee glows at what he took for the ends of the span, a pair at each end, and a larger blob of light he took for a campfire at the north end of the bridge. The rest of the coast immediately ahead was utter blackness. A mile north or so, the beacon lit on the beach drew his attention, and, with a whoosh of relief, by its light he could barely make out boats—barges!—grinding ashore onto the sand and shingle. At least Tarrant and his men where ashore, at last!

Better and better, he thought; *Well,* a little *better. He and his men'll go cautious, scoutin' and skirmishin' in pairs and fours. I've seen 'em do it!* They'll *not get caught in a trap.*

But, if they did, there was nothing he could do to help them.

"Everyone up top, Captain Wiley?" Tarrant asked, breathing hard after a tough scramble up the so-called easier slope, clinging to any immovable rock or stoutly rooted shrub on his way.

"Yes, sir, all up." Wiley told him, un-corking his canteen for a welcome "wet."

"Right, then, first section out forward, and advance with twenty yards between sections."

"Yes, sir," Wiley replied, trotting out to join his company and order the first section of twelve men to scout in skirmish order, two pairs to either side of the road and four men behind them down the middle, one pair on the roadside sprinting forward to kneel to cover the advance of the next.

"Meacham," Tarrant hissed into the dark for the officer in command of one of the Line Companies. "You up? Still have all that damned rope with you?"

"Yes, sir, here," Captain Meacham reported.

"Skirmish order down the road, with one section to keep a sharp eye on our rear," Tarrant ordered. "I'll go with you. Carson, do you stay close, ready to run messages," he said to his orderly.

"Roight on yer 'eels, sir," Corporal Carson whispered back.

The last section of twelve from the Light Company passed by, and Tarrant counted under his breath to let them get at least ten yards in advance of Meacham's company, then snapped "Let's be about it" and stepped off to follow.

Try as they might to go silently, the soldiers could not avoid making noises; stumbling and feeling with their feet along the stone verge along the seaward side of the road, barely eight inches above the dirt of the road. The pairs on the landward side had scrub brush to deal with, and a ditch between the road and the steep slope that led up-slope above them, into which they kept sliding or stumbling, and hob-nailed boots clinked against loose stones in a continual clatter.

Col. Tarrant's breezy estimate of a quarter-hour to land and seize the bridge was right out; it took the better part of an hour before the lead section scouts knelt as they espied the two torches standing at the north end of the bridge, whispering urgently for an officer to come forward, and to warn the column to halt.

Captain Wiley stumbled forward to their summons, bent over at the waist in a furtive crouch, clutching his sword hilt with one hand. " 'Bout a hundred yards, sir," one of the scouts told him. "But I can make out people stirrin' about."

"Damn," Wiley spat. "Half of them should be asleep by now."

"A *lot* of 'em, sir," the soldier hissed. "Goddamn!"

Muskets blasted the night in sharp barks and long, stabbing gushes of red-amber discharge! Men whooped like Red Indians, shouted, and by the light of the torches, Captain Wiley could see the flashes of swords slashing, bayonets stabbing . . . someone!

"Goddamn right!" Wiley exclaimed.

"Firing ashore, sir!" Lt. Grace shouted. "The Ninety-Fourth is taking the bridge!"

Lewrie snapped his telescope to his right eye in time to see muzzle flashes, rather more of them than he'd suspected. But, they were happening at the south end of the bridge, too, and there was no way that Tarrant had snuck his men past the sentries before attacking them from *both* ends.

"Mister Farley, man our boats, and let's get our shore party on the move," Lewrie decided, not waiting for some wig-wagged light. "Off you go, Captain Whitehead, off you go, Mister Rutland!"

Vigilance had crept shoreward since first spotting the boats from *Bristol Lass* grounding onto the beach, finally swinging her bows into the wind to fetch-to, jibs and spanker driving her forward, and her fore course and tops'l laid flat aback to deter forward motion. The leadsmen in the fore chains had found five fathoms in which to drift, and the ship now lay a bit over half a mile offshore, still safely hidden in the darkness.

"Light 'em up!" Lewrie shouted aft to the Afterguard, for them to kindle the two big taffrail lanthorns at the stern. Battle lanthorns along the upper gun-deck were also lit, revealing sailors and Marines swinging outboard onto the nets and scrambling down the sides. "And don't forget your picks and shovels!"

"Who the bloody Hell are they?" Col. Tarrant said between deep gasps for breath after dashing to join the Light Company's skirmishers as quickly as he could in the dark.

"Don't know, sir," Captain Wiley replied in a puzzled growl of uncertainty, "but they ain't soldiers. And it appears that they do love killing Frenchmen."

French sentries who had been awake, either end of the bridge, had been shot, then swarmed over, and, whether dead or not, were bayonetted over and over again, or slashed with butcher knives or old swords. The ones who had been asleep round their campfire, wrapped up in blankets, had been mobbed and slaughtered before most of them could get to their feet and arm themselves. There were two who had surrendered, a Sergeant and a Private, who now stood in a circle of civilians who shook weapons at them, stabbing and gouging, peeling their uniform coats and waist-coats off, and binding their arms behind them.

"My word, I do believe they intend to torture them!" Tarrant exclaimed. "Well, we can't have that. It ain't . . . soldierly."

He stood up and waved his first four skirmishers forward to join him as he cautiously strode forward into the torchlight.

"Hoy, *signores!*" he shouted, arms spread wide to signify his peaceable intent. "Hoy, Italianos . . . Calabrians, *sì?*"

Armed men spun about, spread out to form front, some aiming their muskets or pistols at him.

"I am Leftenant-Colonel Tarrant, British Army! *Inglese Colonnello!* We have come to blow up the bridge, ehm . . . the *ponto?*"

"*Che?*" a large man in a grey coat with a sash about his waist asked, swishing a long cavalry sabre at knee level. "*Il ponte?*"

"*Sì, Signore,*" Tarrant declared, feeling a touch more confident. "We come, ehm . . . *arrivare* to, ehm . . . *destruggare il ponto.* Ehm, *multi* gunpowder, *multi* ah . . . kaboom!" he managed to say, flinging his hands into the air, spreading his fingers to show ruination. "*Sì? Ponto* go boom! *Grande* boom!"

"*Soldati Inglese?*" the man asked, breaking into a tentative grin. "Tomasso, he *parlare Inglese*." He sheathed his sabre, waving a short fellow with a captured musket forward.

"You come destroy the bridge, *Signore Colonnello*?" Tomasso asked.

"Yes, *sì*," Col. Tarrant assured him, smiling himself, now that it did not appear that he'd be shot. "Royal Navy ship, just out there, is to land Marines, gunpowder, and blow it up. The French in Reggio di Calabria will starve if it's gone."

Tomasso turned about to translate that to his fellow partisans, which raised a mighty whoop and chorus of cheers.

"We help you, *Colonnello*?" Tomasso offered.

"If you wish, *signore*, though we have it well in hand," Tarrant replied.

"Good! We help! Soon as we kill these bastard *Francesi*!"

"Oh, I say . . ." Col. Tarrant attempted to say, but half of the mob turned on the two French survivors, and prodded them to the nearest tree to be bound. Shirts and trousers were ripped away, baring them to knife slashes at groins and eyes, making them shriek.

"Carson, run find Captain Meacham, and have him bring all the ropes forward," Tarrant ordered, "and tell him we're secure."

"Good Lord, how ghastly," Capt. Wiley exclaimed as the partisans cheerfully went about their ghoulish task, "I've read accounts of how the Spanish and Portuguese treat French prisoners, but I never thought to see it."

The French Sergeant, recognising British uniforms, screamed his plea for mercy from fellow soldiers, keening like a banshee as gashes were cut all down his body.

"We will *not* include this in our official report to London," Col. Tarrant primly said, "and the least said of it to Captain Lewrie, the better, too."

"Of course, sir," Wiley agreed, "though I expect that that odd fellow, Mister Quill will be delighted."

"To hear of murder?" Col. Tarrant archly said, drawing back.

"That we've found him some Italian partisans who will fight, sir," Wiley said.

"Ah! And so we have," Col. Tarrant said, perking up. "Hmm, I wonder if it's too early in the morning to build a fire of our own. I could really relish a good cup of tea."

CHAPTER NINE

If somebody doesn't come tell me what the bloody Hell happened ashore, I'll strangle someone! Lewrie fumed as he paced the bulwarks of the poop deck, peering first with his night-glass, then with his day-telescope, for any clue as to what was being done ashore. Fires were lit under the spans of the bridge, and once glowing hot, rags were wrapped round lengths of foraged wood as torches were scattered round the centre pillar. He could barely make out picks and shovels dully glinting by the torch lights, but he was too far off to hear the sounds of labour. The sea between ship and shore, and the light surf that cast up upon the gravelly beach, glittered with red-gold and amber flickers like fireflies from Hell.

"Hoy, the boat!" a Midshipman shouted to one of *Vigilance*'s barges emerging from the gloom.

"Rutland!" their laconic Second Officer growled back, and Lewrie clumped down the ladderway to the quarterdeck, then onto the sail-tending gangway by the entry-port to greet him, chiding himself to not appear *too* eager.

"Ah, Mister Rutland," he said as that worthy clambered up the boarding battens to grasp hold of the bulwarks either side of the entry-port. "The Army had a brief fight for the bridge, did they?"

"Oh no, sir," Lt. Rutland told him, heaving a brief gasp for air after his climb. "It appears some local partisans beat them to it. The Ninety-Fourth didn't have to fire a shot, and no one even skinned a knuckle," Rutland said in his usually gloomy way, as if he found the lack of bloodshed de-plorable and dis-appointing. "We need crow-levers, sir."

"Crow-levers," Lewrie echoed.

"To pry the stones of the pillar loose, sir," Rutland said, "the picks and shovels are of little avail. Very little soil for us to dig through, and the base of the pillar might as well be one with the rock on which it rests. We *might* grub enough room for charges to be placed by sun-up, or later."

"You've spoken with Colonel Tarrant?" Lewrie pressed. "Does he know where the guard detail came from, where the rest of them might be encamped?"

"We've shouted at each other, sir," Rutland told him, "he upon the bridge, me in the gorge, but he's not mentioned that, yet."

Lewrie felt a tearing urge to go ashore with Rutland as soon as he gath-ered up some long iron crow-levers that gunners used to shift the tra-verse of their wood carriages, but for once, he forebore; he remembered the description of how one could get up to the bridge by scrambling from one boulder to the next, like a mountain goat, and he didn't think it worth the effort.

Time I get there, Tarrant might not know much more than what I know now, he thought; *Bugger it. I ain't a goat, and I'll not wear my lungs out, shoutin' with him from the gorge.*

"Right then, Mister Rutland, carry on," Lewrie ordered.

"Aye, sir," Rutland said, touching the brim of his hat.

Lewrie pondered where a French encampment might be in the area, close enough for a sentry detail to be sent each night to guard the bridge. The village of Pizzo made the most sense, but two scouts by *Don* Julio, then his man "'Tonio," said not. If there was partisan activity in the area, he doubted if the French troop strength would be less than a battalion, but . . . where could they shelter and defend themselves? And if alerted, how soon might they come to defend the bridge? Lewrie dearly wished that *Tarrant* was thinking about it, for it sounded as if the setting of ex-plosive charges was taking even longer than they'd expected, and if the soldiers were still ashore after daybreak, and his ships close ashore wait-ing for them, then this quick incursion might run into a hornet's nest of trouble!

"Mister Wickersham," Lewrie called out for the Sailing Master, "are we still in five fathoms of water? And do you have any way to determine the distance to the shore?"

"Aye, sir, still in five fathoms, the last casts of the leads," Wickersham replied from a corner of the quarterdeck, "Though, if the wind picks up from offshore, we will have to anchor or brace round the yards to stay off. I *think* we're half a mile offshore, but the sketches gave no height of the bridge, and in the dark, I'd just be guessing, sorry, sir. Trigonometry does not avail at the moment."

"Mister Farley? Hands aloft to take in all sail, and let go the bower and a stern kedge anchor," Lewrie was forced to order. It appeared that they were going to be there quite awhile.

"Might as well be hackin' away in a coal or tin mine," stroke-oar of Lewrie's boat, John Kitch, carped to his mates as he paused to take a sip from his canteen.

"Coal mine'd be easier," another sailor griped as he swung his pick, raising a shower of flinty sparks and a fine shower of stone chips from the base stone he was attacking. "Dammit!" he spat as he felt the ring of iron on stone right up the wooden handle that stung him up his arms to his shoulders. "I know coal. Joined the Navy t'get away from all this, I did. Jesus, we'll be at it all damned day!"

"Put yer backs in it, lads!" a Bosun's Mate encouraged.

"Ah, fuck yerself," Kitch muttered. "I don't see *your* back in it!"

"Crow-levers!" Lt. Rutland was yelling as bundles of gun tools were fetched up from the beach. "Anyone has a gap 'twixt the stones yet, sing out, and try prying with a crow-lever!"

Kitch's team stopped work to inspect what they'd accomplished by the light of a torch, shrugged to each other, and went back to it, without the aid of a crow-lever.

"Look out below!" someone on the bridge called down, a moment before long ropes were dropped over, four from each span, that would hoist the cargo nets full of fused powder kegs up snug beneath them, when the explosives were prepared.

"It gettin' lighter?" someone asked, looking round.

"Close t'false dawn, I expect," another opined.

"Shit," someone spat, then took another swing with his pick. "Should'a brought gloves."

Lieutenant Rutland was back aboard by 7 A.M., just as Six Bells chimed from the forecastle belfry, a sound which made Lewrie grind his teeth each time the bell sounded.

"Any progress, Mister Rutland?" Lewrie asked; wished for, in truth.

"We've two places where we've managed to chip out and lever the outer course of stones out, sir," Lt. Rutland reported, "but there's another course inside those. God only knows how many layers there are to go. Captain Whitehead thinks we should lay the charges now, and hope for the best. He's read that the Romans filled the middle of their bridge pillars with rubble, so the charges *may* succeed."

"Or, it's solid stone right through, and they won't," Lewrie said with equal gloom. "Very well, let's fetch the Marines and all but the Gunner's Mate's men off, and have them prepare the charges."

"Aye, sir," Rutland replied, turning to look about for a likely Midshipman to go ashore and relay that order.

"Still no sign of French troops, sir," Lt. Greenleaf cheerfully pointed out. "We may get everyone away, Scot free, and not one man injured . . . but for blisters, haw!"

Lewrie turned his head to glare at Greenleaf, brows furrowed, and his usually merry blue eyes gone Arctic grey, and Lt. Greenleaf shrank into his coat and found something important to see to.

"Mister Upchurch, you're in charge of signals?" Lewrie called out.

"Aye, sir!" Midshipman Upchurch answered from the taffrails aft.

"Make Dis-Continue The Action, then spell out Recall," Lewrie said, looking up the coast where *Bristol Lass* lay at anchor, waiting for her boats and the soldiers to return to her. Before they had left Milazzo, Lewrie had made sure that Col. Tarrant and his officers had a simplified book of code flag signals.

"*Vigilance* is making a signal hoist, sir!" an Ensign from the Ninety-Fourth piped up. "It is Recall."

"And about time, too," Col. Tarrant said with a firm nod as he peered over the side of the bridge into the gorge to see Marines and sailors gathering up their tools, casting off coats and shirts, and making a weary way down to the boats at the foot of the gorge. "Carson, run tell Captain Meacham to shift his company up the road closer to where we came ashore. Skirmish order, just to be wary, mind. Wiley, let's get your men ready to haul the nets up against the bottom of the spans, soon as the Navy says they're fused and ready."

"Yes, sir," Capt. Wiley replied.

"Ah, *Signore* Tomasso," Tarrant said, turning to his English-speaking interpreter, "we're about ready to prepare the charges and light the fuses. You might tell *Signore* 'Spada' that he might move his men back to a safe distance." Tarrant shook his head at the pretension of the partisan leader's insistence upon keeping his real name secret, choosing instead "Sword" as a sobriquet.

Tomasso relayed that to his leader, then engaged in some more palaver before saying "*Signore Spada,* he ask again if you can spare some muskets, *Signore Colonnello.*"

"Tell him that I cannot spare any at the moment," Tarrant said with a *moue,* "and that if I could, only fourty cartridges could be given him, and then they would be useless. Better for him to take sixty-three calibre muskets from the French, for ammunition for them is closer to hand."

As he waited for that to be explained to "Spada," Tarrant had an idea.

"Tell him that I will relay his best wishes to a fellow by the name of Quill," Tarrant continued, inspired, "who lives in Messina. He is a British agent who urgently wishes to speak with, and aid, anyone in Calabria who fights for liberation from the French. Send a letter to him by smuggler, or send a messenger to speak directly with him. Mister Quill can arrange arms and ammunition for you, and he and your leader can make arrangements for one of our ships to come meet you at some safe place to deliver what you need."

Tomasso's face lit up at the promise of aid, and after he had relayed all that to his leader, so did Spada's face.

"Hoy, the bridge!" someone shouted from the gorge below.

"Yes?" Captain Wiley shouted back.

"Ready t'tail on them lines an' haul taut when we tells ya!" Gunner's Mate Finney bawled aloft.

⚓

Finally! Lewrie thought with rising excitement as the barges with the Marines and sailors returned aboard. One barge remained on the beach, bow barely resting on the sand and gravel, oarsmen holding their oars aloft, ready to stroke away. Lewrie raised his day-glass to study the activities. He could see kegs of gunpowder stacked by the foot of the bridge pillar, dirt and gravel packed in heaps to contain the blasts even a little bit. The cargo nets with more kegs of powder were inching upwards, with his shore party carefully spooling out long slow-match fuses as the nets rose.

Lewrie raised his glass to study the bridge and its approaches; the raggedly-dressed partisans had gone south for safe vantage points, now almost invisible in the scrubby trees and bushes. The soldiers of the 94th had marched away to return to their beach and recovery, leaving only a small party to do the hauling, and Lewrie recognised Col. Tarrant, who had shed his stovepipe shako for a feather-adorned bicorne. Some last lashings, and even the men atop the bridge took up their arms and trotted north away from the blasts to come.

Lewrie pulled out his pocket watch, begrudging the fact that it was now three quarters past eight in the morning, well into the Forenoon Watch.

Now there were only three men left in the gorge, Gunner's Mate Finney, Yeomen of The Powder Gullick and Yates, each with a leftover torch in their hands. They dipped them to the fuses as one, tossed the torches aside, and ran for the boat, bounding down the boulder-strewn gorge to the sand, their feet raising spurts of beach to fling themselves over the bows of the barge even as it was shoved off and stroked astern, so they splashed knee-deep through the surf before getting away. Once in water deep enough, the oarsmen stroked about, turning the barge bows-out, then putting their backs into their oars, raising a bow wave and rushing seaward as if the Hounds of Hell were gnawing at the transom.

Three slow-match fuses were fuming, emitting clouds of smoke as the fires slowly made their spitting, fuming way up towards the slung kegs, to the kegs packed round the pillar.

"How long now?" Lt. Grace wondered aloud.

"Captain Whitehead said they estimated ten minute fuses," Lt. Rutland told him. "Soon now . . . if God's just."

"And everything works," Lt. Greenleaf quipped.

"It must," Rutland said. "Don't be a croaker."

Lewrie pulled out his pocket watch, again, his attention torn 'twixt the passage of time, and the view ashore in his telescope. The barge with the last shore party was almost alongside, and yet the fuses continued to shorten and sputter, closer and closer to the kegs.

Come on, come on, come on! Lewrie fumed; *Go bang, please!*

The smoke and red-hot glows on the fuses reached the suspended nets, and the kegs, at last, and the explosions should have come, but a long breath or two later, there was still nothing . . .

Baroom! and a massive cloud of powder smoke erupted under the bridge, followed a moment later by another *Whoom!* under the northern span, as flame-shot belches of stone soared aloft, lighter material pattering all round the bridge, onto the beach, and raining down onto the sea, raising great splashes. Then came a last gigantic explosion under the southern span, and the whole bridge and gorge were smothered with a towering, spreading blanket of gunsmoke!

Vigilance erupted in cheers of joy as her crew celebrated that destruction, tossing hats in the air, her rigging crowded with hands seeking a better view, and even Commission Sea Officers whooped and huzzahed as loudly and as enthusiastically as the Midshipmen and the ship's boys.

For long minutes there was nothing to see ashore as the smoke slowly dissipated and blew inland on a light sea wind, long enough for Lewrie to look to the north towards *Bristol Lass,* where barges were alongside her on both beams, disgorging Tarrant's two companies to safety aboard their transport.

"Ehm, sir," Lt. Farley drew his attention back.

"Hey?" Lewrie said, returning his telescope to the bridge.

"It, ah . . ." Farley said, coughing into his fist.

The smoke had finally blown clear enough to reveal what they'd accomplished, wisps of smoke still rising as if they'd lit a fire.

The north span of the bridge was almost gone, leaving a stub of roadway from each end, loosened stones still dribbling away to clash into the gorge like the slow fall of leaves from a winter-killed tree. The south span was also gone, though a roadway jutted from the end on the edge of the gorge.

"It appears we've blown a gap of at least thirty feet on the north end, sir," Sailing Master Wickersham opined, "but only about twenty feet on the south span. It could be bridgeable, with enough timber. The ah, pillar, though . . ."

The bastard still stood! Stones in the outermost course where they had managed to pry openings had been blasted away, scattered in the gorge, leaving greater, ragged gouges, with the inner course of stones blackened. But, the base had not been harmed, and the bastard still stood in its ancient Roman-engineered defiance!

"Well, shit!" Lewrie spat. "Just damn my eyes. Mine arse on a *band-box*!"

Now, what the Hell do we do? he asked himself, pounding an impotent fist on the lee bulwarks' cap-rails; *What we do best, I s'pose.*

"Mister Farley, beat to Quarters," he snapped. "Man the larb'd lower-deck twenty-four-pounders. If we can't blow it up, we'll have to *pound* it down with roundshot!"

CHAPTER TEN

*C*ast off your guns!" Lt. Greenleaf's voice roared on the lower gun-deck, barely muffled by distance below. The young Marine drummer and flautist rattled off the Long Roll and a squeaky rendition of "Hey, Johnny Cope." Wooden-wheeled gun truck carriages rumbled over the oak decks as the bowsings of the massive 24-pounder cannon were loosed to allow them be hauled inboard so gun crews could withdraw wood tompions, and prepare to load their charges.

"Mister Page?" Lewrie called out to the nearest Midshipman, "Do you go below and inform Mister Greenleaf to aim small, fire gun-by-gun from bow to stern, and the hands are to consider this a competition, with tobacco and full measures of rum for successful crews."

"Aye aye, sir!" Page replied before dashing for the ladderways.

That's one way t'put a gloss on things, Lewrie thought, still in dis-belief that all that gunpowder hadn't brought the damned bridge down; *Bloody damned Romans, hah! And I used t'like Latin at school!*

The 24-pounders were charged with serge cartridge bags of gunpow-der, wads, then shotted, with a second wad inserted with a thump of ram-rods to seat everything firm. "Run out your guns!" was ordered, and *Vigilance* rumbled and faintly vibrated as thirteen loaded cannon and their truck carriages lurched outwards to thud against the stout timbers of the hull, black, menacing barrels projecting from the gun-ports. Recoil tackle was overhauled for safety in equal bights either side of the carriages, so that when fired, the carriages would rush straight back without slewing and hurting someone.

"Prick cartridge!" Lt. Greenleaf bellowed, followed by "Prime!" and sharp tools were jammed down the touch-holes, the flintlock strikers' pans were filled with fine-mealed ignition powder, the firelocks not yet drawn back to cock.

"Take aim!"

Secondary men of each gun crew used crow-levers to shift right or left, lifting the carriages an inch or two off the deck to align the crude-cut notch sights, and the wood quoin blocks beneath the guns' breeches were either shoved deeper to level the barrels, or withdrawn to elevate them, and gun captains hopped, knelt, and squinted to lay their best aim.

"Lower deck ready, sir!" Midshipman Page shouted, panting from his exertion as he regained the weather decks.

"Very well," Lewrie said, extending his telescope, "my respects to Mister Greenleaf, and he is to open upon the bridge."

"Aye, sir!" Page piped up, dis-appointed that he could not stay on deck to witness the fall of shot, but had to dash below again to relay that order.

"Number One gun . . . fire!" Greenleaf yelled, and the forward-most 24-pounder exploded in a great gush of amber flame and an immense cloud of yellow-white powder smoke, instantly blotting out most of the view. And, with the light offshore breeze, it seemingly took forever for that bank of smoke to thin and drift shoreward. Half a dozen telescopes were snapped to their owners' eyes.

"Clean miss, it appears, sir," the First Officer, Mr. Farley opined, lowering his glass.

"Try Number Two gun," Lewrie snapped, hoping that his gunners would recover their former skills. In his last ship, the *Sapphire,* his gunners had gotten quite accurate. *Vigilance*'s gunners had practiced aimed fire at his insistence, but of late, they had had little reason to stay competent.

Boom! and *Vigilance* drummed and echoed to Number Two gun's discharge. Once more, the target disappeared behind a rolling fogbank of smoke. There was a faint, far-off *Spang!* from shore, though, raising hopes—but that, they could see a minute later, was the result of a near-miss that had struck in the gorge beyond the bridge, the roundshot cracking itself into shards on the boulders, leaving glaring white scars on the dark stone.

"Carry on, Mister Greenleaf!" Lewrie shouted. "Even if it takes all bloody day!"

"Aye aye, sir!" Greenleaf shouted back, not *quite* as enthusiastic as before. "Number Three gun . . . fire!"

Some more last-instant fiddling with crow-levers and the quoin block, the gun captain nervous under the glare of an officer and the jeering, scoffing attention of competitors, and . . . *Boom!*

Lost in the roar and the gush of powder smoke, there came a wee *Crump!* from shore, to which everyone on deck cocked an ear, peering intently to see the result.

"I think I see . . . yes, a hit, by God!" Lt. Farley cheered.

A few feet below the top of the pillar, on the left-hand side, there was a gap in the ancient stonework where a large block had been driven in and knocked askew.

"Number Four gun . . . fire!"

On down the larboard battery the firing went 'til all thirteen 24-pounders had tried their skill, and there had been only three hits on the bridge pillar, the last from the after-most gun knocking down a square stone block which took three more with it as it fell into the gorge.

"Now you've your eyes in, pound it down, lads!" Lewrie cried, and the re-loaded Number One gun far up forward erupted in flames and smoke, and there came yet *another Crump!* as solid iron roundshot struck the bridge pillar. When the smoke cleared, the top of the pillar now looked to be about two feet shorter than it had been, and jaggedly erose.

"Deck, there!" a lookout in the mainmast cross-trees shouted down. "Enemy soldiers on the road! Cavalry t'th' north, an' infantry t'th' south!"

"*Took* 'em long enough," Lewrie scoffed as he pulled out his pocket watch, and was faintly alarmed to note that it was half past ten of the morning. *Damme,* he thought; *this is like 'Church work,' it goes hellish-slow!*

"Could we take them under fire, sir?" Lt. Grace eagerly asked.

"Only if they're stupid enough to stand round what's left of the bridge ends, Mister Grace," Lewrie told him with a grin. "Best would be grapeshot from the carronades, but they'd only reach halfway to the area, more's the pity."

"The upper-deck eighteen-pounders, though, sir," Grace pointed out. "We could put the wind up them."

"Only if they interfere, sir," Lewrie decided, "the main thing is to bring the pillar down." Though, as he turned back to look at the shore, he could not miss the expectant expressions on the faces of the upper-gun deck crews, perched along the sail-tending gangway and bulwarks.

Boom! went the Number Five gun below, and, when the gunsmoke had cleared, there was a large hole in the pillar's seaward face where several blocks of stone had been loosened, exposing an inner course of stone. Number Six gun's captain took longer to fire, making everyone bristle with impatience, then finally let loose. And when the smoke cleared, the ship rang with cheers at the sight of the inner course of stone tumbling away into the gorge, with a flood of rubble and earth cascading down with the blocks as if the pillar was gushing entrails.

"Knew it!" Lt. Rutland cried in rare glee, "Whitehead and I were right. The Romans *did* fill the core with rubble!"

"Will you look at the damned fools!" Mr. Wickersham, the Sailing Master exclaimed as he called everyone's attention to the French officers on horseback who had forced their mounts out to the very end of the stub of the north span to look down into the gorge.

"They won't stay there long, Mister Wickersham!" Lt. Grace chortled, just before another 24-pounder roared.

The bridge pillar which had held up traffic cross the span for untold centuries, slowly began to lose the battle, chunks falling at every shot, now, undermining the upper part which still stood. The pillar, as *Don* Julio and the sketches had described it, was eight feet across on the face that presented itself to *Vigilance*'s guns, and ten feet or more wide, so it was still slow going, but, at last, a roundshot hit in the right place, and the entire upper portion, and both stubs left after the charges had gone off beneath the spans, gave way in a spew of rubble and dirt, and came tumbling down in an avalanche of stone, shortening the pillar by twelve feet or more, Wickersham estimated after fiddling with a sextant and a chalk slate. Further hits weakened the remaining portion, creating yet another slumping, tumbling collapse that cut its width almost in half.

"Hah!" the Sailing Master hooted. "That'll take the bastards *years* to re-build. There's no timbers long enough to span *that*!"

"Perhaps, Mister Wickersham," Lewrie allowed, grinning widely, "but, as long as we're here, we might as well be thorough. It's only shot and pow-der, after all. I'd admire we reduce it to a stub before we sail away."

He looked round for Marine Captain Whitehead, thinking to ask his opinion, since he was the only man aboard who claimed to possess even a smattering of engineering. "What say you, sir?" he asked.

"Oh, well, sir . . . the shorter we make it, the harder it will be, the more timber it will take to build upon that base that remains, and I doubt if a timber bridge would bear a quarter of the weight that the old stone bridge did. Might be damned shaky, too," Whitehead slowly judged as round-shot bowled into what was left, one aimed hit at a time. Whitehead had gone below for a wash-up, and still had a towel in his hands, with which he daubed at his face now and again. "Oh, I say!" he exclaimed as the nar-rower portion facing the sea peeled open like an onion, spilling tons of rubble and earth from its innards, taking another five feet of outer and inner stone courses down with it. "I do believe we're almost done, sir!"

About time, too, Lewrie thought, looking at his pocket watch, again; *it's almost time for the first rum issue!*

"Huzzah!" rose from hundreds of throats, and hats were swung about in the air as a couple of roundshot finally brought at least six more feet of the near pillar down, then the far portion, leaving a stump of ragged-topped stone barely two men's height above the rocks in the gorge.

"Cease fire!" Lewrie yelled down to the deck. "Cease fire! Drop it, lads . . . *dead 'un!*" he called out, using the terminology of the rat pit to urge a game terrier to move on to a fresh kill, and that made *Vigilance*'s people laugh out loud and jeer the hapless French who stood on the shore road.

"Secure your guns!" Lt. Greenleaf ordered, his voice loud in the sud-den relative silence after hours of gunfire. "Swab out well, there, and thumb-stall your vents!" Flintlock strikers were carefully taken off and returned to storage, fall-back linstocks were extinguished in the swab-water tubs, the burned ends of the slow-match coiled round them snipped off and tossed out the gun-ports, the tompions were inserted into the guns' muzzles, the ports closed, and the guns hauled up to thump against the port sills to be bowsed securely from rolling about in a heavy sea.

Seven Bells chimed up forward at the forecastle belfry, and one of the Bosun's Mates looked aft at the quarterdeck, his silver call poised near his lips.

"Aye, carry on, Mister Hopper," Lewrie shouted to him.

"D'ye hear, there!" Hopper roared. "Clear Decks an' Up Spirits!" and the drummer and flautist set up a lively tune to celebrate the arrival of the red-painted and gilt-trimmed rum keg.

The jaunty notes of "One Misty, Moisty Morning" filled the ship as the crew queued up to receive their grog, and Lewrie smiled as he wondered if the French ashore could hear it, and wonder what to make of it.

"Lo, sir," Lt. Rutland commented, "this puts me in mind of the Twenty-Third Psalm. The French, and all, watching us?"

"What, all of it, Mister Rutland?" Lewrie japed.

" 'Thou preparest a table before me in the presence of mine enemies,' " Rutland quoted, " 'thou anointest my head with oil.' "

"And, at the moment, our cups runneth over," Lewrie said with a grin, sweeping an arm to encompass the hands waiting for their rum. "Don't know if goodness and mercy shall follow us all our days, sir, but . . . one hopes it mortifies the bloody French!"

BOOK TWO

We few, we happy few, we band of brothers.
—King Henry the Fifth,
Act IV, Scene 8, line 60
William Shakespeare

CHAPTER ELEVEN

*W*hat an utter pile o' rot," Lewrie gloomed after he had read the last of his official despatches from London. He glared at the untidy pile, their blue, black, and red ribbons and wax seals mingling like a dead octopus atop his day-cabin desk, even emitting an imaginary reek of dead, washed-ashore sea beasts. He took a long sip of cool, lemoned and sugared tea, with an admixture of ginger beer, but what relief that pleasant beverage usually provided might as well have been the cup of bitter gall offered Christ on the cross!

> *One must realise, Captain Lewrie, that landing Operations similar to*
> *yours are being adopted by several Commands in Foreign Waters, which*
> *places a greater Demand upon the Transport Board for ships suitable for*
> *the aforesuch; barges, Naval personnel, taken from King's Ships already*
> *short of men . . .*

Lewrie thought it grossly unfair to blame his successes for the lack of troop transports, a back-handed way of blaming him for others emulating his methods all of a sudden. The letter from Admiralty took note of Rear-Admiral Sir Home Riggs Popham's many raids off the north coast of Spain, for one instance, his taking shore batteries, forts, and massive cutting-out expeditions into French-held harbours to sail out prize merchantmen full of goods that deprived the French.

To read Popham's reports to Admiralty, it sounded as if *he* had invented the idea, and Lewrie's innovations were mere aping!

Starve me, glut them! Lewrie thought with a silent groan.

He also strongly suspected that his enemies in the Navy, and their powerful patrons, begrudged him *any* success after all of their efforts to scotch the formation of his scheme had failed to slow him down, or render his efforts futile. Now, it seemed that they had discovered a *new* way to frustrate him.

Admiralty admitted that they knew how many re-enforcements had been recruited and sketchily trained for the 94th Regiment of Foot, and those soldiers *would* be sent on as soon as possible, but for the lack of available transports of *any* kind, much less ships "bought in" as so-called "armed transports" under direct Navy command, and manned by large naval crews. 'Til then, those re-enforcements might as well be twiddling their thumbs and standing "sentry-go" on the ramparts of Hell! Lewrie had even gotten a letter from Captain Middleton, the poor fellow who had been so helpful in purchasing, discovering and obtaining everything needful the first time round, was about to throw up his hands, get drunk, and sulk over the delays!

Lewrie threw himself back into his chair, and raised his eyes to Mme Berenice Pellatan's flattering portrait of his wife, Jessica, on a forward bulkhead.

Not that she needed *flatterin'*, he thought with a brief, fond smile; *Good God, Jessica, if I'd known this'd be so much hand-to-mouth beggin', I'd of stayed home with you, and* damn *my pride!*

He half-shut his eyes to imagine what life would have been like if he had. High Summer, and weeks at his father's country estate in Surrey, at Anglesgreen; his old mount, Anson, and the tractable mare he would have bought her, and pleasant rides round the parish; ales at the Olde Ploughman tavern; lovemaking and sleeping late into the mornings; London and its in-exhaustible host of amusements, and the comfort of their house in Dover Street?

And his damned former in-laws underfoot for the Season, and his ungrateful, spiteful daughter and her eternal sneering at him and at Jessica (thought more than happy to take his money!) and . . .

"Oh, bugger," he muttered under his breath.

"Midshipman Dunn t'see the Cap'm, SAH!" the Marine sentry outside the doors to his great-cabin barked.

"Enter," Lewrie growled, cautioning himself to *not* bite the calf-head's ears off in frustration.

"M-mm-Midshipman Langdon's duty, sir, and I am to inform you that a note has come aboard from the Army camp ashore, sir," the wee young fifteen-year-old chirped. "Ah, ehm . . . a *note* for you, that is, sir!" he quickly added with a nervous gulp.

"Very well, Mister Dunn, hand it over, and my compliments to Mister Langdon," Lewrie allowed, though still frowning stern enough to curdle the Mid's saliva. "Does he *owe* someone so much that he *has* to stand Harbour Watch?"

It was a given that Commission Officers did not stand Harbour Watches; it was also a given that the older Mids would bully their younger messmates to stand watch for them.

"C-c-cards, sir," Dunn stuttered. "B-bad hands, worth one and seven pence."

"That's what you get for layin' wagers, Mister Dunn," Lewrie chid him. "A caution for both of you. You may go."

"Aye aye, sir!" the lad replied, dipping a brief bow from the waist, then dashing out.

"The *note*, you cod's-head!" Lewrie shouted.

"S-s-sorry, sir, sorry!" Dunn yelped, frozen in mid-dash, then scuttling back to the desk to lay it down. More bowing and scraping, and he escaped, face red to his ears.

"Where the Devil did they dredge *that* fool up?" Lewrie asked the aether as he un-sealed the note, to the amusement of his cabin servants.

"Oh, bugger," Lewrie said aloud once more, louder this time.

Lt. Col. Tarrant of the 94th wrote to inform him that the Army staff at Messina had been most impressed by the destruction of that bridge near Pizzo, had not considered how vital it was to the support of the French in Calabria, and how much it would cost them now that it lay in ruins, what with the difficulty the Royal Navy presented if any supplies were sent by sea, and how only two companies of the 94th had pulled it off . . . with the Navy's help, of course.

A deputation from the Commanding General in Sicily will come to inspect our humble encampment, visit with my battalion, and witness how you and I stage seaborne landings. Hah, the whole dog and pony show, I fear, sir! Might those exalted Worthies now Admit that the 94th amounts to anything other than a Boil on their Bums? I shall provide the Supper. Mr. Quill will join us.

Yr. Obdt. Servant,
Lt. Col. Nicholas Tarrant

"Just so long as Brigadier Caruthers ain't a part of it," Lewrie muttered. "That man's too ambitious, even more so than, well, *me*! And Quill? *That'll* put a damper on the day, poor bastard."

The Army staff in the *Castello* at Messina had made it abundantly clear that Foreign Office spies were not welcome at-table with proper gentlemen, and if allowed to dine at all, were seated below the salt; *far* below, if not at a one-man table out in the hall! Quill was a "spook" in more ways than one, a clumsy, black-clad apparition with no *ton*, gawkingly awkward and off-putting to boot.

Damme, this just might prove t'be entertainin'! Lewrie thought with wicked glee; *And if* Don *Julio shows up, even more so!*

When Lewrie went ashore two mornings later, he witnessed a wee cavalcade coming up the road from Messina; a troop of Light Dragoon cavalry, a General officer on horseback with an aide-de-camp riding alongside him, and an open-topped coach-and-four in which another General sat with his own aides.

"Morning, Sir Alan," Tarrant said as he strode to join him.

"*Buongiorno* to you, Colonel Tarrant," Lewrie responded with a wry grin. "I don't see Mister Quill in the party."

"He and his assistant slunk into camp last night, ahead of all this," Tarrant informed him.

"He's an assistant?" Lewrie asked. "About time, I suppose."

"A fellow name of Silvestri," Tarrant said. "Raised in England, but Italian by birth, from some high-ranking Neapolitan exile family. Bankers, I think they were, to the court of King Ferdinand the Fourth, he says."

"Met him once," Lewrie informed Tarrant. "Ugliest old fart ever I did see, but he knew how to cook seafood."

"Hmm?" Tarrant posed.

"The King of Naples and The Two Sicilies had a seafront fried fish shop.

I ate there with Sir William Hamilton, our Ambassador at the time, and his wife . . . Emma Hamilton. *Very* tasty."

"The fried fish, or Emma Hamilton?" Tarrant sniggered.

"Both, sir," Lewrie slyly boasted. "Both."

I'll never know what it is 'bout me . . . and sailors! Lewrie recalled her panting amid the throes of passion; *A spongy ride, she was, though, half tripes and trullibubs even then!*

"So, who's arriving?" Lewrie asked.

"Leftenant-General Sir Robert Malcomb and his catch-farts," Tarrant wryly told him, "Brigadier Caruthers on horseback, and his aide . . ."

"Oh, damn," Lewrie spat.

"You're bringing your Captain Whitehead ashore, Sir Alan?" Tarrant asked.

"Aye, to give him his due," Lewrie answered, "but not 'til later, and Lieutenant Fletcher from *Bristol Lass,* to explain how your men are berthed, victualled, and debarked into their boats. I s'pose a demonstration's in order this afternoon?"

"Count on it, Sir Alan," Tarrant grimly chuckled. "We must put my 'Tadpoles' through their paces for the staff's amusements."

"Even you are calling them by that name, now?" Lewrie asked.

"It seems to have stuck," Col. Tarrant admitted with a grimace of distaste, "though I wish we could invent something more . . . dangerous-sounding. What predator swims ashore, wreaks havoc, then returns to the sea?"

"Selkies," Lewrie told him, "half people, then seals, by times, though it's an Irish, coastal Scot, and Welsh myth. Hah! *Turtles* swim ashore, but only to bury their eggs!"

"Gad, *that'd* make a damned poor regimental badge!" Tarrant said with a roll of his shoulders.

"Hmm, perhaps only a sea-god's trident, then," Lewrie suggested.

"No matter," Tarrant said, drawing himself more erect, shooting his cuffs and tugging at his waist-length coat. "Let us go greet our esteemed arrivals."

It was not an overly impressive entourage that alit from the carriage; Lt.-Gen. Malcomb was a stout fellow in his late fifties or early sixties, putting Lewrie in mind of that dithering Gen. Dalrymple at Gibraltar years before, called the Dowager by many for his years of military service since he was thirteen, who'd never been in battle or commanded troops in action.

Malcomb's aides-de-camp were nigh as old as he was; a clutch of Majors and Colonels who sported more than their share of grey hair.

"Ah de do, Sir Alan," Malcomb said by way of greeting, "Begad, sir, you're West Country, by the sound o' yer name, what, heh heh? A hardy Cornishman of the old-salt school, hey?"

"My mother's family *are* from Devon, sir," Lewrie answered, thinking Malcomb a garrulous fool, at once, "though I spent all my youth in London."

"Well, that's no matter, sir," Malcomb tittered, waving a hand as if to shoo flies, "You and Colonel Tarrant, here, have created a piratical band of great worth, sir, a most intriguin' crowd o' 'Mer-Men,' what? Confusion to the French, hey?"

"We do what we can, Sir Robert," Lewrie said, hiding his wince, and taking a second to glance at Tarrant to see his expression.

"Ah, and here's Brigadier Caruthers," General Malcomb brayed in good cheer, "Brought him along, d'ye see, since he's experience with landin' troops and gigging Frogs, too. Begad, 'tween the three of you, sirs, it's beginnin' t'sound all salt-watery, hey? Mer-Men, Frog giggin', and tarry sailors together, haw haw!"

"Sir Alan, Colonel Tarrant," Brigadier Caruthers said, bowing slightly and touching the tip of his ornately feathered bicorne hat, "a pleasure to re-make your acquaintance."

"Dare I wonder if your interest in our operations, sir, bodes more, and larger, landings, which the Commanding General envisages?" Col. Tarrant enquired.

"Tut tut, my boy," Malcomb waved off with a laugh, "there's many a gap 'twixt the crouch and the leap, what? Time enough for us to see just how you operate, and report back to our superiors, hey? Might you have anything cool laid by, Colonel? The day's growing warm, and I'm as dry as coal dust."

"We've some nice local wine chilled, sir," Tarrant promised, "packed in ice and snow from Mount Etna."

The Commanding General sent you *to report on us?* Lewrie gawped; *And will ye be sobre enough to remember anything ye saw? God help us!*

They went to the shaded gallery of Col. Tarrant's quarters, and Gen. Malcomb sniffed deep of his offered wine, stuck a little finger in the glass for a tentative taste, and frowned.

"Hmm, sweetish, fruity . . ." he grumbled.

"A Sicilian *Pinot Grigio*, sir," Tarrant told him. "They grow nicely in the volcanic soil near Mount Etna."

"Quite nice," Malcomb commented after a deep sip, "and the ice and such sets it off. Brings out the ah . . . flowery, whatyecall it." He fanned himself with his bicorne hat, drained his glass in one more gulp, and held it out for a refill. "Took out that blasted bridge with only two companies, Colonel Tarrant?"

"The steepness of the terrain didn't lend itself to landing the whole battalion, sir," Tarrant explained. "About one hundred twenty men and officers, all landed at once in six barges, and gotten ashore within half an hour."

"Barges? D'ye mean harbour scows," Malcomb questioned, "like we see in the port of Messina?"

"Twenty-nine-foot Admiralty pattern, eight-oared rowing boats, sir," Lewrie supplied, "not flat-bottomed scows or hoys; the largest in Navy inventory. Usually more suited to use by Admirals. Each of our transports tows six of them. They're a bit too heavy to be hoisted aboard and stowed on the boat-tier beams."

"Whatever all that means, haw haw!" Malcomb waved off with one of his laughs, which had begun to irk. "Half an hour, d'ye say? Hah!"

And both Lewrie and Tarrant had to explain about the boarding nets, and how the soldiers of the 94th went over the side all at once.

"Well, that'll be a sight t'see, hey, Caruthers?" Malcomb asked.

"Indeed it will be, sir," the Brigadier agreed, "and much faster than any of my regiments were got ashore, one boat at a time beneath the entry-ports of *my* transports."

"I thought to employ two companies from one transport to demonstrate the technique later today, after dinner, sir," Tarrant said.

In the co-ordinated raids against an host of small seaports on the toe and sole of Calabria's "boot," Caruthers had cobbled together many transports from God only knew where to put the three regiments of his brigade ashore, but his ships had been crewed by civilian mariners, very thinly manned, and with few cutters and gigs to ferry the troops ashore, forcing his soldiers to do their own rowing. Getting them into the boats had been time-consuming, to the point that one of his regiments was *still* dribbling onto the beach half an hour before a French column had marched down to the commotion, and the third regiment hadn't gotten ashore at all, due to the many coasting trading ships and boats that the Navy had sunk or set afire, precluding the use of town piers as a landing place.

Caruthers had met and defeated the French column, anyway, and in fine fashion, with the Navy's help with long-range gunfire support, and Lewrie's knowledge of captured French howitzers, but even he had realised that it had been a damned close-run thing, and, instead of being hailed as a victor, could have lost his command and his place in the Army.

Had a taste o' fame, did ye? Lewrie speculated as he watched the fellow sip wine and scan round as if looking for new ideas; *Bored by garrison duty, and lookin' for more notice in the newspapers? Want a part in what* we're *doin'?*

General Malcomb mentioned the bridge, again, and half an hour was spent in describing the laying of explosive charges, then the aimed gun-fire from *Vigilance* that had taken out the supporting centre pillar, which led to further explanantion of how Lewrie had had crude sights filed into his guns, and where the idea had come from, to which Gen. Malcomb issued the occasional "Well, I never heard the like" several times. He was offered a tour of the ship to show him, but demurred with a shiver, and swore that he had already seen the interiors of troop transports, so there was no need to plunk his bum into a boat and be rowed out for an inspection.

By then it was time for the mid-day meal, a rather impressive repast that Tarrant had laid on; fish course, roast chicken, followed by lamb in lieu of roast beef, with fresh salad greens and vegetables purchased from local farms, and washed down with glass after glass of suitable wines.

Christ, can he stay awake *enough t'see the demonstration after all that?* Lewrie wondered as Malcomb nodded, belched into his napkin, and swayed on his chair, beginning to slur his words. At least his aides-de-camp, perhaps used to staying sobre whilst their superior drank himself to "snoring happyland," still appeared capable of taking notes.

Once fresh fruit and coffee had been served, everyone, even the General, trooped down to the shoreline, and an Infantry Ensign given the signals chore, hoisted the two-flag hoist that Lewrie and Tarrant had agreed upon as their private code for Land Troops.

"Watch closely now, sir," Tarrant told Malcomb. "The barges, which have been towed astern of the transport, will be pulled up alongside, three to each side by the mast shrouds . . ."

Sailors aboard *Lady Merton* sprang to their tasks doing just that, even as boarding nets were cast overside, and men assigned to the boat crews mustered at the bulwarks above the nets, scrambling down to man their barges the instant they were alongside, taking hold of the nets to keep close to the anchored ship. As Col. Tarrant narrated the procedure, soldiers in stove-pipe shakoes, red tunics, and white cross-belts appeared above the rails, muskets and field accoutrements slung over their shoulders and about their bodies, summoned up from below by their officers' whistles.

Lewrie spent his time watching General Malcomb and Brigadier Caruthers and their aides to see what they were making of the demonstration, and how the aides were scribbling in ledger-sized books.

"At the command, troops from each company will go down into the boats by twelve-man sections . . ." Tarrant droned on.

Lewrie noticed Mr. Quill, and his new assistant, who had slunk down to the shore to stand apart to witness the doings, and, deeming Tarrant able to lecture without his help, drifted over to join them.

"*Buongiorno,* Mister Quill," Lewrie said in a low voice, "and who's your newcomer?"

"Allow me to name myself to you, Captain Lewrie," the stranger smoothly said, doffing his hat, "I am John Silvester, late of Oxford, and London, formerly Giovanni Silvestri of Napoli, 'til King Ferdinand was ousted, when my family sought shelter and exile in England. I am come to aid Mister Quill in all things Italian."

"About time, too," Mr. Quill said. "Especially so, now that we seem to have discovered a band of partisans over on the mainland."

"Aye, Colonel Tarrant told me a little about that," Lewrie responded. "Pleasure t'make your acquaintance, Mister Silvester."

Lewrie gave the new-come a good looking over, wondering if the young man would be any help at all; John, or Giovanni, Silvestri would not be out of place, or thought poorly dressed, in Ranelagh Gardens, the Theatre Royal in Drury Lane, or gambling at the Cocoa Tree back in London. Silvester, or Silvestri, was dark-haired, somewhat too good-looking, in an light-olive complexioned way, dark-eyed, and too full of seeming mirth to play the part of a *paisano* in Calabria, yet . . . his hand, when shaken, was as rough and calloused as any Jack Tar in his crew.

"I am looking forward to returning to my poor country, sir," the young fellow further said, "as soon as I may gather the proper clothes to cloak my purpose, and find transport with this *Don* Julio that Mister Quill has told me about."

"Are ye sure ye can play-act native, sir?" Lewrie asked with a deep scowl. "One slip, and . . ."

Silvestri slouched, launched into a long, incomprehensible palaver in Italian, replete with expressive hands, swiped his long hair into a tousle, and even spat on the ground as if to make a point.

"Well, you convince me, but what do I know?" Lewrie had to confess. "Just so long as you don't turn into a Romney Marsh."

"Ah, *sì sì, Signore* Marsh!" Silvestri enthusiastically cried. *"Il agargiante, et fortunato signore, il leggenda!"*

"Flamboyant and successful, a legend in our service," Quill translated.

"A fellow my instructors speak of with awe, sir," Silvestri said, in a bit of awe himself over reports of Marsh's exploits.

"I've met him," Lewrie responded, most definitely *not* in awe of the man. "He's quite insane, ye know."

"Well, that's what they all said, sir," Silvestri admitted, "but that's what's aided his charmed life."

"Short, grandiose, and sure t'end in tears," Lewrie gravelled.

"I am not his sort, sir, though I do intend to do my bit," the young man promised. "Fisherman, farmer, peasant, labourer . . . whatever is needed."

"Play the guitar, do you?" Lewrie scoffed.

"The mandolin, sir," Silvestri said with a sly grin.

"Once the boats are in line-abreast, they stroke hard for the shore," Col. Tarrant was continuing his explanations, "if necessary, we must launch as far as one mile out, but I'm told that the ships we use as transports can get within half a mile of shore, as we did at the latest landing, see? They draw less water than Sir Alan's ship. In a few minutes more, my troops will be wading ashore, muskets loaded, and ready to skirmish, though the un-opposed landing in the wee hours, when the French are abed, is best. Do take note . . ."

"I see that Brigadier-General Caruthers is here," Quill said.

"I expect he's looking for a way to emulate us and win further acclaim," Lewrie sourly agreed. "If he'd gotten his third regiment ashore at Siderno, I think he'd have marched on Reggio di Calabria after he'd beaten that French column."

"Does he have influential patrons?" Quill wondered aloud.

"With our luck, aye," Lewrie growled. "Bags of 'em."

"Then you might get the ships you need, along with his," Quill posed with a shrug.

"Damn his eyes, he *could*, couldn't he?" Lewrie spat. "And if *my* patron, Admiral Charlton, agrees to having more than one iron in the fire . . . but Admiralty tells me there's little hope for only two more troopers rated as armed transports, with Navy crews, available for a long time in future. Other needs of the Service? Graft? Corruption?"

"Believe me, Sir Alan," Quill was quick to assure him, "I, and Foreign Office, are pressing your case for your recent successes to be re-enforced to the hilt. And now that we have the possibility to have armed and eager partisans on our side, the need for more ships, and more troops for Colonel Tarrant, is even more vital.

"I've managed to arrange arms shipments be sent here for use by the partisans," Quill went on, "both seventy-five calibre Tower muskets and sixty-three calibre French muskets, most of them captured over the years by the Royal Navy at sea . . . Saint Etienne pattern. Once I get *Don* Julio to land them for me . . . or, if you could discover a way to sneak them ashore some dark night, hmm?"

"More than happy to oblige, Mister Quill!" Lewrie exclaimed with delight, "Once *Signore* Silvestri makes the arrangements over there."

They were interrupted by the whoops of soldiers from the 94th splashing shin-deep from the barges onto the beach beyond the wooden landing pier, assembling into four-man groups and dashing forward to screen the landing of the rest, kneeling, and pretending to fire at an imagined enemy in loose Chain Order, with two-man pairs running even farther and taking cover where they could serve as scouts.

"Huzzah, that's the way!" a drunken Gen. Malcomb hooted. "Forth, and give them the bayonet, I say! Onward, you brave Mer-Men! Hic!"

"As you can see, sirs," Col. Tarrant went on, raising his voice to drown out the drunken maunderings of General Malcomb, "the Ninety-Fourth has been trained along the lines of the Light Infantry, with the Line Companies capable of skirmishing as ably as the Light Company. Even the Grenadier Company, yes, them, as well, hah hah! Just as the late, revered General Sir John Moore wished all British soldiers to be. When my re-enforcements *ever* arrive, I intend to form a second Light Company, flesh out the Grenadier Company, and . . ."

"D'ye think they'll take that as sacrilege?" Lewrie quipped.

"I'm sure that that Malcomb fellow will," Mr. Quill rejoined. "He looks as hide-bound and conservative as Cromwell's Roundheads. I do note that Brigadier Caruthers is lapping it all up like a kitten at a bowl of cream.

Yes, he may very well re-train at least one of his regiments the same as Tarrant's troops."

"Now, you'll note that whilst my men have advanced to the objective," Col. Tarrant was telling the witnesses, "the Navy provides security at the beach, and the boats, 'til the raiding party returns after eliminating . . ."

"My cue, I believe," Lewrie said, doffing his hat to Mr. Quill and Silvester/Silvestri. "Good afternoon to you, sirs. Will you be supping with us this evening?"

"Us, at-table with those worthies?" Quill sourly said, "Surely you jest, Sir Alan."

"Oh well, I s'pose I always do," Lewrie admitted with a wry grin and a cock of his head. "Later, then."

"Ah, there you are, Sir Alan," Col. Tarrant said as Lewrie strolled back to join them. "I was just explaining about your sailors standing guard."

"At least nine hands per boat, sirs," Lewrie told them, "and all armed with muskets, pistols, and cutlasses. Each transport will land at least fifty-five of them, Midshipmen and officers included, and my ship supplies seventy Marines, almost a full company, to either stand guard, or augment Colonel Tarrant's soldiers, though they form a solid block in two ranks, in the older style. They're not trained to skirmish in sections, fours, or pairs. Yet!"

The subject of artillery arose, and Lewrie and Tarrant had to confess that they'd found no practical way to get guns, caissons, and limbers ashore in any sort of boat that could withstand rough conditions at sea, and horse-drawn guns would be all but impossible.

"We are not designed, or equipped, sirs," Col. Tarrant pointedly stressed, "to force a permanent lodgement ashore, but to raid and raise Hell, then withdraw."

"And so far we've done it damned well," Lewrie added with some pride.

"I'll drink to that," General Malcomb huzzahed, as if he hadn't already.

CHAPTER TWELVE

*T*arrant's promised supper proved a dead bust. It was too late in the day for the inspection party to ride back to Messina in the dark, General Malcomb was by dusk so drunk that serving him a bowl of soup might have drowned him, face-down, and his aides were not in much better shape, either. They had to be lodged overnight, turfing subaltern officers from their lodgings in their mess, then roused out in the early-earlies and given an indifferent breakfast to speed them on their way, a breakfast that Lewrie pointedly skipped.

If Lewrie expected a quiet morning and a good breakfast aboard his own ship, though, he was wrong, for Mr. Quill and his new-come assistant were still in camp, and, not an hour after the inspection party had clattered away, *Don* Julio Caesare showed up, as if he had been in the vicinity, watching, for just such an opportunity, and Lewrie was summoned ashore once more, un-shaven, with only a sketchy sponge-down.

"Ah, *Signore Capitano*," *Don* Julio amiably cried, arms out wide in greeting from Col. Tarrant's shaded gallery, "You have the visit from *il pezzo grosso* from Messina, hey? Sorry I miss them. I come to speak with *Signore* Quill, *Colonnello Inglese*, and you. I have news of a new place you might wish to strike, heh heh! *Congratulaziones*, about the bridge! The *traffico* is at a complete stop! Nothing is move! Though," *Don* Julio added with a scheming look and a rub of his chin, "with *multi* timber, they might rebuild it."

"Sir Alan has thought of that, *Signore*," Col. Tarrant told him with a confident smile. "He's written his superior, Admiral Charlton, to suggest that a smaller warship cruise close ashore of the bridge every fortnight or so, and take it under fire to daunt the workers on the project, and knock down what they've accomplished. Wood timbers will shatter a lot easier than old stonework, hah!"

"Traffic's backed up either side of the bridge, you say?" Quill eagerly asked.

"Oh *sì*!" *Don* Julio expansively told him. "*Multi* waggons full of supplies north of the bridge, at Maida and Filadelfia, and empty ones at Pizzo and Sant' Onofrio, hah hah! Tempting, but, *povero me, multi, multi Francesi soldati* with them. Alas, I meaning."

"And too far inland for us to hit," Tarrant said with a grim nod, as if he was indeed tempted to try it on, anyway.

Tarrant's orderly made the rounds to refill coffee cups with a fresh, steaming brew, and, whilst *Don* Julio expounded on what some of his men had learned following the raid, Lewrie gave him a look-over.

He's even more prosperous-lookin' than a London banker, Lewrie thought; *Comin' up in the world, are we? Crime does seem t'pay!*

At their first encounter in Messina, *Don* Julio Caesare had been the epitome of a wharf rat, pirate, or poor fisherman, but now he was garbed in fine red-brown boots, dark green corduroy trousers, a white silk ruffled shirt, and long, old-style waist-coat of supple black leather, lined with red silk. Beside his chair, a wide-brimmed tan beaver hat sat. And, of course, he still sported a red waist sash in which he wore his chased pistols and bejewelled dagger sheath.

"Long ago, I mention a place where *il Tedeschi soldati* camp, *sì, Signore* Quill?" *Don* Julio resumed after spooning several spoonfuls of sugar into his cup and stirring it up. "Germans? *Bastardos brutale*!"

"Where, *Signore*?" Quill eagerly asked.

"At Melito di Porto Salvo, west of Cape Spartivento, *Signore*," *Don* Julio informed him, sitting more upright with his elbows on his knees, and getting a crafty look. "Like Tropea, there is the regiment, but only half are in town at any time, the rest looting the *paisanos* in the countryside, collecting the taxes, and storing things of *multi* value in the town's pier-side warehouses. Much grain, pasta, wine, and cured meats, which the *Francesi* in Reggio di Calabria now need even more, *si?*"

"You and your men have scouted it, sounded the waters, and such, sir?" Quill asked him.

"Not yet, *Signore*," *Don* Julio said with hands spread wide in apology, "but if it interests you, I can send 'Tonio to do it."

"Which 'Tonio?" Lewrie just had to ask.

"The 'Tonio who scout your bridge, *Capitano Inglese*!" *Don* Julio said with a sly look, and a hearty laugh.

"Well, alright then!" Lewrie exclaimed happily.

"In the meantime, though, *Don* Julio," Mr. Quill suggested, "I've a wee chore for you to perform for me. Colonel Tarrant ran into some partisans who, quite by chance, attacked the guards on the bridge at the same time as his men were launching their attack. They are led by a fellow who styles himself 'Spada,' the Sword, and I would dearly love to establish connexions with him and his band. The Colonel promised them aid and arms, which I hope will soon arrive."

"Arms, *buono*!" *Don* Julio enthused as if he'd just been promised a keg of gold guineas. "*Multi* guns is good!"

"Before they arrive, though, I've a man I wish to land ashore to make contact with them," Quill told him. "Ah, *Signore* Silvestri, *farsi avanti, per favore.*"

The young man's arrival from inside Tarrant's quarters where he had been waiting made everyone take note of his sudden transformation, and *Don* Julio to sit stiffly erect and squint in suspicion, for he no longer appeared a London dandy. Silvestri now resembled an Italian peasant; hair lank and loose under a shapeless felt hat, in a coarse shirt rolled to the elbows, ragged, dirty trousers, and sandalled feet covered with dust. One day after introductions, Silvestri had grown a suitable stubble on his face, which, like all his bared skin, was a sun-bronzed olive tone.

"*Signore*, allow me to name to you Giovanni Silvestri," Quill said with some smug sense of satisfaction.

"What is this?" *Don* Julio demanded, confused.

"He's my eyes and ears on the mainland, sir," Quill told him, "and will speak with my voice. I wish you to smuggle him ashore near the bridge, and set up places and times to deliver my instructions to him, and retrieve his letters to me."

All *Don* Julio could do for a moment was splutter, then break out into nervous laughter. "Oh, *Signore* Quill," he managed to say at last, "he will not last a *day*! *Sì*, he is . . . *costumed*! . . . to look the part, but as I said before, one must *be* Italian, a Calabrian, to his fingertips, or the *Francesi* and their ass-kissers will discover him, and he is dead! *Finito*!"

Giovanni Silvestri scoffed with a laugh, and launched into a long palaver in Italian, to which *Don* Julio rejoined with what sounded like scorn and sarcasm, dismissing the whole idea. Silvestri gave in kind, which was simply Greek to Lewrie, and even Col. Tarrant's smattering of Italian left him in the dust, smiling tautly and watching the long exchange like a man watching a tennis ball being volleyed.

"Enough! *Abbastanza*!" Mr. Quill demanded at last, raising hands and speaking with more authority than Lewrie thought he had. "I wish you to get him ashore over there, *Don* Julio. It will be worth your time, I assure you, as always. It is vital to the interests of your country, and mine, that he be gotten into service."

"Big risk," *Don* Julio objected, tossing up his hands as if to absolve himself of responsibility. "If you wish this, then it is on your head, *Signore*. He *might* pass, but . . . only God knows. *Sì*, we will set him ashore, but the risk will be worth *multi* guineas. Boats must be off the coast all the time, waiting for letters, making the deliveries of guns and powder. I must obtain more boats, small ones, for that."

"And that will cost, yes, I know," Quill said with a knowing nod of his head, "for which you shall be recompensed, handsomely."

"Hmpf! If he is caught, *Signore* Quill, he may cost you more than you know," *Don* Julio ominously said. "The *Francesi* make him talk, they will know about you, where *Colonnello Inglese* camps, know about *Capitano Inglese* and his ships, and know about *me*! And if I and my men, my boats, are made known to the *Francesi,* then it will be too dangerous for me to sail over there for *any* reason. And then I cannot help you at all, and all is ruined."

And your lucrative smugglin' trade goes smash, too, Lewrie told himself, giving Julio Caesare a leery look; *That's what you're* really *worried about!*

"Then it's up to me to *not* be caught, isn't it, *Signore*?" Silvestri said with a confident cock of his head, and a wee, taut grin.

"It would be much appreciated if you did not," Mr. Quill said, sounding almost jolly.

"*Sciocco* . . . foolish," Caesare pronounced the decision. "But . . . if that is what you want, I will do it for you. How soon?"

"Within a day or so, *Signore*," Quill told him, "pending winds and weather, as Sir Alan is wont to say."

"No, no, it will take longer than that," *Don* Julio objected as he polished off his cup of coffee and rose to his feet, clapping that fine beaver hat on his head. "Must get more small boats, the older and the poorer looking, the better, so no one will suspect. And, I have the business to see to, first."

"*Signore* Silvestri and I will be at Messina, then," Quill told him, rising as well to shake hands on their new deal, "waiting for word from you. He'll be lodging separately, as he has since he came to Sicily."

"Ah, that is best, *buono*," *Don* Julio said with a nod, "else any enemy spies see him with you, and end this before it begins. For now, *arrivederci*, *Signores*." He performed a sketchy bow to all present, then turned to shout at one of his henchmen who had been holding the reins of a pair of horses cropping grass beneath the shade of a tree nearby.

Don Julio swung up into the fine, gleaming saddle of his horse, a tall, sleek hunter of at least fourteen hands, which all of the Englishmen present envied at once, clucked, thumped with his heels, and cantered away towards Milazzo.

"A damned impressive beast he has," Col. Tarrant commented. "I'd imagine it'd be worth over an hundred guineas back home."

"Stole it, most-like," Lewrie sourly commented, "or he's makin' such a pile o' 'tin' from his other pursuits that he can afford it."

"Very possibly, sir," Col. Tarrant said with a wee laugh. "What *Don* Julio said, though, Mister Quill . . . you and your man travelled here together? Might there be people in French pay who . . . ?"

"Not to worry, Colonel," Quill dismissively said, "John lodged at a good hotel in the upper town when he first landed, and he and I came separately."

"And that fellow, and his assumed identity, disappeared once I checked out of my lodgings," Silvestri assured Tarrant. "I return to Messina as a poor *paisano*, in the back of a loaded farm cart, whilst Mister Quill makes his own way. 'Til *Don* Julio's boats are ready, we will play strangers to each other, and Mister Quill sends his little lad, Fiorello, to set the plan in motion."

"Which we should be doing now," Quill said, pulling out his pocket watch and looking aloft to reckon the position of the morning sun. "I do not know which will prove more uncomfortable, the back of a farm cart, or the poor prad I hired to ride out here. The beast simply has no recognisable gait, just shamble, trot, then plod, as it wills!"

They said their goodbyes, then Quill went to his own horse, and Silvestri set off on foot in a shambling, lazy stride down the road to Messina, leaving Lewrie and Tarrant alone at last.

"One must suppose that Caesare will provide us the information on his proposed target, ehm . . . what did he call it?" Tarrant asked.

"Melito di Porto Salvo," Lewrie prompted. "Quite a mouthful, hey? Some of Admiral Charlton's squadron bombarded it from the sea in that big raid a few months ago, but we didn't land and raze it. Hmm, not so far from Reggio di Calabria. We'd have to transit the Strait of Messina at night, with no lights showing, or the French'd be alerted, else. Sail from here just before dusk? But, we'd have to stand off-and-on 'til just before dawn to attack the place."

"Whatever all that nautical talk means," Col. Tarrant dismissed with raised hands, as if perplexed, even after months of dealing with ships and boats. "One would suppose sailing all the way round Sicily would be a deal worse, what? Stage down to Catania or Syracuse, out of sight of the French watchers, and strike from there?"

"We've hit them three times, now, though, sir," Lewrie pointed out, "and they're aware of our presence, and what we can do. Did we sail beyond sight, we'd *have* to go down the Strait, and surely they'd be watching for us. Next thing you know, they're on the alert, from Naples to Taranto. It's not going to get any easier. Which is why we really need your re-enforcements, and I need more transports."

"Or, we need Brigadier Caruthers to fulfill his ambitions, and turn one of his regiments into 'sea-soldiers,' hah hah!" Tarrant rejoined. "Did we have *two* regiments to work with, the French would pull their hair out, trying to determine when and where we strike, at two places at the same time!"

"But, at our cost, sir," Lewrie gloomed, "what he manages to get deprives us. I know he *wishes* to. We're active, he's idle, we've won some fame, and he's only his one battle to boast of since. Probably couldn't do it without findin' a way t'get a horse ashore with him. Caruthers looks good on a horse, and he knows it."

"Perhaps *Don* Julio can steal one and sell it to him," Tarrant suggested, "and a special boat to carry it ashore, as well."

"Hope Caruthers has a deep purse, then," Lewrie sniggered, "for I'm sure Caesare will soak him for it."

"Ah well, Colonels walk or wade, whilst Brigadier-Generals get to gallop, wave a sword, and look gallant. Now, what would be a suitable mount for me, Sir Alan?"

"Oh . . ." Lewrie mused, then grinned. "I could get you a crocodile, so you could *slither* ashore."

"Do you think the French would be impressed?" Tarrant laughed.

"Awed and terrified, sir," Lewrie agreed, laughing, too.

CHAPTER THIRTEEN

W'e're not goin' anywhere 'til Don *Julio tells us,* Lewrie slowly came to re-alise as several days passed with no news forthcoming about the harbour town of Melito di Porto Salvo; *We're bein' led round by our noses.*

He kept his ship's people occupied with cutlass drills, musket practice both ashore and afloat, with yet more exercises at launching boats and land-ing his Marines and armed parties on the beach, then recovering them aboard. Topmasts and yards were struck, then raised back in place and the standing rigging and running rigging tensioned or re-roved through the blocks, not only aboard *Vigilance,* but on all three of his transports, which amused idle soldiers ashore who'd sit, watch, and jeer from the beach.

When those tarry activities palled, Lewrie made arrangements with Col. Tarrant for contests and sports ashore on the broad drill ground. Football, criquet, or rounders, sailors against soldiers, Marines against both, and ship against ship, played out, with each company of the 94th competing against each other to determine which would go for a championship match at each sport against the Navy or Marines. Colonel Tarrant and Major Gittings, just as eager to keep their troops engaged as Lewrie, got into the spirit, even suggesting contests for choirs and soloists, target shooting matches, or dance contests, with tots of grog or twists of tobacco awarded to winners.

The Army drew the line at boat races under oars or sail, though. The Navy was too experienced at those skills.

Naturally, such jocular and amusing diversions drew the local villagers within walking distance of the encampment, and people from Milazzo on the weekends who would sail their fishing boats down for a day, or cram farm carts and waggons with spectators.

That was a risk, Lewrie and Col. Tarrant agreed, but with adequate policing of an underground trade in wine and spirits, they both thought it was worth it. There was already an host of pedlars, dram shop sellers, old women in their all-black clothing to cook and sell their dainties, and washerwomen ready to scrub and rinse uniforms and underclothes in freshwater, even setting up bathhouses behind quilts and blankets hung on the lower branches in the olive groves.

There were prostitutes, of course, among the crowds, as there always would be round soldiers and sailors, and Tarrant and Gittings had fretted the un-looked-for arrival of back pay from Malta, which would be splurged on drink, whores, and food tastier than the Army rations.

There were also pretty young Sicilian girls about, swishing their colourful gowns, sashaying their hips, and flirting with soldiers and sail-ors, in their off-duty hours. In point of fact, more than a few amours had arisen, and Col. Tarrant had had to recognise several marriages, adding to the number of regimental dependents. It did not endear the regiment, or Lewrie's sailors and Marines, to the jealous young Sicilian men who came to watch the contests, though, but what could they do? Young, healthy, and fit young Englishmen with their shirts open and arms bared dashing round at their sports and showing off to the local girls were just too exciting to watch.

Despite his irritation at the long wait for news from Quill's new agent or *Don* Julio's men, Lewrie came to enjoy idle time ashore to watch his men compete. A freshwater bath in a wine vat was more than welcome, as were clean, salt-crystal-free bedding, shirts, and undergarments, and a silver six-pence coin got him sweet pastries and fruity drinks, and a chance to flirt with the young female vendors.

Harmless flirting, of course.

There was his young wife, Jessica, his vows, and that sprig of rosemary in his desk drawer, and . . .

Damn, I'm randy! he thought, stopping in mid-stride round the verge of the drill ground, where sailors off *Vigilance* played football against the 94th's Grenadier Company; *Haven't had a woman in months, since I left my house!*

It did not help that a lissome young woman also slowly strolling round the verge ahead of him was glancing back now and then and making sloe-eyed smiles at him! Her long, dark hair bound back loose at the nape of her neck—a graceful neck!—swayed so tantalisingly upon her shoulders bared by a pleasant blouse, upon bare flesh that seemed to glow warm and temptingly soft to the touch should be . . . !

Almond eyes, dark and mysterious, full lips pursed in coyness, only a hint of a Roman nose, long lashes batting . . . Christ!

As she turned a bit to look back again, firm little breasts were hinted at beneath her thin linen blouse, and aroused wee nipples . . . !

Oh, God! Lewrie thought; *I've got a cock-stand!*

"*Buongiorno, Signore,*" she cooed, as if she knew what effect she was having on him as he tried to brush his uniform coat to cover his obvious lust. "*Una partita eccitante, sì?*"

"Uh . . . ehm," Lewrie gawped, flummoxed, heard a loud cheer, and turned to shout "Well played, lads!" towards the match. "Well played!" "Ehm, *scusa, bella signorina* . . ." he said to her, trying to dredge up enough Italian to make his excuses. To his further chagrin, she took a step or two to stand beside him, looking up in admiration, or something, and cooed something along the lines of "You think me *bella*?"

"*Puttana,*" an old, white-haired fruit vendor spat at the girl, which raised a slanging match 'twixt the pair, and Lewrie slunk away as fast as he could whilst she was diverted.

God, be my witness, I'm tryin' t'be faithful, but . . . my Lord! he thought; *If she was a whore, three shillings or less and I'd be up her skirts against a tree, and . . . no! Sprawled on deep grass out in the woods, naked as Adam and Eve! My cundums are aboard ship, though, so . . . oh, just damn this to bloody Hell!*

Ferociously maddening images of that girl's face, her bare body spread wide to receive him, the sounds she would make in the throes of passion; her on top, rocking to bliss and oblivion, her long hair swaying and thrashing, would not leave his mind. Oh God, her kneeling before him and those luscious lips enfolding his member!

I need a drink, Lewrie determined; *A damned stiff one! Oh, don't even* think "*stiff*"!

Pacing about, though, was difficult since the crutch of his uniform breeches, engorged by a raging erection the like of which he had not experienced in months, pinched something awful, yet he could not pull and tug for roomy relief without revealing his condition to one and all.

I pretend t'pee in the "sinks" and I may not be able to button up my breeches flap, again! Lewrie thought in dread. He fell back on a recitation of *The Articles of War* in his head, which he'd always used to *delay* his orgasms when too excited.

And for the regulating and better government of his Majesty's Navies,
Ships of War, and Forces by Sea, whereon, under the good Providence of
God, the Wealth, Safety, and Strength of the Kingdom chiefly depend;
Be it enacted by the King's Most Excellent Majesty, by and with the
Advice and Consent of the Lords Spiritual and Temporal, and Commons,
in this present Parliament assembled . . .

By the time he got beyond the musketry range, and almost into the fruit groves at the back of the encampment, he let out a sigh of relief that the recitation seemed to be working. Unfortunately, that grove was the site chosen by several soldiers and their doxies to "get the leg over," and their quilts and blankets were used as pallets on the thick grass, not hung for privacy from the boughs. He let out a helpless *Eep!* and whirled round to retrace his steps, with the sight of ordinary coupling by one pair, a stand-up "knee trembler" by another against a peach tree, and the third couple on their knees, and the bare-naked soldier humping away at her bottom like a hound!

This time, Lewrie muttered the Articles in a rushed mutter, and got all the way to Article the Ninth!

If any Ship or Vessel shall be taken as Prize, none of the officers, Mari-
ners, or other persons on board her, shall be stripped of their Cloaths . . .

He feared that, though it had been a long time since he had had to revert to manual stimulation in the dark, there was a good chance he would either begin to squirt semen from his nostrils, or "box the Jesuit and get cock-roaches" that night.

Oh, Christ on a crutch! he quailed as he got back to the drill field and the little booths set up by vendors. Everywhere he looked, he found an enticing young woman to take his fancy, those surely of the "commercial persuasion" and the closely-guarded innocent virgins all but hemmed in by their parents, fathers, and brothers!

He could not stumble about with his eyes shut to temptations, so he pushed through the throng alongside the drill ground to stand before the onlookers of a criquet match between the 94th's Light Company and a party of sailors off *Bristol Lass*, fixing his attention solely upon the bowler, and slowly, finally, returned to a normal flaccidity.

Whew! That was damned close, he told himself, wondering where he might find a glass of the local white wine. And also wondering if going to look for one might put him right back into the midst of the doxies.

"Oh, hello, sir," someone said to his right and Lewrie turned to see his Third Officer, Lt. Greenleaf. "A rather dull match, so far, that," he commented, pointing at the pitch with a leather wine flask in his hand. "The Army's bowlers are all over the place, and when the lads off *Bristol Lass* manage to connect their bats, they dribble off too close for a run. All that Light Infantry scampering makes the Army fielders quick as lightning. The football's better."

"How'd our Vigilances do?" Lewrie asked.

"Lost, sir, nought to one," Greenleaf said, making a face and taking time to lift the flabby wine flask to his mouth and squirt a mouthful into his mouth. "I fear the Army's the better wind, and ran our lads ragged, with their tongues lolling, and gasping for air."

"Oh, pity," Lewrie commiserated, "Anyone hurt?"

"Bruises, mostly, sir," Greenleaf told him, "a black eye or two, a broken nose. Our Surgeon will be busy this evening, but no one was hurt bad enough to be put on light duties."

"Well, good for that, then," Lewrie said.

"Odd sort of war we're having, sir," Greenleaf breezed on after another squirt of wine. "A wee bag of excitement, then right back we come to Fiddler's Green. Music, tasty victuals, wine and spirits, and all the doxies one could wish."

"Aye, the doxies," Lewrie said, those lusty images rising once again in his fervid imagination. It came out more of a grunt.

"None of them particularly refined, but refreshingly simple and eager," Greenleaf prated on, oblivious, "not like what one would find in a larger town. Pity there's such little privacy, except for the one brothel in Milazzo. Can't un-button one's flap where the ship's people can see, after all, sir. Why, out in the olive and the fruit groves . . ."

"Seen it!" Lewrie snapped, hoping the fool would just stop his gob. "Commission officers must eschew such, as I trust you've done, Mister Greenleaf."

"Soul of discretion, sir, I assure you," Greenleaf swore with a leer, "though I cannot speak for the Midshipmen."

"Then you *must*, sir," Lewrie declared, turning to face him. "If not you, then the First Officer Mister Farley. We are *in loco parentis* to the younger lads, and must do what we can to preserve their innocence as long as possible."

You bloody fraud, you hypocrite! he chid himself; *Just* listen *to yourself! I'll be* hymn-singin', *next!*

"Don't know how warnings will go down with the older Mids, but we can't allow the younger ones go home to their families, poxed to their eyebrows, Mister Greenleaf. If all else fails, explain to them about the prevention provided by cundums."

"Cundums, sir?" Lt. Greenleaf posed, head cocked over. "That'd be beyond their wee purses, or pay."

"We're in Italy, sir," Lewrie pointed out, "and it was the Italians who invented the bloody things, *ages* ago, after all. Some of the lads might not understand a man's true nature, and what they have heard in Church, but . . . I'm sure that you and the others in the wardroom will find a way to dance along that narrow line, what? In the long run, virginal innocence is a damned dangerous thing, hey?"

"A lecture, sir," Greenleaf replied, crestfallen to be ordered to do so right after an eye-opening adventure ashore. "I see, sir. If you will excuse me, sir, I will go off and . . . collect my thoughts on the matter."

"Carry on, Mister Greenleaf," Lewrie agreed, and turned back to the amateurish match, just as an Army bowler hurled a shambolic pitch that hit a sailor on the shin. "How is your leg *there*, sir?" Lewrie shouted with the other partisan spectators.

And thank God I don't have t'give that *lecture!* he thought.

Later that day, back aboard *Vigilance*, Lewrie took himself an idle sprawl on his starboard side settee, neck-stock undone, sleeves rolled up, waist-coat hung up, and changing to a looser, comfortable pair of slop-trousers, and old shoes instead of boots. He tried to read, but Chalky was padding round and round in his lap, unable to knead a soft place to curl up. The cat finally let out a human-like *hmpf!* and flopped onto his side, tail slowly curling, and squirming to encourage some "pets." Lewrie obliged him with long strokes down his side from forehead to tail tip, pausing only to turn the page of his book, or take a sip from a mug of a rather unimpressive Italian ale. It was half an hour into the First Dog Watch, late afternoon, and a wee, cool breeze flirted with the ecru sailcloth curtains over the transom windows, came through the extemporised twine-screen door to the stern gallery, whisking away the heat of the day.

Lewrie's mind was not on his book, or the cat's comfort, but on what Lt. Greenleaf had said of the local doxies; how they might not be as refined as the costlier girls in the better brothels in London, but were refreshingly simple and eager to please, and certainly not as coarse and hardened as street walkers or the sort who frequented the low taverns and "cock and hen" clubs for a single shilling.

That girl, that coquette, Lewrie mused, picturing her most vividly all over again, imagining her offered charms *almost* as virginal as a young lover just introduced to lovemaking, and as eager as a new bride, eager and giggling, savouring as much pleasure and passion as she might give. What would a romp be like with one such as her, and might she be at the camp the next sporting contests? Where could he and she find privacy, how many cundums should he carry with him, and might she spend an entire afternoon with him?

"More ale, sir?" Deavers asked as he puttered round the cabins.

"Ah, no, Deavers, thankee," Lewrie replied, irritated to be back in reality; it came out more an *harumpfh*.

"The Eye-talians make some nice wines, sir," Deavers dithered on, "but they need some lessons when it comes to beer and ales."

"Aye, they do," Lewrie grudgingly agreed. To further distract himself from idle lust-dreams, he added, "There's a tale about German monks who posed a question to the Pope about beer, Deavers. They wondered if it was sinful to drink it, or drink so much of it. The Vatican didn't know what they were talking about, so they sent the Pope a barrel of their best, and all the Italian Cardinals, and the Pope sampled it. They wrote the monks and said they could drink it, and it wasn't sinful. It was so different from their wines that they declared it a *penance!* To drink it, like bein' told to recite several dozen Hail Marys!"

"So, if an Englishman drinks himself half a gallon, he's earnin' forgiveness, sir?" Deavers slyly asked.

"No, just a good drunk, and a hard head in the mornin'," Lewrie japed back.

"Midshipman Chenery t'see the Cap'um, SAH!" the Marine sentry announced in a loud voice, and a stamp of his boots.

"Enter," Lewrie said back, laying the book aside, but staying seated; sprawled, rather.

"Ah, thank you for seeing me, sir," Charles Chenery began with his hat held at his waist, turning its brim round and round. "Ehm . . . it's nothing to do with duty, sir. Something personal, rather, and ehm . . . perhaps brother-in-law to brother-in-law, sir?"

"You *know* I do not play favourites, even for you, young sir," Lewrie sternly cautioned him. "In some trouble, are you?"

"Not in trouble, *no sir*!" Chenery nervously exclaimed. "It's ah, d'ye see, ehm . . . it's about *girls*, sir."

Oh, shit! Mine arse on a band-box! Lewrie thought; *I'm givin' that lecture, after all!*

"They're delightfully different from us, for starters," he told Chenery in jest. "What about them?"

"Ashore today, sir," Chenery said, taking a tentative step nearer, and glancing over his shoulder at Deavers, Dasher, and Turnbow who were puttering round the great-cabins. "There was this girl, a local girl. Well, I couldn't make heads or tails of what she was saying, of course, but . . . she was *awfully* friendly, and pretty and . . . fetching, I suppose I could call her. She most-like couldn't make heads or tails of what I was saying, either, but we seemed to hit it off, so *easily*, and I bought us some wine, and . . . but that's not the point, sir! She put her arm in mine, and stood so *close* it made my head reel, and . . . she *kissed* me, just playful at first, and then . . . !"

"Was it your first kiss?" Lewrie asked, almost feeling sorry for his much younger, and in-experienced brother-in-law.

"Ehm . . ." was all Chenery could say.

"Your first that wasn't a peck on the cheek?" Lewrie went on. "Full on the lips, lips slightly parted, lasting for long seconds?" Lewrie prompted, and Chenery nodded his head, reddening. "Did your tongue and hers meet?"

Am I bein' cruel? Lewrie wondered; *It is sort of fun!*

"Aye, it was, sir, and aye, we did," Chenery whispered. "And I got the strangest feeling that I never . . . !"

"Oh, do stop fidgeting and sit you down," Lewrie offered, pointing to one of the collapsible chairs, into which Chenery sank with so much force that the chair squeaked. "It was nice, and exciting, and tempting, was it not?" Lewrie asked. "And you were tempted to do more than just kiss and fondle."

"I was, I was indeed, sir!" Chenery confessed.

God, how much can I tell him without it gettin' back to his father, or Jessica? Lewrie wondered, crossing his legs and turfing Chalky off his lap with a petulant *Mrr!* of complaint; *How much has he been told about sex by his Reverend father? Most-like, not much.*

He felt a serious bout of hypocrisy coming on!

"Hmm, you obviously know about the ways of men and women," Lewrie said. "You've been aboard when the ship was put Out of Discipline."

"Oh, aye sir," Chenery said with a firm nod, "and it was nothing like father told me! That, and well . . . when I and my classmates went to the booksellers after school, we always snuck looks at the caricatures, if we could get away with it. Pooled our pennies and bought a few from street vendors, especially the nude ones, and hid them from our parents . . ."

So he's not *been kept under glass, or a pile of cabbage leaves!* Lewrie thought, feeling hopeful that young Charles Chenery knew a lot more than most lads.

"What *did* your father tell you?" Lewrie asked.

It was the usual pious rot, but what could the lad expect from a father in the ministry, surrounded by older brothers in Holy Orders, his sisters wed to other ministers; keep oneself pure 'til he wed an equally pure bride from a good family; treat all women from the better sort as virginal, innocent, and fragile as Meissen china or crystal stemware; and girls of the lower orders, and looser morals, were to be avoided like the Plague, for vaguely un-specified reasons, and for him to pray often to ask for Heavenly strength to shun temptations if they arose. And, lastly, do not weaken oneself by self-pleasuring and spending one's vital seed and vigour outside of conjugal union.

"Well, all that's good, in the main," Lewrie said, leaning his head back after Chenery had finished stammering through what little he'd been told, "but Life's not quite like that, as you've seen when the temporary 'wives' are allowed aboard," he went on, looking the lad in the eyes. "As you've most-like heard late at night in your mess, when the older Mids . . . spill their seed. The same thing happens belowdecks among the crew, too, when they've been too long without women, and none of them are sapped of their vital strength. So, I'd not make a meal of that, but . . . now. This girl you met. Were there brothers, a father, or an old crone escorting her?"

"Ehm, no sir," Chenery told him. "She was by herself. Well, with two other girls, at first, but they went their own way once she ah . . . cozied up to me."

The poor lad blushes faster than rose buds! Lewrie thought.

"It was good odds that she might have been a girl of the 'commercial persuasion,' lad," Lewrie told him.

"A . . . a whore d'ye mean, sir?" Chenery all but gasped. "But, I thought that most doxies are as plump and haggard as the ones who came aboard *Sapphire*. *Ugly* brutes!"

"Aye, street walkers and dockside whores *are* rather off-putting, but they didn't all start that way," Lewrie said. "It's the life they lead that coarsens 'em. Even girls who look like young goddesses can be prostitutes. Did she try to steer you somewhere private?"

"I did get the sense that she would, sir," Chenery replied.

"In point of fact, I was approached by a very fetching, tempting young woman myself today," Lewrie felt confident enough to admit. "The Army camp draws them like flies to honey. It's a good thing I don't speak Italian, hey? Rather embarrassing, really."

"Aye, it *was*, sir!" Chenery chimed in, perking up. "Mean t'say, more flustering than anything else. *Tempted* to, but not *daring* to . . . have my way with a . . . ? First time and all . . . ?"

"She could have been a 'fireship,' lad," Lewrie told him, turning stern. "Poxed to her eyebrows? You do *not* want to catch the Pox. The Surgeon would charge you fifteen shillings that you don't have to give you the Mercury Cure, your teeth'd turn t'grey chalk and fall out, and no one's really sure that it's a genuine cure. I've seen it happen to fellows I've served with, and there's no guarantee that they'd not pass it on to anyone they married. Hah, try livin' with *that* on your conscience! And, what'd your family say?"

"Oh, I didn't think of that, sir!" Chenery said with a gulp, "though, at the moment I wasn't sure I was thinking at all," he added with a nervous laugh.

"Your 'little' head was in charge, I expect," Lewrie said with his own amusement. "Besides, did the girl think you had a lot of coin in your purse, she might've had a bully-buck partner, ready to cosh you on the head and rob you blind, right down to your stockings. It's a risky thing, associating with the whores, no matter how desirable they look, or how sweet they talk."

"I'm told there are brothels, though, sir," Chenery continued, sounding rather wistful, "where it's safe, and there are physicians to, ah, inspect for the Pox."

"Oh, there are!" Lewrie admitted. "And if one must, and has the funds for it, they are generally safe for young gentlemen."

"And I've heard of protective devices, sir?" Chenery asked.

"Cundums," Lewrie told him, growing wary of his words from that point on. It would not do at all to admit that he had some, or that he had used them in the past. "Sheep gut leather, very thin sheathes one binds on one's member. They prevent infection from the Pox, and it's *said* that, should a married couple not wish, or cannot afford, more children, they're useful at preventing un-wanted pregnancies.

"They're very *dear,* though, and not *always* effective," Lewrie cautioned. "Were I you, Charles," he said, using the lad's first name since they were almost in private, "I'd not risk your health, or your future prospects, without 'em. I fear you'll have to deal with your temptations the best you can 'til you've taken all precautions against future shame. Then, if you simply *must* . . ." Lewrie concluded, flinging up his hands for a moment in a helpless "if."

"It's so very frustrating, though, sir," Chenery said, sighing.

"A lot of Life is, young sir," Lewrie imparted, going for his best "sage" sounds, though thinking himself *such* a fraud.

"Well, I shall go, sir, and thank you for taking time to speak with me about . . . that sort of thing," Chenery said, getting to his feet and tugging at the set of his uniform jacket, which prompted Lewrie to rise as well to see him out. "It's better advice than any I've gotten from the fellows in my mess. Some of the older lads have told the youngest that women have teeth ah, down there," he imparted with a knowing laugh.

"What, that old tale?" Lewrie guffawed. "What rot!"

"I'll take my leave sir," Chenery declared.

"Very well, carry on, Mister Chenery," Lewrie said in reply back to the proper formal relationship. "No need to mention our wee talk with your father, and certainly not your sweet sister. There are things best left unsaid with the fairer sex."

"Oh, of course, sir!" Chenery exclaimed, performing a short bow, and headed for the door, clapping his hat on as he did so.

Hah! Cheated death, again! Lewrie exulted to himself; *I damned well hope, anyway!*

CHAPTER FOURTEEN

Damme, but I used t'be so fond of idleness! Lewrie told himself as he paced the poop deck of HMS *Vigilance* one morning before Clear Decks And Up Spirits was piped. He held his everyday hanger in his hand, swiping it back and forth as if reaping a field of wildflowers, after an hour or more of swordplay with the younger Midshipmen. He paused to look round the anchorage as Six Bells of the Forenoon Watch were struck, hearing the echoing chimes of his three transports mixing with those of his own ship, wondering when they would sail again.

He knew himself, his penchant for boredom if grand doings were not in the offing, but in the past he could at least be bored near tears out on the open sea! Swinging at anchor for nigh a week with nothing to plan for, nothing to *do,* was as close as he expected that he could get to being part of the Standing Officers who safeguarded a de-commissioned ship, and it was chasing him sore. Try as he might, he found himself impatient with others, becoming testy if an evolution did not go well, and in some cases growing downright surly. His skin crawled, his innards seemed to itch with the desire for action, to the point that he could not sit still, or even nap, and found himself forced to prowl the ship, or pace, unable to lose himself in one of his novels, or sleep soundly of a night without more than a few tots of his rapidly dwindling supply of American corn whisky.

Oh, there was Chalky and his antics, though his cat was now of an age, and napped more than he played. And, there were old letters to re-read, and new ones to write when something novel struck him in one of the old ones that he'd glossed over the first time, but Lord!

Greenleaf's right, it is *an odd sort o' war we're having,* he thought, finally sheathing his sword in frustration, looking at it as if he'd never seen it before, and wondering if he would ever draw it, or clap it on his hip except for formal occasions, again.

"Aarrh!" Lewrie shouted to no one, his good old, piratical yell, and clattered down the larboard ladderway to the quarterdeck, where he could dash into his cabins and really vent his frustrations.

"Cool tea, sir?" Deavers offered, "Or lemonade? We've just got two dozen fresh'uns off one of the bum-boats."

"Here, lad," Lewrie said, handing his sword to Dasher for him to stow away. "What d'ye think, Dasher? You're fond of lemonade as I recall."

"Oh, lemonade, aye sir!" Dasher all but squealed.

"Lemonade it is, then, Deavers," Lewrie decided, going to his settee to fling himself onto it. There was a months-old copy of *The Tatler* that his father had sent him on the low, brass Hindoo tray table, and he snatched it up, hoping for some amusement, or a tale of some new scandal; "Prinny," the Prince of Wales, and his doings, were always good for a laugh, and a scandal all to himself.

"Sail ho!" a muted voice wailed down from aloft. "Brig-sloop, hull down, fine on th' bows!"

Lewrie tossed *The Tatler* aside and made a rapid way out to the quarterdeck to snatch up a telescope, then mounted to the poop deck for a view. Yes! He could make out two sets of royals and tops'ls, a hint of the strange ship's courses.

"And why wasn't she hailed when her royals were above the horizon?" Lewrie snarled.

"The drills, sir," Lt. Grace, the Fourth Officer, called back from below him on the quarterdeck, "no one was really looking . . ."

"And the French could've sailed a squadron into the anchorage and no one would've noticed 'til they were *alongside*, sir?" Lewrie snapped, furious and eager to vent on someone.

"I'll speak to the lookouts, sir," Grace replied, humbled.

"Deck, there!" one of the lookouts bawled out. "She's alterin' course, comin' about bows-on, an' making for the anchorage!"

She can't be French, Lewrie told himself, his telescope glued to one eye; *A lone brig-sloop, darin' fire from a sixty-four? Tosh! If they've discovered our anchorage, they'd send a squadron to deal with us . . . and they'd be comin' from the Nor'east, from Naples.*

"Beat to Quarters, sir?" Lt. Grace asked as sailors gathered on the rails and shrouds for a better look.

"No, not yet, Mister Grace," Lewrie told him in a softer voice. "The hands are due their rum, and their dinner, first. It'll be hours before she's anywhere near us. But do keep a closer watch on her, hey?"

"Aye aye, sir!" Grace replied with a firm nod of his head.

And now I'll have t'sham calm and confidence! Damn! Lewrie thought, snapping the tubes of his telescope shut, and sauntering down to the quarterdeck once more to place the telescope in a rack by the compass binnacle cabinet, knowing that *Vigilance*'s people were closely watching him.

"If some damned Frenchman is daft enough t'cross hawses with us, Mister Grace, there's plenty of time for us to oblige the fool," Lewrie said with a confident grin plastered on his phyz. "I'll be aft. Carry on, and keep me apprised."

"Aye, sir."

A tall glass of lemonade sounds good, Lewrie thought as he re-entered his cabins.

"What's this?" Lewrie asked, peering closely at what sat upon his fork that accompanied his roast quail and broad beans.

"The Italians call it *polenta,* sir," his cook, Yeovill told him as he set out the last items from the brass food barge. "It's much like that *couscous* we found at Gibraltar, years ago. It is filling, though a trifle bland without salt, butter, or herbs and olive oil."

Lewrie took a tentative bite, chewed, and set down his fork.

"Puts me in mind of something I got served during the American Revolution," Lewrie decided, "ground corn kernels, blanched in ashes and hot water. Grits, I think they called it, and bland, aye, but . . . whatever you've done with it, it's right tasty."

"Thank you, sir," Yeovill said with a pleased grin, "I'm glad you like it. I'm told it's even better with melted cheese drizzled over it. As to how it's made, well sir . . . I didn't ask, but, if you do like it, it's even cheaper than rice on the local markets, and nigh as plentiful as pasta."

"That means I'll be seeing a lot *more* of it, Yeovill?" Lewrie asked with a mock frown.

"Only every now and then, sir," Yeovill swore, hand to his heart.

"Midshipman Jenner t'see th' Captain, SAH!" the Marine sentry bawled, stamping boots and musket butt on the deck outside.

"Enter!" Lewrie called back.

"Sir, Mister Grace's duty, sir," young Jenner announced, "and I am to inform you that the strange sail shows the Private Signal. She is the *Coquette* brig, and shows Have Despatches."

"Very well, Mister Jenner," Lewrie said, "how far off is she?"

"Ehm, about two miles, sir," Jenner guessed.

"Show her Captain Repair On Board, and I'll speak with her commanding officer myself," Lewrie told him, returning to his dinner.

"Aye, sir," Jenner said, showing himself out.

Good odds she's from Admiral Charlton's squadron, he surmised as he took a sip of white wine to clear his palate; *Fresh news, or fresh orders? Some place Thom Charlton wishes us to attack? Where did I put my Navy List?*

Good as his dinner was, he pulled off his napkin, rose from his chair, and went to his desk to look up the *Coquette* brig and find out who commanded her.

"Good God!" Lewrie exclaimed. "D'arcy Gamble!"

"Sir?" Deavers asked.

"A Mid from my first 'post-ship,' the *Proteus* frigate," Lewrie explained. "He's a Commander, now, of the brig coming to join us."

"Ehm, will you dine him in, sir?" Deavers asked further, fearful of dishing out a second dinner at short notice.

"No, it'll take him an hour or so t'come to anchor, get down a boat, and be rowed over," Lewrie speculated, "but you might set by a serving of dessert for him, if he's peckish."

That drew a faint, audible groan from Dasher, who had hoped for a taste of the berry pie that Yeovill had baked, on the sly once Lewrie was done.

HMS *Coquette* came into the anchorage all standing, rounded up into the wind "man o' war fashion" and let go her best bower anchor even as the last of her canvas was lowered or hauled up and gasketed, a very showy and tarry evolution, and the sign of an exceedingly well-drilled crew. Barely had the anchor bitten into the harbour bottom when *Coquette*'s gig was led round from towing astern to the entry-port for the captain to enter it, and begin stroking for *Vigilance*'s side.

Gamble has "nutmegs" the size o' roundshot, Lewrie thought as he admired the alacrity of the manoeuvre; *I've never had the nerve to try that on. I'd come a cropper, sure! He always was cocky.*

Minutes later, the gig was alongside, the dog's vane of Commander Gamble's hat was peeking above the lip of the entry-port, and the Bosun's calls were trilling as the side-party welcomed him aboard.

"Commander Gamble!" Lewrie cried with a broad grin and a glad hand as Gamble gained the deck and saluted.

"Captain Lewrie!" Gamble replied, clapping his fore-and-aft bicorne hat back on his head and coming to shake hands, beaming fit to bust. "We haven't crossed hawses in a dog's age, sir, and it has been too long! Sir Alan, I must say, rather."

"Oh, tosh," Lewrie dismissed. "You're lookin' fit and healthy."

"As are you, sir," Gamble replied.

"Come to join our endeavour, have you?" Lewrie asked, hoping.

"No, sir, sorry, though it would be a delight to serve with you, again," Commander Gamble said with a brief *moue* of dis-appointment, "Sir Thomas has sent me to follow up on your most recent doings, and . . . bring despatches," he added, indicating the canvas bag slung over one shoulder.

"Let's go aft and catch up whilst we may," Lewrie offered.

"Of course, sir," Gamble agreed.

"Something to drink?" Lewrie enquired once they were seated on the chairs near the starboard side settee. "Wine, cool tea, or lemonade?"

"Your cool tea I always found refreshing, sir, if you please," Gamble requested, "though I was not a regular guest in your cabins in the old *Proteus,* it was a rare treat. One of your officers . . . do I imagine that one of them is Grace?"

"He is, indeed," Lewrie told him as Deavers and Dasher arrived with the requested tea. "You're following up on something we've done?"

"Aye, sir," Gamble said with the sly grin he'd shown of old, "I am to pay a call at that bridge you blew up and take it under fire if the French have made any progress at re-building it. That, and make a perfect pest of myself as far north as the Gulf of Policastro. Shoot up what I can along the coast road, and see if there are any bridges that might need destroying to further harass French supply lines."

"That's a little outside my bailiwick," Lewrie said, "for my intelligence sources don't reach that far. You find any, though, be sure to let me know if there are any promising targets up there, and I and the Ninety-Fourth might have a go at them."

"Ah, your old cat," Gamble said as Chalky showed up, stretching and yawning. "Which one is this'un, sir? I forget."

"That's Chalky," Lewrie said. "The other, Toulon, passed over in 1805. And, the rabbit . . . that's my servant, Dasher's pet."

"Grand times we had in *Proteus*, sir," Gamble reminisced.

"Aye, they were," Lewrie heartily agreed.

"Oh, the despatches, sir," Gamble said, setting down his tea to swing the canvas bag off his shoulder and open it. "There's one from Sir Thomas . . . yes, his knighthood's now official . . . there is one from Admiralty, of which Sir Thomas has a copy, and some personal letters for one and all. Just a few, really," he said with a shrug.

Lewrie accepted them and turned them round to read the senders' addresses; yes, there were two letters from Jessica, which he stuck in an inside coat pocket for later.

"Sir Thomas will be patrolling the west coast of Italy, in addition to the Gulfs of Squillace and Taranto?" Lewrie asked.

"When he can spare the ships, sir," Gamble assured him. "One or two brig-sloops together, sometimes a frigate if he can spare one. The squadron *has* been re-enforced of late, but there are never enough ships to go round, and the Admiral in command of the Mediterranean Fleet has first call upon any new arrivals for doings elsewhere."

"Well, it's not as if the French, or their so-called allies, the Neapolitans, have any naval presence worth speaking of," Lewrie dismissed, "or any plans to confront us if they did. One *wishes* for another Trafalgar, but . . ." he said with another grimace and shrug.

Now that the official business was done, it was time to catch up on old shipmates, and where they were now; Liam Desmond was still Lewrie's Cox'n, but Patrick Furfy had perished; *Proteus*'s old First Officer, Anthony Langlie had just paid off his brig-sloop and was to be made "Post" in a spanking new frigate, which was news to Lewrie. What of Lewrie's sons, and he had re-married? Gamble had to inspect and admire Jessica's portrait, of course.

"Care to go ashore and meet the troops that I was given, sir?" Lewrie asked him. "See how they work?"

"Wish that I could, sir," Gamble demurred, "but I hope to be off your old bridge by dawn, sir, wind allowing. Anything planned, dare I ask?"

"Melito di Porto Salvo," Lewrie told him, "west of Cape Spartivento. All that's wanting is the lay of the land, how many soldiers are garrisoned there, all that."

"I say, I've cruised off that port often, sir," Gamble supplied, "and I do know that the French have a six-gun battery of field guns to protect the harbour. Twelve-pounders, most-like, set out into three-gun redans, either side of the entrance. There are beaches you could land upon, but they're right under the guns, and the land rises rather steeply. Every time we've taken a peek at the place, there's been rather heavy surf on the west side. The town itself straggles uphill beyond the piers."

"Hmm, that doesn't sound too promising," Lewrie commented, rubbing his chin in thought. "Perhaps my local spies will have better news. A damned colourful lot they are, believe you me. Smugglers and thieves, even part-time pirates if the prize is tempting enough. How close ashore did you go?"

"I've stood off at least two miles, sir," Gamble told him. "My nine-pounders aren't a match to their artillery, and their gunners are more than eager to engage any ship that gets too close. After our big sortie all along the coast, and your exploits, it's more than understandable, really, that our presence makes them skittish."

"Hmm," Lewrie said, again, "it sounds as if it'll be the hardest nut we've tried to crack, so far. Perhaps too hard."

"I'm sure you'll find a way, sir," Gamble said, breezily. "You always seem to do so. Well, with your permission, sir, I'll be off. Time and tide, all that?"

"I'll see you on deck," Lewrie offered, "and send for Mister Grace so you can at least shake hands with him."

"That would be fine, sir," Gamble agreed.

After Commander Gamble had been seen over the side, and his boat was bound back to his own ship, Lewrie left the deck and stuck his head into the chart space off the starboard side of the quarterdeck, unscrolling the pertinent chart of the Italian coast to mull over.

Guns in stone redans? he thought, troubled; *Right above the beaches? Heavy surf prevailin' . . . grapeshot and canister, firin' into the boats before they get ashore, into the troops as they wade ashore? Christ, do I want this? There* has to be an easier place.

CHAPTER FIFTEEN

The letters from Admiralty, and from Adm. Charlton, were much more pleasing, though not the sort of news to turn St. Catherine's Wheels over.

> *. . . be pleased to know that an additional troop transport, rated as a hired-in Armed Transport for hostilities only has been obtained for the use of your forces. She is the Coromandel, of 500 tons Burthen, fully Coppered, built on speculation as an East Indiaman, and barely one year old. By the time you receive this missive, she should be fully manned and ready to sail, subject only to the arrival of the re-enforcement troops of the 94th Regt. of Foot from Peterborough. We are given to understand that the Army complement consists of 200 officers and men.*

"Only one," Lewrie muttered under his breath. "One deep-draught barge that can't get any closer ashore than *Vigilance* can? My God, they know what we need, they've known it for *months!*"

Reading further, Lewrie discovered that *Coromandel* would carry six 29-foot barges, be equipped with boarding nets, outfitted with sufficient dog-box cabins for those 200 soldiers, and her crew would consist of 120 officers and sailors.

There was a letter included from Captain Middleton, who had obtained the first three transports and all their needs, apologising that the price of hiring or purchasing ships had gone so high, that so many more were needed to supply General Wellesley's army in Spain and Portugal, and succour various other British expeditions round the world, and, though he had tried his mightiest, he simply could not find suitable vessels, or spare Navy crewmen, and that he hoped that one much larger and capacious ship might suit.

Admiral Charlton's letter expressed much the same regret; no matter how hard he had pressed the matter with London, he could not move mountains, and that even a small addition to Lewrie's command would allow him to stage larger, more daring raids.

Rest assured, old friend, that I have striven to my Utmost to gain you what you Need, not merely what you Wish. After all, your Accomplishments add Lustre to my command, as well. Now, did you and Col. Tarrant achieve some new, noteworthy Successes, worthy of your past Feats, I am certain that Our Lords Commissioners would see their way to Rewarding Victory.

Indeed, what you, and Adm. Sir Home Popham off the North coast of Spain are accomplishing by way of Seaborne Raids just may result in a wholesale adoption of such Raids by both Army and Navy, and you could find yourself swamped with sudden Largesse.

Charlton mentioned his new patrolling cruisers along the Italian coast, and promised some of those ships might be tasked to assist any of his future endeavours, should he find need of them. He had only to request.

Well, that's something, anyway, Lewrie thought, tossing that letter atop his desk and leaning back in his chair. For one wistful moment, he wished that he was in D'arcy Gamble's shoes, cruising along the enemy coast and blissfully shooting to flinders anything that took his fancy, with no greater care in the world than what he could make go smash.

He recalled that there had been two letters from Jessica included in that sparse despatch bag, and reached out to open one.

Dearest Husband,
I trust my latest Epistles find you well and up to Mischief against our Foes, the dastardly French!

Oh, how so sorely I long to receive a letter from you. I know I cannot dare pray for one daily, yet, the Vagaries of our Postal System drives me to Distraction, as I am certain you feel as well.

Suddenly recalling our Supper with Admiral Charlton, and the Advice he gave to me, I took it upon myself to Circumvent the Civil Post and took a hackney to Admiralty itself with these latest, imagining that your Navy might deliver with more Alacrity. Imagine my surprise to meet with one Captain Robt. Middleton, a Commissioner of Admiralty, who, upon Introductions, told me that he knows you well, and, after but a brief Plea for Assistance, most kindly promised that my letters would be included in his latest posts to you!

Imagine!

"Oh, you clever little minx!" Lewrie exclaimed in wonder of her daring, raising his eyes from page to portrait, upon which he gazed longingly and adoringly. Whether he was thought an "old colt's tooth" for marrying a much younger woman or not, at that instant Lewrie was proud to publicly *confess* to being an "old colt's tooth"!

"Midshipman Ingham t'see th' Cap'um, SAH!" the Marine sentry intruded upon his delight.

"Oh, balls!" Lewrie shouted, irked. "Enter!"

Lewrie could hear the Marine's titters, and an audible *Erp!* from Midshipman Ingham before the door opened, and that worthy stepped inside the great-cabins.

"Apologies, sir," Ingham began, "but the signal tower ashore has hoisted a request for you to come ashore."

"It wasn't Captain Repair On Board, was it?" Lewrie asked with a scowl.

"Oh, no sir! It is Request, and Conference, spelled out, sir," Ingham declared.

"They've learned their lesson, anyway," Lewrie said, getting to his feet and tucking his wife's letters into his desk drawer for later. "Show them Will Comply, and pass word for my boat crew."

"Aye aye, sir," Ingham crisply replied, eager to escape whatever snit had prompted that "Oh, balls!"

"Shove me into my everyday, if ye please, Deavers," Lewrie bade, "and warn Yeovill that I don't know how long ashore I'll be, so I may be havin' a very late dinner, if one at all. Charts? Might as well take 'em along, too," he said, patting himself down for the needfuls in his breeches and waist-coat pockets as Deavers fetched his hat and undress uniform coat.

He was greeted at the makeshift pier along the beach by Colonel Tarrant, and a large, wet, and shaggy dog just paddling ashore with a stick in his mouth.

"Welcome, Sir Alan," Tarrant said. "You have no doubt heard?"

"About the new ship, and your re-enforcements, I take it?" Lewrie asked, his head cocked to one side.

"Exactly so, sir," Col. Tarrant agreed with a grim nod. "What the bloody Hell are those fools in London playing at? Or those in Peterborough, too, to be specific. As soon as I got through tearing my hair out, I thought we should confer."

"Aye, no time like the present," Lewrie said. "You're not happy about the number of troops they're sending you?"

"Let's go to my quarters, where I can rant in private," Tarrant suggested, turning seaward for a moment, "Here, Dante, here pup!" and the dog gave himself a thorough shake, creating a cloud of water droplets, and sprang to his master's side, tail wicking, the stick still in his mouth.

"You've a dog, now?" Lewrie asked.

"Yes. Dante just turned up one morning, whining and begging for breakfast. I tossed him some bacon and bread, and he's been glued to me the last week entire. Yes, I'll throw your damned stick for you. There, go fetch 'em up!" as he flung it a good fifty yards inland, and the dog took off in a tear, pouncing on his prize, shaking it between his teeth with happy growls, then came prancing back to rejoin them.

"He's a shaggy cur of no particular breed," Tarrant said as the dog dropped the stick, tongue lolling and tail thrashing for another throw. "Smells better after a dip in the sea, I assure you."

"Good dog, Dante," Lewrie cooed, "and aren't you a big'un?"

A second later and Lewrie was pounced upon, with the dog's front paws nigh on his upper chest, a tongue licking his face, and a strong doggy breath up his nose. He tried shoving him off and down, but that transferred the odour of wet fur to his hands and coat.

"Bad boy, Dante!" Col. Tarrant chid him. "Bad dog!" Which, of course, meant little to the dog, who whirled round in an urgent circle to have his stick thrown again. Tarrant picked it up, flung it, and the dog was off at a gallop to chase it down.

"He must have been some working dog on a farm round here," Col. Tarrant said as they got to the canvas-covered gallery in front of his quarters and took seats. "He didn't know what 'play' was for the first four days, and now he's insatiable at it. With luck, he'll wear himself out in a bit. Wine, Sir Alan?"

"Aye, that'd be welcome," Lewrie agreed, taking off his hat but not sure where to put it down in case the dog found it as tempting as his stick.

"Didn't understand much about petting, and affection, either," Col. Tarrant went on, "and now he simply can't get enough. I swear I don't know why people treat dogs so dismissively.

"Now, sir," Tarrant went on, crossing his booted legs to turn and face Lewrie. "This one new transport they're sending you . . . how many of my men can be put aboard?"

"She's said to be able to accommodate all two hundred, and that's how they'll sail them here," Lewrie told him, "though she has only six barges, the same as the others, so I couldn't get all two hundred of them ashore at one go. There's simply no room in the barges for all of them. That'd be two full, hundred-man companies?"

"Well, no," Tarrant told him. "There are enough *officers* for two more companies, but I thought to use some of the replacements to flesh out the six that I have. Say, eight companies, each of sixty-five or seventy men. Your barges might be crammed arsehole to elbow, but you *might* be able to get them all landed at once, if we don't push it."

"Hmm, that'd be possible," Lewrie said after thinking that over for a bit. "We've cabins for one hundred and twenty, now, on each ship, so room for one hundred fourty'd be possible, so long as we don't have to stay at sea much more than a week, or less."

The dog returned, prancing as proud as punch with himself for "bagging a kill." He dropped the stick by one of Tarrant's boots, sat on his haunches, and whined for more fun.

"Haven't you had enough by now?" Tarrant cooed to his new pet. "Come here, Dante, and sit close for a spell." He extended his hands and the dog placed his head and front paws in Tarrant's lap to get a petting.

"Better your breeches than mine, sir," Lewrie japed.

"Yes, well," Col. Tarrant said with a toss of his head. "Have you heard from *Don* Julio, or Mister Quill, yet, about our new raid?"

"Nothing yet, but the officer of that brig that put in yesterday told me some about it," Lewrie told him as Tarrant's orderly appeared with two glasses of white wine on a silver tray. "Melito di Porto Salvo sounds a tough'un. At least six twelve-pounder field guns in redans either side of the harbour entrance, a German garrison, and the best landing beaches right under their artillery. Steep going, too."

"Damned good soldiers, Germans," Tarrant said with a wince and sucking of his teeth. "Hessians in America, the King's German Legion in Spain . . . they'll be sure to put up a stouter defence than any we have seen yet, and a more alert watch. No surprising them. Canister and grapeshot? They could engage your barges even before they get on the beach. One would hope that *Don* Julio's scouts report with better news . . . or Mister Quill's agent finds us an easier target. Did *Don* Julio say *why* this particular Melito . . . however one says it . . . is so important?"

"Large caches of foodstuffs for the French in Calabria," Lewrie said with a shrug of puzzlement. "Or, perhaps one of his damned competitors is based there, who knows. God, Andalusia in Spain was much easier. The Foreign Office spy at Gibraltar had good connexions with the Spanish partisans, and we chose our *own* places to land, and when, had at least one fishing boat of our own to prowl with, and more men ashore to gather and pass information. Depending on mercenaries and smugglers as we are, well . . . one never knows *what* they might stick us in, or why!

"I brought charts, though," Lewrie offered of a sudden, "just in case we *do* raid Melito di bloody Salvo."

"Yes, let's have a squint at them," Tarrant suggested, "let us go inside, so we can spread them out on my table."

Tarrant's dog prowled round the dining table, paws scratching, to see what the humans were so interested in, but, after a shooing or two, went to a scrap of rag carpet, circled himself several times, and flopped down with an audible *Hmfph!* over being ignored.

"Moderate to heavy surf, there," Lewrie said, pointing at the western beaches with a pencil, "and I expect the artillery is posted somewhere up-slope on the low hills either side of the harbour mouth. The town behind, well, I know little of it, yet, but the charts hint at a rather roundish harbour, with good shelter from storms. A good place for the French to marshal coasting ships."

"It was bombarded from the sea back in the Spring, was it not?" Col. Tarrant asked, using a magnifying glass to peer closer at the chart.

"Aye, but I've no idea how much damage our ships caused," Lewrie agreed. "The narrowness of the harbour mouth limits how long a ship's guns can bear before these low hills intervene. I do know that many fires were set, and some prizes were fetched out, but . . ." he said, tossing off a shrug. "From where we were anchored off Siderno, it certainly *looked* as if we'd burned the place to the ground."

Col. Tarrant set aside his magnifying glass, peered at the chart a bit longer, then went to his desk and rummaged round 'til he found a map of lower Calabria, brought it to the table and spread it out, a sly smile on his face.

"Look here, Sir Alan," Tarrant said. "There's one decent usable road on the west coast, all the way from Naples to Reggio di Calabria, then down to Melito di Porto Salvo. All else are muddy, rutted farm tracks that struggle through the hills. That coast road runs all round the shore, to Catanzaro on the east coast of the peninsula. It's only there that one meets cross-peninsula roads, and they are *below* Pizzo, and that bridge we destroyed. Were I a French general on short commons, I'd divert my supply convoys from round Filadelfia to Catanzaro, *then* west through all those little seaport towns we attacked earlier this year. Hmm, even shorter, did they divert cross the mountains on *this* road from Filadelfia to Monasterace Marina. Perhaps a landing, or a series of landings, from Monasterace to Bova Marina near Cape Spartivento would be easier. Perhaps not even right into the towns themselves, but raids along the road, to stop convoys, drive off their escorts, and set fire to the waggons, kill their draught animals!"

"And, if there *are* bands of partisans in the mountains, they'd have to divert their troop strength farther afield than all of these little seaport towns," Lewrie said, liking the idea at once. "Though, I'd have to land you in the dark, then sail off, so the French don't know you're there 'til you've struck, and there's no way for you to signal me to retrieve you. And, if you run into trouble, I'd not be there in time to extricate you."

"Hmm, there is that," Tarrant said, plumping out his lips in a deep frown. "The risk might be better than attacking Melito di-what-ye-call it. You're quite right, that's a tough nut to crack, no error. Even with eight fleshed-out companies, and your Marines as a ninth, and all my reenforcements as trained and experienced at what we do as the troops I have now, I'd still not wish to try it on."

"There are notes and sketches," Lewrie realised, all but slapping his forehead. "Mister Quill has 'em, and I think I have *some* of them. The results of all the scouting *Don* Julio's men did along the coast before Admiral Charlton's big raid. We'd not be going in *completely* blind."

"Yes!" Tarrant exclaimed. "Troop strengths, warehouses, if any artillery's present, the condition of the landing beaches, and how the towns are laid out! It may not be as much information as we need, but it's enough to allow us to begin planning our *own* raids, and not be totally dependent on *Don* Julio Caesare."

"Well, it's said that 'a little information is a dangerous thing,'" Lewrie quipped.

"Hah! Being led round by the nose is a deal worse!" Tarrant hooted. "I'll get a note off to Mister Quill in Messina this afternoon, to see what he's retained from that earlier mass raid, and I'd admire did you dig into your desk to see if you can turn up anything useful, Sir Alan."

"With pleasure, Colonel," Lewrie gladly agreed. "Perhaps Mister Quill can also tell us if he's heard from his new agent over there, and if and when he wishes his arms to be landed."

"Gad, yes!" Col. Tarrant went on with enthusiasm, "Can Mister Silvestri assemble a larger partisan band, with the weapons he plans to give them, the local Italians could harass the supply convoys in the hills, all along that poor secondary road, as well! Hah! Quite a productive morning, sir!"

"I'll drink to that," Lewrie said, hinting for a refill. He'd even throw a stick for Tarrant's dog, and give him some "wubbies" too, if it got them back into action.

CHAPTER SIXTEEN

*P*erhaps it was Mister Quill's nature, having been a long-term student and librarian at college before his recruitment into Secret Branch, but he was like a "pack-rat," and never threw anything away that caught his fancy, or he thought might be useful in future. He turned up in a light two-wheeled cart the day after Col. Tarrant's request, accompanied by his boy message runner, Fiorello, with a chest crammed full of papers, maps, old letters, and writing materials.

Once ensconced in Col. Tarrant's quarters, and the chest opened, the Colonel's dining table, the sideboard, and the chairs were soon piled high with loose, untidy, and perilously balanced stacks of the stuff, and it didn't help that Dante the hound found it all so intriguingly scented that he had to be shooed out and the doors closed after several collapses and avalanches.

"Fiorello, play with the dog!" Mr. Quill ordered, exasperated, tugging his shirt cuffs and waist-coat back into order. "Sorry about this. My lodgings are just by a sausage shop, and the fish market is not fifty yards off. I expect my papers have taken on aromas simply too tempting. Melito di Porto Salvo, ah . . . it's here, somewhere," Quill said as he roamed from one stack to another, lifting a part of a pile to thumb through.

"We're thinking more about Monasterace Marina, or the villages east of there," Col. Tarrant prompted, while trying to be helpful bent over to scoop up fallen pages and such.

"Don't like the looks of Melito," Lewrie told Quill. "Too tough a nut. The convoys along the roads . . ."

"Ah, the detours, you mean," Quill said, breaking out a smile. "Yes, I've had a letter from Silvestri, which tells of the supplies now going over the mountain roads from Filadelfia to Monasterace and Siderno, then back along the main coast road. The partisans have been watching closely, but haven't been able to do anything about them, so far . . . lack of arms, and numbers. About the arms shipment . . ."

"We want to ambush the supply convoys along the coast road once they cross the mountains," Col. Tarrant reminded Quill, though in a cooing voice; he looked as if he'd save loud shouts for later if the fellow didn't stay on point.

"Hmm, ambushes, well," Mr. Quill mused aloud, standing up and scratching at his chin. "If you can pull that off, more power to you. Don't quite know why you'd wish to traipse about the countryside and play Red Indians, when the seaport towns are still there. Bova Marina, Brancaleone Marina, Locri, Siderno, and on east to Monasterace, they may not have warehouses any longer, but the supply convoys are only stopping for the night, then moving on in the morning."

"How do you know that, sir?" Lewrie asked.

"What, I didn't tell you?" Quill replied, then unfortunately for them breaking out into one of his bray-wheeze-gasping-drowning-man laughs. "Silvestri's band of partisans is in contact with other bands all throughout Western Calabria, and when he asked that fellow 'Spada' or whoever he is about the convoys, he got an ear-ful. Well, there's still stockpiles in each village, oats, grains, and hay for the mule and ox teams. That's what the first convoys carried, d'ye see, so a convoy of waggons could feed their draught animals overnight."

"Quick raids on the towns, then," Col. Tarrant realised, "where we already have information . . . burn the fodder, and whichever convoy happens to be in town at the moment, if luck's with us. Hmm, I say!"

"I would suppose," Quill breezily said, "and if the fodder is lost, hmm . . . the French would have to waste waggons and animals restocking it."

"Delaying the carriage of food and supplies to their troops!" Lewrie exclaimed as if the battle was all but won. "And, if we burn waggons and slaughter the waggon teams, that makes things even more difficult for the French. I doubt the supply of horses, mules, and oxen in Calabria is inexhaustible. Or decent waggons, either."

"And all for the destruction of a single bridge, haw!" Tarrant crowed. "Which would you prefer first, Sir Alan? Pick a village."

"Bova Marina, I suppose," Lewrie said, pushing stacks aside to bare the sea chart beneath them. "It's close to Melito di Porto Salvo, but the land is flatter, the beaches are broader, its harbour is more open, and it's only a long day's march even for ox team waggons from Melito. Almost the end of a long, gruelling trek for the French with the convoy, teamsters *and* escorts, if any. They might be feelin' a bit too cocky, by then. Garrison, though, and artillery," he cautioned.

"I've nothing new since the raids in the Spring," Quill apologised, "but, all that information is in here, somewhere . . . copies of all I sent Admiral Charlton so his ships could prepare for it. Might we have some tea? It may take awhile."

Lewrie heaved a sigh and took off his coat and waist-coat, and hung them on a chair back. He looked round and realised that every chair was taken with stacks of material, so there would be no sitting as they searched for the hidden keys that opened Bova Marina to a new raid. He began to page through the nearest stack on the dining table, wishing that Quill had suggested wine instead of tea, for it looked to be a long morning and afternoon.

Two hours later, and they were still at it. They had found the sketches that *Don* Julio's henchmen had made of Bova Marina; the town's layout, the depths of water off the likely beaches, and a view from sea level. The warehouses were no longer there, of course, pounded to ruin by some frigate's guns, along with half the waterfront dwellings, so that sketch was no longer to be trusted completely. But, so far, they could not find comments on Bova Marina's garrison; how many of them, from which regiment, where they'd been lodged, their nationality, or whether the French had thought to emplace artillery in such a poor place.

"It's close enough to Melito di Porto Salvo," Lewrie hesitantly speculated. "It wasn't a storehouse for an invasion of Sicily like Locri or Siderno were, so . . . perhaps it *had* no garrison of its own, and that regiment of Germans at Melito just tramped through now and then."

"As I recall from our briefings, there were coastal trading ships and large fishing boats in the harbour, though," Col. Tarrant said, leaning back in a chair that he'd finally cleared and now sat upon, rubbing his eyes with the heels of his hands. "Perhaps only one company would be necessary to guard them 'til Marshal Murat up in Naples marched his invasion force down to take ship. And, it most-like *would* have come from the nearest regiment, which would have been the Germans at Melito."

"Nothing left to guard, now," Mr. Quill commented, pinching the bridge of his nose, "and that plan scotched, so there might not be a permanent garrison, as you say, sir."

"I'm fair starving," Col. Tarrant announced. "Let us break for dinner, before my eyes glaze over."

"Amen to that," Lewrie seconded with enthusiasm.

"Just so long as it ain't fish," Quill dared to say. "The fish market at Messina? My poor stipend? Ah, me. Why, I may be growing *gills* by now, hah hah!"

Don't . . . do not . . . *laugh!* Lewrie implored, dreading another bout of Quill's donkey-like hee-haws as they made their way out to the front gallery, sunlight, and fresh air. Lewrie had been on his feet for the better part of an hour before he'd cleared a chair for himself, bent over the dining table, and he had a faint crick in his lower back, which he bent and twisted to relieve.

"I wonder, though, sirs," Quill began once they were all seated in much more comfortable collapsible campaign chairs round a locally obtained farm table, and sipping on fresh glasses of fruity white wine, "Are you gentlemen a bit daunted by the presence of German allied troops at Melito?"

"The terrain, the narrow beaches, the prevailing surf," Lewrie ticked off on the fingers of one hand, "and the six twelve-pounders that cover the beaches. One'd think *Don* Julio'd realise that it's *indeed* too daunting, at present, even if he isn't a soldier."

"That, and the fact that, so far, we've spent far too long in camp . . ." Tarrant added.

"Swingin' round our anchors," Lewrie stuck in.

"Waiting, idling," Tarrant went on, with a slight bow to Lewrie, "and totally dependent upon news of places that *Don* Julio wishes us to strike.

He's picked all our targets, save the big raids on Locri and Siderno, where these vast supply depots were, and I'd much prefer choosing for myself. You must feel the same dependence, sir."

"Oh, indeed, Colonel Tarrant, I have!" Mr. Quill answered him with almost world-weary resignation. "He, and the services he offered, literally fell into my lap, within a month of my arrival at Messina. Quite *dear* services, mind. Fifty guineas here, an hundred guineas there, 'Such a risk will cost you, *signore*.' I need more boats, more guns, more time, more *everything*! Now the arms I requested ages ago have finally arrived, their delivery to the partisans over there in Calabria will cost me even more! If I can find him."

"What, he's disappeared?" Lewrie gawped.

"Off somewhere on his own criminal enterprise," Quill groused, "out of touch for the present. I've spoken with some of his men . . . all those damned "Tonios,' and none can say where he's gone, or when the scouts come back from Melito di Porto Salvo, either. Did I hear from Mister Silvestri through *Don* Julio's men? No, sirs. The partisans sent a little fishing smack cross the Straits to Messina and delivered his letter themselves. They even named a beach where they can accept the arms, the dark of the moon coming up, but . . . without *Don* Julio's boats, I can't make the delivery."

"Ehm, how many?" Lewrie idly asked.

"Two hundred stands of arms," Quill lamented, "Is that how you describe them? Two hundred refurbished French Saint Etienne arsenal muskets, French cartridge boxes and belts, and twenty thousand rounds of pre-made paper cartridges."

"Well, Sir Alan has boats aplenty," Col. Tarrant tossed off. "He could deliver them, surely."

"Eet weel cost you *multi* gold, *signore*," Lewrie japed, though he secretly thought it high-handed of Col. Tarrant to volunteer his services so blithely.

"You could, Sir Alan?" Mr. Quill gushed. "That would be just capital!" They're stored at the *Castello* in Messina for the nonce, all crated up, ten to a box, One, perhaps two, of your rowing barges could carry them nicely!"

"And Mister Silvestri and the partisans could begin to curtail supply convoys in the mountains!" Col. Tarrant enthused.

"Ahem," Tarrant's orderly announced, "dinner is served, sirs."

"Topping!" Tarrant cried. "What are we having?"

"Sardines and mussels in wine sauce, sir, with rice and beans, and a loaf of that nice, crusty *ciabatta* bread with seasoned olive oil dipping sauce, along with a crisp lettuce salad."

Lewrie looked to Quill, who at that moment was heaving a sigh that it would be fish, after all, and hid his smile of glee that the man was to be dis-appointed once again.

"I was quite impressed with the mien of the partisans that I met the night we took the bridge," Col. Tarrant said as his orderly fetched out grapes, apricots, and sweet bisquits for "afters," and a fresh bottle of that white wine. "Quite fearless. Swashbuckling, even. Now you're in contact with them, Mister Quill, grand things may be afoot."

"As I have dearly wished, sir," Quill replied, savouring his wine, "though the Italians *seem* as spirited as any, I cannot in good conscience put too much trust in their resistance."

"Oh? Whyever not, sir?" Col. Tarrant asked, sounding let down.

"Well, consider their history, sir," Quill began, looking skyward to gather his thoughts for a moment. "The history of Iberia, rather, in the first instance. The Spanish and the Portuguese were for hundreds of years at war with their Moorish invaders, the Gothic Vandals before them, and with each other, at times. The various kingdoms *were* able to unite, though, and co-operate against the Moors in the *Reconquista. El Cid?* All that martial glory, in the name of God? Then, when they packed the last Moors off in Fourteen Ninety-Two, and Ferdinand and Isabella united all the kingdoms under one banner, there was relative peace within their own borders, under one monarch, with a *sense* of themselves as Spanish or Portuguese, so . . . when the French marched in and their gutless Francophile ministers sold them out, they were *livid*!

"The Italians, though . . ." Quill went on, leaning back in his chair, toying with a knife and an apricot, "once Rome fell, and the Empire in the West fell into chaos, the Italians have known nothing but war, invasions, one new tyrant after another, city-states like Florence, Padua, Naples, and others invading other city-states nigh as often as one changes shirts. Occupation, rape, robbery, murder, pillaging, starvation? Vikings, Normans, Moors, Vandals, Spanish conquerors, Ottoman Turks, and now the French, and it's all of one piece to the Italians."

"Better to sit back and hope they're left alone 'til the next conqueror comes marching in, d'ye mean?" Lewrie asked him.

"Occupation by the French, Sir Alan, is nothing to get offended by. They're just another plague of locusts to be borne 'til they go away, and someone else takes their place, yes. Why take up arms, why resist, after so many centuries of supine complacency? They see their dukes and counts and leaders collaborating, so . . . why bother? I fear, sirs, that the Italians can be excitable, but only over a horse race, or a festival. There will be some who rise up, but . . . don't count on the same scale of resistance as we've seen in Spain."

"Then why do you wish to give them *arms*, Mister Quill?" Lewrie demanded.

"Upon the belief that, perhaps, this time they will, and that with our arms and encouragement, this time the spark will take light and kindle *real* rebellion," Quill sadly told him.

"Good God," Col. Tarrant commented, "I do not envy you your mission, Mister Quill."

"I might have better luck separating Spanish colonies from the home country, indeed, sir," Quill answered. "But, I must try, and hope, that my efforts will be rewarded."

"Ah, well," Tarrant said with a sigh. "Back to the mining of your papers, I fear. Shall we, gentlemen?"

By four that afternoon, they had found what they had searched for, and yes, it had been one company of a German regiment that had garrisoned Bova Marina when it had been an invasion port for the taking of Sicily, there to guard the many boats, but there had never been any artillery emplaced there, and most-likely would not be any, now that the small, sleepy seaport contained nothing in need of protection.

To Col. Tarrant's chagrin, Lewrie decided that they would not sail directly down the Strait of Messina to make the raid, in full view of enemy watchers ashore on the mainland, but would go North, then West-about Sicily, to strike from the open sea. By now, his ship and the transports were known to the French, and the sight of them would alert the whole Calabrian coast.

To atone for that, Lewrie invited them to dine aboard *Vigilance* that evening, promising them that his cook, Yeovill, would provide a succulent repast. He assured Mr. Quill that it would most certainly *not* be fish!

⚓

Once back aboard in his great-cabins, Lewrie sat at his desk, and slowly sipped on a mug of ginger beer, mulling over whom he would send with the arms shipment. His junior officers, Rutland, Greenleaf, and Grace had participated in all of the troop landings and fighting, so far, earning his praise in reports to Admiralty, which the papers in London had re-printed, most especially *The Gazette*. Advancement to higher rank or more-responsible postings depended on a man's reputation with Admiralty, and the general public. In his own younger days, Lewrie and his fellow Mids, his fellow Lieutenants, had almost come to blows over which of them would be granted the opportunity to shine and make names for themselves. Bravery, skill, and "neck-or-nothing" daring gained a fellow honour, and glory.

Aye, I relish seein' my name in the papers, too, Lewrie admitted to himself; *And I wish I could go with the muskets myself.*

He recalled how delighted Brigadier Caruthers had been during the battle with the French regiment at Siderno, back in the Spring, when he had crowed that he had had a horse, a captured French horse, shot out from under him, as if it was the grandest thing.

Of course it was; it would look brave in the London papers!

Sadly, though, Lewrie realised that he was too old, too senior, now, to risk life and limb chasing more fame, or satisfying his lust for action; no, that would be his junior officers' place these days.

Farley, he thought; *He's not had his chance, yet.*

As *Vigilance*'s First Officer, Lieutenant Farley held an elevated position, but an onerous one. His job was to act as second-in-command and present Lewrie with a ship ready to go to sea at a moment's notice, a somewhat *happy,* well-drilled, and superbly organised ship, with her crewmen assigned to the tasks to which they were most suited. Under his eagle eyes fell the proper material condition of just about everything, a thankless, unending chore, but one which groomed him for promotion to his own command, someday.

Lewrie recalled his impressions of Lt. Farley from their brief time together in the *Thermopylae* frigate, in the Winter of 1801, in the Baltic, and the Battle of Copenhagen. Farley and his old shipmate from their Midshipmen days, Lt. Fox had been quite a waggish pair, but nigh "tarpaulin men" and good leaders on duty, and Farley had distinguished himself during that cruise, especially after the frigate's First Officer, Lt. Ballard had been killed in battle.

Farley it is, Lewrie thought, making up his mind; *And if I know him well enough by now, he'll* leap *at the chance.*

"Dasher?" Lewrie said.

"Aye, sir?" Dasher asked, looking up from feeding his bunny a lettuce leaf.

"Go pass word for the First Officer, would you? I have need of him," Lewrie told him.

Aye, he'll leap, Lewrie thought as Dasher left the cabins; *And God help his hopeful arse.*

CHAPTER SEVENTEEN

*T*here had been wind, rain, and moderately heavy seas during the passage along the south coast of Sicily 'til HMS *Vigilance* and her transports cleared Cape Passero, the island's extreme sou'eastern tip. From there on, the last afternoon of the voyage had turned smoother, a great relief to the men of the 94th, who, despite their experience with ships, boats, and landings, had yet to expose them to open seas for days at a time, especially in rough weather. For the most part, they had abandoned their dog-box cabins belowdecks and had clung to the bulwarks along the weather decks, green-gilled and "casting their accounts to Neptune," to the amusement of the naval crews aboard the transport ships. Buckets were passed up from below to be emptied overside, then back down the hatches like a make-shift fire brigade, for those too ill to come up for fresher air, and the soldiers didn't understand the admonitions to hurl over the leeward side 'til wind-whipped puke was blown back into their faces when attempting to use the weather rails.

"Do you imagine our 'Mer-Men' will be recovered enough to make the landing, sir?" Mr. Wickersham, *Vigilance*'s Sailing Master, cordially asked Lt. Rutland, who stood the Watch.

"Tonight's a Banyan Day supper," Rutland replied, "so they may be up for a bite or two. Nothing too greasy, nor anything that will scratch on the way back up."

"Hah!" Mr. Wickersham said with a bark of a laugh, half in appreciation for Lt. Rutland's jest, and half in amazement that the dour man had actually made one.

"Hallo, you're early," Wickersham commented as Lt. Farley came trotting up the lee ladderway to the quarterdeck.

"Too stuffy in the wardroom," Farley told him, taking a deep sniff of fresh air. "Ah, that's better! Besides, up-dating the Muster Books began to pall. Plenty of time for those after we've made our raid and head home. And as soon as I set foot ashore, I hope that the local food vendors are open. Street food in Messina was eye-opening."

Wickersham and Rutland shared a look behind Farley's back, as if to roll their eyes and sigh, sure that a fresh account of his covert mission would be forthcoming.

"Toothsome, *and* hellishly cheap, too," Farley said, unaware of their looks. *"Arancini*. They've the *colour* of oranges, which is why they're called that. Rice balls, stuffed with meat and vegetables, and a dash of saffron, rolled in bread crumbs and fried in olive oil, so tasty and satisfying! *Muesa* something or other, couldn't catch its full name? Organ meats, but lighter than liver, with sprinkles of strong cow milk cheese on bread! Just marvellous!"

"And did the partisans serve those, too, Mister Farley?" the Sailing Master asked him, tongue-in-cheek.

"Uhm no, not a morsel, sir," Lt. Farley said gruffly, aware that he was being twitted. "How do we fare, Rutland?" he said, turning his attention to the Second Officer for the particulars of course, speed at the last cast of the log, the Captain's orders for the evening, and whether sail would be shortened after full dark.

"Cap'um's on deck!" one of the Midshipmen of the Watch called.

"Don't mind me, sirs. Carry on," Lewrie told them all as he went up a ladderway to the poop deck with his telescope. He scanned the skies, the sails aloft, and the stream of the commissioning pendant, then extended his telescope to look aft at *Bristol Lass,* the largest transport ship and the one closest astern.

Think they're done heavin', he told himself as he espied soldiers on the weather deck, bareheaded in their shirt sleeves, strolling or idling, and no longer bent over the bulwarks in misery. Aft upon *Bristol Lass*'s quarter-

deck, he could make out men still in red coats; Col. Tarrant and the officers of the two companies carried aboard her, conversing with Lt. Fletcher.
And Col. Tarrant's large dog, Dante, frisking about them all, hungry for
"pets" and attention. Tarrant had told him that Dante might run off if he
left the dog in camp whilst he was away, for he'd only had the beast such
a short time, unsure of its loyalty, and he would be heartbroken if that happened, for where could his new dog find a better, surer home?

Hope he leaves it aboard, Lewrie thought; *It was hard enough hoistin' the
dog aboard in the first place.*

As he lowered his telescope, Lewrie thought of Bisquit, the dog that
had become the *Reliant* frigate's mascot, then his own dog in all but name
aboard HMS *Sapphire*. He felt a sudden ache of longing for the silly beast,
and a pang that he'd left him in London with his wife. It was the kindest
thing to do, for drills on the great guns had always made Bisquit shiver
and whine in fear, even if the drills were without live firing. Bisquit had
loving people to look after him, and he and Jessica's cocker spaniel, Rembrandt and the kitchen ratter terrier, Bully were inseparable now, but . . .
Lewrie felt a sense of loss for those loving brown eyes, that whisking tail,
and a prompting muzzle against his knee. Chalky, and all of his previous
cats, were just as adoring and affectionate, but there was something different about a dog, and most specially, Bisquit.

He shook that feeling off and raised his telescope again for a look at the
trailing transports, then at the western horizon and the skies above it. He
and Tarrant, when laying their plans, had taken the phase of the moon,
and its expected rise, into consideration, even if the weather on the night
of landing was unknown to them, and beyond their control. He heaved a
tentative sigh of relief that the clouds were thinning as the heavy weather
of the previous days were blowing inland on gentler winds. Seven Bells
were struck up forward at the forecastle belfry; half past three in the
afternoon, and almost the end of the Day Watch. Two Mids, Malin and
Charles Chenery, cast the chip log aft at the taffrails, and turned the half-
minute glass.

"Eight and one-half knots!" Midshipman Malin called out to the officers
on the quarterdeck. "Eight and a half, sirs!"

Lewrie had pored over the charts in his cabins, and in the chart space
off the quarterdeck, for hours already, and grunted with satisfaction that,
if the winds remained constant and steady, they'd be off Bova Marina
well before dawn, and, according to the *ephemeris,* the moon, a waning

half-moon, would have risen round half past eleven tonight. With clearing skies, perhaps a partial overcast scudding by, there would be just enough light to see by to get the ships anchored and the boats manned in the dark, and if God was just, the soldiers, Marines, and armed seamen could sneak ashore un-noticed, and all four ships would be almost invisible.

And a ruddy, bloody sky at sundown'd not go amiss, either, he wished to himself.

Four fully darkened ships ghosted along the shoreline, sailing under re-duced sail, with men in the fore chains heaving their leads to feel their way into shallower water, groping almost blind for the five-fathom line indi-cated on the charts.

"Five fathom, sir! Five fathom t'this line!" was relayed aft to the quar-terdeck in urgent whispers.

"Put your helm hard down, Quartermasters," Lt. Farley snapped to the helmsmen. "Hands aloft, trice up and lay out to take in all sail! Stand by the anchor party!"

Lewrie stood at the windward corner of the quarterdeck, wincing at the noises as the ropes round the drum of the double helm groaned, as the ship herself creaked and gave out weary, protesting noises as she came about, fearing that watchers ashore could *hear* them coming. Even with the light of a half-moon, occluded for long moments as the thin clouds slowly scud-ded shoreward, he could see topmen scrambling up the rat-lines of the shrouds and making their way out the foot ropes of the yards that still bore exposed canvas. Jibs and stays'ls came slithering down, their halliards singing in the blocks, and loosened sails fluttering and snapping as loud as gunshots.

Down both beams, below the sail-tending gangways, Marines and sailors stood almost elbow to elbow, swaying and shuffling to adjust to the cant of the decks, and canteens and cartridge pouches, bayonet sheathes thudded against slung muskets and cutlass hilts, making him wish he could hiss a loud *Sshh!*

"No helm, sir!" the senior Quartermaster on the helm told Lt. Farley as softly but urgently as he could.

"Pass word forrud, let go the best bower!" Farley said, leaning over the cross-deck hammock stanchions, and the roar of the hawser as it rushed out, and the loud splash of the anchor was as loud as a broadside, to Lewrie's ears.

Blessed, covert silence reigned for a long minute as the quarterdeck officers waited for the snub and jerk in sure sign of the anchor biting into the seabed, even as more scope to the cable paid out from the hawse holes.

"Ship's at anchor, sir!" Lt. Farley reported, sounding almost breathlessly relieved. "All sails taken in, and ready to proceed."

"Haul the boats alongside, rig the boarding nets overside, and stand ready to debark the Marines," Lewrie snapped back. He simply had to go up to the poop deck for a better view, and dashed upwards with one of the night-glasses.

They had spotted the town lights of Melito di Porto Salvo as they had tiptoed past that seaport, and there were some lights lit ashore in Bova Marina, too. But not too many, Lewrie hoped. Rectangles of dim amber glows from windows in houses or taverns where a single candle was lit; barred, slitted windows where the shutters were closed, but someone stirred at that early hour; some weak lanthorns hung outside a wealthier house, or scattered along the quays to light the piers for pre-dawn fishermen preparing to set out for a morning's catch; that was all he could see, and as yet, hopefully, none of these were wending their way to their boats.

"Nets are rigged, and the barges are alongside, sir!" Farley hissed from the quarterdeck below him.

"Very well, Mister Farley," Lewrie replied, striving for a calm and reassuring tone, "Man the boats and prepare to shove off."

"Aye aye, sir!"

Now, what the bloody Hell's that? Lewrie asked himself as he swung his telescope about to either side of the little village. He strained to make sense of the odd lights a bit inland, damning the limitations of the night-glass, which showed everything upside down and backwards. There were dull amber and dim red lights that seemed to flicker.

Campfires? he wondered, sucking air past his teeth; *A French troop encampment? Mine arse on a band-box, what have we stumbled into, and how many?*

He looked aft, peering hungrily for any sight of the transports, hoping that they had not yet debarked their troops, but, to his alarm, saw the tiny specks from hooded lanthorns announcing that they were already sending off their loaded boats.

"Boats manned and ready to shove off, sir!" Lt. Farley said as loud as he dared.

Oh, Christ! In for a penny . . . Lewrie thought, groaning; *It was too late to call it off.*

"Shove off, aye!" he snapped, with the forlorn hope that the French were sound asleep, and could still be taken by surprise. He raised his night-glass again, eyes straining.

Well? Maybe? he thought, taking note that the campfires were burning low, as if nought but a few yawning sentries were tending to them. One fire seemed to erupt in a rising shower of sparks as someone fed it more wood, and beyond it . . . !

Laundry on a line? he puzzled as he espied several rectangular shapes briefly revealed by the flare-up of the campfire; *Who in Hell dries bedsheets at night?*

Before the campfire returned to a sullen red-orange, it struck him that those supposed bedsheets were badly in need of a proper washing, for they seemed as parchment-coloured as old sailcloth.

"Waggons?" he exclaimed, suddenly realising what he had seen. "Canvas-covered waggons!"

Lewrie swung his night-telescope back and forth, searching for more rectangular shapes, and found them on either side of the town. There appeared to be *two* supply convoys encamped for the night, resting their draught animals, and sleeping off supper. Were there troops escorting them? He imagined that the guards might be cavalry, which caused a small, tight grin to spread on his face. They'd be asleep at that hour, their mounts un-saddled, the troopers bootless for the most part, and most weapons un-loaded, for safety's sake.

"Now, do we get ashore quiet, and surprise 'em!" he whispered. "Just thankee Jesus!"

He looked for his landing force, but that was all but impossible to spot. Dark-hulled barges on black water were invisible . . . wait! In the few moments that the clouds allowed the waning moon's light to glitter on the sea's ripples, he could make out eerie greenish glints like widely scattered fireflies. *Phosphorescence!* he thought, a "break-teeth" word he doubted he could spell with a gun to his head. There were wee things in the seawater that would glow when disturbed, something he'd seen more often in the Caribbean or tropical waters, but it *was* High Summer in the Mediterranean, so whatever caused that glow was thriving now. He could almost conjure that he could hear the oars creaking in the thole pins as each long stroke created irregular gashes of green, and faery-like droplets from each blade as it rose to be swung forward for the next stroke. Each rudder, each transom, made a wee light as they passed through the sea. The clues were faint, and only dimly seen, but Lewrie could identify three gaggles of barges off to his left, loosely grouped, and nowhere in any orderly fashion, all bound for a boot-black shore. A bit to his right, barges from his ship seemed to be headed for the few lights lit in Bova Marina itself, as if Captain Whitehead meant to land his Marines right onto the quays.

Lewrie fretted whether the Mids and tillermen, the Army officers, could also see where each of their barges roughly were to each other, and make adjustments. Could they see the shore and the beaches upon which they would land? Could they also spot where the supply waggons were? Once more, Lewrie cursed his rank and seniority, wishing that he could be right among them, urging the boats into proper line, giving alerts as to the presence of the waggons.

Shrouded by the dark that swallowed his ship, Lewrie pounded a fist on the cap-rail of the poop deck's bulwark, bemoaning the fact that he was in command of all, yet in control of nothing, and would have no word of success or failure 'til dawn or later, fearing the first sounds of gunfire that might mean anything!

"They *must* be ashore by now," Lt. Farley muttered, loud enough for Lewrie to hear.

"I think I could almost see them," the Sailing Master chimed in.

"That odd, green stuff?" Farley added with a chuckle.

"Sshh!" Lewrie hissed down to the quarterdeck, ready to curse the both of them. When he returned his intense gaze to the sea once more, everything had disappeared. The wee green fireflies were gone, and the shore was a darker black than the sea. A wider bank of clouds made it even worse, smothering the faint moonlight.

"Dammit!" he groused, pounding the cap-rail again.

CHAPTER EIGHTEEN

*C*olonel Tarrant stepped onto the gunn'l of his barge to leap to the beach, but landed badly, taking a tumble onto wet, gritty sand and gravel, just as a wave broke and flooded inland, soaking his breeches to mid-thigh.

"Right, then," he said, getting to his feet. "A damned good thing that I didn't wear my good boots, hah! Colour party? Where the Devil's the Colour party, Corporal Carson?"

"Next boat off t'th' roight, sir," Tarrant's orderly reported.

"All boats ashore?" Tarrant asked, looking up and down the beach, unable to make out much. He could hear his company officers and the senior non-commissioned officers, though, growling and swearing as they herded soldiers into company groups, then into sections. He could also hear wet boots squishing, musket butts thumping against canteens and accoutrements.

"Colour party, here," Col. Tarrant dared order aloud, summoning those men to him. "Battalion will advance!" and skirmishers set out, up a slight rise from the beach, boots and legs thrashing through the low undergrowth above the hard-packed beach, into the softer dry sand, and onto the dirt coastal roadway.

"'Tallion, halt!" he ordered, fetching a pocket telescope from the rough canvas rucksack slung on his right hip for a look-see. As he did so, he thought he heard a mournful dog howling from somewhere; in the town, perhaps, or somewhere ahead of them? No, it was a howl too faint to be anywhere close. "Oh, the damned hound!" he muttered with a chuckle; it was *his* dog, baying at being left aboard ship.

Tarrant now could make out the splendid sight of a group of waggons, dozens of them, spread out in front of him and his soldiers, all lined up in neat rows, tongues down to touch the ground, with harness laid out upon the tongues and alongside them to speed the hitching of draught animals in the morning. There were low campfires burning, and some tents erected near them, for enemy officers he imagined. Round the fires, he could see supine blanketed forms. Only a few sentries paced about in overcoats or draping blankets, muskets slung off their shoulders, and most of them stayed close to the fires.

"Ah, perfection!" Tarrant said in delight, drawing his sword, "Colour party, bare the Colours! 'Tallion!" he roared as loud as he could of a sudden. "Fix bayonets! At the double quick, advance!"

Another sight delighted Tarrant; the gape-jawed stupefaction of the French sentries as they were frozen in their tracks for long seconds by the sudden appearance of six whole companies of *Anglais* infantry storming down upon them, with muskets pointing at them, and reddish glints of firelight on steel bayonets. Some shots were fired, aimed in the general direction of the British, hastily snapped off, half-blinded by the campfires round which they had huddled, instead of standing proper guard out beyond where their eyes could adjust to the dark, but who knew, or would even suspect, that such a sudden attack could come as if from the blue?

Sleeping soldiers were flinging aside their blankets, groping for their weapons, cartridge pouches, and shoes, confused as to which they should tend to first. Un-loaded weapons were urgently clawed at, paper cartridges bitten, and powder poured down the muzzles, bullets spat down after them, and wooden butts thumped on the ground with no time to draw out their ramrods.

"Skirmishers!" Tarrant roared. "Volley!"

There were a few shots from the panicky French, quickly answered by British muskets as the skirmishers out in front of each advancing company slammed themselves to a halt, cocked their firelocks, and let off a storm of musketry that swept away harshly awakened Frenchmen.

"Ninety-Fourth!" Tarrant almost screamed. "Charge!"

What courage the French had fled them, and the quicker among them broke and ran, threading their way through the neat rows of waggons to escape. The slower ones, still trying to pull their boots on, or trying to gather their personal belongings, were prey for British steel, buttstrokes to the head, or a musket ball. Col. Tarrant saw a French officer stumble from one of the tents, hopping on one foot to draw up a tall cavalryman's boot, with a drawn sword in one hand, shouting for his men to stand fast, Tarrant imagined. Before he had his boot pulled up, a soldier of the Light Company slammed him in the head with his brass-mounted musket butt, sprawling the officer on his back. Reversing the musket, he thrust eight inches of his bayonet into the man's belly. The officer raised both arms and both legs to fend that off, shrieking, as he jack-knifed and died.

"Cavalry, cavalry," Col. Tarrant muttered, taking note of how many saddles were strewn around, used in lieu of pillows or headrests by the flung-aside blankets, and the badges on the front of the many abandoned shakoes. "Ware, cavalry! Ware, cavalry!" he warned his men. He could smell beasts, now, horses, mules, perhaps oxen, out of sight beyond the lines of waggons. "Root them out of the waggon lines! Go to it, Ninety-Fourth! And, light some afire, to see by!"

Bova Marina's waterfront did have an ancient stone quay, but none too long, or high above the water. To either side of the oldest part, there were lower wooden piers, then gritty beach, where nondescript fishing boats were drawn ashore for the night. Capt. Whitehead led his Marines onto the stone quay, their barges bows-on to the quay, parting the few larger fishing boats that were tied up alongside.

Marines stood shakily on the gunn'ls, reached up and rolled to the top of the quay, then offered a hand to the others who followed. Ten men were directed to the left end of the street fronting the quay, ten to the right, as skirmishers, while Whitehead directed others to the few buildings where lights shone from the windows. At his nod, doors were smashed open and Marines dashed inside. There were civilian shouts and womanly screams of alarm from some, then gunshots from another.

"Public 'ouse, sir!" Sgt. Daykin crisply reported. "Three Frog sodgers inside, drinkin'. Or they wuz. Cavalrymen by th' look of 'em, sir."

"I hope they enjoyed their last brandies," Whitehead sniggered. "The other houses?"

"One wuz a h'ordinary, gettin' ready fer th' breakfast trade, sir," Sgt. Daykin told him, "t'other's a private 'ouse."

"Well, we seem to own the town, now, Sergeant," Whitehead said.

"Yes sir," Daykin agreed, peering about for trouble.

"Mister Grace?" Whitehead called out.

"Aye, sir," Lt. Grace, in charge of the boats and landing party spoke up.

"The town's yours, sir," Capt. Whitehead told him with a grin, "for what *that's* worth. I'm taking my Marines up through the town to see what's beyond. Find the coast road, proper, see if . . ."

He was interrupted by gunfire, first a flurry of muskets, then a crackling storm of it, and the roar from men's throats as they were ordered to charge.

"First honours to the Army, sir," Lt. Grace said.

"Guard my back, Mister Grace, whilst we go see what sort of Devilment we can get into," Whitehead replied. "Marines!" he shouted to his men. "Loose column of twos up this street, past the church square, Leftenant Venables . . . ten men with you as skirmishers out front. Go!"

Boots tramped on cobblestones, accoutrements rattled and banged, as the Marines trotted forward, muskets aimed at windows and doors as the little seaport of Bova Marina came awake, as window shutters were flung open, and candles and lanthorns were lit. Civilian heads popped into sight for brief moments, wide eyes and gaping mouths saw strange soldiers in red coats rushing by their houses, and voices called out in alarm and astonishment. Someone in the church began ringing the bell with an urgent clanging as the Marines tramped past it, through the square, and beyond.

Lt. Grace watched them go, then turned to his own duties, posting armed sailors at either end of the waterfront, and in the mouths of the three narrower streets that led into the town. Some sailors he ordered to search the boats along the quay, then remembered that Sgt. Daykin had reported a public house. He went to the door to the establishment, poked his head inside, and saw the sprawled corpses of three French cavalry troopers, took in the overturned tables, broken chairs, and a large straw-covered demijohn of wine slowly gurgling out its contents.

"Ooh, too bad for them, sor," Cox'n Desmond said from behind his shoulder, crowding up to take a look for himself.

"Better them than us," Stroke-oar Kitch agreed, beside him.

"Here, this won't do at all," Lt. Grace said. "The men will get in here and drink themselves senseless. Desmond, Kitch, do you two guard the door, and make sure our people aren't tempted. Can I trust you to do that?"

"Aye aye sor, ye can!" Liam Desmond swore. "Me Bible Oath on't!"

"Cap'um Lewrie trusts us, Mister Grace," Kitch seconded, "and so can you."

"I'll leave you to it, then," Grace decided, frowning as sternly as he could, "but be warned. No drink, hear me?"

At their sobre nods, Grace took hold of his sword hilt and went on up the street to have a look-see of the town.

"Arrah, but he's a young'un, ain't he, John?" Desmond whispered with a snigger.

"Like foxes guardin' th' hen house, aye, Liam." Kitch laughed. "Wonder if Eye-talians know what rum is?"

"If they don't, there's sure t'be some brandy about, a bottle'r two o' *good* wine, or some o' that *grappa*," Desmond speculated, peering inside the tavern.

"Oh Christ, no," Kitch objected. "*Grappa*'d be th' ruin of us. I'd rather drink horse liniment, and *not* wake up blind. Hmm," Kitch said, leaning in to scan the tavern. "D'ye think them Frenchies might have some coin on 'em?"

"Souvenirs t'sell once back aboard, if there's no coin," Desmond said, perking up over a possible profit. "That feller there, he looks t'be a Sergeant or somethin'," he said, pointing at the body that lay closest to the door. "His rank badges might be worth a penny'r two."

"I'll stand guard whilst you have yerself a nip'r two, and a go at their pockets," Kitch volunteered.

"Faith, but ye're a kind man, for an Englishman, John Kitch!" Desmond declared. "And certain t'be rewarded in Heaven!" He entered the tavern, turned the French Sergeant over onto his back, and began to feel for pockets to slash open. Diagonal chevrons and shoulder tassels from the corpse's uniform coat went into his own pockets, before he reached for the overturned demi-john to sample its contents.

"Just don't be takin' too long, Liam," Kitch hissed from the side of his mouth as he pretended to stand stern guard over the door. "I've a hellish thirst, meself."

⚓

Marine Captain Whitehead halted his column once past the last sealed and silent row of houses that fronted the main road behind the village of Bova Marina, feeling the hairs on the nape of his neck go stiff, from a feeling that he was being watched from behind the shuttered windows of the houses. Some of his Marines faced rearward with their muskets aimed at those windows, where candlelight shone.

Off to his left, Capt. Whitehead could see long, flickering shadows cast by the burgeoning glows of waggons set afire, and could almost make out soldiers of the 94th sneaking among the waggons that had not yet been set afire, weapons levelled, and bayonets shining amber and gold. In front of him, there were fields of scraggly crops of some kind, individual plots separated by low stone walls or woven branches of coastal scrub bush. To his right, off in the darkness beyond the flickering firelight, he could barely make out more waggons, what he took to be an entire second road convoy that had not yet been attacked. Were there people moving among them?

HMS *Vigilance* carried a Marine complement of two Corporals, two Sergeants, and seventy private Marines. Such a complement rated three officers to oversee them all: himself, and two subaltern Leftenants, Venables and Kellett, both of them relative "newlies" aged twenty-four and nineteen, respectively.

"Mister Venables, Mister Kellett, to me," Whitehead hissed in the darkness, and sensed a shuffling and the tread of boots. "There's Frenchmen among those waggons yonder. The Ninety-Fourth is advancing upon them from our left. Take charge of your platoons and incline to the right, forming two-deep ranks. Once formed, we will advance to take that waggon convoy in flank. Right? Go."

Whitehead stepped forward, then over a knee-high stone barrier into a field of some crop that swished and tugged at his boots, with an un-cocked pistol in each hand, wishing that he could shout to his men for quiet, for their separation into two elements, then the advance ahead and to their right made one Hell of a racket.

"Cavalry to the front!" Whitehead heard some officer bellow off to his left, heard the jingle of saddle and bridle, harness, and the scrape of sabres being drawn. "Form ranks! Prepare to receive!"

Capt. Whitehead thought that *something* was moving to his front, large forms half-guessed-at in the darkness, coalescing into almost recognisable shapes at they grouped together and approached the fires set among the first waggon convoy.

"Marines! Halt!" he shouted of a sudden. "Cavalry to our front! First ranks, cock your locks . . . level and take aim! Fire!"

Whitehead screwed his eyes tight shut as his men's Tower muskets roared and spat long flames. He opened his eyes to search for the results of that volley, but heard more than he saw: horses screaming in sudden pain, their riders crying out in shock, the neighs of mounts rearing in panic.

"Second ranks, level . . . fire!" Whitehead yelled, forgetting to shut his eyes this time. He heard another, much louder and sustained crash of musketry from the left from the 94th, then the unbelievable order of "Charge! Give them the bayonet!"

"Huzzah!" Capt. Whitehead shouted to his men. "Infantry charging cavalry, lads? Reload, and . . . advance at the double!"

That was much harder to do, almost comical, as muzzle-blinded Marines stumbled into low stone walls, sprawled and tripped over the dry branches that delineated individual plots, and, whilst the 94th was rushing forward over level ground and howling their battle cries, *Vigilance*'s Marines cursed aloud, yelped and stumbled, some going arse-over-tit when their feet met the obstructions.

When closer to the burning waggons, it was easier to find their way, at last, out of the last scraggly farm plots and onto the main coast road, where the Marines could see the results of their volleys; there were at least two dozen horses down, most dead but some of them still thrashing and trying to get back on their feet. Among them were French cavalrymen, some shot dead, some clawing at their death wounds, and a few pinned under the weight of their dead mounts.

"Who goes there?" a loud voice demanded.

"Whitehead! Marines!" he shouted back.

"Oh, Whitehead! Good show!" Col. Tarrant called out. "A damned good show! Came up through the town, did you? But of course you did, good fellow! Took them in flank and shot the courage out of them, I dare say, hah hah! They *might* have managed to charge us had you not, and with us unable to form square, things might have gotten a touch grim, but . . ."

"No one'll ever believe it, sir," Whitehead managed to say, elated to receive such praise, and still in awe of the results. "Infantry charging cavalry, and driving them off?"

"Yayss, well it makes our foes look rather lame, don't it?" Col. Tarrant crowed, sheathing his sword at last. "They must have been Italian, not French. Take any prisoners, did you, Whitehead?"

"Ehm, no sir," Whitehead had to admit, cringing at the image of his men and their own laughable "charge." "I *believe* I saw some of them galloping off to the right, to the east, but I couldn't swear to it."

"We managed to nab a few," Col. Tarrant told him, "though God knows what we'll do with them. Strip them as naked as Adam and turn them loose, I suppose. Good fellow, Wiley!" Tarrant turned to shout to one of his officers who was directing his company to set fires on waggons of the eastern convoy. "Plenty to do 'til dawn, sir," Tarrant said, turning back to the Marine officer.

They both started of a sudden at the sharp barks of gunshots as men of the 94th put wounded, screaming horses out of their misery.

"I would admire, sir," Col. Tarrant bade, "did you, along with one of my companies, set out piquets to the east of town to alert us of any French response."

"Of course, Colonel, gladly," Capt. Whitehead responded.

"Now will come the nasty part," Tarrant said with an unhappy sigh. "All these animals . . . cavalry mounts, horse and mule teams, the yokes of oxen, must be slaughtered. No sense burning the waggons and the supplies in them, else. The French in Calabria must be deprived of everything that can feed or support them in any fashion."

"Piquet duty suddenly sounds delightful, sir," Whitehead said. "I grew up in the country, where my family breeds horses and mules."

"Off you go, then, sir, and the blood will be on my hands, as much as I care for horseflesh myself," Tarrant said with a shrug of his shoulders. "Perhaps I may find a bowl and a pitcher of water, and emulate Pontius Pilate, and wash the guilt away? Who knows?"

"*Now,* what the Devil is happening?" Lewrie snapped to the men on the quarterdeck. Six Bells of the Middle Watch sounded from the belfry up forward and he began to grope for his pocket watch to tell the time, even though it was still too dark aboard to see. He cursed his enforced idleness and ignorance of what was transpiring ashore for the hundredth time. There had been what sounded like a pitched battle behind the town to the western edge, then minutes of silence before some fires were lit, so he could *hope* that Tarrant had seized the field and was carrying out his plans. But then, there had come another crash of musketry, shorter but just as intense as the first *behind* the town, with hundreds of muzzle flashes in two directions!

Now, there were two growing, spreading seas of flames ashore, where Lewrie had imagined the waggon convoys had laid up for the night, which sight *should* have assured him that the landing force had gained the desired results, but . . . every now and then he could hear firing, as if the French were staging a last-ditch battle on the fringes of the town and the convoys to save even a scrap of the supplies, or a smidgeon of their honour.

He raised his telescope to his eye yet again, and there was the seaport town of Bova Marina, its buildings, church steeples, and its waterfront silhouetted starkly black against the rising sea of flame. But, it was still too dark to spot the signal post which Lt. Rutland would set up, or make out any flag messages.

Even semaphore wouldn't work! Lewrie thought, exasperatingly; *Lanthorns against all that fire? Shit! Maybe if they wig-wagged from the quays, where it's dark?*

Then, of course, there was the problem that only one or two of the officers in the 94th even *knew* the proper positions of a semaphore tower's arms to spell out anything, and only one or two people aboard *Vigilance* who knew how to read them! And that in broad daylight!

"I do believe there's a hint of greyness to the skies, sir," the Sailing Master dared speak up, knowing Lewrie's black mood.

"Hmm? Oh," Lewrie said, lowering his telescope and peering all about. He could almost make out a hand held up before his face. He pulled his pocket watch out, held it under his nose, and could make out the white dial, and make a guess at where the hands stood.

"About bloody time," Lewrie grumbled, still un-satisfied.

"Oh, I say there!" the Sailing Master exclaimed as loud booms sounded from the shore, and billowing flame clouds soared aloft as some waggons bearing kegged gunpowder blew up. Another, then another, filled with pre-made paper musket cartridges, took light, sending up a shower of fireworks and a fusillade of pops that resembled a *feu de joie* on the King's birthday.

"Huzzah!" several Midshipmen cried out, waving their hats with delight, and making "Oohs" and "Aahs" as each new waggon exploded.

All Lewrie could do was glower at them, and drum his fingers on the cap-rails in impatience.

⚓

Desmond and Kitch were quite pleased with their haul of loot by dawn. The three dead Frenchmen sprawled on the floor of the tavern had been carrying a fair amount of silver coins, and the Sergeant near the door had two gold Napoleons sewn into the cuff turnbacks of his coat, along with a wedding ring and a pocket watch.

They had also found a squat glass bottle of peach brandy, which they had shared back and forth, sparingly, knowing that there would be Hell to pay did they go back aboard "three sheets to the wind," but it was tasty, heady, and almost worth the risk to sip at, not guzzle.

Once all the shooting was over, though, and the people of Bova Marina dared come out of their houses and hiding places, they found it impossible to keep the civilians out of their own tavern.

One moment, they had the place completely to themselves, then the next, they were mobbed by revellers who flooded through the door, talking a blue streak, dancing round and clapping themselves on the back, and drinking like *they* had won a great victory, themselves.

They clapped Desmond and Kitch on their backs, almost fought for the honour of shaking the *Ingleses'* hands, all the while speaking loud and vociferously in an incomprehensible babble of joyous Italian. Some music was struck up from outside, and the band members pranced inside the tavern, setting all the crowd dancing, as well.

"They're takin' all th' wine an' ev'rything!" Kitch bemoaned in a loud voice. "Liam, we're bein' robbed!"

"We still have th' brandy, arrah," Desmond told him, shouldering his way toward the tavern door. "A last swallow or two, me lad, and I think it's time t' scamper, 'fore we're up on charges."

This time they did guzzle, gave the still half-full bottle a sad eye, and set it down on a table before going outside and slinging muskets from their shoulders so they could pretend to stand guard. It was a good thing that they did, for who should stomp up to peer closely at them than dour Lt. Rutland.

"Who placed you here?" Rutland demanded, scowling.

"Mister Grace did, yer honour, sir," Kitch replied, "t' keep our lads from drinkin' th' place dry."

"*You* two? Hah!" Rutland barked in dis-belief. "That's a farce! You've been drinking?"

"Not 'til th' Eye-talians come, sor," Desmond told him, trying to stand sobrely erect, "an' started t'party, and 'twas them who forced us t'take a sip or two. Their tavern, sor, an' we couldn't stop 'em."

"None of our lads got in past us, sir," Kitch pointed out.

"Bein' sociable, like, with th' locals, sor," Desmond declared.

Rutland would have said more, even asked to smell their breaths, but several civilian men staggered out of the tavern arm-in-arm, and cheering fit to bust, with bottles of wine in their hands. A song was struck up, and the street began to fill with revellers. Then there was that bottle of peach brandy again, thrust at Lt. Rutland.

"Bravo, bravo, il Inglese!" a man shouted close enough to sling spittle on Rutland's coat. *"Salute! Il Francesi . . . morto!"* he cried with a slashing motion cross his throat, which caused many revellers to roar agreement and raise bottles to their lips.

"Well, if I must," Lt. Rutland said, frowning, and took a short sip of the brandy. As he handed it back, the civilians urged him to take another, then offered it to Desmond and Kitch.

"Permission, sor? They mean well, and all," Desmond asked, and Rutland allowed them a sip each. "Ah, right tasty that is, sor."

"You two get down to the quays, now, and wait there for the Marines to return," Lt. Rutland ordered, then called out to their backs as they made a quick escape, "And keep the hands from getting drunk in celebration with the damned Italians, hear me?"

"Aye aye, sor!" Desmond sang out.

"Good God, Liam, we forgot the dead men's shakoes!" Kitch said of a sudden. "There'd be money in those!"

"Ah, but we've got a pocketful o' their buttons t'sell, John," Desmond reassured him, "and we got ourselves a snoot full, hah hah!"

At last! Lewrie thought as black night gave way to pre-dawn greyness, enough light by which to make out Bova Marina's buildings and the low stone quay, now crowded with fishing boats and *Vigilance*'s barges. Armed sailors strolled or sat at ease all up and down the seafront street, and halfway up the centre of the three streets that led inland from it. Up that main street which led to the public square and the church, there was a horde of civilians, all dancing round a bonfire of some kind. Beyond the church steeple, the coastal road and anything behind it was a sea of foul black smoke rising from the fires. Some men came rushing from that ebon stage curtain of a smoke pall with some heavy burdens, the arrival of which set the mob into cheers and whistles that Lewrie could almost imagine he heard. He raised his telescope, a day-glass this time, and smiled in relief.

"They're roasting whole sides o' beef!" he marvelled aloud. "I believe we've won completely, gentlemen."

If soldiers and Marines slaughtered draught animals, and local Italians felt safe enough to butcher an ox or two, that meant that the French had been killed, made prisoner, or driven off . . . long enough for a feast, anyway. All that was wanting was the return of the 94th and his sailors and Marines to the ships, perhaps within the next two hours, and his wee squadron could up-anchor and clear the coast before the enemy could respond from Melito di Porto Salvo or Brancaleone Marina. *Then,* Lewrie assured himself; *Then! Someone would tell me what had happened ashore, and show me a list of casualties.*

He knew that they had won, but won what?

CHAPTER NINETEEN

A half-hour out to sea, steering Sou'east to leave the coast behind, and there had been too much to see to for Lewrie to take the time to listen to Captain Whitehead's verbal report. At last, he turned the deck over to the officer of the Forenoon Watch, passed word for the Marine leader, and went aft to his cabins for a late breakfast and a welcome hot cup of coffee.

"You sent for me, sir?" Whitehead asked minutes later after he was admitted to the great-cabins.

"Join me for breakfast, sir, and tell me all that transpired," Lewrie eagerly insisted. He set aside his bowl of oatmeal and got out paper and pencil to make notes for his report.

"Oh, sir, it was a complete rout!" Whitehead began, as Deavers and Turnbow set out oatmeal, butter, treacle, and bisquit for him, and poured the Marine his first cup of coffee.

He could not speak for what Colonel Tarrant's troops had done in the first minutes, not 'til they had met up after taking the second convoy's wag-gons, delighting again to relate the novel act of infantry charging cav-alry, and how the first convoy's escort troop had been run off horseless and weaponless, and the second troop of cavalry had been decimated by the combined volleys of musketry.

"As the sun began to rise, sir, when we were standing piquet to the east of town," Whitehead said, "we could see thirty or fourty men on horseback, just sitting there watching us, but, even as we and one company of the Ninety-Fourth were recalled to the boats, they didn't make a move towards us. Colonel Tarrant's men took several prisoners, and they turned out to be French escorting the eastern convoy, and were Italians guarding the second."

"Did he fetch any prisoners off?" Lewrie asked, impatiently signalling for a refill of coffee.

"A few officers, I believe, sir," Whitehead told him. "As for the rest, we left their wounded in the care of the town surgeon, and let the rest go, after they surrendered their boots and accoutrements, which Colonel Tarrant had burned, along with every saddle we could find, and all the waggon harnesses."

"Quite thorough, good," Lewrie commented, making quick notes. "Now, had we any casualties?"

"Light injuries, mostly from stumbling round in the dark, and tripping over things, sir," Capt. Whitehead said with a laugh. "Among the armed sailors, none, sir. You may have to wait 'til we're back in port to ask Colonel Tarrant about his losses, though. I did not *see* any as the regiment came off, but their beaches were too far off for me to take note of much."

"Enemy losses?" Lewrie asked, getting to the meat of things.

"We counted fifty-two enemy dead, sir, though some of them were civilian waggoners, I'm sure," Whitehead said, digging in a pocket of his soiled red coat for his own hastily scrawled jottings. "Eighteen wounded left in Bova Marina to be tended to, out of one hundred twenty troopers in their two cavalry troops. I *think* sixty men in a troop of cavalry is the average number, sir, but I wouldn't swear to it. As to material losses, we burned, ehm . . ." He paused to puzzle over what he had written in the dark. "Aha. Sixty waggons in the western convoy, and fifty-four in the one to the east of town." Which sum made Lewrie scribble, then pause with a prompting brow up.

"It cut rough with some of my Marines, sir, to slaughter horses and mules," Whitehead went on, puzzling some more over his notes. "The Colonel told me his count was four hundred and twenty horses or mules shot, along with thirty-six oxen, and about fifty cavalry mounts. It was the Army's doing, thank the Lord."

"Hmpf!" Lewrie sniffed, regretting the death of so many horses; like all English gentlemen, he thought horses one of God's more magnificent creations.

"Damned shame, really, sir," Whitehead commented between bites of breakfast, "espcially the cavalry mounts."

"Oh, I agree, Whitehead," Lewrie told him. "So, barring losses among the Ninety-Fourth which would detract from our success, I'd say we had a very productive morning. Once you're back in your wardroom, speak with Mister Rutland and Mister Grace about any names you'd wish to be mentioned in despatches in the margins of my report."

"I shall, sir," Whitehead replied. "Oh, I forgot to mention the weapons we captured. Sabres, musketoons, and such? Ehm, sixty sabres and sixty-six firelocks . . . all carried away and dumped into the sea as we rowed back to the ships, sir. As to what weapons, supplies, or gunpowder were in the waggons, there's no accounting. We were a bit too busy setting them afire to take an inventory, though I'd imagine that the bulk of it was food and drink."

"I agree," Lewrie said again. "The French and their unwilling allies in Italy may be well armed, but starvin' 'em's the important thing. In Calabria, anyway, so they can't launch another invasion of Sicily. I just wish we had the force to do the same thing in the rest of Southern Italy."

"With us as an example, sir," Whitehead said, "Admiralty and Horse Guards will see the value of our raids, and put together more squadrons like ours."

"Pray God, indeed, sir!" Lewrie said.

Once Capt. Whitehead had finished his last cup of coffee and departed, Lewrie had a spell of play with his cat, Chalky, on the settee, all the while forming the proper phrases for his report on the action in his head. He would have started it that instant, but the lure of fresh air was too great. With a last poke at Chalky's belly, which prompted quick, slashing claws, an annoyed *Mrr!,* and a roll and run for the dining coach, he rose and went out to the quarterdeck, where a delightfully cool early morning breeze stirred his hair and flapped the turnbacks of his lapels. A glance aft satisfied him that all of his transports were sailing in-line-astern of *Vigilance* at a neat two-cables' separation, Union Jacks and commissioning pendants streaming like snake's tongues as they slowly hobby-horsed across a brilliantly blue sea under a sky blotted with blotches of white clouds.

"Went well, Mister Rutland?" Lewrie asked the officer of the watch.

"Ashore, sir? Aye. Some skinned elbows and knees, but other than that, we had it easy," Lt. Rutland told him. "The lads didn't get many chances to pick up souvenirs from the French, but the Marines did. No one got into local wines or spirits, either, and everyone came off sobre. Mostly. Desmond and Kitch stood guard over the only tavern in town and kept our lads out."

"Desmond and Kitch?" Lewrie asked. "Desmond and Kitch guarded the tavern? *Really?*" He had to burst out laughing at that news, for it was simply too implausible. He was sure that they'd come aboard most carefully, but at the least half-drunk. "Sly lads, them."

The Sailing Master, Mr. Wickersham, emerged from the chart room on the larboard side of the quarterdeck, said his good mornings, then went up the ladderway to the poop deck for a moment before clumping back down. "About six miles offshore, now, I make it, sir. Do you wish to come about anytime soon?"

"Hmm, let's put Italy below the horizon before we do so, sir," Lewrie decided. "Then we'll wear about to Due West," He glanced up at the commissioning pendant to gauge the direction of the wind.

"Round-about Sicily again, sir?" Wickersham asked.

"No, not this time," Lewrie told him, breaking out a wide grin. "I intend to sail right up the Strait of Messina, to rub the French noses in it. Let 'em see us pass by. And when we do, sirs, I will have a broom hoisted to the mainmast truck of each ship. We've made a *very* clean sweep. Let the snail-eatin' bastards eat *that*!"

"Deck, there!" a foremast lookout called down. "Strange ship in harbour . . . anchored, an' sails gasketed!"

HMS *Vigilance*, five miles off the coast of Sicily, and twelve miles short of Milazzo, was plodding along under reduced sail at the head of the column when the lookout sang out, perking the interest of the watch-standing half of the crew, and the idlers off-watch crowding the forecastle and sail-tending gangways to gawk and speculate.

Lewrie left his post at the windward bulwarks and trotted up to the better viewpoint of the poop deck. Planting his feet against the slow roll and hobby-horsing of the ship, and leaning his chest into the cross-deck hammock stanchion racks, he raised his day-glass for a long look. The first thing that sprang to mind was that the bastard had his anchorage where *Vigilance* always sat. The strange newcomer couldn't be French, either, he assured himself, for what sort of fool would invade a foe's harbour and *anchor*, then lower, or bind his means of propulsion in harbour gaskets? At twelve miles or better, there was little to make out, with the stranger halfway hull-down, and only a forest of masts and yards showing; if there was a national flag aloft, or a long company or commissioning pendant showing, they were invisible at such a distance. Was she naval, or a civilian merchantman?

Whoever or whatever she was, she was big, though, seeming to be about as large and bluff as a Third Rate 74-gunner, or . . . dare he hope . . . an Indiaman? An expectant grin grew at the corners of his mouth.

"Ehm . . . should we go to Quarters, sir?" Lt. Grace asked from below on the quarterdeck.

"Not 'til we're much closer, no, Mister Grace," Lewrie called down to him, lowering his telescope for a moment to face him. "I do believe that she's the *Coromandel*, the transport we've been promised. And if she ain't," he added, "she'll yield and let us have our best anchorage back . . . at the point of a gun if we have to."

"Very good, sir!" Lt. Grace said, sounding relieved and pleased.

"When we're within a mile or so, I'd wish to signal the other ships to enter harbour and anchor, and we'll haul out of line to let them," Lewrie said on, lifting his telescope once more. "We should have anchored farthest out, anyway, long before, in case the French try to raid us."

"I will have the Afterguard make up that signal, sir," Lt. Grace promised.

"Very well, Mister Grace," Lewrie replied, eye glued to the ocular. "And pass word for Mister Severance."

"Aye, sir," Grace said.

A long minute or two later, Sub-Lt. Severance came out from the great-cabins, where he had been making copies of Lewrie's latest reports to Admiralty, and trotted up to the poop deck to join him.

"Mister Severance, I'd admire did you look up *Coromandel* in the latest Navy List," Lewrie bade him. "Knowing her number'd make speaking her easier on the signalmen. They'd have to spell out Strange Ship, or Hey You, else."

"I'll see to it, sir," Severance said with a grin, doffed his hat, and dashed back below. He was back to report within a minute, shaking his head.

"She's too new to the Fleet, most-like, sir. The list doesn't show a *Coromandel*. Ours is over a month old."

"Oh, very well," Lewrie said with a shrug. "Hey You it'll have to be 'til we're close enough for her to make her number to us."

"They look to be about five miles off, now, sir," Midshipman Kinsey of *Coromandel* reported to his commanding officer, Lt. John Dickson, who at that moment was shirtless and sponging himself off with fresh, cool water fetched from the Army camp ashore.

"Oh, very well, Kinsey," Dickson growled. "You may go."

"Aye, sir," Kinsey replied, bowing himself out of the cabins.

Dickson shot a silent sneer, and a sad shake of his head, at the departing Midshipman's back. What sort of fool did it take to be over thirty-five years old and still a Midshipman, living on the miserly £6 annual pay, and seemed lark-happy to get it? Dickson had dismissed Kinsey early-on; the man had no conversation, no wit, a poor education, clumsy manners, and most importantly, absolutely nothing to justify a hope for promotion.

Lt. Dickson towelled himself dry, felt his cheeks to satisfy himself that he was closely shaved, then snapped "Shirt!" to his servant, Ordinary Seaman Ryder.

"Hah hah, by Jove, just look at that!" Sub-Lieutenant Clough could be heard braying to the crew on deck. "They're all sporting brooms at their mastheads! Gone and done something grand and glorious, I'd wager!"

Dickson winced, for Clough grated on him, too; for being only twenty, and boyishly enthusiastic about everything. Clough was a better seaman than Kinsey, by miles, but he was so *young*, had perhaps too *much* conversation, too much wit of the schoolboy variety, exquisite manners and the social grooming of a well-off, well-connected family, like Dickson's. They should have gotten along like a house afire, but Clough *would* chatter and prate like a magpie, and felt that the slightest period of silence *must* be filled with something. Despite all that, Clough's prospects for advancement were sterling, for his family, like Dickson's, had the best sort of "interest," which was the mother's milk of a successful career in the Fleet.

So what, Dickson asked himself for the hundredth time, was Clough doing aboard a hired-in armed transport that didn't mount a single gun, carrying smelly *soldiers* from here to there and back again? It was as if someone at Admiralty had set them all up to be blighted, or for a failure. *Coromandel*'s crew had come from receiving ships at Portsmouth, from paid-off warships, and from the Impress Service, and none of them were worth a damn, to Dickson's lights: drunks, malingerers, feeble ignoramuses, and gaolhouse sweepings.

Dickson sullenly stuffed his shirttails into his breeches and carefully tied his black neck-stock before a mirror. "Waist-coat," he said, and his cabin servant offered it up, slipping it onto his spread arms.

Dickson was the third-born son of his family, and had had no say about his chosen career. At least no one had thought of his taking Holy Orders, like his younger brother, thank God! And if he had had to be in the Navy, going aboard his first ship at age twelve, then he had determined to make the best of it, and to be the best he could at it, no matter how stultifyingly boring sea life was, how dull and ignorant his fellow Mids were, or how dirty, ignorant, and low the common seamen were.

With good family friends' influence and favour, he'd made Lieutenant by nineteen, and was now twenty-four, and should have been appointed into a *proper* warship. Everyone had noticed him for his navigational skills, seamanship, his coolness under pressure, and his instinctive leadership qualities; he was marked for great things, all of his patrons had confided to him.

To mollify his dis-appointment of commanding *Coromandel,* they had pointed out that it *was* a sea command, and while it was certainly not an attractive posting, he could, on the side, do his patrons a favour.

First of all, he could observe and report to them as to what it was that an amphibious landing force actually *did;* did it work, or was it worthy of expansion and wholesale adoption, or a mere experiment sure to fail sooner or later? Admiral Sir Home Riggs Popham was doing grand things on the north coast of Spain, but he had not had to resort to specialised ships, or armed transports, and used normal-sized ships' boats and his squadron's Marines and armed sailors, not Army troops.

Secondly, if it was determined that the cost was worth it, it would be a plum command for someone much worthier than this fellow, Lewrie. Dickson was to keep his eyes and ears open to see if the man had any flaws that could result in his replacement with someone of *their* choosing. It was hinted that this Lewrie fellow was already in bad odour with other influential people in the Navy, and government, and that it would be most desirable for the man to be "beached," or caught out and assigned to the "Yellow Squadron" of incompetents and fools.

Well, if so many senior officers and powerful people who could advance Dickson's career wished the man laid low, then John Dickson would oblige them, so long as such an onerous job got *him* advanced!

After buttoning up his waist-coat and donning his best-dress uniform coat, Dickson looked round the great-cabins he occupied. For a week or so, so much space, so much hard-to-find privacy, seemed an advanced reward, but that had palled quickly when he realised that he must share the grand cabins with four Army officers, walled off with deal and canvas partitions, along with Sub-Lieutenant Clough, and the jumped-up Master's Mate turned Sailing Master. Unfortunately, with more than an hundred sailors aboard, and expected to carry over two hundred soldiers, even a grand East Indiaman, built to carry hundreds of tons of cargo, and so many well-paying passengers, there was not room aboard to swing the proverbial cat, and *every* meal was a communal meal, including that lout Midshipman Kinsey. At least he swung his hammock at night down in the bread room, where he could be swarmed by the ship's rats. At least *one* of the quarter galleries was set aside for Dickson's sole use, but his share of the cabins was only a slightly larger dog-box of a sleeping space.

"Your sword an' 'at, sir," his cabin servant said in a flat, dis-interested voice. Truth be told, he'd come to despise Lt. Dickson as much as Dickson despised everybody else.

Dickson bound the white leather sword belt round his waist, and closed the double snake's head clasp, easing the set of his expensive Wilkinson's smallsword upon his hip, then took the fine bicorne hat and set it upon his head, looking again in the small mirror over the wash-hand stand, tilting the hat to his favourite rakish angle.

Dickson had always thought of himself as a sterling example of a proper young English gentleman of the better class, handsome and well set up, popular with his early schoolmates and young ladies of the better sort; impressive, too, to those beneath his social standing who would spread their legs to satisfy his desires. He admired himself in the mirror for a bit, then rehearsed a sterner face. How to probe Lewrie would be tricky. Perhaps he could try toadying to ingratiate himself, first? Well, perhaps a touch of hero worship would suit; this Lewrie *had* made some sort of name for himself, hadn't he?

"I shall be on deck," Dickson told his servant, and stepped out onto the quarterdeck, blissfully missing the scowl and quiet-mouthed curse his cabin servant threw at his back.

The lad, Ordinary Seaman Ryder, had been a topman aboard his last ship, and dearly missed the easy camaraderie of life among his peers, of serving far aloft as one of the reigning kings of any crew. But this Dickson shit had looked over a group of idling tars and just pointed at him and told him that he needed a cabin servant, a "catch-fart," and that Ryder was it, and that was that, whether he knew the first thing about the duty or not.

During the time in Portsmouth to assemble the crew, convert the Indiaman to a trooper, then on the passage from there to here, whereever here was, Ryder had kept his eyes and ears open, and had learned just what a back-stabbing, curt, and sneering pack of fools *Coromandel*'s officers were. *All* officers were, to his lights, but this lot?

"I jus' 'ope th' Devil takes th' lot o' ye," he muttered.

"The best bower is holding, sir," Lt. Farley reported after some nervous moments about anchoring farther out than usual, in un-familiar holding ground. "Six and a half fathoms depth, and we've paid out four-to-one scope of cable. Same with the kedge astern."

"Very well, Mister Farley," Lewrie said with a satisfied nod, and a deep breath let out in relief that the same mud, sand, and gravel bottom could be found almost a mile offshore of their usual spot. He looked shoreward and watched as soldiers seemed to pour like treacle down the sides of the transports, eager to return to their encampment, where they could boast of their deeds to the few men who'd remained to guard the empty camp, and show off their souvenirs taken from the dead Frenchmen.

"And there goes the Colonel's dog, sir," Farley said, laughing, as the shaggy hound was slung over the side in an enfolding cargo net and lowered into one of the barges.

"There'll be an idle day for the Army, I'd expect," Lewrie said, "and the civilians will be swarmin' 'em by dusk, cooks, whores, and all. I think we've earned one, too, right, Mister Farley?"

"Aye, sir," his First Officer gladly agreed.

"General signal to all ships, then," Lewrie decided, "show Make And Mend, 'til sundown. Then, at Seven Bells of the Forenoon, hoist Splice The

Mainbrace. An idle morning and afternoon, *and* a good rum issue, seems t'be in order.

"Has *Coromandel* shown her number yet?" Lewrie asked, turning to look aft at Midshipman Gadsden, who was in charge of the signalling party.

"She has, sir!" Gadsden sang out. "It's Nine-Six-Four, sir!"

"Hmpf," Lewrie commented, looking at *Coromandel* with his telescope, now that she lay close by. He *could* hoist a signal with her number preceding Captain Repair On Board, but . . . he was curious as to what sort of transport the Navy had finally sent him.

Lewrie leaned over the starboard bulwarks to watch the Bosun, Mr. Gore, pointing and yelling for on-watch hands manning the lifts and braces to make adjustments to square away the yards to a taut and mathematical perfection.

"Mister Gore?" Lewrie shouted, cupping hands round his mouth. "I wish to borrow your boat once you're done!"

"Aye, Cap'um sir! Won't be a minute!" Gore shouted back.

"No rush, Mister Gore! Square her away pretty!" Lewrie called back. And a few minutes later, the barge was alongside the larboard entry-port, the Bosun puffing his way to the decks, and a side-party hastily assembled to see the Captain off.

"Steer for *Coromandel*, the big new'un, Mister Page," he told the Mid aft by the tiller as he settled himself beside him.

"So that's what the boarding nets are for?" Sub-Lt. Clough said after watching the hundreds of soldiers scramble down into the barges alongside, and then be rowed ashore to a rickety-looking wooden pier on the wide beach. "They look . . . skilled at it."

Clough could hear them singing, too, whooping and laughing to be returning to their huts. He recognised the song as "Nottingham Ale."

Lt. John Dickson cleared his throat, rather loudly, in comment. Once all ships were anchored, the flagship had fired off two swivel guns to announce a General Signal, then had hoisted Make And Mend, but, after that, had paid *Coromandel* no notice, and he found himself standing idle in his best-dress uniform, slowly sweating it up . . . and it had cost his parents a pretty penny, too . . . in the rising heat of a late Summer morning.

"Ehm, is that boat making for us?" Midshipman Kinsey wondered aloud. "That'un there. Bless me, I think I see a Post-Captain aft in her sternsheets!"

"Oh, Christ," Lt. Dickson spat. He had expected a summons to go aboard for a first meeting with this Lewrie character, but this was novel. "Mister Clough, organise a side-party. Ryder!" he shouted over his shoulder to the great-cabins. "Open a bottle of white wine, and get out two glasses. *Clean* ones, mind!"

Aft in the great-cabins, Ryder rummaged through the inlaid wine-cabinet, pulled out a bottle of Rhenish, and pulled the cork with some difficulty; his usual way of opening a bottle was to smash the neck on something, then pour it into a mug. Curious, and for a vengeful lark, he put the bottle to his mouth and drank off a glug or two, sniggering.

"At least it ain't 'Miss Taylor,'" he muttered over the taste, compared to the cheap, raw Navy issue white wine.

On deck, Dickson waited and waited as the boat, a 29-foot barge, came alongside. There was something to be done, but Kinsey was not doing it. "Kinsey! Challenge?" he prompted through gritted teeth.

"Oh!" Midshipman Kinsey gasped. "Boat ahoy!" he roared over the side, in a passably good quarterdeck voice that could reach from aft to the forecastle.

"Aye aye!" the barge's bow man shouted back, holding up a hand showing four fingers, though the barge was close enough for anyone to see that a Post-Captain of more than three years' seniority, wearing two gilt epaulets, was aboard.

The boat thudded against the hull by the mainmast chains, and a quick glance overside showed an officer in an old-style cocked hat reaching for the chain platform and shrouds, then stepping onto the boarding battens, hands seizing the man-ropes. Dickson thanked God that the battens were freshly sanded, and the man-ropes were white and new, with neat Turk's Head knots at the ends. He had to peer overside again, realising that *Coromandel*, built for the East India trade, had straight sides for greater cargo volume, and no tumblehome to ease an ascent. He winced and leaned back inboard, praying that this Captain Lewrie didn't slip, fall, and crack his head open on his barge!

There! The dog's vane emblem of the arriving officer's hat was above the lip of the entry-port, and *Coromandel*'s Bosun began a long, complicated call on his silver pipe, and the side-party was called to attention, doffing their tarred straw hats.

Dickson took a deep breath, let it out, then stepped forward to greet Captain Lewrie, his bicorne hat raised in salute. "Welcome to *Coromandel*, sir," he began as the arrival took hold of the bulwarks either side of the entry-port, gave a stamp and jerk, and landed two feet inboard before removing his own hat to salute the flag aft, and answer Dickson's salute. "Captain Sir Alan Lewrie, I suppose?"

"Last time I looked, aye, sir," Lewrie responded with a grin on his face. "And you are?"

"Lieutenant John Dickson, Sir Alan. Might I offer you a glass of something? The great-cabins are this way," Dickson said, trying to appear pleasant.

"That'd be welcome, aye, Mister Dickson. Lead on!" Lewrie said with enthusiasm.

What had he expected to see, after the disparaging remarks he'd heard from his patrons? This Lewrie was . . . odd.

Dickson thought that Lewrie was about three inches shy of six feet tall, and might have weighed twelve stone, with good shoulders and a trim waist for a Post-Captain of obvious means who could set a good table and over-indulge, as many did.

He'd been told by his patrons that Lewrie had been in the Navy since 1780, and was surely in his late fourties, but he appeared to be younger than that, spryer, and with a jauntier step than men who had been in the Navy nearly thirty years. He was said to have been uncommonly lucky at prize-money, but didn't appear wealthy; his coat was a plain undress coat, the gilt lace upon it gone verdigris green with exposure to sea air, as was the lace on his cocked hat. Upon his hip he wore a slightly curved hanger sword, its dark blue leather scabbard worn and nicked, and seashell hand-guard and lion's head pommel bright, polished silver, but also marred by hard use, or desperate combat. And Lewrie wore tailored white slop trousers, stained from tar and galley slush used to soften running rigging, stuffed into a good pair of Hessian boots, minus the usual decorative gilt tassels.

"My apologies for the meanness of my quarters, Sir Alan," Lt. Dickson said as they entered the great-cabins, "but I am forced to share them with the Army, and my juniors. It's like being in a wardroom, only messier and more crowded. I fear there's little in the way of furniture, so we must sit at the dining table."

"No matter," Lewrie said, taking off his hat and pulling out a chair, and

Dickson noticed that there was a faint scar on one side of Lewrie's cheek, and a slight blemish on his forehead. He also took note that the man's eyes were a merry greyish-blue, and that Lewrie's hair was still thick, of a mid-brown, almost chestnut colour, and wavy over his ears.

Ryder arrived with the bottle of Rhenish and two glasses, and Lewrie took time to thank him as he reached for one. Dickson saw a gold band on Lewrie's left hand, wondering what sort of a termagant wife he had who'd insist that a husband wear a wedding ring; it was almost unheard of!

"Ehm, you came in flying brooms, Sir Alan?" Dickson asked, by way of beginning.

"We made a night landing over on the toe of the Italian 'boot' and burned two road supply convoys," Lewrie told him with some glee. "A few weeks back, we blew up a bridge on the only coast road from Naples to Reggio di Calabria, and the French have been forced to go the long way round. That's what you'll be doing, Mister Dickson, along with the rest of us . . . harassing the French, burning up goods warehouses, putting troops ashore for quick, in-and-out raids. Now, today's a Make and Mend for the squadron as their reward for a job well done . . . as will be the signal to splice the mainbrace that'll be coming at Seven Bells, but tomorrow . . . we'll set you and your hands to work at learning our trade. I note you've stored all six barges on your boat-tier beams?"

"Aye, sir," Dickson replied, after a sip of wine.

"Best get 'em in the water, let 'em soak and seal the seams," Lewrie instructed. "We usually tow them astern, and draw 'em up to the chain platforms, either side, so the boat crews, then the soldiers, can scramble down the nets and get aboard as quick as they can. We'd spend half the day gettin' the troops ashore, else. There's a Brigadier Caruthers over in Messina who raked up a gaggle o' transports for a landing months ago, put his three regiments ashore . . . tried to, anyway, but with too few boats, and only civilian sailors to man them, so he had to fight his battle with only two regiments, no artillery, and *then* blow up two big supply depots for an invasion of Sicily. Grand muck-up *that* was, but it came off right in the end, and our Admiral, Sir Thomas Charlton, won his knighthood for it, and some of his warships made some money off the many prizes they towed out."

"Has there been any naval opposition to your raids, Sir Alan?" Dickson asked, hoping for a shot at some sort of combat.

"None that we've seen, no," Lewrie told him, "but, do we goad 'em hard enough, there's sure to be some French ships, or leftovers from the Nea-politan Navy, still fit for sea at Naples, Taranto, or Brindisi over on the Adriatic coast. . . . Hell, maybe they'd move some down from Venice, sooner or later, though Admiral Charlton's ships keep a close guard all up and down the coasts.

"If it comes down to it, sir," Lewrie went on with an assured grin, "old *Vigilance* can deal with 'em. I've trained my gunners well, well enough to fire accurate, aimed broadsides to support the troops ashore. They can hit an open gun-port at one hundred yards."

Dickson thought that a vaunting boast, for he'd never heard the like of *aimed* naval gunfire, but he let it pass. "And when we do land troops, sir, can I expect to see some action ashore?"

"Fire-eater are you, Dickson?" Lewrie hooted. "Good for you! Your boat crews will be armed so they can stand guard over the beaches and the boats 'til the Army is done with their work and comes back to re-board. If you wish to command that party whilst your juniors stand in your stead aboard *Coromandel*, you're more than welcome, though in most instances so far, the armed parties have had little to do."

"I just may, sir," Dickson declared. "Once my juniors, and my crew, thoroughly understand their duties, that is," he added hastily.

"'Nother glass, sir?" Ryder asked, noting that both officers' wine glasses were empty.

"Aye, I'd . . ." Dickson began to say.

"I'd much rather get a tour of your ship, sir," Lewrie intruded. "We've begged and pleaded so long and hard for her that it'll be like a Christmas treat, as proof we really have her, ready to go!"

"Well, of course, Sir Alan," Dickson replied, pushing back his chair, though he really would have relished another cool drink on such a warm day. "Happy to show you round her," he feigned equal eagerness, think-ing that his new commanding officer was an energetic sod.

After they left the great-cabins, Ryder had himself another nip of wine, re-corked the bottle, and sprawled in a chair at the table.

Up and down the weather decks and gangways, from taffrail to the knightsheads and forecastle, it was Lewrie who led the inspection, intent on seeing everything, poking and prowling through the below-decks troop quarters, the state of the capstans and pumps, then down to the orlop to squeeze through the stored victuals and water butts.

As he did so, he and Lt. Dickson met many of *Coromandel*'s hands and was briefly introduced in passing. Both men discovered something about the other, from the way the sailors responded. Dickson was made aware that this Lewrie character was a lot better known in the Fleet than he'd been led to believe, that his presence seemed to impress his sailors, and that one or two, here and there, had served aboard a ship under Lewrie before, and were glad to see him, expressing delight that if they were under his command, they'd surely see some action.

Well, of *course* Captain Lewrie had been knighted for doing *something* brave and daring, but Dickson didn't know the particulars, but he vowed to ask others about it—other officers of the squadron or aboard *Vigilance*, certainly *not* his own sailors!

Upon Lewrie's part, what little he could glean of Lt. Dickson's character was dis-appointing. The man behaved curtly, brusquely, and dismissively when dealing with his sailors, or when introducing Lewrie to Sub-Lt. Clough or Midshipman Kinsey.

Oddest pairing ever I did see, Lewrie thought by the time they were back on the weather decks; *One's a high-flown sneerer, t'other's a chatterbox, and their Mid's a cod's-head.*

That made him wonder if *Coromandel* was a welcome gift from Heaven, or a burden to be borne. He suspected that Dickson would be a hard man, a Tartar, to his men, for whom he evinced little respect or regard, and wished that he could take a peek at the transport's punishment book to see if Dickson kept his crew in line with the frequent use of the lash and other punishments. Sub-Lt. Clough might be too new to his temporary rank and duties as Dickson's First Officer to step in and speak for the men. As far as Lewrie was concerned, Clough seemed too silly and too much a "Popularity Dick" to be respected and obeyed by the crew. As for Kinsey, well . . . he *might* be a typical "tarpaulin man" masquerading as a dolt; Lewrie hoped that was so. He'd seen the sort ever since his first ship, especially in men risen from the lower deck who were inarticulate, poorly schooled, and with crude "country" manners, but consummate seamen. *Coromandel* certainly needed one!

Lewrie had also met Dickson's sort, too, especially among the younger officers coming up through the ranks too quickly through patronage and "interest," and there seemed to be more of them than there were when he was a Lieutenant. To their sort, even Able Seamen with years of experience were little more than thoughtless, biddable scum from the lowest, meanest class, who must be driven, or frightened, to do their duty, *things* to be tolerated, like livestock, and each man as replaceable and un-interesting as a single sheep in a flock.

"Might I interest you in another glass of wine, Sir Alan?" Lt. Dickson smoothly offered as they stood near the entry-port.

In answer, Lewrie pulled out his pocket watch, then stuck it back in a waist-coat pocket. "No, Mister Dickson, it's nigh eleven of the morning, and I'd not wish to deprive my boat crew their issue of rum by staying aboard longer."

Get the point o' that, you coxcomb? he thought.

"Well, I trust you found my ship in proper fig, Sir Alan," the man replied, almost smarmily.

"She'll do," Lewrie gruffly answered, "but the proof of the pudding'll be how well, and how quickly, you can bring her up to snuff."

"We shall endeavour to do our best, Sir Alan," Dickson promised.

"Startin' tomorrow, once Colonel Tarrant's sorted his new men out into equal-sized companies, they'll be coming aboard, by the nets. So, don't let *too* many of 'em drown, right?"

"Er, right, sir," Dickson said, taken aback.

"Well, I'm off," Lewrie told them, noting that Sub-Lt. Clough had to prompt Midshipman Kinsey to call for the side-party to muster with a poke in the ribs.

Don't let them be as hopeless as they look, please Jesus! Lewrie thought as he descended the man-ropes and boarding battens to his waiting boat.

"Back to the ship, Desmond," Lewrie ordered. "The grog's bein' mixed, and time's a'wasting."

"Shove off, Hicks!" Cox'n Desmond shouted. "Out oars, starb'd, now out oars, larb'd, and *row* ye bastards! My full issue o' rum is dependin' on it!"

"We'll be first in line," Stroke-oar Kitch warned them, "or I'll have yer slackin' nutmegs off!"

CHAPTER TWENTY

*I*t was really two days later when the first embarkation drills were held, for Colonel Tarrant and Major Gittings had to sort out their troops into eight companies of about seventy men each, adding newly-arrived soldiers to flesh out their now-experienced veterans, and arranging accommodations in tents fresh from England 'til they could be turned into semi-permanent wood huts rooved with canvas.

More dependent women and children had come, too, with the lucky men whose mates had drawn the long straws, and accommodations had to be made for them, too. The encampment bustled with energy as labourers arrived from Milazzo with nails and lumber and saws built; as new-come women argued with women from the original complement over trivial matters; and boys haggled, bullied, and teased each other, to the point of fist fights. And of course, the local Sicilian vendors showed up in droves, drawn by the promise of newcomers with coin in their pockets, who were enticed by the aromas of strange new cuisine, more fresh fruit than most of them had ever seen, and the lure of wine, or the infamous *grappa*. Among the new bachelor soldiers with coin, the local whores had a field day.

When the embarkation drill actually commenced, the beach and the pier teemed with boats from *Coromandel*, and one from *Vigilance* to take Col.

Tarrant out to watch and oversee. Lewrie took another barge close to the new transport to watch, and his boat and Tarrant's ended up side-by-side.

"Everything sorted out to your satisfaction, Colonel?" Lewrie cheerfully asked, amused by a large parasol that Tarrant had wedged in place to keep the sun off. "And how's Dante?"

"Oh God," Tarrant said with mock gloom. "The damned hound. He's no better sailor than I am. He *hated* his time aboard ship. Dante's a fond dog, mind, but he can be a trial."

They could hear the dog, who paced the shore frantically, howling fit to bust, looking as if he'd leap in and paddle out to be with his master.

"I've sent Lieutenant Fletcher aboard *Coromandel* to explain it all to her people," Lewrie told him.

"And I've put some experienced officers, sergeants, and corporals among my newlies, as well," Col. Tarrant told him. "Lord, I do hope they show better than we did at Malta, the first few practice landings. For a while there, I wasn't sure that my lads would *ever* catch on, or if the whole idea was worth it."

"Just so long as you don't stop to brew tea, sir," Lewrie japed, "or poach the local goats and chickens," reminding him of the initial landing from the sea in Mellieha Bay on the nor'west coast of Malta.

"Correct me if I dis-remember, sir," Col. Tarrant said back with false archness, and a grin on his face, "but I do recall that one of our 'bag,' a tender kid goat, graced *your* table that evening?"

"*Touché,*" Lewrie replied. "Damned tasty he was, too."

Whistles blew and sergeants roared as the barges full of troops came alongside the chain platforms of *Coromandel,* three to each beam, and sailors who had boated their oars reached out to take hold of the boarding nets. Soldiers' faces looked upwards, fearfully, as they were urged to step on the gunn'ls and begin to climb up hand over hand.

"I don't suppose it's worth the effort timing them," Tarrant said, lounging back against the transom of his boat. Lewrie just laughed.

"Up ye go, laddies!" one particular Sergeant loudly roared over the rest. "Grip with two hands, step up, foot at a time, then shift yer grip higher!"

For this initial exposure to how they would get aboard or ashore, the new soldiers of the 94th did not sling muskets over their shoulders, or wear cartridge pouches, rucksacks, or even canteens, to ease their burden. Even so, their slow progress upwards put Lewrie in mind of the oozing of cold treacle on his oatmeal, or the old saw about "Church Work—It Goes Slow."

"By *Noon,* ye clumsy rascals!" the Sergeant fumed. "By Saint Geoffrey's Day? Git a bloody *move* on! You, too, Captain Wellman, sir!"

"How do you like your new company officers?" Lewrie asked.

"Eager . . . young . . . raw as fresh beef," Col. Tarrant commented. "Were we a proper two-battalion regiment, I'd have had a chance to vet them first. They'll learn, once their shine wears off. Yours?"

"Early days," Lewrie told him, unwilling to voice his worries about *Coromandel*'s officers before his sailors. "We'll just have to keep our fingers crossed 'til they catch on, as you say."

"Ehm, sor?" Cox'n Desmond piped up. "Permission t'tap the water barrico? Th' day's gettin' warmish."

"Aye, go ahead," Lewrie allowed. "And no laughing at the new soldiers, right lads? They've enough on their plate at the moment. Even if they *are* amusin'."

"By the way," Col. Tarrant said, "there was a letter from Brigadier Caruthers waiting for me when we got back. It seems he's now quite enthusiastic about our doings, and was full of questions about procedures and such requirements."

"Caruthers?" Lewrie queried. "Why? Is he hopin' t'turn one of his regiments into 'tadpoles'?"

"I suspect so," Col. Tarrant said with a faint frown. "Just to get back into action. His victory at Siderno, and the whiff of fame it brought him, must have given him the itch to do something more than drilling and garrison duty round Messina 'gainst a French invasion that'll most-like never come."

"Faint hope of *that,*" Lewrie spat. "Where'd he get the ships for it, when it was like milkin' stones for us to get one new one!"

"Well, I gather that he has the ear of his Commanding General at Messina," Tarrant breezily said, "staff officers who can bask in the warm glow of Siderno, and family and political connexions. Recall, he had no difficulty dredging up more than a dozen merchant ships for his brigade. Wasn't *all* your Admiral Charlton's work, don't ye know. Even if they were the wrong kind, with too few boats to get his men ashore, even in dribs and drabs, he obtained them, somehow."

"Perhaps he's rich enough t'hire them," Lewrie snidely drawled, "or buy them outright."

"If he *does* possess that much wealth, more power to him," Col. Tarrant replied with a wee laugh, "and if he finds the transports, and converts just one of his regiments, he's more than welcome to. For my part, having *two* landing forces, able to strike two places at once, would drive the French to utter distraction."

"He'd need an escort like *Vigilance,* or a large Fifth Rate, for gun support," Lewrie pointed out, "and that may be harder for him to lay hands on than a clutch of troopers. Even if he did, I doubt the gunners aboard her would know the first thing about aimed fire."

"I gather from his letters, though, that he's still keen on discovering some way to get field guns ashore, some sort of big barges, like the sort one sees on the Thames," Col. Tarrant told him.

Lewrie popped his mouth open to scoff, but stopped, remembering the day long ago when he'd taken his first frigate, *Proteus,* down the Medway from Chatham to the Nore, trying to navigate round the many bends of the river, which had been frightening enough, made even more risky by continual confrontations with strings of sailing barges full of coal or grain, whose masters didn't give a damn for giving way!

By God, he lays hands on some o' those, Caruthers just might land artillery, guns, limbers, caissons, and all! he told himself; *More to the point, could we get some, and beat him to it?*

Lewrie had made so many demands upon Captain Middleton in outfitting the first three transports that he had, Middleton most-like would have gone grey-headed, or torn his hair out, finding the new one for him, already. Dare he write and make a further request?

"Oh, do shut up, Dante!" Col. Tarrant shouted shoreward, sitting up to cup his hands. "Daddy will be coming back. Stop fretting, boy! Be a good doggy!"

The hound did stop his incessant demanding barking, cocked his head, to hear his master's voice, but then began to whine longingly, just as loud. Sailors from *Vigilance* in both boats tittered and hid their grins behind their hands.

"I can see why you prefer cats, Lewrie," Tarrant said with a sigh. "I've some ginger beer in my canteen. Care for some?" He produced a small bright-pewter mug and poured himself a drink.

"No thank you, sir," Lewrie replied, hellishly tempted, but he could not partake before his sailors in something they couldn't have. "Water's fine for me."

As if on cue, Desmond passed Lewrie a dull brass and much-dented cup of water, which he sipped slowly, then handed back. At least the water was fresh, fetched from shore but a day before.

"Hah!" Col. Tarrant exclaimed, "It seems they've all managed to get aboard, with no one drowned or injured." Lewrie turned to watch as sailors scrambled up the boarding nets to the deck, much more quickly and agilely than the raw soldiers. Once they were all inboard, there was about five minutes of quiet before whistles began to blow again, and the sailors returned to their boats, followed more slowly by an oozing flood of red-coated soldiers.

"We'll keep doin' it 'til ye can do it in yer sleep!" the loud Sergeant promised. "Yer officers'll be timin' ye this time!"

"Didn't know wot they wuz volunteerin' for, I'd wager," Kitch sniggered.

"Shouldn't o'joined, if ya can't take a joke," Desmond agreed.

The boarding drills continued 'til noon, and a respite for the soldiers to eat ashore, then resumed in the afternoon for another two hours or so, before *Coromandel*'s barges rowed their charges ashore, and returned to be tied up alongside the chain platforms, the boarding nets hauled up the ship's sides and stowed for the night. Colonel Tarrant instructed that his new men would spend the next day at the firing butts and in the fruit groves, to hone their skills at chain or skirmish order fighting, but, the day after that, the newlies would spend their time in the boats and on the nets, this time in full kit with muskets.

Lewrie had not watched the afternoon practices, spending hours in his cabins getting finger cramp and ink stains on his hands, writing letters and going over ship's books. In the privacy of his day-cabin and dining coach, he could at last have some wine with his dinner, and savour his cool tea with lemon and sugar after that, with no one but his servants to see him do so, and envy, or feel deprived.

"Boat ahoy!" a Midshipman of the Watch called out, and Lewrie heard a faint return cry of *Bristol Lass*, and a request to come aboard.

Now what? Lewrie asked himself as he sanded his letter, and began to fold it over itself so he could seal it with wax and inscribe the address. He considered donning his waist-coat and rolling down his shirt sleeves, but the day, and the air in the cabins, were too warm.

There was a shout for a side-party, then the *fweeping* of the Bosun's calls. Lewrie leaned back in his desk chair to see who was coming to call.

"Leften't Fletcher of th' *Bristol Lass*, SAH!" the Marine sentry bawled.

"Enter!" Lewrie shouted back, finally getting to his feet.

"Good afternoon, sir," Lt. Fletcher said, hat under his arm as he stepped inside. "Thank you for seeing me."

"Anything wrong, Mister Fletcher?" Lewrie asked, noting that the man's old limp, which had taken him from a frigate to being the Agent Afloat for a small convoy of cavalry transports back in 1805, seemed to be back.

"Nothing dire, sir," Fletcher said as he came forward to the desk.

"Care for some of my cool tea?" Lewrie offered, sweeping an arm in the direction of the starboard side seating arrangement. "Take a pew, do, sir."

"I'd relish something cool, aye, sir," Fletcher said, seating himself primly in one of the collapsible chairs.

"Deavers, tea for Mister Fletcher, and I'll have a top-up," Lewrie bade, taking his tall glass to go join him. "Nothing dire, but . . . what?"

"A minor dispute, sir, 'twixt me and Mister Dickson," Fletcher said as his tea arrived. "I got the impression that he did not care for my presence aboard his ship, today, sir, ordering his crew about, and . . . supplanting his authority as to how to best go about boarding and leaving the ship. Once the drills ended, he invited me to his cabins and expressed his displeasure."

"In what way, sir?" Lewrie demanded, an angry brow up.

"He demanded the date of my commission, to see who was senior in rank, sir," Fletcher said with a wee, weary grin, "and when he found that I was senior to him by more than five years, he said that since his ship is much larger than the other transports, it would make eminent sense that *he* should command the doings of all four, seniority notwithstanding."

"I *see*!" Lewrie spat, glowering. "I trust you set him straight upon that head, Mister Fletcher."

"Not completely, sir," Fletcher had to admit, shifting in his chair and crossing his legs. "He was still quite adamant about it, and I left him at loggerheads. I fear that in my surprise over the matter, I told him that he and his crew must get much better, more organised, than they were before they became a useful part of the squadron, which did not go down well, at all, sir."

"Were they *that* bad, sir?" Lewrie asked. "From where I sat, they didn't look all that clumsy or cack-handed, for their first attempts."

"It's more . . ." Lt. Fletcher paused to gather his thoughts, looking up at the overhead for a moment. He took a long sip of his tea to begin again. "*Coromandel*'s crew are not so much *led*, sir, as they are *herded*, like a flock of sheep. Bosun and his Mate, petty officers and such, were much too free with their rope starters, for one thing. *And* their threats of punishment. Dashing about like collies, nipping and barking? And . . . well, it's hard for me to criticise how other fellows command their ship, but, ah . . . Mister Dickson is not well-served by his juniors, and I gathered that he's aware of their shortcomings, but doesn't . . . or can't . . . do much about it.

"Her sailors, sir," Fletcher went on, "I'm certain they sense the same thing, *know* they're badly led, and answer that lack with truculence, and dumb, rote obedience. It's only the constant threat of corporal punishment that keeps them moving at all, sir!"

"Hmm, I did get the impression that her juniors, that Clough and her Mid, Kinsey were . . . odd choices," Lewrie carefully said, aware that he could not interfere in how *Coromandel* was commanded, shuffle more-capable officers into her as replacements, demote or dismiss as sorely as he might wish. Nor could he speak *too* ill of fellow officers, undermining their standing with others. "And, I did not sense that Lieutenant Dickson held *them*, or the common seamen, in all that much regard, either, but . . ." he said, leaning back into the settee cushions and letting out a long, bitter sigh. "They're what we've been given to work with, Mister Fletcher, and that's all there is to it."

"Sadly, sir, aye," Fletcher morosely agreed, taking another sip of his cool tea.

"I will straighten him out on the question of seniority," Lewrie promised him, "no matter Dickson came to us in command of a converted First Rate. He's too new to our ways to imagine that he's in charge of the transports. I'll speak to him, aye.

"*And*, if *Coromandel*'s efficiency does not improve before the next raid," Lewrie also promised, "or come up to *your* standards, and mine, I'll want you, sir, aboard her for every drill, 'til that ship is able to perform her duties as ably as the rest. Does that suit you, Mister Fletcher?"

"Completely, sir," Lt. Fletcher firmly said, nodding, as if he would look forward to lighting a fire under Dickson and his officers.

"I noted you limped a bit when you came in, sir," Lewrie said. "Does your old wound trouble you? Should I have Mister Woodbury take a look at you?"

"Oh, I'm fine, sir," Fletcher said with a wee laugh. "Really. The wound's fine, completely healed long ago. I merely came close to turning my ankle, getting into my boat this afternoon. Some liniment, and binding it snug, and I'll be dancing by tomorrow Noon, hah hah."

"Whilst you're aboard, let my Surgeon see you, anyway, Mister Fletcher, just t'put my mind at ease," Lewrie offered. "Can't have you goin' lame on me, when I depend on you for so much."

"I suppose I should, then, sir, whilst I'm aboard," Lt. Fletcher grudgingly agreed. "And thank you for the sentiment, sir."

"Dasher?" Lewrie summoned his cabin servant. "Do you go forward and pass word for the Surgeon to attend us."

"Aye aye, sir!" Dasher cried, running off to the door.

Once Lt. Fletcher had been seen by the Surgeon, and departed the ship to be rowed back to *Bristol Lass*, Lewrie remained on deck after the departure ceremony. He went up to the poop deck for a breath of breeze, plucking at his waist-coat and shirt, staring at the ships anchored inshore of his, at *Coromandel*, with a frown on his face.

What are you, Dickson, who are you, and where'd you come from? Lewrie wondered; *Did some of my enemies in the Fleet pluck you, and your lack-wits from the fool academy and sic you on me? You here to sink me and the "experiment"? Pig in a poke, thorn in my side, or a wolf at my breast,* which?

"Mine arse on a band-box, I'll not have it!" he whispered with heat. "You'll serve me chearly, or I'll break your arrogant arse!"

CHAPTER TWENTY-ONE

*T*he next morning, *Vigilance*'s barges carried her Marines ashore to practice their musketry at the 94th's firing range, and Lewrie took an idle morning off to go witness, and get a little practice of his own with his Ferguson rifled musket and his pair of double-barrelled Manton pistols, weapons that had been stowed away idle far too long, to his likes. Even as a youngster, he had always been a good shot, and when he and his father, Sir Hugo had been invited down to the country estates of his father's friends, he had excelled with a fowling piece.

The 94th's newlies seemed to have had only the sketchiest training before sailing from England, barely able to get off three shots a minute, and many of them turning their heads away from the flashes of the pans when "Fire!" was ordered, and God only knew where half their musket balls went, for the long canvas target sheets, painted with an array of enemy soldiers shoulder-to-shoulder, showed little damage.

"*Four* rounds a minute, lads!" an exasperated new-come Captain roared. "You'll have to load faster, and when I say, 'Level,' you must try to look down the barrel at the target. When I say, 'Fire,' squint if you like, but you must *try* to aim!"

"Water break," Major Gittings ordered. "Ten minutes in the shade, men. We'll let the Marines have a go."

"Thank you, sir," Marine Captain Whitehead said, then ordered his men to the butts. There was some muttering from the Army troops, some jeers about the superiority of Redcoats over "Lobsterbacks." The Marines ignored them, stepped to the lines, and, at the order to load, drew paper cartridges from their pouches, bit off one end, and primed their pans. With the firelocks closed, the rest of the powder was poured down the barrels, and ramrods twirled to ram the charges snug. Balls were spat down the muzzles, the wadded up cartridge paper was rammed down atop them.

"Make ready . . . cock your locks . . . level . . . fire!" Whitehead snapped, looking at his pocket watch held in one hand, an expensive one with a second hand. Seventy muskets barked almost as one, then the muskets were lowered, butts on the ground, and reloading began.

"That's four!" Capt. Whitehead crowed after the last volley. "In one minute! Now, tap-load, lads, and we'll do five!"

And instead of ramming powder, ball, and wadding down, musket butts were thumped hard on the ground to settle everything snug, and the ramrods were only used to force the wadding down against the ball.

"That's five!" Capt. Whitehead shouted after the end of the second minute. "And that's how to do it! Cease fire!"

It took another minute or so for the gunsmoke to roll away, so the target sheets could be seen, revealing shot holes all along the breast-high silhouettes. The Marines had been shooting from fourty yards' distance, but Whitehead ordered his men to turn round and go to the fifty-yard posts, where they fired another three volleys at the target sheets, then did the same from sixty yards. Lastly, the Marine officers paced long steps farther away to an estimated seventy yards, far beyond the posts which marked any range, and filled the target sheets with another two minutes of rapid fire, tap-loading at five rounds a minute.

"Twenty-five rounds expended per man, sir," Whitehead proudly reported to Lewrie. "Permission for a water break, sir?"

"Aye, and well done, sir!" Lewrie heartily agreed.

"You new men," Major Gittings said to them as they got to their feet from their rest, "the rest of the battalion can aim and fire as well as the Marines, by now, and get off four, sometimes five, shots a minute. They can *aim*, too, as much as 'Brown Bess' allows. Now, get to the fifty-yard posts, and show me that you can do that, too!"

"Damned good shooting, Whitehead," Lewrie told him as the Marine strolled over to join him. "I trust our lads'll show as well when it comes to skirmishing."

"Thank you, sir, and they will if I have anything to say about it," White-head replied with a grin, taking a swig of water from his wooden canteen.

"Do we have enough ammunition?" Lewrie asked.

"We came ashore with eighty rounds per man, and there's plenty more aboard ship, sir," Whitehead told him, "and I'll send for some, if we run short. I say, sir, that fellow on the two-wheeled cart over yonder . . . is that not that 'gallows bird' ghost from Messina?"

Lewrie turned and spotted the cart, drawn by a light-coloured mule, and Mr. Quill holding the reins, as it came over the make-shift bridge over the freshwater stream.

"Aye, it is," Lewrie said, "Mister Quill, our resident Foreign Office spook. Damn, and I wished t'get some shooting in. I suppose he's fresh news for us. I'll have t'go speak with him. Carry on, Whitehead."

He'd be a lot more anonymous if he didn't wear black all of the time, Lewrie thought as he turned from the firing range to go to the dirt track that ran to the encampment; *The man must only have the one suit, and that like "dominee ditto."*

"Hoy, Mister Quill," he called out as the cart drew level with him, and Quill pulled on the reins. "What's brought you from the joys of Messina?"

"Aha, Captain Lewrie!" Quill gladly replied. "The very man that I wished to see . . . without taking a boat out to your ship, that is. How convenient that I catch you ashore. Care for a short ride? Just to Colonel Tarrant's quarters."

"It ain't that far, I'll walk," Lewrie told him.

"Congratulations on your most recent raid, sir," Quill said as he shook the reins to get the mule moving again. "And, do I see that you've received re-enforcements since I was here last?"

"The battalion, too," Lewrie said as he trudged alongside the cart. "Only the one ship, but, once Tarrant's got his new men up to snuff, he'll have about six hundred men t'work with, almost the full strength of a battalion that's been in the field in Spain for a few years, less casualties, sickness, and desertion." Lewrie filled him in on *Coromandel*'s origin, tonnage, and much greater berthing space for troops and crew.

Quill drew rein, again, by the trees round Col. Tarrant's offices and lodgings, and tied the reins round the wooden brake lever as one of Tarrant's orderlies came over to tend to the mule. Quill then got down, most awkwardly, his long spindly limbs putting Lewrie in mind of a black spider spinning his web.

"Ah, that's better," Quill said, tugging his clothing back in proper set, sounding relieved. "Hope we're not interrupting him."

"Well, that'd depend on the nature of your news, Quill," Lewrie drolly joshed. "For good or ill."

"Oh, it's good . . . mostly," Quill tried to assure him.

"Well, let's announce ourselves," Lewrie said.

They were offered seats in Tarrant's campaign furniture, which had arrived with his new draught of soldiers, on the raised wooden patio under the long, wide canvas fly, and a pot of tea was brought out from indoors, along with sugar, sliced lemons, or the choice of fresh milk. Just as they got settled, up bounded Dante, Col. Tarrant's dog, all exuberance, tail whisking, rump wiggling, and whining with glee. The dog, now groomed, clipped, and bathed, was head, legs, and paws in Quill's lap in an instant, sniffing him all over.

"I say now, down dog, down I say!" Quill pleaded, both hands high in the air holding cup and saucer out of harm's way. "And where the Devil did this beast come from?"

"Hallo, Dante, here boy," Lewrie, enticing the dog with clacks of his tongue and hands patting his thighs. "He's Tarrant's dog, who just showed up one morning, a farm stray he thinks. Yes! Good morning to you, Dante! What a big, fine puppy!" he coaxed as the dog left Quill and went for Lewrie's lap. "It appears they dote on each other."

"Ah, there you are!" Col. Tarrant exclaimed as he came out to the shaded gallery. "Down, Dante. Don't mess up our guests' clothes. Yes, you adore company, don't you, you silly hound! Stick, Dante?" Tarrant offered after a moment or two of embracing his dog who stood on its back legs against his chest, licking his face. The dog *would* like to play fetch with his stick, dashing fifty yards off in chase.

"Milk and sugar for me, Carson," Tarrant told his orderly. "Ah! So, what news from the *Castello*, Mister Quill?"

"No one at Army headquarters tells me a blessed thing, Colonel Tarrant," Quill sulkily told him, drawing his feet under his chair and pulling his elbows in to protect his chest and tea as Dante came galloping back with his stick in his mouth. "But I have heard from our Mister Silvestri, and another new source of information." If his hands had been free, Quill would have tapped the side of his nose in a sly promise. "By the way, congratulations on destroying those road convoys at Bova Marina, sir."

"Hit our stride with that one," Col. Tarrant boasted, tugging at Dante's stick 'til he let it go for another long toss.

"The arms which Sir Alan was good enough to land for me have proven useful, as well, with supply convoys, sirs," Quill told them. "Oh, some are still stashed and well-hidden, but at least half have been distributed to that 'Spada' fellow and his band, and some other partisan bands. The dirt track . . . can't call it a proper road . . . through the hills roughly 'twixt Filadelfia and Serra San Bruno, on the way to the coast at Monasterace Marina, is the shortest route for supplies, now the bridge at Pizzo is gone, and at least two convoys have been attacked and burned. It's very twisty, with many narrow defiles, simply perfect for ambuscades. And, if the escorts are too strong, the partisans still manage to delay things with fallen trees or rock falls. The French have to use infantry as escorts since the country's just too steep and wooded for cavalry."

"Hmm, that ought to work to the partisans' advantage," Tarrant said. "Should we send them some gunpowder and slow-match fuses for their roadblock work?"

"It appears they have all they need from captured French goods, sir," Quill informed him with a satisfied air; until the dog came back near him, and he tensed up, again. It appeared that Mr. Quill did not much care for dogs and their antics—odd in an English gentleman.

"You mentioned a new source of information?" Lewrie prompted.

"Ah, yes," Quill said, perking up again. "Recall the night that you met with *Don* Caesare and all his ' 'Tonios,' in my lodgings in Messina? His . . . under-bosses I suppose one could call them, his *capos* and some of his smuggler captains. Well, the one who didn't say much at all that night, the burly one with the scar on his forehead, and the darker complexion . . . a real *brutta faccia*, that 'un, hah hah . . . turns out to be a tad more patriotic than *Don* Caesare. A sly one, too. Well, he has kin, and business relations, over in Calabria, and he can manage to get news from them now and then. He approached me, on his own, and offered to use them to gather information on troop movements, when supply convoys set out from Reggio di Calabria on the return journey, and what the French are up to generally over there."

"And how much does *he* charge you?" Lewrie sarcastically asked, glad to know that they had a new source of news, but skeptical.

"Less than *Don* Caesare," Quill said, surprising Lewrie. "As I said, he's more patriotic than *that* criminal. I still don't know his real name, so he still goes as 'Tonio, but . . . I suspect that 'Tonio has his eyes on supplanting *Don* Julio sometime down the road. 'Uneasy lies the crowned head,' what? For all the kisses on the cheeks, the hugs and vows of loyalty, Sicilian criminal gang life is a cut-throat business, with all of them from the *capos* to the lowly sailors on the smuggling boats scheming for advantage over someone else."

"Hah! Like watching the doings in Parliament!" Tarrant hooted.

"Or the Navy," Lewrie chimed in, considering his own opponents.

"Now, 'Tonio is doing this for us all on his own, *sub rosa,* and I must conjure you both to never let slip this new arrangement to *Don* Julio," Quill sternly told them. "We must all guard our tongues when speaking of the source of any information that came from 'Tonio when *Don* Julio is around. We must say that Mister Silvestri has discovered it, by building up a network of informants all his own. I fear that if *Don* Julio gets wind of it, 'Tonio might just be found floating in the harbour at Messina. Working for us without *Don* Julio's approval might make the *Don* imagine that there's a plot against his leadership . . . and his fortune, and very life, and the man can be vicious when threatened."

"Hmm, then before we hold another meeting with Caesare, we must have one of our own," Col. Tarrant decided after a long moment to mull that caution over. "To almost rehearse what we say, and what we can't, in his presence."

"In essence, yes, Colonel," Quill sombrely agreed.

"Speaking of," Lewrie piped up, "how is the scamp, and have you seen him lately?"

"Oh, yes!" Quill said, rolling his eyes in sorry recollection. "He's quite wroth with us, do you see. First off, we didn't use his boats, or people, to deliver the arms to the partisans. He made his rant that *amateurs* would give the game away by our clumsiness, can you imagine? He said if I wished to maintain a working network, I'd best leave such to the ones who know how to go about it!"

"What gall he has!" Col. Tarrant sniffed.

"He's also still in a pet about Mister Silvestri representing us over on the mainland," Quill went on. "He's sure that he will be caught by the

French, sooner or later, or some *paisano* will turn him in in hopes of a cash reward. And, lastly," Mr. Quill told them, "he was very dis-appointed that we hit Bova Marina, not Melito di Porto Salvo. It makes me think that Melito is much like Tropea, a place where one of his competitors stores his loot and smuggled goods. He has *some* hidden agenda for us to attack the place. Went all angry that we didn't use the intelligence he'd gathered for us, and that he'd have to send his people to survey it all over again, at a great risk."

"And that'd cost you even more, naturally," Lewrie smirked.

"Oh, but of *course*, sir!" Quill exclaimed. "He's made a pretty penny off Foreign Office funds so far, and I imagine he'd not like to lose the in-come, which is most-like going straight into his personal accounts, not into his syndicate's."

"Carson," Col. Tarrant called over his shoulder. "I think we've had enough tea. Fetch out some white wine, instead. Given the news," Tarrant said to his guests, "I'd break out the brandy, were it later in the morn-ing. This seems serious. Ah, Mister Quill, what have you heard anent Brigadier Caruthers?"

"Well, not much, sir," Mr. Quill told him, cocking his head in puzzle-ment. "As I said, I've little doings at the *Castello*. My sort isn't welcome there, and I've no real source of news there. Why the Brigadier, Colonel?"

Colonel Tarrant explained Caruthers's new enthusiasm for getting into the amphibious landing work, of converting at least one of his regiments into ship-borne soldiers, and obtaining ships of his own with which to do so, mentioning the letter that Caruthers had written asking for more par-ticulars as to how to go about it.

"He wants to get in the game with us, one way or another," Lewrie said. "Duplicate what we're doing, which'll end up costing us what we need."

"Equip and train at least one of his regiments, and obtain five or six transports," Col. Tarrant added. "That might just be for starters, 'til he commands an amphibious brigade."

Quill got an odd look on his long, narrow face, a squinty frown at first, then a smile, almost a gawping one as he mulled that over.

"Mean t'say, sirs," Quill said, almost tittering, "you wish me to spy on our own Army, on Brigadier Caruthers?"

"Well, yes," Tarrant shyly replied, cocking his gaze skyward as if to distance his words. "If you put it that way. Not *spy*, really, but . . . keep an ear to the ground. No skulking, or . . . whatever it is you do when *actually*, ehm . . . *sort* of spying?"

"Keep track of his doings in that regard," Lewrie translated.

"Bless my soul," Mr. Quill said, shaking his head, and drawing himself up with feet neatly tucked, elbows in, and balancing his wine glass as primly as a drawing room guest. "Colour me dumb-struck, sirs. And, at the moment, I haven't the first clue as to how to go about it. There's no one on his staff I could bribe, or blackmail, for the very good reason that I don't know any of them from Adam. I can't sneak into his offices and copy his correspondence."

"No throats to cut?" Lewrie helpfully offered, winking.

"Oh, not in my line of work, at *all*, Captain Lewrie!" Quill replied, in all seriousness as if he didn't, or couldn't realise that Lewrie was japing. "I suppose, though, that if I manage to draw him out . . . did he give me the *briefest* time of day . . . and mention that my branch of government was desirous of expanding the reach of our raids, and could put in a good word with both Admiralty and Horse Guards, he *might* just start babbling about his plans, enthusiastically."

"Hmm, that sounds a bit risky," Lewrie told him. "If it's not done cleverly, you might just put him on guard, and make Caruthers suspicious. He knows that you deal with us almost exclusively."

"Well, there is that," Mr. Quill admitted. "Organising is more my forté, after all, and spending money to get other people to carry out what I plan, not . . . actual, ehm . . . spy work. Ferreting things from people, midnight assignations?" Quill seemed as stand-offish of bloody-handed espionage and intrigue as Tarrant had in making his request.

"So, it's not on the cards?" Col. Tarrant said, blowing out his breath in dis-appointment.

"Well, I didn't say that, Colonel," Quill replied. "I may find a way. I just can't think of how to go about it quite yet. Subtlety is required, and that must be planned."

"I just want to know what the ambitious bastard's up to," Col. Tarrant grumbled, waving at his orderly for glasses to be re-filled.

"Haw! Sic *Don* Julio on him!" Lewrie hooted. "I'd wager *he'd* get the truth out of him! Or, would that cost too damned much?"

"Hmm, tempting!" Tarrant said, laughing out loud. "Pulling his fingernails, hot pokers and tongs, and many sharp knives?"

"Good Lord, Colonel," Mr. Quill exclaimed, "you sound as if you should be in *my* trade!"

Unfortunately, Quill found the idea so amusing that he began to bray, gargle, and break out his horrid donkey-like laugh. Tarrant's dog, which had been sitting close to his master's boots, and quiet for a change, leaped to his feet and started to bark madly, unsure if what he was hearing was a threat or not.

"Hush, now, Dante," Tarrant cooed to soothe him. "Good puppy. Come here and get some pets. Good, brave fellow, yes!"

"Keen on emulating your successes, is Caruthers?" Quill asked, once he got his breath back. "There's an easier, cheaper way to go about it, sirs. It's obvious, really. He only has to trade one of his regiments and have yours transferred to his brigade."

"Mine arse on a band-box!" Lewrie barked, astonished.

"Oh . . . my . . . sweet . . . Christ!" Col. Tarrant breathed out in shock. "Pray God, no! Not that!"

"Havin' him breathin' down our necks on every raid? Usin' us t'have himself another grand battle?" Lewrie almost raged. "He can't *help* but turn a raid into a lodgement, darin' the French t'come and give him another hot fight! Oh, Jesus *weep*!"

"Carson, fetch out the brandy, will you?" Col. Tarrant bade his orderly. "I fear I've a good sulk coming on."

"Did I say something wrong, sirs?" Quill asked, all asea by the reaction.

"Oh, *Hell* yes!" Lewrie spat.

The firing range was at last empty, and Lewrie and Tarrant went down there to get some practice in, Col. Tarrant bringing his orderly, Corporal Carson, along to serve as gun-bearer and re-loader. To ease Mr. Quill's unease after his unfortunate statement, they invited him along as well, even though he had no weapons of his own but a short-barrelled pocket "barker." And the idea of Brigadier Caruthers's seizure of the 94th was most definitely not spoken of again, though the possibility hung in the air like sour powder smoke on a windless day.

Lewrie went through all his pre-made paper cartridges for his pair of Manton pistols from the ten-yard posts, then reverted to his powder horn and pouch of loose ball: eighty, an hundred shots at the silhouette of a

French soldier, quite riddling it and turning his hands numb by the time he expended all of it.

Col. Tarrant was a good shot with his own pair of pistols, then turned out to be amazingly accurate with a smooth-bore Tower musket, even from the sixty-yard mark. Mr. Quill, however, barely knew how to load his one wee piece, expertly aided by Cpl. Carson, and hopelessly inept at shooting.

When Lewrie wished to try his eye with his rifled Ferguson musket, Tarrant all but danced in place for a chance to fire it as well, first from sixty yards, then paced off eighty, then one hundred yards, crowing with delight over the accuracy of the Ferguson, and how it was loaded from the breech. Which enthusiasm left Quill with nothing to do but sulk and watch them rave and congratulate themselves. He at last wandered off to see what the black-clad old women were cooking and selling to those soldiers who were idle.

"Poor fellow," Lewrie commented as they began to run out of the paper cartridges Lewrie had brought ashore for the Ferguson.

"Who? Quill? Is he gone?" Col. Tarrant asked, looking round. "Good."

"Always the odd man out, I'd expect," Lewrie said, borrowing a dry rag with which to mop his face which felt gritty, blackened from the priming powder in the rifle musket's pan. "Gawky, awkward, and bookish. Public school and university must have been a trial for him. He might be good at criquet, but . . ."

"Well, he's odd man out with me!" Col. Tarrant snapped, taking a drink from his wood canteen. "Steal my regiment, be damned. Christ, I tell you, Sir Alan, I'll not have it. I'll fight tooth and nail to keep them out of Caruthers's clutches. And God rot Quill for even saying anything about it!"

"If he does, though . . ." Lewrie mused.

"By God, I'll resign my commission!" Tarrant fumed. "And I am certain Major Gittings and half my company officers would as well. Caruthers is a glory-hunting butcher. Were it not for you, he'd have gotten half his regiments knackered at Lucri and Siderno. Give him free rein, and he'll come a cropper. His luck will run out, and I'd not care to be with him when it does."

"Well, if only t'see the look on his face," Lewrie quipped.

Col. Tarrant cocked his head to peer at Lewrie, a grim grin on his face. "It might be worth it, at that, but for the fact that the Ninety-Fourth would suffer Caruthers's fate and be annihilated along with him. Oh, well. Care for dinner?"

"Be delighted, sir," Lewrie told him with relish. "I must own to be peckish by now."

"Let's gather it all up, Carson," Tarrant ordered his man, "and we'll clean them before we eat. And wash the taste of gunpowder away with another bottle of that delicious white wine.

"Mind, now," Tarrant went on, turning sterner, "I'll demand we speak of *anything* . . . utter foolishness and bad jokes . . . other than what Quill blurted."

"I doubt I have more than an hundred good jokes, sir," Lewrie said, grinning, "but I do try and tell them differently each time."

And, by the time they reached Col. Tarrant's quarters and the welcome shade of his front gallery and its canvas fly, Quill's mule and two-wheeled cart were no longer tethered under the trees. He was well on his way cross the bridge on the road to Messina, made to feel, Lewrie was certain, like a *pariah* dog.

"Good riddance," Tarrant growled.

BOOK THREE

Me nulla dies tam fortibus ausis
dissimelem arguerit; tentum fortuna secunda
haud adversa cadat.

Never shall time prove me unmeet for such bold
emprise; so but fortune prove kind, nor cruel.
—*AENEID*, BOOK IX, LINES 231–33
VIRGIL

CHAPTER TWENTY-TWO

*B*oarding drills, boat work to take soldiers aboard and row them to the beach to splash ashore and form by companies for manoeuvres in the fruit and olive groves, and armed boat crews standing guard on the beach and their barges 'til the soldiers returned and boarded them to be rowed back aboard; both Lewrie and Lt. Fletcher oversaw every evolution aboard *Coromandel*, and went ashore as far as the beach with the armed sailors, no matter what Lt. Dickson thought of their being there.

Truth was, *Coromandel*'s people *were* slow to catch on, and slower than the other transports when performing their required duties; they needed a goad, and Lewrie was more than happy to give them one. He had already taken Dickson aside to explain why he, and *Coromandel*, were not the command ship of the transports.

"I chose Mister Fletcher long ago t'be the senior officer for the troop ships," Lewrie had explained to him, "because he's senior to Mister Hoar of *Spaniel*, and Mister Creswell of *Lady Merton*, and the arrangement's worked well, so far. Besides, you and *Coromandel* are new to our game, no matter your ship is nigh as big as mine, so . . . put that thought out of your mind, and work up your people 'til they're as efficient as the rest."

But *damn* Dickson, if he still proved truculent over Fletcher's presence over every exercise!

"It is confusing my crew, Sir Alan," Dickson protested as far as he had dared, "whether to follow the orders of Mister Fletcher or me and *my* officers. His presence undermines our authority."

"And does he not brief you on the day's work beforehand, sir?" Lewrie had asked, "And point out the things to be improved and seen to?"

"He does, Sir Alan, but . . . I, we, feel it un-dignified to be ordered about on our own decks," Dickson had groused.

"You came to this squadron, sir, with only the haziest idea of what it is we do," Lewrie pointed out, controlling his temper damned well, or so he thought, "and you and your officers are learning just as the other troopers did before we made our first raids. A skill to be learned, a level of efficiency to be gained, before I can deem you a useful unit of the squadron. You have no trouble with *me* directing your hands to the proper way of doing things, do you, sir? I do not undermine your authority by coming aboard to witness? Good. Then, consider Mister Fletcher my voice, and my eyes 'til he and I feel that *Coromandel*'s a fit member, ready to go. Now, let's be at it."

It was well that they did not hear from Mr. Quill for some time whilst *Coromandel*'s people slowly gained proficiency. He no longer visited, ashamed perhaps. Col. Tarrant and Major Gittings drilled their new-come soldiers, both ashore and aboard ship, 'til they were as proficient as his older, original troops, and could at last be shuffled round into the ranks, and lodgements, alongside the veterans. As for Quill's new chore of spying on Brigadier Caruthers and what he intended, they heard nothing, either.

To broaden his sources of information as to Caruthers's plans, Lewrie wrote Peter Rushton's brother Harold at the Secretary of State for War, asking if anyone in His Majesty's Government was pressing for more troop ships be sent to Sicily for *anyone's* use, and wrote to Captain Middleton and his old friend in Foreign Office Secret Branch, James Peel, wondering if *he'd* heard anything. It might take weeks to receive any letters in reply.

And, in the meantime, they had no fresh raids envisioned, and Lewrie was getting antsy and bored again, itching to do *something*.

He went aboard *Bristol Lass* to speak with Lt. Fletcher, went ashore to speak with Col. Tarrant, with a plan in hand.

Did Lt. Fletcher feel that *Coromandel* was ready enough for some sort of graduation drill at sea? Grudgingly, Fletcher thought that the latest drills showed promise and an acceptable level of ability. Of late, night exercises had come off with no one drowned or harmed, with the troops of the two new companies boarding in the dark, then being rowed ashore with the barges in passable line-abreast, and all done under arms with full canteens, rucksacks, and ammo pouches.

"Then let's do it!" Lewrie had decided. "We'll land on that beach east of here, near Villafranca Tirrena, after a night at sea. I wonder if the Colonel would care to come along . . . minus his damned dog, of course."

A last supper ashore in Col. Tarrant's quarters, with his new company commanders, Captains Lyndon and Wellman, Lt. Dickson and Sub-Lt. Clough to firm up the plans for the drill, and they were off, *Coromandel* escorted by HMS *Vigilance*, as she would be when performing the real thing on the Italian coast.

The two ships put out to sea early the next morning, steering North and Nor'-Nor'west to spend a day prowling round Volcano and Lupari Islands in the Aeolian chain, for the very good reason that those fabled isles of ancient Greek legends piqued Lewrie's curiosity from his schoolday reading, and he wanted to take a squint at them. Like all myths and legends, though, they proved less than enchanting, for they were rocky, with few landing places, and stank of sulphur far out to sea.

With favourable winds, the two ships reversed course, reducing sail to time their approach to the wide, sandy beach near Villafranca Tirrena well after Midnight, taking advantage of moonlight and starlight to give the green soldiers, and *Coromandel*'s crew and landing parties, barely enough illumination to work by.

The mid-day meal, then supper, was served aboard both ships, and the passengers aboard *Coromandel* were ordered to turn in early for a few hours of sleep. Lewrie hoped that the soldiers took to their quarters belowdecks, for he had ordered the four-man dog-boxes altered as soon as *Coromandel* had arrived, before the troops tore them apart to fit *their* notions.

Usually, each dog-box featured thin wood plank partitions from the deck to the overhead, and the front of each likewise boarded in, leaving only a doorway. Lewrie had the lowermost planking ripped out below the lower of the solid bunks, and opened up the spaces above the upper bunks to within eight inches of the thin mattresses, to improve the circulation of air. The front panelling was torn out, as well, to leave the soldiers easier access to the midships spaces which created a wide aisle where they could mill about or loaf, with easy access to the water butts and the weapons racks.

It here must be pointed out that Lt. Dickson did not see the sense of those alterations, claiming that what the dockyards built for troop quarters was the norm, and was good enough for other troop transports, so why accommodate, or pamper, them?

At least they were getting Navy rations to eat!

After dining in *Vigilance*'s First Officer, Lt. Farley, the ship's Marine officers, the Surgeon, Sailing Master, and two Mids who would be going ashore with the barges, Lewrie took a long time on the calm of the poop deck, savouring the cool night winds after a warm day at sea, a *rare* day at sea after sitting idle too long at anchor waiting for information on places to be raided and plans to be laid.

He closed his eyes and leaned against the cross-deck hammock stanchions, swaying with the motion of the hull as it snored along at seven knots, listening to the creaks and groans of timbers upon timbers, the faint squeaks from aloft as the many turning blocks of the running rigging worked to the ease, then strain. Even at that fairly slow speed, there was a rushing, waterfall sound as the hull parted dark waters, the cutwater and forefoot far up forward chuckling as the ship shoved her way on, before the wake creamed down her sides to burble and blend in the wide, white bridal train of her wake.

He opened his eyes and turned to pace aft to the taffrails where the lanthorns were lit for the night, their amber glows creating an almost "homey" snugness against the darkness beyond. Clinging to one of the lanthorn's posts, he could almost make out that wake, broad and a faintly eerie blue of phosphorescence. And there were the lanthorns glowing aboard *Coromandel*, roughly two cables astern, now and then occluded by masts and sails.

At least Dickson can keep station, Lewrie thought, still unsure of the man's competency. Dickson was *someone's* pet, else he'd not have command of a rowboat at his age. He hadn't done anything, so far as Lewrie could learn, grand or brave enough to explain it, else.

Turning away, Lewrie paced back forward on the windward side of the deck, looking cross the low coach-top amidships of the poop that provided light and air to his great-cabins, and it was amusing to see his cabin servants through the shallow glass panes at their work, at a much more leisurely pace than if he was still below.

And there on the larboard side sat his most lubberly wood and canvas collapsible deck chair, and for a moment, Lewrie was sorely tempted to ease down into it, stretch out in the dark, and rest for a spell. No, men on watch in the Afterguard were about, and he had no good reason to play idle before them.

He went back to the windward corner of the hammock stanchions, breathing deep of the innumerable odours of a warship under way, and of the sea itself: some admittedly foul, some pleasant, and all such a part of his life.

Thirty years in "King's Coat," he told himself; *and I can't say it's been all bad. Or, maybe my idea of what satisfies was warped a long time ago, hah! Let's see what the morrow brings, though.*

Both ships' crews, soldiers, and Marines were roused from their hammocks or bunks at Six Bells of the Middle Watch, a full hour earlier than the usual "All Hands" at 4 A.M. when the watch ended. Lewrie had drowsed fully dressed with his uniform coat for a coverlet in his hanging bed-cot, napping then waking, napping then waking. He rolled out groggily and stumbled in the dark in search of the wash-hand stand groping like a blind man for the filled pitcher and bowl so he could splash water on his face, scrub up, and wake himself. He was feeling about for a towel when Deavers, Dasher, and Turnbow entered the cabins and managed to get a couple of candles lit.

"Morning, Captain sir," Deavers said, yawning widely. "Yeovill says to tell you he'll have your coffee ready in the shake of a wee lamb's tail."

"Umph," was Lewrie's response to that as he poured more water into a handy glass to sluice the sleep taste and dryness from his mouth. "Ah, that's a bit better. Some, anyway. How's the weather and sea?"

"Too dark t'tell, sir," Dasher told him.

Lewrie snatched his old cocked hat off a high peg and went out to the quarterdeck to take a sniff, stiffening the backs of the men at the helm, and the officer of the watch, Mr. Greenleaf.

"Morning, sir," Lt. Greenleaf said. "We're steady on Sou'-Sou' East, half Sou'east. Last cast of the log showed six knots, and the sea and wind are a tad lively. The moon is setting, and the skies are mostly clear."

"Thankee, Mister Greenleaf," Lewrie said, peering over the side to see if he could spot white caps and white horses on the crests of the nearest waves, barely illuminated by the taffrail lanthorns. "Do you feel any roughness, or hobby-horsing?"

"Ehm, there's a bit more scending," Greenleaf opined. "Long-set waves, but perhaps no more than four or five feet high so far, sir."

Lewrie went up to the poop deck to peer aft in search of *Coromandel*, hoping to judge the sea state by watching her movements, but all he could make out were her taffrail lanthorns, which did not sway or pitch much at all.

"Lookouts aloft?" Lewrie asked once he regained the quarterdeck. "Any reports from them?"

"They espied faint lights ashore, sir," Greenleaf said, "much the same farm lights we saw when we last made practice landing on the beaches, and on pretty-much the same bearings as the last time. I'd reckon that we're within six or seven miles of the coast, but that'll be up to Mister Wickersham to decide."

Even as he said the man's name, the Sailing Master emerged from his sea cabin on the starboard side under the overhang of the poop deck, shrugging himself into a grogram watch coat.

"Ah, good morning, sir," Wickersham called out, recognising Lewrie in the faint light from the compass binnacle cabinet. "I trust you slept better than I did. I'll borrow a night-glass if I may?"

He took one from the rack on the cabinet and went up to the poop to peer shoreward for a long minute, then clumped back down, loudly clearing a phlegmy throat. "I make us about six miles off the beach, Captain, and, unless the locals have moved their bedroom windows, we are spot-on to where we landed our people the last time. Damme, are the galley fires lit yet? I'd gladly throttle someone for a cup of coffee."

"At six knots, we'll be coming to anchor round five A.M.," Lewrie estimated aloud. "Almost pre-dawn grey. Not too bad."

"Aye, sir," Wickersham agreed, making a grunt-yawning noise.

More shoes clumped on the larboard ladderway from the waist to the quarterdeck. It was Yeovill, bearing a battered old coffeepot by its bail, and lidded brass barge usually used to fetch Lewrie his solitary breakfast. "Morning, sirs," he said.

"Once you've poured mine, Yeovill, do fetch Mister Wickersham and Mister Greenleaf a mug of coffee," Lewrie instructed.

"That I will, sir!" Yeovill promised.

"Thank you kindly, Captain sir," the Sailing Master said, seconded by Greenleaf's, "Thankee amen, sir."

"I'll be aft, then," Lewrie told them, re-entering his cabins to avidly accept a mug of sugared black coffee from Yeovill.

"If you're feeling peckish, sir, there's a boiled egg and some of last night's shore bread," Yeovill told him as he quickly poured two more mugs to carry out to the quarterdeck. "Oh, and there's some sausage for Chalky in the barge, and some sliced cabbage for Dasher's rabbit."

"You do us proud, as always, Yeovill," Lewrie made it a point to tell him, for personal cooks as talented as Yeovill simply must be praised if one wished to keep them.

"Some butter f'r yer bread, sir?" Turnbow offered, setting out a plate on which Lewrie could shell his egg. "'Tis only a week old."

"Aye, Turnbow," Lewrie said, sitting down at his table. "Think it might turn out to be a good morning, after all."

The moon had gone under the horizon, and the sea and sky were beginning to be revealed by the faintest hint of lighter grey light when both ships rounded up to the wind, coasted to a stop, and let go their best bower anchors, even as hands aloft took in the last scrap of sail.

"Draw up the barges, Mister Farley, get the boarding nets over the sides, and prepare to dis-embark troops," Lewrie ordered, then went forward to the cross-deck hammock stanchions at the forward edge of the quarterdeck to look down into the ship's waist. "All ready to go, Whitehead?"

"Ready, sir!" the Marine officer called back, looking cheerful, "And the signals party, too." There they were alongside Lt. Rutland and Lt. Grace, the tall canvas sea bag stuffed with signal flags, and the long spar which would be planted on the beach, upon which the flags would be displayed. This morning, it was Midshipman Langdon, the oldest, and Midshipman Chenery, who would man it. Langdon, at twenty-five, looked as if he would

take it all in professional stride, but younger Charles Chenery still looked
boyishly cock-a-whoop.

"Damned good navigation, sirs!" Lewrie praised the people on the
quarterdeck as he raised his telescope to look at the beaches, recognising
a church steeple in Villafranca Tirrena, a tall stone barn, and a dead, bare
tree from their earlier landings. They were indeed, spot-on! He crossed
the quarterdeck to look at *Coromandel*.

"So far so good," Lewrie muttered under his breath, for the transport's
boarding nets were being laid out overside, and barges were being drawn
alongside from being towed astern in trots. It looked seamanlike and efficient for once, which elicited a pleased grunt from him.

"Very well, let's be at it," Lewrie said louder, shouting aft to the hands
at the signal halliards. "Hoist the signal to man boats and land the landing force!"

A moment later, and *Coromandel* showed the same, lone signal flag,
two-blocked at the peak of the halliards.

"Barges alongside, nets deployed, and ready to go, sir," First Officer
Farley reported.

"Aft there, strike the hoist!" Lewrie yelled, ordering the Execute. "Sailors, man the boats!"

Oarsmen, Cox'ns, Midshipmen scrambled over the bulwarks to swarm
down the boarding nets to their waiting boats, followed by bundles of
weapons with which to guard the barges and the landing beach once the
Marines advanced inland.

"Land the landing force!" Lewrie shouted, cuing the Marines to go over
the side to enter the manned and waiting barges.

Lewrie turned his attention to the *Coromandel*, peering closely at her
activities; he was sure that his sailors and Marines had it all down pat by
now. What he saw made him frown.

There in the ocular of his telescope was Lt. Dickson and Sub-Lt.
Clough, dashing from one side of their quarterdeck to the other, peering
over the sides with some urgency. His sailors were in the barges, and the
soldiers of the 94th were going down the nets, but for one wee group,
larboard side aft, who were still gathered along the bulwarks and sail-
tending gangway, not moving at all.

"Shove off, there! Line-abreast, and . . . stroke!" Lt. Rutland was
ordering *Vigilance*'s barges to get under way, and Lewrie spared them a
glance, taking note that the waters 'twixt the ship and the beaches looked

a little rougher than he'd expected, but nothing that they had not experienced before.

No, Lewrie's attention was rivetted to *Coromandel*, where those soldiers were still on deck, as were sailors in the right numbers to make up a barge crew, standing and shrugging at each other in dumb show. Her boats were stroking away from her side, at last, delayed by some confusion that had Lt. Dickson in a howling dither, flailing his arms and yelling something. Three boats from *Coromandel*'s starboard side were slowly making way, sorting themselves out in line-abreast, then resting on their oars for the rest to come round her bows and join them. One came round, then a second, then . . . nothing.

Lewrie did a quick count, swinging his telescope to eye the one nearest. Five barges and . . .

"Why's that boat being rowed by only six oars?" he pointed out to his quarterdeck staff. "There's two men near the bows sittin' on their bloody hands, by God!"

"Two, three, four, five . . . where's the sixth?" Lt. Farley asked aloud. "Oh, don't tell me they've gone and lost one of their boats!"

Lewrie did another quick count, gawping in dis-belief.

"You cack-handed *lubbers*!" he roared, hoping that Lt. Dickson could hear him cross the quarter-mile separation. "You've gone and lost a *barge*? Mine arse on a bloody *band-box*!"

"Mean t'say I *won't* pass the exam, teacher?" Lt. Greenleaf, ever a wag, sniggered. "And I studied *so* hard! What'll pater say?"

"You miserable, incompetent, 'no sailor' babes!" Lewrie cursed, astonished. "My bloody *cat* keeps better watch of his *toys*! Comin' out o' your bloody *pay*, Dickson, hear me? If it was rainin' soup, you'd have a bloody *fork*, and you'd drop *that*! You jumped-up . . . *Arrh*!"

He wanted to be aboard *Coromandel* instanter, so he could seize Dickson by his coat lapels and shake him like a dust rag, but he had no means to do so. All of *Vigilance*'s boats were away, rowing hard for the beach, and were still at least an hundred yards off before the line of breaking surf. It would be minutes before the Marines and armed sailors exited them and freed one up to return to the ship.

"Well, I never," the Sailing Master said, sadly chuckling.

"Just going to say," Lt. Farley chimed in, breezily, holding in outright laughter with some difficulty.

"There's not a boat in sight, sir," Lt. Greenleaf said after a long scan seaward with his telescope. "God only knows when in the night that it went adrift. *Might* spot it when the sun comes up," he added hopefully. He shouted aloft to the lookouts in the cross-trees, but after a long moment, they could not spot it, either.

"As soon as our boats are grounded, hoist a signal for one boat to return aboard, Mister Farley," Lewrie said, managing to put a lid on his anger, for the moment, at least. "I've a bone to pick with *Coromandel*'s commanding officer. A *monumental* bone."

"Aye, sir," the First Officer said, taking note that Captain Lewrie's usually merry grey-blue eyes had gone the iciest Arctic grey.

Lt. Farley had seen that odd change only a few times serving under Lewrie, in the *Thermopylae* frigate back in 1801, and rarely at all in *Vigilance*. Thankfully, the Captain's anger had never been directed at him, but Lt. Farley was mortal-certain that Lt. Dickson was going to get the roasting of his life, and a well-deserved one, too.

Under a lighter grey sky, with only the faintest hint of colour below the eastern horizon, Lewrie took the salute of the side-party at *Coromandel*'s entry-port, doffing his hat to the flag aft, then to the assembled officers.

"Good morning, Mister Dickson," he began.

"Sir Alan," Dickson said, bicorne doffed high and half bowing from the waist. His face was flushed with embarrassment.

"Lost a whole barge, have you, sir?" Lewrie asked as he placed his hat back on his head. "And some oars, too, I noticed?"

"I simply don't know how such a thing could happen, sir . . ." Dickson tried to say, but Lewrie cut him off.

"No, I don't know how that could happen, either. Sir!" Lewrie drawled. "Let's go aft, shall we?"

"Aye, sir," Dickson said, looking like a hanged spaniel.

In the privacy of the cabins, Dickson tried again.

"Before we left harbour at Milazzo, sir, my Acting Bosun made an inspection, and assured me that everything was in order," Dickson said. "The boats secured for towing astern, everything needful in the barges bundled together, and . . . may I offer you something, Sir Alan?"

"No," Lewrie firmly said, glowering. "You may not."

"As I said, sir, everything *was* seen to," Dickson repeated.

"You did not inspect yourself, sir?" Lewrie demanded.

"I trusted my petty officers and Bosun, sir, and feel badly let down by their slip-shod . . ." Dickson almost stammered.

"'Tis a poor workman, blames his tools," Lewrie snapped. "It's all your responsibility, Mister Dickson. The ship, your people, and the details of an important exercise. Had this happened during an actual landing against the enemy coast over yonder, it might have proved t'be disastrous. Sir. Was no one posted to keep watch over the tow during the night?"

"Ehm, no, sir," Dickson had to confess. "We assumed . . ."

"Well, assuming was a dead bust, wasn't it," Lewrie sneered. "It's standing orders aboard *my* ship that the Mids casting the chip log on the half-hour keep an eye on the tows, and sing out at once if something's amiss. Slip-shod, d'ye say? Aye, all that in *spades,* sir!"

Lt. Dickson's chin was protectively tucked snug against his neck by then, and he badly needed a drink of something wet to cure the dryness of his mouth, but could not indulge if Lewrie wouldn't.

"I am most heartily sorry to dis-appoint, Sir Alan," Dickson said, almost grovelling. "My fault, entirely."

"Aye, it is," Lewrie sternly rejoined. "At the least, you got *five* barges manned, and landed the troops on the beach. *Most* of 'em. We'll cancel the exercise. Do you hoist your number, and Recall to your boats ashore. Then, once everyone's back aboard, you can spend the rest of the day, and night if it takes that long, swanning about to find your missing boat, and recover it before the local pirates make off with it and call it Christmas Day. Sir."

"Aye aye, Sir Alan," Dickson answered, almost venting a long breath of relief. "Sorry."

"Indeed," Lewrie frostily pointed out. "I'll remain aboard to watch the return of your barges, and the troops. *My* barge can stay below your starboard main chains 'til I depart. God knows, there's *room* for it."

"Aye, Sir Alan," Dickson said with a nervous nod. "I will see to that signal, directly."

"Go," Lewrie said, "but don't think that this is over. Sir."

That stopped Dickson in his tracks and spun him about to face Lewrie, again, worry about his career plain on his phyz.

"I've four *very* competent Lieutenants in *Vigilance*'s wardroom, Mister Dickson," Lewrie threatened, "all experienced with the work we do, and sound seamen, all. Perhaps *Coromandel* might benefit from an exchange . . . unless taking you aboard might be to my ship's detriment, hmm? Go. Hoist the signal."

"Aye aye, sir!" Dickson said, goggling, swallowing nervously, before stumbling out to the quarterdeck, fearing that it might not be *his* quarterdeck much longer, and cursing his patrons for placing him here, under his breath, thinking himself a total fool for taking the bait of a ship to command!

Lewrie followed him more leisurely, mounting to *Coromandel*'s poop deck from where he could see all.

The requisite signal was quickly two-blocked, and a matching one was wig-wagged from shore to indicate that they saw it and would obey. Down *Coromandel*'s hoist went to order the Execute, and soldiers from the 94th began to trudge back to the beach, and armed boat crews got out their oars, ready to depart.

Here now, that's . . . odd, Lewrie thought as he studied the men still aboard, going about their duties; *Damme, are they grinnin' like schoolboys?*

There were many hooded looks and winks, sailors leaning close to whisper to each other and silently snigger. And, as the barge crews came up the boarding nets at last, damned if they acted that way, too!

It's a Goddamned silent mutiny! Lewrie realised.

Coromandel's brow-beaten, herded, threatened, and even lashed people had had enough of Lt. bloody Dickson and his ways, and had at last found a way to scupper him! A poorly tied tow line on the last barge astern of a trot of three, oars misplaced from another.

I'd wager a month's pay they'll find ten oars *in that missing barge!* Lewrie told himself, stifling his amusement, for it wouldn't do for a Post-Captain to show that he was in on the immense joke!

"Boats secured, nets taken in, and all hands accounted for, sir," Sub-Lt. Clough reported to Lt. Dickson, who took the report, and then turned to Lewrie for further orders.

"Make sail for Milazzo, Mister Dickson, discharge the troops, then make sail, again, to hunt down your missing barge," Lewrie told him. "The last time I was with Captain Middleton in Portsmouth, and outfitting the other transports, the cost of a twenty-nine-foot barge with ev'rything all found, was over one hundred fifty pounds, so . . . good luck recovering it, or you might have to answer to Admiralty for its loss."

"Aye, sir," Lt. Dickson tautly replied, looking miserable.

"Once back in harbour, I will give you my decision. Sir," Lewrie told him, leaving Dickson under an uncertain threat.

"Aye, sir," Dickson managed to rasp out, and Sub-Lt. Clough raised his brows and peered about, wondering what that meant.

Christ, but that felt damned good! Lewrie told himself, once he was seated in the sternsheets of his barge; *Now, who can I spare? Grace, Greenleaf? We'll just have to see. But, Dickson aboard my ship? He's pure poison! His attitude towards the hands might make my Vigilances mutiny!*

CHAPTER TWENTY-THREE

*E*ven before *Vigilance* got within sight of the other transports anchored off Milazzo, Lewrie had finished a letter to Adm. Sir Thomas Charlton informing him of his decision to temporarily relieve Dickson of his command and replace him with one of his officers. It would be a dicey act, for though Lewrie was in command of all the squadron, he had not been appointed a Commodore's authority, and was under the command of Charlton, wherever he was at that moment, hundreds of miles away. He hedged his bets by asking whether Charlton thought he had the authority to do so, or if Charlton thought that there might be a better solution to *Coromandel*'s problem. Dickson had powerful patrons, and Lewrie was already the target of *other* people's spite; dare he do something to turn a whole new set against him? If Charlton approved, Lewrie asked for a reply to show that he concurred, or not.

That letter was sanded to dry the ink, but not yet folded over itself to form an envelope; the sticks of sealing wax and Lewrie's personal seal were still in a drawer of his desk. It lay flat on the desk top, making Lewrie wonder if he would ever mail it.

Cooler head, he told himself; *that's what I need. Spur of the moment, gone off at half-cock like a two shilling pistol? Dickson's that ship's real problem, but . . . can I do anything about him? Just 'cause I despise the bastard? It'll look un-justified, and spiteful.*

With a long sigh, he slipped the letter into the central drawer of his desk and shut it. "I'll be on deck," he told his retinue.

Lt. Rutland was officer of the watch, glooming over the windward corner of the quarterdeck, his dour face screwed up in even more dismal thoughts than usual.

"Captain, sir," Rutland said, touching the brim of his hat as he surrendered that post to stand in front of the compass binnacle cabinet.

"Mister Rutland," Lewrie acknowledged.

"A shambles, sir," Rutland commented after a long silence.

"*Coromandel?*" Lewrie asked with a snort of sour humour.

"Aye, sir. A badly run ship," Rutland sneered. "Pity."

"They're *close* to competent," Lewrie told him.

"Their hearts ain't in it, though, sir," Rutland went on. "From the top down. Were they better led, well."

That's the most I've ever heard him say! Lewrie marvelled; *He usually has less conversation than a pile o' roundshot.*

A long, uneasy silence followed that. Finally, Rutland cleared his throat and said, "Talked with them."

"Aye?" Lewrie prompted, wondering where he was going.

"Clough, sir," Rutland expounded. "He's not that bad. On the young side, but mostly capable . . . if he could ever stop jabbering. Her Mid, Kinsey, too, sir. A 'tarpaulin' fellow, playing dumb 'cause he doesn't like Mister Dickson, and won't go out of his way to help him. Might enjoy riling him."

"Well, he fooled me," Lewrie said. "I thought he was hopeless."

"Need a better officer in command of her, sir," Rutland said.

Christ, I haven't even said anything in front of my crew yet, Lewrie all but gawped; *and news o' what I might do has already made the rounds?*

"I could straighten her out, sir, if need be," Rutland told him, looking far forward at the dip and rise of the jib-boom and bow-sprit.

"You'd volunteer, Mister Rutland?" Lewrie asked, amazed. "You'd leave us?"

"If needs must, sir," Rutland said, finally turning his head to look at him. "Good of the Service, the good of the squadron. Wouldn't *enjoy* it, but . . ." he concluded with a shrug.

"I'm tempted," Lewrie confessed, "but I haven't decided, yet. I may not have the authority. And here I thought you *liked Vigilance.*"

"Oh, I do, sir, immensely," Rutland assured him, though his expression did not change from his usual spare sternness. "But, it would be grand to have actual command of something, and make her as smart as paint."

"A satisfying accomplishment," Lewrie said.

"Exactly so, sir," Rutland said, then turned to face forward again, as if that would be all he had to say on the subject.

"I'll let you know if I do decide," Lewrie assured him.

Makin' Coromandel *a happy, taut ship'd be an accomplishment, indeed,* Lewrie thought; *Aye, if Dickson don't improve.*

Astern of HMS *Vigilance* by two cables, sailing right up the warship's wake, *Coromandel*'s people and the two companies of soldiers from the 94th could almost be thought to be in glad takings now that the exercise was over. Stiff leather collars were undone, and red coats were un-buttoned, with white pipe-clayed straps and bandoliers temporarily stowed below in the four-man cabins. Those who chewed tobacco were gathered round the spit kids, and men who smoked pipes lazed on the leeward sail-tending gangways. Soldiers and sailors made free with the dippers at the scuttlebutts for sips of water as the day warmed, and the mood aboard was slyly jovial.

The same could not be said about the mood upon the quarterdeck, however, where the air between the officers almost tingled like the prickly aura of a lightning strike.

"You have badly let me down, sirs," Lt. Dickson gravelled, his voice a'rasp with warning. "Let the ship down. Made me look like a perfect fool!"

"Wasn't *our* doing, sir," Sub-Lt. Clough objected. "Neither I, nor Kinsey, had anything to do with securing the tow lines, or the missing oars. All was in order before we sailed."

"Saw to everything myself, sir," Midshipman Kinsey grumped.

"Quick glances, were they?" Dickson accused. "Someone in the crew shifted those oars somewhere, somebody undid the tow line, and I want to know who they were!"

"Well, it's not as if someone went down the tow line from the stern in the dead of night, hauled the second boat up to the first, got in it, and untied the tow to the third. It'd take a circus acrobat to get back aboard after doing that, and . . ."

"Or a topman!" Dickson spat. "Any of those bastards are that agile.

We're going to get to the bottom of it, hear me? More to the point, *you* two will get to the bottom of it. I want names, and I will have them up on charges. By God, sirs, our idiot Bosun will be up all night, making up cats o' nine tails for the punishments I mean to hand down! I will make this crew *howl* before I'm through!"

"Beg pardon, sir," Midshipman Kinsey dared say, "but that might be too harsh. A *few* truly deserving, maybe, but . . ."

"Are you 'Popularity Dick' now, Kinsey?" Dickson sneered. "I'd have thought that was more Clough's line."

"Sir!" Sub-Lt. Clough exclaimed, stung by the accusation.

"As if you wouldn't rather josh with the crew than enforce any discipline, or uphold your authority," Dickson said in heat. "I've seen you do it, Clough. This ship's crew's a hodgepodge of malingerers, drunks, petty criminals, and ox-heads as stupid and ignorant as so many *cows*! Dredged up from the cast-offs of a dozen ships, and sent here to bedevil me with their vile, lazy ways! They must be forced to do their duties, properly, efficiently, and have their backs laid open with the lash if they don't. This ain't an antic, a schoolboy prank, you fools! It was close to mutiny, and it *will* be tamped down and eliminated. They will learn to respect and obey their betters, or they'll pay for it. And if you can't get to the root of it, then I will write Admiralty and request your replacements!

"Now," Dickson said, softening his rant a bit, "be about it, and bring me the names of the instigators. Go! Get out of my face!"

Dickson stomped off the quarterdeck, out along the windward sail-tending gangway, to glower at his disreputable crew, eagerly seeking someone who was not doing his duty, someone who smirked or was too jovial, whom he could punish.

"Jesus weep," Clough muttered, after letting out a long pent-up breath. "Who'd be a sailor on *this* barge!"

"Remember the *Hermione* frigate?" Kinsey asked. "Her Captain, Pigot I think his name was, was the same sort of Tartar. When his crew mutinied, they murdered him in his bed."

"You don't think . . . !" Clough gasped. "No, not under the guns of the *Vigilance*. Surely not! Wasn't *Hermione* sailing alone?"

"Seen a lot of officers in my time in the Navy, man and boy," Kinsey said with a sad shake of his head. "I *know* we're not to say anything about a senior officer, seeing as how it's dis-loyal, and a court-martial offence. But . . . I swear he'll be the ruin of us."

"Dasn't even mention the word 'mutiny,' either," Clough warned him. "Unless we see one brewing, of course. He said it first," Clough added, sounding like a schoolboy's plaint to Kinsey's ears.

"God, finding who did it's nigh impossible," Kinsey told him. "The whole crew could be in on it, for all we know, and not one of 'em will admit to it, or point a finger."

"Have to try, though," Sub-Lt. Clough said with a long sigh of frustration. "I don't know what he'll do if we don't, or can't, get results."

"Aye, I suppose," the elder Midshipman gloomily agreed. "Here now . . . recall what Captain Lewrie told Dickson as he was leaving the ship? Something about giving him his decision once we get back from hunting our missing barge? I wonder what that was all about."

"Hmm, Lewrie *did* give him a cobbing, I expect," Clough said, in well-hidden amusement over his commanding officer's predicament, "and Dickson looked as happy as a hanged spaniel when they left the great-cabins. A formal complaint to Admiralty, or Rear-Admiral Charlton, a threat to have Dickson exchange with another officer? No idea."

"Could be welcome news for some," Kinsey said with a brief bit of hope as he rubbed his unshaven chin, "or bad news for someone in particular. Well, I think I'll go below and see if I can turn up those missing oars, before we go laying blame on anyone."

"I'll keep us from running aground 'til the change of watch," Clough promised. "Good luck to you."

"Anchored securely fore and aft, sir," Lt. Farley reported to Lewrie, "five-to-one scope paid out on the hawsers in five and a half fathoms of water. Ehm . . . do you still wish to hold cutlass drill, sir?"

"No, I think not, Mister Farley, not today," Lewrie decided, after a long moment of thought. "Best we inspect our barges, and see to their painters and tow lines for chafing or wear. It wouldn't do us any good to tear a strip off one ship for laxness, then go and lose a boat, ourselves, what?"

"Oh no, no good at all, sir!" Farley said with a snigger. "I'll see to it, directly."

"Be sure to point out the markers to the harbour watch, so we can tell if the anchors drag," Lewrie said, having a look-round for a large barn three points off the starboard bows, and a church bell tower three points off the larboard quarter, in the village of Milazzo, "The flagpole in the Army camp'll do for one, as well as the signals post by the docks."

"And Mount Etna over yonder, too, sir," Farley pointed out.

"Very well, I'll be aft," Lewrie told him, but only took two steps toward his door before pausing, and going up to the poop deck to watch *Coromandel* as she completed anchoring closer inshore near the other transports, and putting the boarding nets overside to send her temporary complement of soldiers ashore.

Since she would soon be departing to hunt up her missing boat, Dickson had only let go her best bower, ignoring a stern kedge anchor, and Lewrie watched closely to see how much scope he'd let run through the hawse-hole. There was a light wind off the sea, but *Coromandel* was a big ship, with a lot more freeboard than the other transports, and even a light wind could shuffle her about. Had he taken into account for a possible swing that might put his ship crunching into *Spaniel* or *Lady Merton*, anchored fore-and-aft nearby?

Go on, Dickson, smash something up so I can dismiss you, Lewrie thought as he peered closer with a telescope; *Some damnfool, lubberly idiocy that I can justify as good cause!*

From his vantage point, *Coromandel*'s stern *seemed* hellish-close to *Lady Merton*'s bow-sprit and jib-boom, but no one aboard the smaller trooper was scurrying forward in concern, or shouting warnings as the wind made *Coromandel* swing round her anchor to point her bows higher into the breeze, and her stern at the beach.

I'm bein' perverse, wishin' for that, Lewrie chid himself; *Fine, so I'm perverse! But! If he's slow gettin' his anchor up and sails set, he can* still *put her stern aground!*

But, ever so slowly, *Coromandel*'s barges returned from the beach and the boarding nets were hauled up over her bulwarks. Jibs and staysails were hoisted, along with the spanker aft, and the ship drew up to her anchor 'til the hawser was "up and down," and, after a brief stern board, the bower was being rung up to the catheads, and she was under way with a faint mustachio of foam under her forefoot.

Oh well, better luck next time, Lewrie thought, collapsing the tubes of his telescope and clumping down the ladderway to the quarterdeck. He entered his great-cabins, shedding hat, coat, waist-coat, and neck-stock, delighted to find that the transom sash windows' upper halves were open for a breeze, as was the wood, glass-paned door to his stern gallery, and, out of the late morning sun, his cabins were relatively cool and comfortable.

His cat, Chalky, sat by the tight mesh of the strung twine door to the stern gallery, jaws chittering and making wee hunting noises. His paws worked on the taut twine as if he was playing a harp.

"Something cool before dinner, sir?" Deavers tempted.

"A mug of ale, if we've any left, thankee," Lewrie told him, going to his fiddled rack of books to find something amusing to read, as Dasher hung his shed clothing on pegs too high for the cat to get to and "adorn" with white fur. "Here, Chalky, leave the seabirds be. You ever do catch a gull, he'd peck your eyes out like raisins in a duff. Here, puss puss! Lap!" he invited, and Chalky finally left off his dream of killing something and trotted over to the starboard side settee, sprang up atop the cushions with his tail up, and pawed his shirt sleeve with talons sheathed.

"There's a good catling, yayss," Lewrie cooed, petting him.

I may re-write that letter to Charlton, Lewrie told himself; *Who knows? I may still have to send it.*

CHAPTER TWENTY-FOUR

$\mathscr{T}$he next morning, HMS *Vigilance* did hold the delayed cutlass drill, whilst her officers and Midshipmen practiced with the heavy blades or their personal swords on the poop deck. Older Mids who had been exposed to a fencing master's *salle* showed off, instructing the younger lads to the double threat of cutlass in one hand, and their dirks, which were normally worn as a sign of their dignity and their status as officers-to-be, in the other. The ship rang with the sounds of steel clanging and slithering on opposing steel, though the drill steps stressed footwork and balance on the thrust, return, slash, and counter, slowed down from the furious melee of the real thing. Lewrie long before had been trained well in the two-handed work of smallsword and dagger, or the cloak draped over his left hand as a shield and a trap for a too-confident thrust.

Lewrie delighted in sword practice, for it was one of the few ways for an officer to keep somewhat fit in the confines of a ship at sea; they were not required to manhandle guns and carriages, tail on to hoist in cargo, lift boats off the cross-deck beams, or clamber aloft to handle sail or strike topmasts. There were only so many laps of the ship one could walk! He considered himself hale and fit, even at the advanced age of forty-seven years, but was secretly glad when Lt. Farley called for a water break at the scuttlebutts, and a chance to regain his breath.

"Pointless, really, sir," Lt. Rutland commented as they stood at the forward edge of the poop deck, looking down into the waist, where sailors and Marines still practiced in facing rows. "As soon as they swarm and board an enemy ship, half their learning goes by the board, and they fight like they were in a tavern brawl."

"But, better skilled than the French, who've not been out of port two weeks, and half of 'em still green round the gills," Lewrie joshed.

"Deck, there!" someone in the main mast cross-trees shouted. "Sail on th' horizon! Two points off th' larb'd bows!"

Lt. Farley was quick to dash down to the quarterdeck to seize a brass speaking trumpet and shout back. "Can you make her out?"

"Hull down, sir!" was the reply. "Only showin' tops'ls!"

"From the East, Nor'east," Lt. Rutland speculated as he took his turn with the long dipper. "*Coromandel* must have found her barge, at last."

"Took him long enough," Lewrie said, uncharitably.

"Ehm, you've given my offer some thought, sir?" Rutland asked, pretending that it did not matter which way Lewrie decided.

"I may give Mister Dickson one last chance to prove himself, Mister Rutland," Lewrie told him. "But, if he messes up once more, I may place you in command of her. May be temporary, mind. Admiral Charlton may over-rule me."

"Depending on Dickson's, and Grace's, dates of commission, it may delight Mister Grace to be made Third Officer," Rutland sniggered, showing a faintest bit of rare humour.

"Deck, there!" came another hail from aloft. "I kin only see *two* tops's! Looks t'be a brig!"

"So he *hasn't* found his boat, yet," Lewrie chuckled. "Perhaps *Don Julio* scooped it up and is holdin' it for ransom?"

"Who, the smuggler, sir?" Rutland asked. "The one who scouts our missions for us? Never met him."

"Consider yourself fortunate, then, Mister Rutland," Lewrie told him. "He's an oily, cut-throat who'd kill his children if the price was high enough."

They returned to their sword practice after everyone had had a dipper or two of freshwater. This time, Lewrie squared off against Midshipman Charles Chenery, his young brother-in-law.

"Put your dirk away, Mister Chenery," Lewrie told him, "and we will simplify things."

"Light hanger against a heavy cutlass, sir," Chenery said with an impish air. "I'd hate to break your sword, sir."

"It's a Gills', and stouter than you think. Guard yourself!" Lewrie shot back, and for the next ten minutes, 'til Six Bells of the Forenoon rang out, and the drill was ended for the day, Lewrie found himself all but overwhelmed by Chenery's quickness and supple wrist, though he did manage to dance him backwards and get inside his guard with low-held thrusts or half-slashes, even able to step up chest-to-chest and shove his hanger's hilt and guard upwards against the lad's chin. If it had been for real, he would have knocked him sprawling, open to a killing stroke.

"Desperate men never fight fair, Mister Chenery," Lewrie crowed, panting. "Elegance against a garlic-breathed Frenchmen'll get you killed."

"I'll keep that in mind, sir," Chenery said, still smiling.

"Go sponge yourself off, and get ready for the rum issue," Lewrie told him, sheathing his hanger at last, and going below for a full mug of cool tea and ginger beer, and a sponge-off of his own.

"Deck there," he heard as he re-donned his damp shirt. "Th' sail on th' horizon's almost hull-up! She's makin' her number!"

A moment later, one of the Midshipmen of the Harbour Watch was at Lewrie's door to inform him that the strange sail was a warship, one of their own, the HMS *Coquette*.

"Huzzah!" Lewrie exclaimed. "D'arcy Gamble's coming! Now we can find out what's acting up the coast!"

He looked at his desk, where his amended letter to Admiral Sir Thomas Charlton sat atop a pile of personal letters that he'd hoped to post to England.

You're goin' anywhere near the squadron, Malta or Gibraltar, you're a Godsend, Commander Gamble! he happily thought.

Hours later, HMS *Coquette* came to anchor a quarter-mile off, and in fine style, taking in all her sail by the time she coasted to a stop with her bows in the wind, and letting go her bower at the same time, an impressive feat of seamanship.

Within moments, *Coquette*'s wee gig was under way, bearing her captain to *Vigilance*'s starboard side and entry-port. Lewrie stood by the beginning of the sail-tending gangway near the entry-port, eager to see Gamble aboard, impatient with the ritual of hailing the supposedly "strange" boat, the shouted reply, and the permission to close the ship yelled back.

The gig thumped against the hull by the main chains, and a long moment later, the hint of a hat above the lip of the entry-port brought the side-party to attention as Bosun's calls trilled. Once inboard, Commander Gamble doffed his hat to the flag and his welcomers, with a slight bow from his waist.

"Commander Gamble, *very* welcome aboard!" Lewrie said, stepping forward to offer his hand.

"Captain Lewrie!" Gamble said, smiling broadly as he shook with him. "I trust you keep well?"

"Quite well, sir," Lewrie replied. "Come aft, take a pew, and a glass of something, and tell me all your latest news."

"Delighted to do so, sir," Gamble said.

Once seated round the low, brass Hindoo tray table, and Dasher fetching glasses of cool tea mixed with ginger beer, Gamble slung his sword out of the way to settle into the settee cushions. "I did not compliment you on the fineness of your cabin furnishings last time I was aboard, sir. It's all quite homey."

"God, don't tell Admiralty, then," Lewrie japed, "else they'll think me a luxury-loving Corinthian, and I'll get 'beached' forever! A fair amount of it's my wife's taste, truth t'tell. Dame Lewrie is an artist, and has an eye for such things."

Gamble turned his head briefly to glance at Jessica's portrait on the forward bulkhead. "You are a most fortunate man, sir. Now! Your bridge!"

"Aha, have the French repaired it?" Lewrie asked, shifting forward in his chair.

"Every time I've passed it, sir, I've lingered to pound at it, as have the other brig-sloops which patrol the coast north of Reggio di Calabria," Gamble reported with some glee. "They've tried to make a start at replacing the central pillar with wood timber frames, and when that got shot away, a weird triangular bracing tower, but that got shattered as well. There's quite a pile of broken timbers in the gully, by now. And, as soon as they spot a sail coming close, all their civilian workers scatter, whether we fire on them or not. The last time *Rainbow*, another of our sloops, fired on it, all her captain could see was uniformed French engineers, and they ran off just like the local Italians, hah hah!

"A few days ago, though, sir," Commander Gamble said, turning, graver, "when I closed the coast to have another go at it, there were artillery batteries either end of the bridge, or a single, mixed battery . . . four twelve-pounder guns, and a brace of howitzers with explosive shells. I had to haul off once they got the range of me, sorry to say."

"Well, we knew the situation wouldn't last," Lewrie said, saddened to hear that. "They score any hits on you, were any of your men hurt?"

"Some splashes a long musket shot off, one explosive shell off my starboard, another far over on my larboard, and I determined that discretion might be the best course. No one hurt at all, though we got the wind up when those shells burst."

"Good," Lewrie replied. "If only there was a way to fire explosive shells aboard ship, though the storage might prove a problem."

"The French *have* tried to move supplies south from Naples by sea, sir," Gamble went on, "small coasters and commandeered fishing boats, mostly, but our continued presence forces them to skulk along the coast, in sight of land, and duck into any fishing port or inlet that's handy when they see *any* strange sail to seaward. I doubt if some of them make sixty miles a day."

"Just as they did off northern Spain," Lewrie agreed.

"And, just as you did off that coast, sir, we've been reaping a rich harvest of them," Gamble boasted, with a nod of his head to honour Lewrie's past accomplishments. "Most of the crews have turned out to be Neapolitans, people from that kingdom's navy, out of work now, and in need of some income. The ones we've captured seem quite happy to be imprisoned on Malta, out of French clutches. Some of the prisoners are French sailors, rounded up from idled warships, and they're none too happy. What part of their fleet that was sent to Naples is still in harbour, too fearful to sortie. Frigates mostly."

"Hmm, if they haven't yet re-built that bridge, their supplies must still come by road, the long way round," Lewrie said, glad to hear of it, and gave Gamble an account of the attack at Bova Marina, and the destruction of the road convoys. "All the rough dirt tracks cross the mountains to shorten their journeys strike the main coast road at Monasterace, still. I assume you're rejoining Charlton?"

"Aye, sir," Gamble agreed.

"Then I wonder if anyone assigned to bombarding Monasterace back in the Spring kept their notes on the place," Lewrie said, "for that seems the best place to hit. Our spies and informants were not asked to smoak the place out, since I, and the Army, weren't going to land troops there. Hell, I just may take all my ships to sea and cruise off the place, just t'put the fear o' God in 'em!"

"Once back with the squadron, I'll ask, sir," Gamble promised. "By the by, I ran into one of your ships on my way here."

"*Coromandel*," Lewrie stated.

"Aye, sir," Gamble said with a laugh. "Rather an embarrassment, that. We espied her at about fifteen miles, and once we were in signalling distance, we made our number to her, she put up hers, but she's not listed in my latest book, so we thought we were up against a French two-decker seventy-four, hah hah! I was ready to haul wind and flee, even after she hoisted a Union Jack. But then, *she* turns away, as if my little sloop is a danger! But, after we hoisted our National Colours, she came back on course, and I closed her to speak her."

"And how'd that go?" Lewrie asked.

"Her commanding officer is a little terror, sir," Gamble said. "Imagine, he was angry with me for giving him such a fright! Well, I put him in his place, right smartly, and told him if he *was* a part of your squadron, he was sailing the wrong way about. He said that he was searching for a missing boat?"

That made Lewrie smile, and relate the details of that latest incident. "And had he found it, yet?" Lewrie asked.

"No, he was still casting about for it, sir," Gamble laughed, "and I'd not seen hide or hair of it, either. Lord, how *does* one lose a whole barge?"

"Through a wee, sly bit of a prank played on him by his crew," Lewrie told him, explaining the mood he'd seen aboard. "And, upon that head, I've about made my mind up to exchanging him for one of my officers, before a real mutiny breaks out. I've a letter to Admiral Charlton, and I'd much admire did you bear it to him when you join the squadron."

"Is he really that bad, sir?" Gamble had to ask, a brow up in wonder. "I've *seen* that sort of attitude towards our sailors before, but only among new-come Midshipmen still wet behind their ears. After a time aboard any decently run ship, *most* discover the real value of our men, no matter how they entered the Navy. This Dickson fellow sounds like the haughtiest sort of aristocrat. From a noble family, or a rich one, is he?"

"I don't know much about his background," Lewrie told him, surprised some by Gamble's statement, for when they had served together in the *Proteus* frigate, D'arcy Gamble's background, and family, was of the best of well-to-do landed gentry, though by the time that Lewrie got him as a Midshipman, Gamble had been in the Navy for several years, and had had that top-lofty air knocked out of him, if indeed he had ever felt that way about the lower classes.

"If you do intend to exchange him, sir," Gamble said, after requesting a refill of his tea and ginger beer, "one hopes that an exposure to *your* way of commanding a ship, and its men, will make an improvement in his nature. Oh, well hallo, puss!"

Chalky, bored by the lack of seabirds alighting on the stern gallery railings, had come to the settee and hopped up to greet the new arrival.

"That's Chalky, do you recall him?" Lewrie asked.

"Oh aye, sir, him and your other, the black and white one. What was his name?" Gamble said, essaying a pet on Chalky's head, to which the cat submitted.

"Toulon, where I got him," Lewrie said.

"What I remember most, sir, was the Marines' pet mongoose, Private Cocky," Gamble reminisced happily. "He was better than a terrier or any cat when it came to ratting. It damned near emptied the bread room of 'millers,' and left the Midshipman cockpit with none to eat on the sly. We learned to never wager against Private Cocky!"

"Speaking of victuals, sir," Lewrie offered, "would you care to dine aboard? My cook is a marvel."

"I fear not, sir, but thank you for the invitation," Commander Gamble said. "I just popped in to give you the latest information on your bridge, and must get back with the squadron. Oh, I quite forgot. North of the bridge, round Eufemia Lamezia, there's quite a backlog of supply convoys, so much so that they're running some of them as far as Catanzaro, on the south coast. It's a much longer route, but the road's better. An attack there might prove productive, if I may suggest, sir."

"How'd you learn that, sir?" Lewrie asked, enthusing.

"All rather 'under the rose,' sir," Gamble told him, leaning forward and sounding conspiratorial. "We overhauled a fishing boat 'tween there and Pizzo, a boat that seemed as if they *wished* to be caught and made prize.

There was a fellow aboard who had a little English, and he told us of it, via some fellow named Silvestri, to pass on to someone named Quill? All very mysterious."

"I know both of them," Lewrie told him, filling Gamble in on the local espionage and information arrangement. "I shall pass that news on to Mister Quill in Messina, instanter."

"Well then, I'm glad it did not completely slip my mind, sir," Gamble said with a wee laugh as he shifted about to rise. "I must be off, sir, but I hope to accept your invitation to dine some time in the future. And I must say, I have had your cool tea before, on a rare occasion, but somehow it tastes even better this time."

"A fortunate accident, that," Lewrie told him as he got to his feet to escort Gamble to the deck. "There wasn't enough tea when I had to go ashore at Locri and Siderno, so Deavers topped it off with some ginger beer in my wood canteen."

"Aha!" Gamble said as he clapped his hat on his head, "I've had my stewards brew cool tea for me, but I haven't seen ginger beer in ages, more's the pity.

"Remember this, sir?" Gamble said, lifting his sword off his hip. It was a rather plain smallsword with a brass hand guard over a wire-wrapped hilt and a lion's head pommel, in a black leather scabbard with worn brass throat and drag. "The night of the fight we had with the *l'Uranie* frigate off Cape Town? You came to me with several dead French officers' swords and said, 'Choose,' when you made me an Acting-Lieutenant after Mister Catterall was killed."

"My word, you still wear it?" Lewrie marvelled. "I'd have thought that your family would have bought a better one once you were confirmed."

"Oh, they did, sir, damned near as grand as a presentation blade, rather embarrassing, really, for it's much too fancy. But, I have always preferred this one, sir. Cherished it, in point of fact. For the moment that made me."

"Then, may you wear it for a long time, Commander Gamble, and let it carry you to your Captaincy and beyond," Lewrie told him in all sincerity.

"Thank you for that, sir," Gamble said in return, then cleared his throat, as did Lewrie, for it was perhaps too sentimental a moment for English gentlemen to discuss, or even admit to. "I suppose that I should be going."

"Bide long enough to allow my people to gather up their letters ready to go, along with mine here, Commander Gamble," Lewrie said. "Dasher,

go pass word a mail sack's departing ship, then round up an empty bisquit bag for them to put their letters in."

"Aye, sir!" Dasher said, running out to the quarterdeck like a bolt of
lightning.

"Ehm . . . you keep rabbits in your cabins, sir?" Gamble asked, spotting the wood cage, and Harriet.

"The lad's pet," Lewrie explained, grinning shyly, "Better it's kept in
here than in the manger, where it'd be mistaken for an *eatin'* rabbit. And
it gives Chalky something live to pester."

Once all outgoing mail had been gathered up, the side-party and the
Bosun re-formed. To the trills of the silver calls, Commander Gamble
left the ship as all hands on deck doffed their hats to him. Lewrie stood in
the open entry-port, leaning out and looking down to bid Gamble a fond
farewell.

"Vaya con Dios!" he called to the departing boat. *"Arrividerci,* and fare
thee well! *Bonne chance,* and *Dosvidanya* for good measure!"

" 'Ere, whas 'e goin' on h'about, den?" a sailor from the side-party
asked his mate.

"Ya got me, Tom," the other whispered back. "Off'cers, 'ey allus gotta
show orf d'eir eddy-cation."

After Gamble had left the ship, even as that worthy was climbing the
boarding battens of his own ship, Lewrie was penning a note to Mr. Quill,
summoning a Midshipman, and when one arrived, bade him take one of
the boats and deliver it to the Army camp for relaying to Messina.

Then, he went to the chart space on the larboard side of the quarterdeck to delve into the many sea charts and land maps stored there, looking for ones that depicted Saint Eufemia Bay, hoping that a landing near
Eufemia Lamezia might prove fruitful, before the French finally got the
bridge repaired sturdy enough to use again.

When last Lewrie had talked with Quill, mention *had* been made about
an attack on Monasterace Marina, where supply convoys converged after
crossing the mountains, down to the easier coastal plain and a decent road
near the shore. But, even Quill had never thought to gather detailed information about Monasterace, as Lewrie had told Gamble. That had been

someone else's pigeon, and not a landing, but a bombardment from the sea. Either place, Monasterace or Eufemia Lamezia, might suit, but, with *Don* Julio off on some of his own dastardly doings, and in a pet that Lewrie and Quill had done something without him, even put an agent in Calabria that he didn't have total control over, no amount of golden guineas would convince one of *Don* Julio's under-bosses to go scout either place for them. Julio Caesare's wrath might be more of a risk than being nabbed by the French!

Lewrie used a magnifying glass, poring closely along the shoreline on the pertinent sea chart, noting the estimated water depths near the town of Eufemia Lamezia, but the chart didn't tell him much, for it was a copy of an Italian-made chart done only God knew how long before, copied and re-copied. There was ocean in white, the land and beaches rendered in tan, with the coast road drawn in black, the town and the hills roundabout rather sketchy as to topography and heights, indicated by a series of lines, followed by a great blank space leading inland, with another set of prominent hills and peaks beyond. In that great blank gap there might as well have been a caution that "here be dragons," for what could not be plainly seen from sea level and the deck of a ship simply didn't matter to mariners.

The landsman's map of the area—also a copy of an Italian map—was drawn with north at the *bottom*, for God's sake! Topography was indicated by inverted Vees, the more closely clustered the steeper the land, he imagined, and the town and its port was rendered more like a gridded rectangle, with churches and wayside shrines marked by little crosses. If he wanted to read the labels attached to anything on the map, he had to spin it round 180 degrees! There *seemed* to be beaches either side of the harbour entrance, but, above one of them was a steep hill of some kind, and above the other was an enigmatic square done in heavy black ink; a fort, he wondered?

Damn it to Hell! Lewrie groaned to himself, tossing the magnifying glass atop the slanted chart table, and standing up from a too-long crouch; *This place needs scoutin', too, else we'll be sittin' on our numb arses 'til* next *Epiphany!*

And, Alan Lewrie, it must here be noted, was not a man to sit idle for *too* long!

He stepped out of the chart space to the quarterdeck, placing his hands in the small of his back and arching, wondering if a long life at sea was getting to his bones, at last, as it seemed to do in officers he'd known who were near his present age.

"Oh Lord, will you look at that!" Midshipman Gadsden who was reluctantly standing Harbour Watch instead of one of the younkers who'd refused to be bullied into doing it, said in amusement. "Boat ahoy, hah hah!"

Lewrie leaned over the larboard bulwarks to see what the Mid was guffawing about. "Aha!" he exclaimed. "Our prodigal's come home!"

Coming down the coast from Milazzo was one of that small port's typically scruffy, paint-peeled, un-lacquered fishing boats, with three locals aboard, looking as if it was altering course to approach HMS *Vigilance*. Astern of her, though, was a 29-foot Admiralty barge, on a short tow line; *Coromandel*'s missing boat had been found. She was unmistakable, for unlike the barges of the first three troop transports, *Coromandel*'s barges had been painted with matte-black hulls and grey gunn'ls to lessen the chance that they might be spotted as they rowed inshore laden with troops at night.

"Have you any Italian, Mister Gadsden?" Lewrie asked.

"*Un poco*, sir," Gadsden replied. "Very little at all. I could send for Mister Bingley. He's caught on to it rather well."

"Aye, do so, sir," Lewrie bade, "and *wave* them alongside, if you have to. I think a reward's in order."

Lewrie went to his cabins, unlocked one of his desk drawers, and got out his wash-leather coin purse. There were a few gold guineas in it, silver shillings, and his usual fall-back specie for interaction with the locals, silver six-pence, along with wadded up paper money, which everyone suspected was a governmental sham, and stuff that foreigners would have nothing to do with. He sorted out ten shillings, stuck them in a slop-trouser pocket, and put the coin purse back in the drawer, locking it again.

"*Signore*, ehm . . . *andiamo!*" Gadsden was shouting overside when Lewrie came back to the deck. "*Entrare*, rather? Ah, Bingley! Tell 'em to come alongside, there's a good fellow."

Midshipman Bingley was one of *Vigilance*'s older Mids, over twenty years in age, a rather stout and full-faced fellow who so far had not done much to distinguish himself with Lewrie and the other officers. He could sling the lingo, though, with a beguiling smile.

"*Andiamo lato, signores! Congratulazione! Meraviglioso! Andiamo* and *ricevere mancia competente!*" Bingley shouted to the boatmen, then turned to

Lewrie. "Gadsden said I should tell them there would be a reward, is that alright, sir?"

"Aye," Lewrie agreed. "Silver shillings for all."

"Signores! Inglese d'argento . . . uh, *scellinos!"* he shouted.

The scruffy local fishing boat came alongside the larboard mainmast chains, bows on to the platform, and one of the fishermen hauled the barge's tow line up 'til the barge was nuzzling their boat's transom.

"Here, Mister Gadsden," Lewrie said, handing over a stack of coins, "three shillings apiece for them, and tell 'em the other's for their wine. And secure that line to the shroud dead eyes. We do *not* want t'lose that barge, again!"

"Aye, sir!" Gadsden said, pocketing the coins for safekeeping as he went down the battens and man-ropes.

"Grazie!" Lewrie shouted down. *"Molto grazie, signores!"*

Once Midshipman Gadsden distributed the coins, they all pulled off their hats or head coverings and bobbed their thanks, trying to hug Gadsden in joy. Once he got free of their clutches, they began to shove off, rowing off a few yards to set a much-patched lateen sail still, looking over their shoulders and waving and babbling gratitude.

"I couldn't understand much of what they were saying, sir, but I did get the impression that the barge was a gift from someone named *Don* Julio? They thought it a fine boat, but they would not dream of keeping her for themselves, I take it."

"Aye, *Don* Julio Caesare has that effect on people," Lewrie told Gadsden with a wry expression.

And I can't wait t'see the look on Lieutenant Dickson's phyz when he returns to port, Lewrie thought, looking over the side and gloating to note that there were *ten* oars in the barge, not eight, as he had expected; *If he returns to port, that is!*

CHAPTER TWENTY-FIVE

Oh, God," Lt. Dickson said with a groan, "Just damn it to Hell," as *Coromandel* stood into Milazzo's anchorage two days later and espied their missing barge tied up alongside the Army's beachfront pier.

They had quartered the seas from the extreme eastern tip of Sicily almost within sight of Milazzo, and as far north as the Aeolian Isles, half of each watch division aloft in the tops or the cross-trees with their eyes peeled for anything afloat, and *Coromandel*'s crew had taken almost fiendish delight, it seemed to Dickson, to cry "ho!" over every breaching pod of dolphins, the rare basking whale, or shark fin that cut the water in chase of balling, swirling small fish that made churning eddies on the surface.

His crew! They were going about their duties as well as could be expected, brailing up courses, lowering stays'ls, and reducing the size of the top'ls so *Coromandel* could round up into the wind before letting go the bower anchor. But, to Dickson, they were performing those duties in a cheeky manner, glancing forward over the bows, and pointing out the missing barge to their mates, taking cruel amusement in their commander's dismay, the churlish bastards! Dickson wished that he could charge the lot of them with mute insubordination and have them bound to upright hatch gratings and given two dozen lashes each! By *God* he'd make them howl like gut-shot *dogs*!

The next'un who looks aft at me and grins, and I'll . . . ! he furiously thought, if only to stave off his dread of what awaited him from Captain Sir bloody Alan Lewrie, bloody Baronet after his fruitless, nigh frantic search.

"Well, there's nigh two hundred fifty pounds we won't be dunned for!" Sub-Lt. Clough had the nerve to say aloud, with a titter.

"You'll stop your gob and attend to your duties, sir!" Dickson snapped. "And Kinsey. Stand by with the kedge anchor. We will come to anchor neatly, or I'll know why not!"

"Aye, sir," Midshipman Kinsey replied.

Dickson continued his quiet fuming, back stiff, hands clasped in the small of his back, rocking on the balls of his feet, feeling a *tad* of relief that the lost barge *had* been found. The Counsellor of The Cheque was remorseless when it came to retrieving Admiralty funds. He himself knew of a fellow appointed Commander into a prize shortly before the Peace of Amiens in 1802. He'd been a promising officer, had a doting Captain and a Vice-Admiral of the Blue, both relatives, who'd plucked him from the flagship's wardroom and given him a plum command. It had lasted six months before the Peace, and then Admiralty had not confirmed his advancement, and it had damned near been the ruin of him, for the Counsellor of The Cheque ordered him to return the difference in pay, casting him upon the mercy of his creditors, who'd had none, and ended with a spell in debtors' prison before one of his aunts had paid the difference and cleared his arrears.

Coromandel ghosted past HMS *Vigilance,* bound inshore to join the other troop transports anchored nearer the beach, and Dickson stared straight ahead, not daring to even glance over at the 64-gunner, for fear of seeing Captain Lewrie. But he had a tingling at the back of his neck that told him he was being watched most closely, much like the old adage of feeling a rabbit running over his grave!

"'Bout here, sir," the Acting Sailing Master opined as to the proper place to round up and let go the bower.

"Very well," Dickson replied with a *harumph.* "Helm hard down, Quartermasters! Fetch her right up to the wind. Kinsey, let go the kedge and let the hawser run free! Ready, bow party!"

No one will fault me on seamanship! he assured himself; *And if these dolts try to make me look bad . . . !*

No one did, and *Coromandel* slowly swung up into the eyes of the wind, brought to a crawl by the drag of the kedge hawser rumbling out the aft hawse hole, and the reefed tops'ls, now pressed flat aback to the masts. The jibs still standing began to flutter as their angle to the wind became too acute, streaming down the centerline of the ship.

"No bite t'th' helm, sir," a Quartermaster announced, whirling the wheel back and forth with ease to show the lack of pressure.

"Let go the bower!" Dickson shouted forward, and there came a great splash as the anchor went overside, dropped from the larboard cathead beam, and another hawser cable rumbled, as the ship came to a full stop and began to make an infinitesimal leeway.

"Come on, *bite*, damn ye," the Acting Sailing Master hissed as *Coromandel*'s sternway made chuckling sounds round the impotent rudder.

At last, there was a jerk and a snub as the bower dug into the harbour bed, and the run of the anchor cable was controlled to allow at least a four-to-one scope. Dickson turned about and glared at Midshipman Kinsey to signal him to take up the long slack of the kedge cable. Round and round the aft capstan sailors tramped, shortening the scope 'til *Coromandel* lay near abeam the wind, almost parallel to the shoreline, and was at last at a secure rest, with all her sails brailed up in harbour gaskets, and her jibs handed and stowed.

"Ehm . . . *Vigilance* is showing a signal, sir," Clough announced. "Our number and . . . Captain Repair On Board."

"Very well, I shall, dress," Dickson said, as if it was of no matter. "Haul a boat up 'neath the starboard main chains for me."

Before going aft to his cabins, he had to cough to clear his throat, for it suddenly felt very dry.

It did not help Dickson's fretful mood to know that he was being stared at by his crew as he went down into his boat to be rowed over to *Vigilance*. Straight, dumb-show faces would, he was mortal-certain, break out into gleeful smiles as soon as he quit the deck. Worse for his nerves was the silent attention paid to his arrival by the crew of the flagship as his boat came alongside, dozens and dozens of sailors and Marines peering down from the sail-tending gangways as sobre and stiff as men would be when summoned to witness punishment. It was as if everyone aboard *Vigilance* already knew his fate. So, it was not the exertion of scaling the ship's side that brought him to the deck and entry-port red-faced and sweaty.

"Lieutenant Dickson of *Coromandel*, come aboard as ordered," he said to the officer on deck who gravely doffed his hat to him with all the cheer of a mourner at a funeral to a widower. "Farley, First Officer. The Captain is aft in his cabins, Mister Dickson. If you will follow me?"

All Dickson could do was swallow and nod.

The Marine sentry stamped his boots and musket butt to announce their arrival, the door was opened, and Dickson tucked his elegant custom-made bicorne under one arm and entered.

Dickson got a brief impression of wealth and style to the cabin furnishings; linseeded overhead deck beams, polished brass or pewter lanthorns and candle stands, fine Axminster or Turkey carpets atop the black and white deck chequered canvas, rich red cushions on the lazarette storage cabinets beneath the transom sash windows and on the settee and chair grouping to starboard set round a low brass tray-table.

In the centre of the tableau stood a highly polished oak desk with a single chair before it. Atop it sat a white cat mottled with grey splotches, which stared at him unblinking, and behind the desk stood Captain Lewrie, hands in the small of his back . . . waiting. It put Dickson in mind of a court-martial, with only his own sword on the desk top lacking, point towards him in condemnation.

"Reporting aboard as ordered, sir," Dickson said, wishing for something with which to wet his mouth and throat.

"Sit down, Mister Dickson," Lewrie began, indicating the chair before the desk. "A glass of something?"

"That would be welcome, aye, Sir Alan," Dickson said.

"An ale for each of us, Deavers," Lewrie ordered, and two tall mugs of beer were fetched from a keg somewhere in the dining coach, and Dickson could not help turning round in his chair to see, noting a woman's portrait on the forward bulkhead, an incredibly fetching young woman, and it was all he could do to tear his eyes away from the portrait.

The mug was placed on the desk in front of him and Dickson took a deep, refreshing draught, grateful for the wetness.

Quite the dandy prat, ain't ye, Lewrie thought as he beheld Lt. Dickson, for the fellow had taken time to don his best-dress uniform, with a silk shirt on under a snow-white waist-coat, with a pressed neck-stock round his throat, un-stained breeches, and well-blacked Hessian boots with gilt lace trim and tassels. And on his hip, Dickson sported an ornately gilt smallsword worth at least £50, at a rough guess.

"You lads can go skylark on deck for a while," Lewrie idly said to his cabin servants, and they trooped out to the quarterdeck, which almost made Dickson choke on his swallow of beer. He set the mug on the desk and moved his hands to his lap.

"Now, sir," Lewrie said, setting aside his own mug, and giving the cat a stroking. "You really made a muck of things, sir. Losing a boat? Some fishermen from Milazzo brought her in, else you would be out a pretty penny for her loss."

"Sir, I . . ." Dickson began. "Sir Alan, rather . . ."

"I don't quite know how your crew did it, Dickson, but they got the missing oars in the barge before they let it slip free, so you've all ten back, to boot."

"Sir, I am saddled with the absolute dregs of the receiving ships at Portsmouth," Dickson replied with some heat. "Drunks, idlers, whiners, and scapegraces . . . gaol sweepings, petty criminals, sneaks, and . . ."

"I told you once, it's a poor workman blames his tools, sir," Lewrie cut him off sternly. "But, it's an arrogant, disdainful fool who'll bully, browbeat, and *lash* his crew to competence, if only for abject fear of punishment. Recall Pigot and the *Hermione* frigate?"

"Sir, I . . ." Dickson tried to say.

"I expect if I looked through your punishment book I'd find a litany of defaulters lashed," Lewrie went on. "I've served under many Captains, some good, some bad, and one or two bloody awful, but in all that time, I've never met one who went out of his way to turn his crew into resentful skulkers. I don't know who you had as examples who taught you to despise your junior officers, *and* every man and boy aboard, or whether you came into the Navy with that top-lofty attitude, but the only thing that I can see that you've accomplished so far is to lose every shred of respect from your men by your harshness, and your dismissive sneers."

"Sir, I must protest . . . !"

"Protest all you like, Mister Dickson," Lewrie coldly shot back. "A fine way to fuck up your first shot at command, I must say! There was an Italian writer—how apt for us—who wrote advice for budding rulers that it's better to be feared than loved, but you've taken that to a sublimely ridiculous extreme. I've found that respect from sailors must be earned, not demanded, and to gain that, one must *show* respect for one's men, for what they know, and instruct them if they don't yet know . . . *without* scaring them silly.

"Firm but fair," Lewrie continued, "Recall that 'un? Punish if necessary, but only for true faults. Reward for good behaviour, or their successes. Give them a *reason* to be proud of themselves, and of their ship, no matter how humble her role will be."

Lt. Dickson had gone even redder in the face, looking as if his neckstock was strangling him, with his head cocked back to look down his nose, nostrils flaring in controlled rage to be berated so.

No, he ain't gettin' it, but he will, Lewrie assured himself.

"You brought me an imperfect instrument, Mister Dickson," Lewrie told him. "I badly need well-organised transport ships with which to stage raids over on the mainland, but *Coromandel* isn't up to my standards yet, and I have serious doubts that you're the man to improve her."

"You . . . you would take away my *command*, sir?" Dickson gasped, letting some of his rage come to light. "You *can't*! It simply . . . !"

"I can, and I shall, Mister Dickson," Lewrie harshly told him. "I *must*, for I have no belief that you would be able to turn things round. You've poisoned the well. My Second Officer, Mister Rutland, will replace you aboard *Coromandel*, and you will exchange with him and come aboard *Vigilance*. What is the date of your commission?"

Dickson had gone slack-jawed, utterly stupefied, and stumbled out the date, wondering why he had first thought that Lewrie's eyes were merry blue, for they had gone frosty, Arctic grey, and flinty.

"That will make you Fourth Lieutenant here, sir," Lewrie told him. "My current Fourth Officer, Mister Grace, predates you by some five months."

"It simply isn't *done*, sir, I protest!" Dickson yelped. "I will write Admiralty . . . !"

"You're free to do so, sir," Lewrie went on. "I strongly urge you, sir, to watch and learn how my officers and Midshipmen deal with our people. Use of the 'cat' is rare aboard *Vigilance*, and everyone, Commission Officer to ship's boys, have come to rub together as well as anyone can expect, by now. I'd even go so far as to say that she is a *happy* ship, but that's taken diligence, hard work, and 'firm but fair' discipline, leavened with *respect*. There are lessons that you should take to heart, Mister Dickson, and I conjure you to do so."

"Sir, I . . ." Dickson said, gulping, gone cold inside.

"Make the most of this, sir, see it as an opportunity," Lewrie said. "But I must warn you, sir, that I will not have *Coromandel*'s ways brought aboard *Vigilance*. Understand me?"

"Aye, sir," Dickson managed to croak.

"Good," Lewrie said with a nod of his head. "Now. You may return to *Coromandel* and pack your dunnage. Mister Rutland will be boarding in an hour or so. He will not read himself in formally, but the both of you will, with all good grace, summon your crew and announce that you are exchanging. That will be all, Mister Dickson. You may go."

Dickson sat for a moment more, too numbed to stand, or speak in his defence, just nod his head, eyes un-focussed, before he drew in a deep breath, placed his hands on his knees, and levered himself to his feet. He remembered his high-born manners and bowed from the waist, then turned to clump to the great-cabin door, not daring to look back, and lost in what felt like a fever dream.

Lewrie picked up his mug and took a deep draught of beer, for his own throat was as dry as a desert. "You've the one chance to improve yourself, Dickson," he muttered to the far cabin entrance, now shut, "and if you fuck up this one, then God help you."

CHAPTER TWENTY-SIX

I think we should go to sea," Lewrie told his assembled officers over a rare breakfast in his cabins, which raised some hearty cheers in agreement.

"We've a new place to raid, sir?" Lt. Grace asked.

"No, but Mister Quill is gathering intelligence for us on two promising places," Lewrie told him. "Monasterace, where all of the convoys converge after crossing the mountains, and Eufemia Lamezia, up above our bridge, where the road convoys diverge from the main coast road, and there's a jam-up. Commander Gamble in *Coquette* brought news about how far along the French repairs on our bridge are going, and I wish to go get some much-needed live gunnery practice. There will be opposition, this time," Lewrie promised.

"Enemy ships, sir?" Lt. Greenleaf hopefully brayed. "Huzzah!"

"Enemy artillery, actually, Mister Greenleaf," Lewrie said with a shrug. "A mixed battery of field pieces and howitzers firing explosive shells. Those guns, the French engineers, and their latest efforts should be swatted away t'keep the bastards honest."

"Except for three or four water kegs that need re-filling, the ship is ready in all respects, sir," Lt. Farley announced. "If we can forgo dry-fire drill on the guns this morning, I can have us bung full before Noon, sir."

"Fruit, sir," Grace was quick to suggest. "If we're out several days, or a fortnight, oranges and grapes would be welcome with our people."

"Then speak with the Purser as soon as you can today, sir, and let's think about enough fresh loaf bread for at least two days. That *ciabatta* doesn't spoil as quickly as most," Lewrie added to the list. "Aye, weather and wind permittin', let's stand ready to make sail by Noon tomorrow."

"I will volunteer to sail to Milazzo, sir," Lt. Grace quickly offered. "Take the Purser along to the town market, and the bakers? The sutlers round the Army camp won't have enough ready made."

"And might that involve seeing the baker's fetching young daughter, Grace?" Lt. Greenleaf teased. "She *is* a rare beauty."

"Well," was all that Grace could say, blushing and ducking.

"Dickson, I'll thank you to see to the watering party," Farley said, looking down the table at their newest.

"And when you do go ashore, Mister Dickson, I'd thank you to go see Colonel Tarrant," Lewrie added to Dickson's duties. "We'll be having a look into Eufemia Lamezia as a possible place to raid, and I'd think that an officer from the Ninety-Fourth should come along. You'll extend the invitation, and inform the Colonel that we will be putting to sea by Noon tomorrow.

"And, before you do that," Lewrie went on, "I must get a letter off to Mister Quill in Messina, telling him that we'll be away for a time, so he doesn't waste a ride out here expecting a conference to relate anything he's learned so far. You can hand Colonel Tarrant my note, and he'll see it gets off."

"Aye, sir," Dickson replied, practically the first thing that he had said since sitting down to his pork chop and eggs.

Seven Bells chimed far up forward at the forecastle belfry to mark half past seven of the morning, presaging the start of the Forenoon Watch, and its chores.

"If anyone's still hungry, too damned bad," Lewrie jested as he pulled off his napkin and tossed it aside, "there's some toast left in the bread barge, but let's be about the day's duties, what, sirs?"

With a scraping of chair legs, they rose from the table as Lewrie rose, gathered their hats from the sideboard, and made their way to the cabin doors.

"Ah, Mister Farley, bide a moment," Lewrie said.

"Aye, sir?" the First Officer said, a brow up in fret that some detail had been missed.

"How's our newest fitting in?" Lewrie asked once the others had left.

"Hmm, that's rather hard to say, sir," Farley answered, after a long moment. "Half the time, one hardly knows he's here. He keeps to himself, doesn't say much, and with no watches to stand whilst we're in harbour, there's no way for me to assess his seamanship. He plays a recorder, sir, a rather nice one. Quite talented at it, if I am any judge. Our sing-alongs in our mess already had Greenleaf's violin, and my poor strummings on my mandolin, so Dickson's a welcome addition, in that regard."

"What of his interactions with our people?" Lewrie asked, more to the meat of it.

"Hmm, subdued, I'd say, sir," Lt. Farley told him. "He doesn't waste time with useless orders and such, but he doesn't slouch about or neglect anything, either. Puts me more in mind of Mister Rutland and all his eternal gloom, sir!" Farley added with a laugh.

"Well, I s'pose that's the best we can expect straightaway," Lewrie said with a shrug. "He'll either fit in or he won't. Once we get to sea, we'll learn more about him. Thank you, Mister Farley, you may go about your duties."

"Aye, sir, and thank you for a tasty breakfast," Farley said, bowing his way out.

"Chalky, get off the table," Lewrie snapped, clapping his hands to deter the cat from licking every plate for meat scraps, egg, and hashed potato bits. "You've *had* your share and more!"

And when Dasher and Turnbow tried to gather up the plates, the cat *stood* in the middle of one plate, licking like mad to get all that he could before being picked up and set aside, or shooed off.

"You're such a glutton," Lewrie sighed, exasperated, as Chalky made off with a pork chop bone and dashed beneath the starboard side settee with it.

When Lt. Dickson brought the last full water butt alongside to be hoisted aboard in slings, he also fetched Captain Bromhead of the 94th, one of the Line Company officers who had been with the regiment the longest, and had taken part in all their landings. Space was made for him in the officers' wardroom, in the slightly larger dog-box cabin right aft on the starboard side, which would be a Captain's when *Vigilance* carried a First Rate Commodore or Rear-Admiral. He would dine with Lewrie, though, for suppers, but would take the bulk of his meals with the ship's officers.

Late in the afternoon, round the start of the First Dog Watch, Lt. Grace returned from Milazzo with a heaping boatload of bread and fat sacks of fruit, including lemons that some of the ship's sailors used to liven their grog. The Purser, Mr. Blundell, was aggrieved by the extra expense for everything, especially so since he could not resell the bread to the hands, but had to issue it in lieu of dry, hard ship's bisquit. At least he could sell the oranges and lemons for tuppence apiece, but he'd barely break even. Ever since the Army had built their encampment, and the squadron had made the bay their anchorage, their joint demands upon local produce and livestock had driven prices higher, despite what warnings *Don* Julio Caesare had given them about price-gouging.

"And is the baker's daughter as pretty as they said, Grace?" Lt. Farley teased as Grace gained the deck.

"Ravishing, sir," Grace said with a wide smile, "though her father has an eagle eye over her, and her virtue. Much like all his pastries . . . look, but don't touch!"

"Unless you're buying, hey?" Greenleaf said, smirking.

"The girl is so fetching, one is mightily tempted to court and marry, sir," Grace told him.

"The Navy's not fond of marriage," Lt. Dickson ventured to say, "especially for junior officers. I was surprised to hear that Mister Rutland is married."

"Aye, married with children, and nought beyond his Navy pay," Greenleaf told him, "poor Devil. It's no wonder he's so glum."

"Anyone caught your fancy back home, Dickson?" Farley asked him, and they all perked up their ears to learn something personal about their taciturn newcomer.

"Oh no, no one special yet," Dickson replied with a shake of his head. "Young ladies of good family in my neighbourhood have eyes on 'salt free' beaus," he attempted to jape, sounding almost wistful and open for a moment, then caught himself and turned his attention to a sling load of fruit rising over the bulwarks.

"That'll be the last lot," Grace said, looking over the side at his barge below the larboard main chains. "You lads secure, and come up, once the boat's ready for towing in the morning."

"You've a working-party to stow it all, Mister Blundell?" the First Officer asked the Purser.

"Aye, I have," the Purser replied, still grumbling over what it had cost him.

"Then we're free to go below and tap our keg of ale," Farley suggested. "Liquor our boots for sailing in the morning, what?"

"Aye, to start with," Greenleaf laughed, "followed by wine *and* a bowl of punch, if I've a say in it. Come on, Dickson. Let us see what contribution to the punch you will make."

"Would a pint of gin do?" Dickson said with the first grin he had essayed since coming aboard.

"It'd do just topping!" Greenleaf hooted.

Mid-afternoon the following day found HMS *Vigilance* out at sea under all plain sail, a few miles offshore of the site of their first raid, the small port of Tropea, and bound for Pizzo and beyond, for the bridge they had shot to pieces.

The ship had not yet been called to Quarters, but Dickson, trying to appear diligent, was already below on the lower gun-deck among the heavy 24-pounders, where he would direct their firing as Fourth Officer. An elder Quarter-Gunner in charge of several guns together was strolling along his charges, tugging at run-out and recoil tackle ropes, checking the bowsings that held the barrels snug to the hull.

"There's enough swab-water in the tubs?" Dickson asked him.

"Cummins, sir," the fellow replied, "Quarter-Gunner," he added, touching his brow by way of a salute. "You're new to th' ship, so's I expect you'll be wantin' t'learn people's names an' all. Aye, Mister Dickson, ev'ry tub's full, th' slow-match fuse is laid by handy, an' th' ready shot for *my* guns is rolled for proper roundness. I checked 'em meself."

"What are these notches in the breeching rings?" Dickson asked, intrigued, and wondering if they were intentional.

"Rough sights, sir, same as on the muzzles," Cummins said with a cackle. "Capum Lewrie's high on accurate gunnery, an' had us cut th' notches soon's he come aboard. We knocked down an old stone fort at one place, blew down a stone bridge up where we're goin', once, an' back in th' Spring, shot th' Bejeesus out of a French infantry regiment nigh a whole *mile* away! I hear tell in his last ship, him an' his squadron took on four big frigates, an' his gunners were puttin' shot right into French gun-ports, at half a full cable, not close aboard! Chaw or pipe tobacco for the best crews, out o' his own pocket, too. Put us to it e'en afore we got t'Malta."

"Surely, you exaggerate, uh Cummins," Dickson said.

"Just you wait 'til these brutes light off, sir," Cummins said in boast. "We might be a trifle rusty, laid up in port so long 'tween raids an' all, but, once we get our eyes in, you'll be seein' a thing t'see, sir!"

"Right ye are, an' amen t'that," a gun-captain chimed in from a mess table on the larboard side.

Dickson looked round and took note that sailors were gathered at the mess tables, which were still lowered, not strapped to the overhead out of the way of gun crews when Quarters was announced. He reckoned that not all the off-watch hands idling below were members of the gun crews, but all down the ship's starboard side, younger hands were listening to slightly older men, near the massive 24-pounders they likely served, talking low but boastful, rubbing horny hands in anticipation of action, and grinning evilly over what they'd do to the French.

"These men to starboard . . ." Dickson asked the Quarter-Gunner.

"Ready an' willin', sir," Cummins told him with a gap-toothed grin. "They knows we're goin' t'shoot up that bridge we knocked down last time, that the Frogs have batteries there, now, and we'll be closin' th' coast starb'd side to, an' they wanna be th' first t'run out and engage."

"Lord, sir," a young gunner piped up, "ain't no way t'keep anythin' secret 'board ship. It's clear as day wot we're goin' t'do."

"I see," Dickson said, disguising his amazement. *His* sailors hadn't been eager about *anything*, or had the *wits* to anticipate and make preparations beforehand. He put it down to the difference between a warship and an un-armed transport, but . . . there was something surprisingly different about *Vigilance*.

Dickson also felt hundreds of eyes boring into the nape of his neck, of being assessed. No one who mattered was watching him being diligent, and he felt like an interloper, so he strolled back aft to the ladderway to the upper gun-deck, and fresh air, conducting only a cursory inspection of guns, gun tools, and tackle.

Once there, he noted that each of the starboard 18-pounders on the upper gun-deck was halfway manned, as well, and men were tinkering with their charges, lounging with their elbows resting on the sun-warm barrels, or sprawled on the oak decks close by, just waiting for the first rattles of the Long Roll from the Marine drummer, the urgent trill of Bosun's calls.

He mounted to the quarterdeck for a look-see at the Calabrian coast which was about eight miles off, nodding greetings to Lt. Grace, who had the watch.

"Been below?" Grace asked as Dickson stood by the bulwarks for a better view outboard.

"All's well, and everyone's eager," Dickson told him. "Just had a look-round to see if everything's in order."

"It will be," Grace assured him. "Captain Lewrie's a stickler for good gunnery. Powder smoke is like a fine *cigarro* to him! He's a real fighter, and our people know it by now. Do we come to anchor and let the crews fire one at a time, there'll be free tobacco and a full measure of rum for those who shoot best, too."

"Where did he get the idea for cutting sights on the guns?" Lt. Dickson asked. "I never heard the like."

"Oh, he heard of another Captain who . . ." Grace began to say, but was interrupted by Lewrie's arrival on the quarterdeck from his cabins. "Captain's on deck!" Grace announced, then crossed over to the lee side of the deck, yielding the windward.

"No no, Mister Grace," Lewrie said. "Stay where you are whilst I have myself a look-see from the starboard side."

Lewrie stood there for a long time with his telescope to one eye, studying the shore as it glided by. When done with that, he peered aloft to the commissioning pendant and its streaming, judging direction and strength of the winds, and the proper set of the sails.

"We're almost level with Pizzo," Lewrie announced at last, "and the bridge isn't far beyond. Haul our wind three points and close the coast, sir. And I'll have the courses brailed up."

"Aye, sir!" Grace snapped, then turned to bawl forward to send hands to sheets and braces, and for topmen to man the course yards.

"About that time, sir?" the Sailing Master, Mr. Wickersham asked jovially as he bestirred himself from a cat-nap in his sea cabin and came onto the quarterdeck.

"Indeed, Mister Wickersham," Lewrie told him. "Hands to the fore chains to toss the leads if you please."

Vigilance's jib-boom and bow-sprit swept round to the right as the yards aloft were re-angled to take the winds more abeam, slowing as the courses were hauled up. Minutes later, the ship was squared away, now ghosting at about five knots and bound inshore.

"Mister Grace," Lewrie finally said. "Sound Beat to Quarters."

Vigilance, which had been gliding along in relative silence, as if hushed and waiting, erupted with sudden noise as the Marine drummer and flautist rattled out the Long Roll and struck up an urgent tune. Bare feet and shod feet thundered on the ladderways leading below, as men ran to their stations for battle. Already, bowsings were being cast loose to allow truck carriages to be hauled to the centreline with the roar and rumble of a cattle stampede, and the hog-like squeal of un-greased wooden wheels and axles. Hundreds of door-slams sounded as deal and canvas partitions were struck down, furniture was carried below out of harm's way, and the gun decks were turned into long alleys bare of any human comforts. Just guns, carriages, and men.

Dickson disappeared below to his station, as did Lt. Grace and Lt. Greenleaf. Lt. Farley came to the quarterdeck to second the Captain and Sailing Master. And bare minutes later, Midshipmen scampered up from below, from both bow and stern, to make their reports to the officers remaining.

"Sir, the ship is at Quarters and ready for action," Lt. Farley solemnly announced.

"Very well," Lewrie said, just as gravely. "Have the guns loaded, open the ports, and run out. Mister Wickersham, your recollection of the coast is still fresh? You can conn us within a quarter-mile like we lay last time?"

"Aye, Captain," Wickersham replied, peering shoreward with his telescope. "You'll wish to anchor?"

"Hah! Not this time, sir, no," Lewrie replied, "I don't wish to give the French gunners a stationary target. We'll cruise by slowly, then turn out to sea, circle round, and do it again 'til we've done as much damage as we can."

"Guns run out, ports open, and ready to open, sir," Lt. Farley reported. "I think I can almost make out the bridge from here, damned if I can't," he added, extending his own glass. "Just round that high point, and it'll be in full view. About two miles away?"

"Hmm, about that, aye, Mister Farley," Wickersham agreed.

"It looks different," Lewrie commented as the high point of land that partially blocked the view slowly inched half a point farther to the right of the ship's bows.

They've been lumbering, Lewrie thought, taking in the sight of steep hills that had been thickly forested when they had come here before. There had been trees on the seaward side of the coast road that almost hid it, either side of the bridge, but now there was a field of stumps and bare earth and rock, and the steep slopes that had forced the road out to the edge of the precipices were just as bare.

"Aha! They've been as busy as a whole tribe of beavers!" Farley joshed as the bridge came fully in sight.

Lewrie spotted crane hoists, either end of what was left of the bridge, with teams of oxen yoked and harnessed to do the heavy hauling. On the north end, just off the stub of stone span that still stood, a large timber dangled from the hoist as if they had caught the French in the process of lowering it down into the ravine. Farther out on the road there was a large timber waggon, also drawn by oxen, loaded with rough-milled wood baulks. And, there was a half-battery of artillery sited on the road, protected by a redan of logs, with two openings for firing. Lewrie imagined that he would see the same arrangement on the south end when it came into view.

"Busy running," the Sailing Master said with a snort of humour.

Indeed, the road from the bridge teemed with workers in their shirt sleeves, tools in their hands and over their shoulders, fleeing in scurrying packs, some shrugging into their uniform jackets, with their shakoes set on their heads at any old angle.

"I see smoke," Lt. Farley warned. "Furnaces for heated shot?"

"We've been in sight long enough for them to do so," Lewrie said, his stomach muscles tensing in dread of red-hot cannon balls smashing into *Vigilance*'s sides, sticking in the dents they would make, and the tarred, painted timbers igniting. His ship could be burned to the waterline, and no amount of stroking on the wash-deck pumps would be of any use.

"I don't think the smoke's coming from the batteries," Lewrie said, half in hope. "No, it's from down in the ravine, under the old bridge." He recalled that Commander Gamble had told him that damage from various bombardments had left piles of broken timber down there, but Lewrie was at a loss as to why the French would set fire to it, except to create a smoke screen too thick for any ship to fire at the bridge. And that didn't make any sense to him, either. That dense a smoke pall would blind the gunners who were there to protect it.

Vigilance swam slowly on, within a mile of the shore by then, and a mile or so short of the bridge and the re-construction work, and the south end of the bridge came into view, a duplicate of the activity on the north end; a log redan for a half-battery of artillery, a crane hoist, various waggons, yoked oxen, and un-harnessed mules and draught horses. Another horde of fleeing workers and French engineers could be seen almost galloping towards the village of Pizzo.

"Pass word below, if you please," Lewrie said, studying the half-battery closest to them, "we will engage the enemy batteries, first."

As he watched, there came a sudden burst of yellow-white powder smoke ashore, followed a second later by the thunder clap of a cannon firing, then the rustling keen of a roundshot approaching the ship.

Lewrie clenched his jaws and compressed his lips as the cannon ball's wail rose in pitch as it neared. *Splash!* went the roundshot as it struck the sea a quarter-mile short of *Vigilance*, throwing up a tall and feathery plume of spray as it plunged into the water.

"Howitzer," he commented. "Plunged straight down, and didn't skip from First Graze."

Boom! as the smouldering fuse in the shot reached the interior powder charge, and the explosive shot blew up deep under water, making a white foam *mound* of disturbance for a second before a thicker, even taller plume of spray shot through with smoke erupted.

"Aye, howitzer," Lewrie said again. "The fuse was cut too long."

They won't make that mistake again, he grimly thought, wondering if he had bitten off more than his ship could chew.

"A mile to the closest battery, I make it, sir," Mr. Wickersham said with his sextant to his eye, "A long-ish shot."

"We'll wait," Lewrie told the people on the quarterdeck. "Half a mile's better."

The French battery opened fire once more, this time with a pair of 12-pounder field guns, their shot flying in much flatter ballistic arcs, striking the sea far short of *Vigilance*, then bounding up from First Graze to dap closer like skipped stones, losing momentum each time, finally succumbing to gravity and their own weight and sinking from sight at least a full cable short. Then came another burst of gunsmoke, the slamming sound of the howitzer firing, and the *Skree!* of its shot on the way. Lewrie tensed again.

Crack! went the shell as it exploded just above the sea, about two hundred yards short, leaving a dark grey and black blotch above the water, and flinging shattered iron bits all about, foaming a wide patch of water beneath it.

One o' those square in the waist, and I won't have an upper gun-deck left! Lewrie thought.

"Half a mile, sir," the Sailing Master said, after some quick scribblings on a chalk slate.

"Mister Farley, pass word below," Lewrie snapped, eager to reply to the French artillery at last. "All guns to fire as they bear."

"Aye, sir!" Lt. Farley said, sounding a tad relieved himself, and shooing Midshipmen to run below with the order.

"Seems unfair, sir," Wickersham commented.

"What, sir? Howitzers?" Lewrie asked him.

"No, sir. What they're about to receive!" Wickersham tittered. "Three guns against twenty-six much bigger ones!"

"On the up-roll!" Lt. Greenleaf on the upper gun-deck could be heard to bellow. "*As* you *bear . . .* fire!"

Up forward, a 24-pounder on the lower gun-deck roared, followed by the sharper sound from an upper deck 18-pounder, and the firing stuttered down the ship to the stern-most gun-ports. Before a bank of powder smoke masked everything between *Vigilance* and the shore, Lewrie saw roundshot striking all round the log redan, the waggons and beasts on the road, and the slopes both before and behind where the French guns were emplaced. He slammed a fist on the bulwark's cap-rails in impatience, wishing for a stronger wind to blow all the smoke away so he and his gunners could see the results of their first shots.

There came a muffled roar in the relative silence after the last guns had fired, then a keen of an explosive shell approaching. Where it went Lewrie had no idea, nor did the French, for the shell burst somewhere between ship and shore in the midst of the smoke pall that drifted downwind.

"Stop yer vents! Swab *out!*" Lt. Greenleaf was shouting. "Charge your guns!" forcing Lewrie to look down into the waist to watch the gun crews leaping over their duties, ship's boys scampering up from the magazines with fresh powder cartridges in wood or leather containers, and gun-captains choosing the roundest shot for reloading.

"Shot your guns!" Greenleaf bawled. "Ready? Run out, and prick cartridge! Prime! Take aim!"

The smoke was thinning as it was blown closer to shore, giving hints of what damage they had done with their first shots. Lewrie got a tantalising glimpse, forcing him to raise his telescope for a closer look, just as the forward-most guns on both gun-decks began to roar once more. Smashed and overturned waggons, stampeding horses and mules, some splotched with blood, dis-embowelled, the triangular crane hoist smashed and blown onto the upper slope above the road, and the two-gun redan . . . "Oh, dammit!" he muttered for the fresh gunsmoke blotted out his view! Even scrambling up to his usual post on the poop deck would not avail. The guns below the quarterdeck went off, making an even thicker pea soup fog, and he took a deep breath and held it as he was wreathed in the rotten egg stink of it.

He looked round the quarterdeck, and made out the Sailing Master and he had to laugh, for the man was fanning his arms to blow the gunsmoke away as if assailed by a plague of flies!

Lt. Greenleaf was crying his un-ending litany; Stop vents, Swab, Charge your guns, Overhaul recoil tackle, Shot your guns, Prick cartridge, all smothered and anonymous like a town crier in a street near the Thames, lost in the night and fogs.

"I think I can see . . ." Lt. Farley hesitantly said. "Yes, I can. The log redan looks shattered, sir. Strewn about like a handful of twigs, and one of their field pieces looks to be dis-mounted!"

It was like peering through a haze, but Lewrie could make out the emplacement at last, and smiled at the sight. The logs had been little protection to the men serving those guns, and one of them *had* been dis-mounted, a wheel of the carriage shattered and the gun now canted over to one side and out of action. He looked for artillerymen to be serving the intact piece, but there was little movement or sign of the crews; a hint of a shako above the log piles where someone was sheltering, perhaps.

What a horrid position! Lewrie thought, before his guns fired once more. The steep slope behind the road, the narrowness of that road, and the steep slope in front had forced the officer in charge of that battery to site his guns right on the road, and place all of his caissons and limbers practically steps away! His howitzers had been set up almost atop the trails of the field guns' carriages!

"We're in range of the guns at the north end of the bridge," Lt. Farley directed their attention as far-off explosions sounded. Through the smoke, Lewrie could see quick flashes of red and amber as that half-battery opened fire. There was a shell splash so close to the ship that a pillar of spray rose and pelted the quarterdeck like a brief summer shower. Through his boots, Lewrie could feel the shot thud into the hull with a faint sound.

"Steer a point to larboard," Lewrie ordered to expand the gun arcs to reach that half-battery, for the angle his guns could reach was limited by the narrowness of the gun-ports. "Pass word for the guns to aim for the new battery, once the smoke clears."

Vigilance's guns crashed and boomed, and truck carriages lurched back from the ports in recoil, creating a rumble as loud as an avalanche of stones, some guns leaping inches off the deck as the barrels heated up.

There was a sudden blast of fire leaping high into the sky amid the nigh impenetrable smoke pall, a livid flash of yellow that turned red in an eye blink as something substantial ashore blew up, forcing Lewrie to curse again that he couldn't see what it was that instant, yet crewmen on the upper decks cheered and swirled their hats in the air, even if they couldn't see what they'd accomplished.

There was a sharp crack of an explosive shell going off, far beyond *Vigilance*'s un-engaged side, out to sea.

"Check fire for a moment, Mister Farley!" Lewrie snapped, eager to *see* what was happening. "Let the smoke clear!"

"Six fathoms!" a leadsman in the fore chains yelled aft, in a wail like a ghost. "Six fathoms t'this line!"

"About as close as we should get, sir," the Sailing Master cautioned, "with this total lack of visibility."

"Fine with me, Mister Wickersham," Lewrie agreed.

"Thus, Quartermasters, and nothing to loo'ard," Wickersham told the helmsmen.

"Nothin' t'loo'ard aye," was the response, and some firmer grips on the wheel spokes.

"Look at that!" Lt. Farley crowed as the smoke finally began to thin. "I do believe we hit their powder supply!"

Indeed, the whole south end of the bridge where the half-battery had sat was now a sea of billowing, boiling black smoke, shot through with red flames, the caisson waggons exploded, limbers turned to kindling and well alight, the log redan a game of pick-up-sticks strewn down the steep slope and both field pieces and the howitzer were dis-mounted, their wooden wheels and carriages burning. Of their crews there was no sign. The fire had even spread to the crane hoist which was also afire, and what progress the French had made to shore up the approach from the south end over the stump of the old stone span was burning.

"You may open upon the other battery, Mister Farley!" Lewrie ordered with a note of triumph in his voice. He raised his glass to gloat over the ruin they had caused, noting how many deep divots had been blown from both the lower and the upper slopes round the guns.

"May we have another half a point free, sir?" Farley suggested.

"Aye, do so. Helmsmen, half a point to windward," Lewrie said.

Gun-captains serving the upper deck 18-pounders bent to peer down their guns' barrels, knelt to wiggle the quoin blocks an inch or so to shift elevation, to place the sight notches in line with their targets, finally stepping back and aside from recoil, with flintlock strikers cocked and the trigger lines drawn taut in their hands.

"*As* you *bear* . . . fire!"

The French had already fired, and Lewrie heard a roundshot soar over the deck, and felt the air disturbed by its passage. There was a second roundshot that struck the ship somewhere up forward, and the keen of a falling howitzer shell, which made Lewrie shrug into his coat in dread. *Boom!* as a pillar of seawater shot skyward about one hundred yards short, the shell laid and fused almost perfectly. One more like that, and *Vigilance* might take *real* damage! But, she was serving out much worse upon the French, and before her gunsmoke laid a curtain cross the scene, Lewrie could see roundshot striking close to the half-battery, flinging clouds of dirt, rock, and gravel high in the air, causing part of the lower slope to slide down to the beach.

The ship sailed on, slower now that the massive concussions of her guns had shot the wind to zephyrs, as the guns always seemed to do, and the smoke pall took even longer to waft shoreward and dissipate.

"One more broadside, and we'll be past the battery," Lt. Farley opined, coughing a bit on the thick smoke. "It's a bit aft of abeam, now, sir, the last I could see of it."

"I know, Mister Farley," Lewrie agreed. "We'll have to stand out to sea and come back to finish the work."

And that'll be no fun, he told himself; *with our starboard guns unable to engage, and havin' t'take what the French serve us in the meantime.*

"Now what the Devil?" Mr. Wickersham exclaimed as the smoke

began to thin enough for him to raise his telescope and examine what they had accomplished. "I do believe they're running away, sir!"

Lewrie eagerly put his own telescope to his eye and began to chuckle under his breath, for the ground and the stone verge of the road round the enemy battery was chewed up as if a myriad of rabbits had been digging, the log redan in front of the guns knocked aside and no taller than the bottom log. The field pieces and the howitzer lay fully exposed, still upright on their carriages, wheels intact, and surrounded by their ancillary waggons full of shot, powder, and explosive shells and un-set fuses. But the surviving gunners were pelting up the road away from their charges as fast as their legs could carry them, sure that they would suffer the same fate as their compatriots in the other half-battery.

"Cease fire, Mister Farley!" Lewrie cried in delight. "Let the gunners take a rest, and a turn at the scuttlebutts. It appears as if the French have chosen discretion over valour."

"Might not even be French, sir," Mr. Wickersham hooted. "Sure to be some of their Italian allies. Poor, unwilling conscripts."

"Let's get a way on the ship, gentlemen, and stand out to come round and finish the job," Lewrie said.

And, as HMS *Vigilance* swung up onto the wind to gain speed for a tack which would carry her back to the bridge for another run, Lewrie went up to the poop deck for a better look at the structure that the French engineers had cobbled together to support road traffic along that stretch of coastal road.

"What in the Devil's that?" Lewrie said aloud.

"Damned loud, but most entertaining, I must say!" someone on the quarterdeck below him was crowing.

Lewrie looked down and spotted Captain Bromhead of the 94th. He had not seen him since breakfast, and had completely forgotten that he was aboard!

"Loud, was it, Captain Bromhead?" Lewrie asked him, making the Army officer look up.

"I was standing with Captain Whitehead of your Marines along the rails," Bromhead replied with a laugh and a shake of his head as if he was trying to clear his ears. "Right above the middle of all of your cannon, sir. I wish someone would have suggested candle wax in my ears beforehand, hah hah!"

"Know anything about construction, sir?" Lewrie asked him. "If you do, please come up and help me make sense of what I'm seeing."

"Well, gladly, Captain Lewrie, though I know little of engineering," Captain Bromhead said. "My math skills were hopeless for entry into Woolwich. Artillery, engineering, whoo!"

He trotted up, though, and pulled out a smaller, silver-chased pocket telescope and trained it on the bridge, now astern of the ship. The smoke from *Vigilance*'s broadsides had thinned to a fine mist, by then, and the bridge lay stark and almost clear.

"They building a chimney?" Bromhead puzzled after a long study. "A long, tall box most chimney-like, I'd say. Logs?"

"Stout oak tree trunks, perhaps," Lewrie said, just as puzzled. "They look as if they've been milled square, somewhere nearby. Interlocking at the ends, like cabins I saw in the Americas. They must be twelve feet long or better, and thick. Foot and a half thick, do you think?"

"Hard to tell at this distance, sir," Bromhead said, shrugging. "Very thick and stout, to bear as much weight as heavily-laden waggons crossing the bridge. Bless me! Is that a forge down in the ravine? That smoke there, sir."

"Aye, I noticed that before we opened fire," Lewrie agreed.

"Well, they can't just stack them up without some sort of nails or heavy spikes," Captain Bromhead enthused over the idea. "I'd wager their engineers have used the artillery battery forge waggon to make long and stout iron spikes to keep them from shifting under the weight whenever a waggon goes across!"

"And there's still a good fire in it," Lewrie said, getting an idea. "Lots of hot coals, bellows to stoke with . . . hmm."

"We can go ashore and set it all alight, sir!" Bromhead urged. "We've driven off any opposition!"

"We can, indeed, sir!" Lewrie said with a laugh. "Mister Farley! Mister Wickersham! We will anchor, this time, and complete the destruction of their artillery. We will also land the Marines to go start a huge fire! Pass word for Captain Whitehead."

"Aye aye, sir!" the First Officer called back, eager for more action, but he had other duties to see to, first. "All hands, ready to tack! Hands to sheets and braces!"

Vigilance had stood out to sea at least three miles, hard on the winds, and gathering sufficient speed with which to complete a tack cross the eyes of the wind, and not get caught "in irons," missing stays, and brought fully aback to drift down onto a lee shore before making a second try.

"They're getting their courage back, sir!" the Sailing Master said in an idle moment allowed from stern concentration on the tack.

Sure enough, the French workers and engineers, the artillerymen from that second half-battery, supposed that the *Anglais* Devil ship was done with them for the day, and was sailing away. They were cautiously drifting, skulking, back closer to the bridge to repair what damage had been done. Lewrie smirked as he watched them once *Vigilance* crossed the eyes of the wind and hauled her wind to run a beam reach down the coast as if bound South, then began to fall off the wind to make another run, setting off a new stampede to safety.

Scurry, mice! he thought gleefully; *The cat ain't done yet!*

Once anchored by bower and kedge, close to where she had come to anchor the first time they'd attacked the bridge, a quarter-mile offshore, the upper deck 18-pounder guns began to roar, from bow to stern in carefully laid shots at the abandoned half-battery on the north end of the bridge approaches, with idle hands, ship's boys, and gun crews whooping and cheering over the accuracy of each shot, or jeering a poor one.

Captain Whitehead and his Lieutenants, with an eager Captain Bromhead along, took all the Marines and the armed boats crews ashore, onto the gritty beach at the foot of the ravine. Muskets, bayonets, and cartridge boxes were laid aside, and coats and hats stripped off so they could pump the leather bellows to stoke the forge fires into bright, yellow-hot coals, while others opened ten-pound kegs of gunpowder to strew round the chimney-like bridge timbers. Fine-mealed coal was fed to the forge to make even more sizzling hot chunks which were shovelled over the vast piles of broken timbers from other raids, onto the milled timbers waiting to be hoisted into place, and tossed high up onto the timbers already erected, which were smeared with some sort of preservative. Great, sputtering flashes erupted round the base of the centre pillar as the loose gunpowder took light and spewed enormous clouds of yellow-white smoke reeking of sulphur and rotten eggs.

Slowly, the erected timbers began to burn on the outside, and the piles of milled timbers began to flare 'til the whole ravine was belching dense grey and black clouds of smoke and flame, fires and smoke so thick that the Marines were driven back to their boats on the beach.

"I do believe that thing is beginning to act like a chimney, sir!" Lt. Farley cheered.

Their joy was interrupted by a massive explosion as an 18-pounder shot hit one of the caissons of the half-battery on the north end of the bridge, and that explosion transmitted itself to the rest, one so strong that a French 12-pounder artillery piece was driven over the low stone verge of the coast road to tumble down the steep cliff to smash itself to kindling on the rocks below.

"Hoist the Recall signal," Lewrie ordered. "Let's get our people back aboard. Once the boats are secure, we'll turn the lower deck twenty-four-pounders loose on what's left of the bridge."

"Aye aye, sir!" Lt. Farley replied, then coughed into his fist.

"Aye, it *is* gettin' a tad thick," Lewrie said, as the smoke off the fires ashore began to cover the entire area, the raw, oily stink of it even reaching the ship despite the onshore breeze.

He could, however, make out Captain Whitehead of the Marines waving his arms widely in acknowledgement of the Recall signal, and summoning his men into the waiting barges. With muskets and accoutrements re-slung, the Marines helped the armed sailors push the barges off the gravelly beach and leap aboard, arms, legs, and oarsmen all entangled as the boats drifted into slightly deeper water.

"Secure the upper deck guns, sir?" Lt. Farley asked him.

"No," Lewrie told him. "They're to hold their fire 'til all of our people are back aboard, and then we'll haul up the boarding nets and re-open upon what's left of the bridge with all guns."

"Aye, sir," Farley said.

It was a joyous pack of sailors and Marines who clambered up the boarding nets minutes later, joshing and laughing with each other, and taking long looks at their handiwork once they'd gained the decks before drifting off in small groups to stow away their arms and queue up at the scuttlebutts for a welcome drink of water.

"Nets secured, sir," Lt. Farley reported, "and all boats aft and ready for towing."

"Very well, Mister Farley, you may open on the bridge," Lewrie ordered, before trotting up to the poop deck with his telescope.

"All guns! Stand to and make ready! Individual fire on the chimney-looking thing!" Lt. Greenleaf bellowed on the upper gun-deck.

One at a time, much like the tolling of a doleful church bell, the guns on both decks erupted, spearing gushes of powder smoke shot through with embers from the flannel powder cartridges and long tongues of red and amber fire. Errant iron roundshot made spanging and bonging noises as they struck rock in the dry ravine, whilst other rounds created parroty squawks when they struck wood. One roundshot smashed the forge, creating a cloud of fireflies spreading outwards like the burst of a fireworks rocket as hot coals flew about.

Slowly, the upper reaches of the construction got shaken apart, scattering long, thick milled timbers far aside, some to tumble over and over before crashing down into the morass of bright flames, and the interlocking beams of the pillar were shortened, the whole thing shaken and loosened, beginning to come apart with groans. At last, there was nothing left to shoot at but a jumbled pyre little taller than the mast of a sailing lugger, with the fierce wind that the fire created revealing hints of the original Roman stone pillar inside, and it, too, looked shorter than the last time they had seen it, as the heat of the fires ate the ancient mortar, allowing the weight of the dirt and rubble-filled centre to push outwards and collapse that, too.

"Cease fire, Mister Farley," Lewrie called down to the deafened men on the quarterdeck below him. "I think we've done enough."

"Aye, sir," Farley agreed, plucking candle wax from his ears.

"And I'll have reports from both gun-decks about the accuracy of individual crews, for tobacco and rum rewards," Lewrie added.

"Aye, sir!"

"Swab 'em down good, lads!" Lt. Greenleaf roared, full of good cheer. "Not a speck of powder smut on your guns, from muzzles to the cascabels before the tompions go back in! Good shooting, damned fine shooting! We've done a grand day's work today!"

After a last, triumphant look at the carnage they had created, Lewrie collapsed the tubes of his telescope and sauntered down the ladderway to the quarterdeck to stow it in the rack on the compass binnacle cabinet. Captain Bromhead of the 94th, with nothing to do but stand round as a spectator, came aft from his vantage point by the starboard entry-port, wiggling fingers in his ears.

"Protect your hearing better this time, Captain Bromhead?" Lewrie asked him.

"Ah, no sir. No time to melt some wax before the guns started up again," Bromhead replied, tilting his head far over. "Lieutenant Greenleaf said I should press my hands over my ears and keep my mouth open, but it didn't help all that much."

"Let's pray we didn't deafen you permanently, then," Lewrie said with a slight grin. "Join me for some cool tea, ginger beer, or ale?"

"I'd be delighted, sir," Bromhead gratefully told him. "I find my mouth is coated with powder smoke. Ehm . . . we will be looking in at Eufemia Lamezia after this?"

"Not today, no," Lewrie said, pulling out his pocket watch. "I think a nice, quiet night out at sea will do for us, stand off-and-on the place 'til dawn, then sail in to look it over tomorrow."

"Oh, good!" Bromhead replied. "Time and enough for word of what we did here today to reach the town, and make them shake in their boots at their first sight of us, haw!"

"Aye, our arrival will, won't it?" Lewrie said, quite pleased at the prospect. "Though, when word reaches Naples or Reggio di Calabria, I'd imagine it'll be more anger than fear in their senior officers. In point of fact, our success here might result in some courts-martial for whoever was assigned to guard this place."

"Might we relish the thought, sir, that we've ruined Marshal Murat's dinner," Bromhead teased, "or, when word reaches Paris, we put Bonaparte himself off his feed, hah hah?"

"Death, confusion, and frustration to the French!" Lewrie said, and had himself a good laugh.

CHAPTER TWENTY-SEVEN

*T*here was a fairly bright moon and a clear, starlit sky the evening after they had destroyed the bridge for good and all, and, as HMS *Vigilance* stood off-and-on in the Gulf of Saint Eufemia, there was a celebration in the ship's waist. Sailors and Marines lined the sail-tending gangways to look down upon the revelry. The Marine drummer boy, the flute player, and a skilled fiddler served up lively tunes and jigs, with a contribution from Cox'n Liam Desmond and his *uilleann* lap pipes. Spry men and ship's boys stamped round in *contre-dances,* and contestants took over the mid-ship hatch gratings to vie for which was a champion at hornpipes. Old, favourite songs were belted out, along with the slower laments for home and missing loves, but in the main it was a most cheerful evening from the middle of the Second Dog Watch 'til the 9 P.M. call for all lights to be extinguished belowdecks.

Younger Midshipmen held their own dances and songs on the fore-castle, whilst the ship's officers looked on from the quarterdeck and the forward edge of the poop, above. There was dignity to be lost if they participated, of course, but at least they could sing along and sway, grin and laugh over the sillier songs, and carefully touch the corners of their eyes when a lament was sung.

Lt. Dickson crammed himself into the lee corner of the poop deck, hard up against the bulwarks with an arm round one of the thick tarred mizen mast stays, looking down in wonder, and now and again glancing down to see what Captain Lewrie was doing, and thinking some hard and painful thoughts, for the day and now the evening were eye-opening.

In his previous ships, Third Rate ships of the line, an older three-masted Sloop of War, then a 74-gunned two-decker under his distant kinfolk, he had not seen all that much combat; a shot under the bows of a fleeing merchantman or privateer, followed by a quick surrender, and one passable stand-up fight with a French corvette in the Bay of Biscay that had not lasted quite half an hour before the French captain had struck his colours, his guns fired mostly for the sake of his, and his nation's, honour.

Today, though, he had been in a ship that had been fired at, with explosive shells to boot, and none of his gun crews on the lower deck had paid any more attention to danger than they would of a shower of cold, cooked peas. And they served their guns accurately, too, steadily and unceasingly getting off three shots every two minutes, cheering their aim and their results when destroying the French artillery, and whooping with delight to see the make-shift bridge crumble under their weight of metal. And tonight they were singing and dancing in a manner that Dickson had never experienced aboard the other ships he had served. Oh, the recruiting posters always promised "music and dancing nightly" along with oceans of prize-money, but it was a rare thing for that promise to be observed.

Vigilance was a highly effective warship, and evidently a happy ship, too, with every hand well-trained and *proud* of their roles, and of their ship, *without* being driven to it like dumb cattle too ignorant to understand the finer sentiments of patriotism, service, and dedication that only men like himself could understand, or feel.

The Master at Arms and his Ship's Corporals finally took up their lant-horns and called for all other lights to be doused at Two Bells of the Evening Watch, raising good-natured complaints among the revellers as the off-watch hands went below to roll into their hammocks for a few hours' sleep, and the instruments were put aside.

Dickson had the Middle Watch, Midnight 'til 4 A.M. that evening, so he slowly sauntered down to the quarterdeck to go below to the wardroom for a short rest, himself, listening to the Sailing Master grumble over the last puffs from his pipe before tapping the bowl's contents overside, and the low banter of his fellow officers.

"Goodnight, Captain sir," Dickson dared say to Lewrie.

"Ah, goodnight to you, Mister Dickson, short though your rest will be," Lewrie said back, as pleasantly as he bade the others. "I'll wish t'be wakened at Eight Bells."

"Aye, sir," Dickson replied, touching the front of his bicorne hat in parting salute, and feeling as if he was accepted aboard as a full member of the wardroom, and the crew, with no grudge held against him. So long as he did not muck up.

"Beg pardon, sir," Midshipman Charles Chenery said as soon as Lewrie stepped out onto the quarterdeck after his breakfast, "the men wish a favour, sir."

"And what would that be, Mister Chenery?" Lewrie asked him.

"Ehm . . . the crew would like permission for a broom to be lashed to the mainmast truck, in sign of another clean sweep, sir," Midshipman Chenery said. "So the French in Eufemia Lamezia see it, and know who we are."

"And they put *you* up to the asking?" Lewrie wondered, grinning. "Why not Midshipmen Langdon, Cummings, or Upchurch? They're the eldest. Even the Bosun, Mister Gore?"

"I would suppose, ehm, because I am your in-law, sir?" Chenery said, tucking his chin into his shirt collar.

"Well, no harm in the doing, I suppose," Lewrie told him. "But, whoever goes all the way to the truck I conjure to do it most carefully. No sense falling to their death, hear me?"

"Aye, sir!" Chenery answered with a relieved grin.

"And Mister Chenery," Lewrie added, stopping him from dashing to the waist, "just because we *are* in-laws, I'll not have our people thinking that *you* can work your way with me for any damnfool request. Make sure they know it."

"Aye, sir!"

"Ah, good morning, Captain Bromhead," Lewrie said to the Army officer as he made his way to the quarterdeck by the same ladderway that Chenery took to descend. "Ready to smoak out Eufemia Lamezia? We have worn about to sail in close. There's a sea chart and a landsman's map in the chart space we can refer to."

"Ready and willing, sir," Bromhead told him, "though I may wish to borrow a stronger telescope than mine."

"Of course, sir," Lewrie told him, then turned his attention to the base of the mainmast trunk, where a fifteen-year-old topman took up a fresh broom, lashed a few turns of light rope round it, and then bound it to his left arm, as other sailors gathered round to cheer him on. Lewrie felt a shiver in his groin as the young fellow sprang to the top of the windward bulwarks, swung out onto the mainmast stays and rat-lines, and began to climb, as agile as an ape.

Better you than me, Lewrie thought. In his Midshipman days he had spent half of each watch he stood aloft in the rigging, making or taking in sail alongside the hands, and he had hated every bloody minute of it! Up to the cat harpings where the sets of shrouds crossed each other, out to hang upside down like a true sailorman from the futtock shrouds where larboard shrouds dead-eyed on the starboard side of the fighting top, a claw up and over the rim, then up the narrower shrouds to the cross-trees, then onward to work on the royals and the t'gallant yards. But, he had *never*, even for a hefty wager or a challenge, shinned up to the mainmast truck, or even *thought* of standing upright on the wee button cap, hundreds of feet aloft with nothing to grab on to for support as the ship swayed and the wind gusted!

"Watch this," Lewrie told Bromhead, pointing the feat out to him. "And say a prayer?"

"Whatever is he doing?" Capt. Bromhead gawped. "Oh, my word!"

The topman made it to the cross-trees, shared a joke with the lookout posted there, then went on up 'til he was wrapped round the mast top, shinning that slim pole, then removing the broom's lashings from his arm to transfer them to the truck, with the broom straw jutting skyward. Then, with equal agility, he descended to land on the sail-tending gangway to loud whistles, cat-calls, and applause.

"Mister Acford," Lewrie bade the nearest Midshipman on the quarter-deck, "do you go find that game fellow's name and tell him he's a full measure of rum this morning, no sippers or gulpers."

"Aye aye, sir!"

"He did that for *rum*, sir?" Bromhead marvelled.

"For pride of the ship, sir," Lewrie corrected him.

⚓

Once *Vigilance* closed the coast, though, and cruised only one or two miles offshore of Eufemia Lamezia, the prospects for a raid to burn the backup of supply convoys looked less than desirable.

For one, what beaches there were appeared too shallow for landings. There were rocks awash fronting the most promising one on the north side of the port's entrance channel, leaving only two narrow and dubious passes through them and the lively surf to the beaches, which looked little deeper than two barges' length before they ended in even more rocks, and what looked to be a rather steep scree slope up to the hill behind them.

On the southern hill which dominated the entrance to the town and its harbour, that enigmatic black square that Lewrie had found on the land map *could* be a fort.

"Old, stone-built," Capt. Bromhead muttered, peering shoreward with a borrowed glass, "walls sure to be thick. An old monastery, or nunnery, perhaps? Might *not* be a fort. The windows . . ."

"Not arrow slits," Lewrie commented.

"No, too big for archers or crossbowmen, but just about big enough for light cannon," Bromhead said, sucking his teeth. "*If* anyone thought to put troops and guns in there. And the slopes up to it . . ."

"Totally un-suitable," Lewrie decided aloud. "Too steep for men to climb easily, and the beaches below the hill are even worse than the ones to the north. You could land the whole battalion, perhaps, but you'd have to spend all the morning securing that place and the heights, and by then all the convoys would have scampered, and we'd have nothing t'show for it."

"And if the French *have* thought to guard the town with troops, we'd lose a lot of men for that nothing," Capt. Bromhead agreed with a strong *moue* of dis-appointment. "And your armed sailors, hah! Why, there's barely enough room on the southern beaches for them to stand!"

"Even a cutting-out party using two of our barges to sail in in the wee hours might have a rough go of it," Lewrie said, collapsing the tubes of his telescope with a finality, and a faint hiss from the air inside. "I doubt there's anything worth taking in there, some fishing boats and such. We've convinced the French that sending supplies by sea is out."

"If we wanted to burn road convoys, sir," Bromhead said, "then it would have to be done from inland, and I doubt if the local partisans are well-armed enough, or determined and organised enough, to do it. A nice suggestion, but . . ." he said, tossing up his hands with futility.

"Back to Milazzo, then, and see what else our spies have come up with," Lewrie agreed. "Mister Grace? Bring the ship onto the wind and shape course for Milazzo."

"Aye aye, sir!"

At least we can still crow over our "clean sweep" broom, Lewrie thought.

It felt a lot less victorious the next morning when *Vigilance* came to anchor in the bay off the 94th Regiment's encampment, for it was drizzling a dull, steady rain from clouds so low and slow-scudding that the usually visible snowcap of Mount Etna was hidden in fog. A grey haze hung over the land, the forests and olive and fruit groves, mingling with the smoke from the Army's cookfires, turning lush Sicily to the drabness of an Irish coastline.

As soon as the anchors were set, and the yards squared away to the Bosun's satisfaction, Lewrie went ashore with Capt. Bromhead to report to Col. Tarrant, and it was a miserable boat ride, for the morning was too warm to wear a boat cloak against the rain, so Lewrie and Bromhead had to suffer a soaking. Once on the make-shift pier, Lewrie looked back at his ship and heaved a sigh, for the upright broom at the masthead looked vain on such a day.

From long use, there was a path through the grain stubble in the field that had been taken over for the camp, and it was muddy, with a puddle here and there, as if the rain had been heavier overnight.

"Oh God, no!" Bromhead exclaimed as they neared Col. Tarrant's headquarters. "No, dog, no! Down! Down, I say!"

Tarrant's hound, Dante, was overjoyed to welcome them, bounding at them with his tongue lolling out, and his large paws and forelegs seemingly *made* of mud. Bromhead's admonitions did no good, for the hound stood on his hind legs, planted his paws on Bromhead's fairly immaculate uniform coat, and tried to lick his face.

"Down!" Bromhead barked loudly, shoving the dog aside. "Damn your eyes! Down!" he roared in a voice that could be heard over the sound of a pitched battle.

Dante whined, backed off, and looked at Lewrie.

"Don't even think of it!" Lewrie growled, pointing a finger.

The dog galloped off towards the headquarters, barking madly as if to announce their arrival, and after a moment, Col. Tarrant did step out onto his covered front gallery and wave to them.

"Aha! You two have come in 'Pudding Time,' sirs," Tarrant said as Dante padded circles round his master, tail and hind end wiggling. "Mister Quill came into camp last night, looking for you. Come in, come in, and dry out."

"Capital!" Lewrie said at that news. "Let's hope he's brought us useful information. Ehm, you don't have a boot scraper, do you?"

"I've no carpets to worry about, Sir Alan, just plain sawn wood boards," Tarrant told him with a laugh. "Do come in. Hang up your coats to drain, and we'll sample a keg of ale just come from England. Mail from home arrived with it, by the way. Yours is at the officers' mess, Bromhead, and yours, Sir Alan, is aboard *Bristol Lass*."

They entered, though the air was warmer indoors than out, even with all the canvas covers on the windows rolled up. Tarrant's man, Corporal Carson, was there in a twinkling to take their hats and wet coats for a sponge-down. Col. Tarrant himself fetched three tall mugs from a sideboard and meticulously tapped the keg, leaving everyone a nice one-inch head on their ales.

"Now, what have you two been up to?" Tarrant asked after taking a deep sip of his ale. "Tell it all to me."

He was delighted to hear that the bridge re-construction had been completely scotched for a good, long time, but had to sigh with dis-appointment when Bromhead described Eufemia Lamezia.

"It's simply not on the cards, sir," Bromhead told him. "By the time we'd get our troops atop either of the hills, the supply convoys would have dispersed, and if their escorts combined and stayed to give us a fight, it would be too costly for us."

"We up-dated the charts and maps," Lewrie added, "and we made a few sketches of what the place looks like from the sea. He's right, it's not worth the candle, Colonel."

"Well, that's alright," Tarrant replied. "It sounded tempting, at first. Mister Quill has gotten word from his agent over there that he's having trouble keeping the local partisans to do much more than make pin-prick raids, even with their new arms, and if we did land at Eufemia Lamezia, we'd have no help from them. They seem satisfied to ambush foraging parties and mounted messengers, then melt away as if scared by their own daring."

"Has Mister Silvester managed to send us copies of the orders and such from those messengers, sir?" Lewrie asked.

"A few, of little import so far," Col. Tarrant told him, after another sip of his ale. "Whoever's in charge of re-building the bridge has boasted of his progress, and his defences, and his superiors are confident that they can use the coast road from Naples soon in the future, hah hah! Well, you put paid to *that*!"

"Captain Lewrie said he smelled a courts-martial for that fellow," Bromhead said with a wee laugh. "And, now that we've scouted out the approaches to Eufemia Lamezia, the French might have to think it's at risk, and waste troops to garrison the place. Fewer troops available for other places we might attack. Or, troops for convoy escorts."

"Good thinking, Bromhead, yes," Tarrant said in praise of the idea.

"What has the regiment been doing in my absence, may I dare ask, sir?" Bromhead said, shifting in his chair to cross his legs.

"Besides the usual close-order drill?" Tarrant answered with a grin on his face. "Why, we held a little route march. Just got back last night before the rain set in. About fifteen miles east near the beaches we practiced on, went into camp, dossing down rough overnight, then marched back here the next morning. Hah! Our poor sutlers and vendors! You never saw the like!"

Both Bromhead and Lewrie leaned forward in their chairs, expecting a gay tale.

"They showed up, as they always do, round breakfast," Tarrant began, "setting up their little booths and such, but we were already formed in ranks, and marching out, and you never *heard* such a caterwauling and wailing, sure that we were leaving for good and there'd be no more money to be made off us, hah hah! Up pops the handcarts and donkeys, chasing after us! The old black-clad women galloping along on their bare feet with their goods slung on their backs, or balanced on their heads to keep up with us, hoping we'd stop and buy something! Locals streaming ahead of us to cry their wares? Then, when we camped for the night, the strongest and the fastest had to camp out with us, with no blankets or shelter, to flog what they had left. We left them in our dust in the morning, the poor devils, for they were simply spent, with their tongues lolling out, and had to eat what they meant to sell, or go hungry! I expect the laggarts limping along far behind us simply got drenched in the rain!"

Tarrant was right; it was an amusing picture, and all three of them got a good laugh out of the tale. That laughter ended, though, when Dante began to bark outside, and they could hear Quill vainly trying to keep the dog from greeting him with muddy paws.

"I do believe I hear the call of an ill-omened bird," Tarrant said in a stage whisper to his guests; he had not forgotten the suggestion Quill had made about Brigadier Caruthers absorbing his regiment.

"Best let him in," Lewrie said with a shrug.

"Do you go rescue him, Carson," Col. Tarrant bade his orderly.

A moment later and Mr. Quill appeared in the room, preceded, though, by Dante, who took time to shake himself almost dry, then go to each guest and his master, and sniff crotches and try to place his head and paws in any welcoming lap.

"Dante!" Tarrant snapped, pointing to a filthy quilt over in one corner of the room. "Beddy by! Go to your pallet!" And, amazingly the dog obeyed, though not without a wee whine of protest. He circled on the quilt, then threw himself down with a huffing sound, to lay his head on his paws.

"There, that's better," Tarrant said. "Welcome, Mister Quill."

"Good morning, sir," Quill replied, taking off a black riding duster and his hat. Dante had managed to smear the duster with mud, so Corporal Carson came to take it for a sponging-off.

"What's new in Messina?" Lewrie asked.

"Ah, sir, to quote the Bard, 'there's something rotten in Denmark,'" Quill said with a put-upon sigh. "*Don* Julio Caesare is back from whatever he's been up to, and he's rather wroth with us, and with some of his under-bosses. In his long absence, I paid some of them to go gather information for us, make contact with Mister Silvester and the partisans . . . pass on a letter and fetch off any from them? Well, *Don* Julio said that any money from me was his, and his alone, and that 'Tonio had no right to be making decisions without his permission, or getting any big ideas, the greedy bastard. *Don* Julio, not 'Tonio, I mean as the greedy bastard. He tongue-lashed me to deal only with him, or he'd pull all his co-operation. I'd given 'Tonio fifty pounds, and *Don* Julio made him hand it over in front of the others. Is that ale, sir? I'd greatly admire a taste."

"But of course, Mister Quill," Col. Tarrant said, finding a fresh mug and pouring it full himself. "That doesn't sound like a good way to motivate his own people, I must say. Why, one might imagine that this 'Tonio, whoever he is, *has* gotten some ideas after a humiliation like that."

"Perhaps something's gone amiss with some of his businesses," Lewrie opined. "*Don* Julio's always struck me as shrewd, dangerous, but ingratiating, and clever enough to keep people in line without insulting them. How co-operative *is* this 'Tonio?"

"Very," Quill said after a long draught and a loud "Aah!" of pleasure. "I told you all before that he's much more patriotic than his boss, more eager to see the French out of Italy, and Calabria in particular. I get the vague suspicion that most of the under-bosses, the *capos,* are Sicilians of long standing, and that 'Tonio and some few of the others are originally Calabrians, and might still be considered Calabrians, no matter how long they and their families have resided this side of the Strait."

"Well, you said *Don* Julio has business dealings over there, and some of his *capos* who run things for him in Calabria *have* to be locals, not Sicilians lording it over them," Lewrie speculated. "Like the man whose son got us the sketches of the bridge in the first place was a Calabrian *capo,* right?"

"Yes, but it now seems to me that someone other than Sicilian can be useful, but never can be trusted to run the whole show," Quill replied, shrugging. "Second-class people. Recall how much *Don* Julio despises anything or anyone from Naples. Competition? Themselves so insular that they'd sneer at Sicilians?"

"Gad, it sounds very much like *all* of Italy," Col. Tarrant said with a wee laugh. "It's a wonder the *Romans* held it together without every little town going at the next one down the road with hammer and tongs!"

"You get the sense that this 'Tonio might have big ideas of his own?" Lewrie asked. "Might he aspire to be a *Don* himself? Over in Calabria, or all of *Don* Julio's fiefdom? Hmm. That might be useful, and a lot more co-operative with us."

"If that happens, Sir Alan, I imagine we'd all be grateful," Quill said, "but . . . as a Calabrian, he could never supplant Caesare. I cannot be seen to encourage his aspirations. Too dangerous."

"But, you could sympathise," Col. Tarrant stated in a slow, calculating drawl.

"Well, I suppose I could, Colonel," Quill said, just as slowly, "but if *Don* Julio hears of it, then 'Tonio is surely done for, and we lose *all* co-operation with *any* of *Don* Julio's organisation. Frankly, sirs . . . without them, we might as well pack up and go home. We are completely dependent upon their good will."

"And we have yet to hit our stride, sirs!" Capt. Bromhead said in protest. "We haven't hurt the French as dear as we could!"

"Upon that head, sirs," Mr. Quill pressed, "have you gentlemen any good news for me?"

"We finished off the bridge for good and all," Bromhead boasted at once, and went on to describe the action, the destruction of the French artillery, the impromptu landing by the Marines and the fires they had set.

"Well, that will force the French to continue routing their road convoys the long, rough way round," Quill said, somewhat enthused by the account. "And, did you have a peek at Eufemia Lamezia, Sir Alan?"

"Aye, but it was a dead bust," Lewrie had to tell him, giving Quill the many reasons why a landing there would be fruitless, and quite dangerous in terms of casualties to the 94th. "The only two places that seem worth the candle would be Monasterace, or Catanzaro, and we still don't know much about either place. Admiral Charlton's squadron might have some information from when they bombarded Monasterace, but that's yet to come, hopefully."

"Have you dug up anything on either, Mister Quill?" Col. Tarrant asked him.

"Before *Don* Julio got back, 'Tonio *was* putting together an expedition to Monasterace," Quill told them, "but that's scotched, now, and I'll have to wait for *Don* Julio to get over his pet before I can approach *him* with the request, and I can guarantee you that it will *not* be 'Tonio who goes. *Don* Julio still has a flea in his ear about Melito di Porto Salvo."

"That again?" Lewrie hooted, rising to go re-fill his own mug. "You've already told him once about why it may be too tough a nut to crack, Mister Quill? What the Devil's there that he wants, the Crown Jewels, the Holy Grail, or the bloody Ark of the Covenant?"

"A competitor's storehouses, I'd expect," Quill gloomed.

"Well, we're having none of *that*!" Lewrie declared. "From what we've seen of it from close offshore, it looks t'be as well defended as Reggio di Calabria or bloody Naples."

"We do, however, Sir Alan," Col. Tarrant said with a frown on his face, "need to strike someplace. This whole endeavour is an experiment, and to continue in existence, it must be seen to be doing something grand, now and then."

"Believe me, Colonel, I *know*!" Lewrie all but spat in agreement. He did not return to his chair, but slowly paced to the front of the quarters to look out a window with the canvas drawn up, to sip at his ale and moodily study the anchorage, the moored ships, and the beachside pier, all misted and distanced by a fresher round of rain.

If this fails, will I even keep my ship? he sadly wondered; *If Admiralty cancels us, would I end up ashore on half-pay? Being back in London with Jessica'd be so sweet, but* . . . damme *if I'll let all the people who'd love t'see me humbled have a chance t'gloat!*

For one daft second, he had a thought to sail off instanter and have a go at Monasterace *without* proper information and preparation, but realised that would be simply *too* rash, and sure to get a lot of good men killed or wounded, and a clumsy failure he'd have to confess to Admiralty, which might end his command just as quickly.

"Something you said off Eufemia Lamezia, Captain Bromhead," he said without turning round. "About how them seeing us so close offshore might alarm them?"

"Yes, sir?" Bromhead hesitantly replied.

Lewrie turned, with the hint of a smile, and with the merest sketch of a plan. "I could take *Vigilance* and all four transports to sea, round-about Sicily, then make an appearance off Catanzaro, as if we're going to land. Then, put back out to sea and show up off Melito di Porto Salvo and do the same thing, then up the Strait of Messina to do the same off Eufemia Lamezia."

"A long time at sea for my men," Col. Tarrant said, puzzled.

"No troops," Lewrie countered, "transports only. The French know by now what the sight of us might mean. They would have to move troops and guns to re-enforce every place we're seen, and thin them out. In the meantime, Mister Quill can arrange a scout of Monasterace, which I shall definitely *not* visit, and Admiral Charlton may supply us with as much information as he has by the time I return.

"Hell!" Lewrie declared, "I may even come to anchor and get in some gunnery practice to convince them that the Devil and all of his Imps have come to breakfast!"

"Confusion to the French, ah hah!" Col. Tarrant huzzahed with a lift of his mug. "But, why sail round Sicily, when you can trail your colours right under the noses of their generals in Reggio di Calabria, sir? Right down the Strait, with bands playing!"

And it'll look *like we're doin' something productive!* Lewrie could assure himself.

Back aboard *Vigilance,* though, Lt. Dickson was penning a long letter to one of his principal patrons. With no duties at anchor in port, and with nothing to do on a rainy day, he was doing the bidding of the people who had placed him under Capt. Sir Alan Lewrie, sending them his observations of amphibious operations, how they were conducted, and whether the diversion of badly needed troop transports, and the valuable Navy crews who manned them, was worth the doing, and if the whole scheme was worth the expense of Admiralty funds.

Of course, Dickson prefaced his accounts with a long complaint of being removed from command and being placed aboard *Vigilance* as her *Fourth* Lieutenant before getting to the meat of the matter, but he had already sent off several letters expressing his embarrassment.

"Good God, a 'sea letter'!" Lt. Greenleaf commented as he came out of the quarter gallery, headed to the wash-hand stand to clean his face and hands. "You must be *very* sweet on the girl, Dickson."

"He's not even writing on the back of the pages," Lt. Farley, the First Officer teased, looking up from his never-ending alterations in the Muster Book, "nor cross the first lines, either."

Dickson shrugged into himself and laid a forearm as if to shield it from view. "It you must know, it's to my father, with a page or two to sisters and brothers included, to save them postage," Dickson said in explanation. "A little bit for everyone to be shared out when they get together for Sunday dinner."

"It'll weigh nigh a pound before you're done," Greenleaf said. "That'll be a five shilling *log!*"

Dickson flashed a brief, polite smile. He was still walking on tiptoes round his fellow wardroom mates, waiting for the first sneer, the first pointed comment, for they all knew the reason for him being among them. In truth, Dickson *expected* guarded derision, feeling as if he went about stoop-shouldered, waiting for the blow to fall, but, so far, though he'd not won any new friends (nor did he care to do so) he had not made any enemies, so long as he fulfilled his duties with professional skill.

He had laid out the details of all the previous landings that he had gleaned from his fellow officers, then portrayed their latest off that bridge above

Pizzo, and the demonstration off Eufemia Lamezia, paying suitable praise for the impromptu landing of the Marines to set fire to everything under and round the bridge.

It strikes me, though, that, as daring as the operations have been, they have been few and far between, with weeks on end languishing in harbour before sailing off to strike again. One could assume that the squadron could be put to better use by cruising the Calabrian coast, looking for advantageous places to land, and burn; semaphore towers, enemy batteries, and such, or any town that had a garrison & destroying anything that floats in the ports, as we see in accounts of the doings of Adm. Popham on the N. coast of Spain. Instead, we must bide until adequate information can come to us from a shadowy, frankly criminal gang of smugglers & cut-throats, all under the aegis of a spectral minion of Foreign Office in Messina, a most odd bird or so I am told, and all is done for money, when I imagine that if spies are needful, more trustworthy agents of British blood could be doing the information gathering. Frankly, gentlemen, what little I have seen has been most stultifying, and boresome, so far. I fear, for all his former gallantry, that Capt. Lewrie plays the game too cautiously to be in command of such an experiment.

There, he told himself after signing it; *now we'll see what my patrons make of this. With luck, they'll find a way to take Lewrie down a peg or two, and get me a command back.*

CHAPTER TWENTY-EIGHT

Lay on a special dinner for today, Yeovill," Lewrie told his cook over breakfast the next day. "I'll be having Mister Farley, Mister Wickersham, and the officers in command of the transports. Eight, all told."

"Very good, sir," Yeovill replied, his head cocked over to one side in thought for a moment. "Ehm, how would chicken Parmesan suit, with pasta, peas or broad beans, and garden green salad?"

"What the Devil's chicken Parmesan?" Lewrie had to ask.

"Well, normally, it's a boneless chicken breast smothered in a marinara sauce, with slices of Parmesan cheese atop, sir," Yeovill explained, "but I can de-bone a decent-sized bird, and add the meat to a serving bowl of pasta, with the sauce and cheese. A little will go a long way. And, may I suggest a *monte pulŗiano* to wash it down?"

"You always amaze me, Yeovill," Lewrie said in awe of how quickly the man had come up with a solution, seemingly from the top of his head. "I think you could cobble together a feast at the North Pole!"

"Only do you care for whale or seal meat, sir," Yeovill said.

"Very well, let's serve that," Lewrie decided, imagining an oil and vinegar sauce for the salad, some wee young Roma tomatoes on the side, perhaps even a sprinkling of goat cheese, which he had come to like. As

he finished the last bites of his breakfast, dabbed at his lips with his napkin and pulled it free from his shirt collar, Lewrie patted his stomach, then
kneaded his abdomen, wondering if his cook did him *too* proud. Would
he at last batten up like an Autumn hog, and become as rotund as many
Post-Captains he had known? No, once he stood to go to his desk, he could
still get two thumbs inside of his breeches' waistband, and they did not
feel a bit snugger than they had before.

Somewhat assured, he sat down and wrote out invitations to all the
transports' commanding officers, folded them over, then sent one of his
servants on deck to summon a Midshipman.

"Sent for me, sir?" Midshipman Fairfoot reported minutes later.

"Aye, Mister Fairfoot," Lewrie told him. "I need you to deliver invitations to transports. Take a boat and a rowing crew. No need to t'seal 'em.
Just keep 'em dry and smudge free."

"Aye, sir," the lad replied, knuckled his brow and went out on deck,
bawling for a boat crew to be assembled, and buoyed by his bit of free-
dom from the ship and worse tasks.

"More coffee, sir?" Deavers asked. "There may be a cup's worth left in
the pot."

"Aye, thankee, Deavers, and I think I will," Lewrie told him.

At the appointed time, First Officer Farley and the Sailing Master came
aft to the starboard entry-port, and four barges stroked out from the inshore anchorages of the transports. Lt. Fletcher off *Bristol Lass* came aboard
first, followed by Lt. Rutland off *Coromandel*, then Lt. Hoar of *Spaniel*,
and then Lt. Creswell off *Lady Merton*. They mingled, doffing hats to each
other, then shaking hands more cordially, with Lt. Farley and Mr. Wickersham joshing Rutland about his new assignment aboard *Coromandel*, before the door to the great cabins opened, and Deavers bowed them in.

After surrendering hats and swords to Dasher and Turnbow, they took
seats down either side of Lewrie's twelve-place table, Fletcher and Farley
at the top of the table near Lewrie at the end, which made Lewrie cock a
brow at Rutland in query.

"I thought you would be senior, Mister Rutland," he said.

"I do supercede Mister Fletcher, sir," Rutland replied, "but he has been
senior over the rest of the transports from the beginning, and that's gone
so well that I saw no reason to claim seniority."

"Well!" Lewrie said, a tad surprised. "If you do not stand upon pride of place, and things continue to go as well as they have so far, your arrangement with Mister Fletcher is fine by me. Gentlemen, we'll begin with a white wine, if you will. You may pour, Deavers. I trust you do not mind if I make this a working dinner?"

"It had crossed our minds that your invitation precedes a fresh operation, sir," Lt. Fletcher said for all of them.

"It does, indeed," Lewrie said, "though Mister Quill and his sources of information haven't gathered enough to make solid plans, as yet. No, I thought we'd just go on a cruise to keep the French on their toes. We will not even be carrying troops, this time."

That made them sit up straighter and share glances with each other. It was Lt. Rutland who was the first to evince a sly look.

"Demonstrations, sir," Rutland said. "A whole series of them? Those will keep the French up nights, worrying where we may strike."

"Indeed, Mister Rutland," Lewrie congratulated, "you got it in one. Right down the Strait of Messina in full sight, then out to sea 'til we stand in and make our appearances. As circumstances allow, I may even come to anchor and fire on something, here and there."

"And we could form lines of boats and pretend to row ashore!" Lt. Creswell enthused. "Even with none but our armed sailors aboard them, we'll sow bags of panic."

"Entirely the point," Lt. Farley chimed in. "Just gonna say."

"Ehm, how far afield, sir?" Lt. Hoar of *Spaniel* asked.

"I was thinking as far east as Catanzaro," Lewrie told him.

"If we are to stir things up, sir," Lt. Fletcher suggested, "I would think Crotone needs a visit. We've been told that Crotone is a garrison town, with a fort or two, and enemy shipping in its port. Perhaps Admiral Charlton's squadron has 'smoaked' it in the past, but never made a real threatening move against it. Might the French there need waking up, sir?"

"That would freeze the garrison in place, aye," Lewrie agreed, "and keep them from dispersing to protect other port towns closer to us down the coast. From there, we *could* close Catanzaro, where some of the roads meet the coastal supply route. Five or six miles off from the rest of the small towns 'til we get to Melito di Porto Salvo, and come to anchor to give them a scare."

"We could see what you did to the bridge above Pizzo, sir," Lt. Hoar said with a snigger.

"Your salads, gentlemen," Deavers said as he and the other cabin servants fetched out plates, and Lewrie wondered if Yeovill could read his mind, for yes, there were crumbles of *feta* cheese atop his salad!

"Even farther afield up north," Lewrie hinted with a brow up.

"Oh, this won't be the first time I've wished that our so-called 'armed transports' really had some guns!" Lt. Creswell bemoaned.

"I imagine we're going to have a hellish lot of fun!" Fletcher hooted.

Yeovill had even thrown in a humble bread pudding in lieu of a duff, but one made with orange slices and lots of fruit juice. Nuts, sweet bisquits, and a soft cheese came with the Port bottle.

As the meal at last came to a convivial end, Lewrie bade Rutland stay awhile longer, to ask how *Coromandel* was shaping up. They went to the starboard side settee and chairs to sip cool tea.

"So, finding your feet over there, are you, Mister Rutland?" Lewrie asked him once they got settled and comfortable.

"I believe so, sir," Rutland said, nodding and looking thoughtful. "I feel that my ways suit her people better than Dickson's ever did. For all his complaints, I find them a decent lot, no better or worse than one could expect. I've allowed no easing of proper discipline . . ."

"But you haven't played 'Popularity Dick' either," Lewrie interjected, grinning. "That's *certainly* not your way."

"Ah, no sir," Rutland replied, knowing that people took him for a gloomer, "but so far I've found very few reasons to have hands up at 'mast' for discipline problems, and certainly none of them worthy of the 'cat.' Rum or tobacco stoppage, mostly. Bless me, sir, they've even begun to skylark and sing in the Dog Watches, and when at boat and net drill, the hands have become quite efficient."

"Your officers, whom Dickson despised?" Lewrie asked.

"Hah, sir!" Rutland exclaimed with humour. "I get the impression that Clough and Kinsey *enjoyed* twitting Dickson with their ways. Oh, Clough will still jibber-jabber, but he saves it for meals aft, now, and Kinsey may be more of a tarpaulin sailor than any man I've met in the Navy. Under a jumped-up patrician, he couldn't *help* but to be surly and put on his dumb-show, but he'll do, now. Do right well. Ehm . . . may I ask how Dickson is doing aboard *Vigilance*, sir?"

"Getting a well-needed education, Mister Rutland," Lewrie told him.

"Pray God, it'll stick with him when he goes aboard his next ship, or gets another command. He's playin' turtle . . . half-drawn up in his shell, and says little. I must admit that when he's on duty, he seems as good as anyone else aboard, but . . . it may be just a sham."

"I simply can't imagine where a young fellow learned to despise common folk, sir," Lt. Rutland said with a shake of his head. "It's not as if he's 'The Honourable' son of someone titled, from what I could gather, and Sub-Lieutenant Clough told me that Dickson didn't attend a public school, but was home-tutored for a spell, then went to a local grammar school before he joined the Navy. Even if his family is well-to-do, they're only country Gentry, not Peers of the Realm."

"Maybe his grammar school was full of farmers' sons and coal-heavers' lads," Lewrie said with a chuckle, "and they saw him as one of the Quality to be teased and get away with it."

"You may have a point, sir," Rutland said, nodding sagely. "I fear, if we are to sail in two days, sir, I must get back aboard my ship and see that all is in readiness. I thank you for the dinner, sir," he added as he finished his tea and got to his feet. "Your man Yeovill is a marvel, though I must confess that Italian spices set my heartburn off. Delicious, but . . . ?"

"I'll not keep you, sir," Lewrie said, seeing him to the door. "And, one hopes that your ship's people will take as much amusement from our prank against the French as our officers do, hah hah!"

"I am certain that they will see the fun of it, sir," Rutland promised.

Crotone was a lovely harbour, wide and open to the sea, ringed with beaches perfect for landings. It had been, according to the Ship's Surgeon, Mr. Woodbury, one of the principal settlements of the ancient Greeks, dating to five centuries before Christ, and a cultural center with a large temple dedicated to Hera.

"You, ah . . . won't shoot it up *too* badly, will you, sir?" Mr. Woodbury timidly asked as *Vigilance* crept to within a mile of the town, with the transports astern of her even further reducing sails and speed as if they would come to anchor.

"Well, I don't know about temples, sir," Lewrie answered him with his telescope to one eye, "but that seafront castle looks more of a good target. It doesn't look *that* old."

"Sixteenth century, my guidebook said, sir," Woodbury told him, appalled that the castle made too good a target.

"Guidebook?" Lewrie snapped, lowering his telescope. "You have a guidebook? With street plans and such?"

"Just descriptions of things worth seeing, sir," Woodbury answered, "suitable inns and such, that some travellers on their Grand Tour of the Continent compiled."

"Deck, there!" a mainmast lookout shouted down. "Enemy soldiers marchin' outa th' town! With artillery!"

"There, sir!" Lt. Farley pointed out, stabbing an arm outwards. "Deploying on the beaches west of the main part of town! I see . . . at least six horse-drawn guns."

"I see 'em, Mister Farley, thankee," Lewrie said after a long look. "Mister Wickersham, can we get within three quarters of a mile?"

"If these Italian charts are to be trusted, sir, we can get within half a mile," the Sailing Master said.

"Conn us in if you please, Mister Wickersham," Lewrie ordered. "Hands to the fore chains t'sling the leads. It seems the French are offering up something better than castles and temples, Mister Woodbury. Ye don't mind if we kill a few, do you?"

"Death to the French, sir," the Surgeon said, relieved.

Lewrie took another look at the French troops flooding out of the town and forming just above the overwash barrows of the beaches, counting the number of company banners as they formed ranks three or four deep as if to repel a landing with massed musketry, and 12-pounder guns to use against the barges as they neared the shore. It looked as if an entire French regiment was there; the entire garrison of Crotone, he wondered?

"Lord, here comes cavalry, too!" Farley hooted as several troops of horsemen cantered along the coastal road above the beaches, behind the infantry, then wheeled into four ranks above their left flank. A flash of light along their front, and hundreds of sabres were drawn, ready for the killing charge once the French infantry had done their own preliminary slaughter.

"There's a Goddamned fool over there," Lewrie said, lowering his telescope, "who's about t'learn a very painful lesson. Mister Farley, we will open at half-mile range. Double-shot the guns and have both decks stand ready."

"Aye, sir."

"Soldiers!" Lewrie spat. "They never learn what ships can do!"

The Sailing Master was standing close to the Quartermasters at the double-wheel helm, his attentions torn 'twixt the compass bowl, the commissioning pendant high aloft that indicated the direction and strength of the wind, and the shouts from the leadsmen up forward who were sounding the depths. One of his Master's Mates had his sextant to his eye, scribbling observations on a chalk slate to measure their distance from the shore.

"Half a mile from shore, sir, and in five fathoms of water," Wickersham reported at last, with a wee *Whew!* of relief.

"Open the ports, Mister Farley," Lewrie snapped. "Run out and take aim. We will fire in broadside."

The First Officer relayed those orders below and *Vigilance* rumbled loudly as 18-pounders and 24-pounders were run out. More thuds and thumps as crow-levers raised heavy barrels so the elevating wood blocks, the quoins under the breeches, were adjusted, and whole gun carriages were shifted a bit to angle ahead in the narrow gun-ports.

"Ready, sir!" Farley reported, sounding excited.

"You may open, Mister Farley," Lewrie said, enthusiasm in his voice, too, for he had always loved the roar and stink of the guns.

"By broadside . . . fire!" from Farley, and the titanic thunder began, accompanied by a huge pall of gunsmoke that a quartering wind rapidly blew away towards the bows.

Vigilance was only making about five knots, a leisurely cruise along the coast, but it was fast enough to force gun-captains to shift the aim of the gun carriages more abeam once they were loaded and run back up to the ports. "By broadside . . . fire!"

Impatient to see what damage his guns were doing, Lewrie rushed up to the poop deck and pressed himself most unseamanlike up against the starboard bulwarks to steady his telescope. The smoke pall was thicker after the second broadside, wafting away ahead of the ship, but leaving a dense haze. Just as he thought he could see, hog stampede rumbles sounded from below as the guns were run out for a third broadside, and he had to lower his glass.

"By broadside . . . fire!"

Lewrie looked down the side of the ship, up on tiptoes to lean far out to watch the guns erupt in smoke and stabbing jets of flame as the guns recoiled inboard out of sight.

"Beg pardon, sir!" Lt. Farley shouted up to him from the deck below, "The next broadside may have to be angled too far aft in the ports for safe firing!"

"Cease fire, then, Mister Farley," Lewrie ordered. "Let's see what there is left to shoot at, first."

"Aye aye, sir!" Farley replied, then bawled the cease fire order below to the gun-decks.

Come on, come on! Lewrie thought, willing the smoke pall to disappear. He pulled out his pocket watch and took note that they had gotten off three broadsides in two minutes and a bit, even from the massive 24-pounders, which fact made him grunt with satisfaction.

At last!

The smoke was being blown clear, and the haze was thinning, just enough to reveal what they had wrought.

"Just bloody beautiful!" Lewrie hooted in wicked glee.

There were still six field pieces standing where they had been positioned before the infantry lines, but the caissons and limbers at their rears were smashed, and there was not a single gunner in sight. Panicked horse teams which had been led far behind the infantry were galloping hither and yon, and the surviving French infantry were not that far behind them, scattering in small packs. Lewrie caught a wee glint of gold atop a pole in the centre of one pack that was running back into town; the gilded eagle that Napoleon gave to each regiment that was supposed to be as sacred and inspiring as any that the ancient Romans had bestowed upon their legions. Unfortunately for this French regiment, it looked as if a third of its soldiers lay strewn dead or dying on the sand. Off to the left flank where the infantry had formed, there were dead horses and cavalrymen, though it looked as if the cavalry had had the good sense to wheel about and gallop away from the slaughter. Lewrie could see a crowd of dazed horses and riders milling about a quarter-mile farther west down the coast road, sabres still glinting as if they slashed air in frustration and hot anger.

"I do believe that Crotone is in need of an entire new garrison, Mister Farley!" Lewrie called down to the quarterdeck, whooping with delight. "Secure the guns, and stand down from Quarters. Let's not press our luck, Mister Wickersham. Helm down and bring her up to windward, and signal the transports to alter course in succession and make sail conformable to the weather!"

And, as the gun-ports were shut and sealed, HMS *Vigilance* rang to a new noise, the cheers and jeers of hundreds of men.

Catanzaro was a different story, the town itself not a suitable target for bombardment, for the town proper lay inland from the coastal road, and its subsidiary outlet to the sea was a much smaller fishing port of Catanzaro Lido, where the roads over the mountains came down to the relatively flat plains and met the main route, and there was nothing much there to take under fire.

The squadron's approach from the sea could be seen for hours before they got within range, giving what enemy garrison might be present with bags of warning. And surely word of the disaster those ships had wrought at Crotone had had time to travel down the coast, so there was no sign of resistance this time, no troops, no guns in waiting, no galloping cavalry.

Vigilance and the transports came to anchor within a mile of the shore, anyway, *Vigilance* with her ports open and her guns run out in show, whilst the transports hauled their barges alongside from being towed astern, with boarding nets hung overside. Armed sailors scrambled down the nets and manned their boats, then stroked into a rough line and slowly made their way towards the beaches.

There had been several escorted convoys visible on the coastal road when they first approached, but by the time the barges got close to a landing, they were long gone, dashing hastily back into the dubious safety of Catanzaro itself, back up the road towards the hills, or east or west away from the dread sight of the ships and the barges, at a speed that raised great clouds of dust from the arid soils of Calabria. Even ox teams seemed to be goaded into lumbering trots, which everyone aboard delighted to see, sure that all the draught animals would be so exhausted before they reached what they deemed safety, and useless for days after. From the upper decks, Lewrie and his officers could see escorting cavalry keeping up with their convoys, positioned behind the last waggons as if they could guard their charges from there, eating pounds of dust at the trot or the canter, now and again wheeling about to form ranks as if they might charge right down to the beaches and futilely make a show of defiance to salve their honour.

The barges ground their bows onto the sands, and armed sailors from the transports leaped out to draw them more firmly ashore, then deployed in skirmish lines, tactics they had learned from the 94th at the Army encampment, even daring to cross the now-empty road and do some for-aging, and there was not a French or allied soldier within two miles of them, and not a single waggon in sight by then!

After half an hour of that demonstration, Lewrie had two guns fired for the General Signal to all ships, and hoisted Recall. And Lewrie was most satisfied with it all, for he could use the strongest telescope aboard and look deep up the main road down from the hills, and grin at the sight of fleeing convoys of waggons facing one way, and the ones coming down jammed up in general confusion. The landing parties rowed away from the beaches and the coast road, where not one vehicle or draught ani-mal stirred, and the road stretched vacant and quiet for as far as the eye could see.

"I *still* don't like the look of this place," Lewrie told Farley as they peered long and hard at Melito di Porto Salvo as the squadron closed the coast under reduced sail, and slowly angling shoreward for a close pass at about a mile's distance. "The beaches are right under their guns, and the slopes look too steep to assault."

"Rather a boisterous surf today, too, sir," Lt. Farley pointed out, "es-pecially to the west of the town. Perhaps not *too* rough to the east."

"But, those beaches east of the town and the harbour entrance are too far," Lewrie gloomed, leaning both elbows on the bulwarks. "Even if we tried landing there in the middle of the night, the French would have enough warning to march down there and offer a stiff fight, defeating our whole purpose. The road convoys'd be safe and snug in town for the night . . ."

"Just going to say, sir," Lt. Farley interjected.

". . . We couldn't get at 'em, and there'd be nothing moving on the roads for us to burn," Lewrie continued. "And forewarned, we'd never manage t'get into the town to do any damage. Damn *Don* Julio."

"Our favourite criminal, sir?" Farley said with a snigger.

"He's insistent that this place gets savaged," Lewrie told him, "only God knows why. A competitor's lair, or a treasure trove to be looted? If the French weren't there, he might even gather up all of his men and boats, and have a go at it, himself."

"He may be welcome to it, sir," Farley said, raising his glass for another look. "Will we be anchoring the transports as we did at Catanzaro?"

"I think not, Mister Farley," Lewrie said with a shake of his head. "I intend to cruise by, exchange fire with the shore batteries, and see how many guns they have."

He craned his neck to look aloft at the set of the sails and the commissioning pendant, squinting in the early morning light, frowned, then looked astern to the transports.

"No sense in risking the transports," he said. "Make a signal for them to alter course and stay to windward of me by at least one cable. Once they answer, we will Beat to Quarters."

"Aye, sir!" Farley replied, turning to the nearest Midshipman on the quarterdeck to hoist the signal.

Lewrie looked aft once more to see the signal flags soar aloft on the halliards and break out in bright colours. Moments later, a matching set of signals appeared on the lead transport, *Bristol Lass*, repeated right down the line to *Spaniel* at the rear of their column.

"Strike it for the Execute," Lewrie ordered, and the signal, two-blocked at the peak of the halliards, was rapidly run down. "Now you may Beat to Quarters, Mister Farley."

As *Vigilance* drummed to the rush of hundreds of crewmen going to their fell duties, Lewrie went up to the poop deck for a better view of Melito di Porto Salvo, still wondering what was so vital to Julio Caesare. In his day-glass the seaport town looked much of a piece with the many other coastal towns in Calabria. Hills, beaches, a snug harbour, and a rather neat waterfront lined with houses, stores, and warehouses, and a layer cake of more buildings and streets that marched up the slopes behind the sea, with public squares surrounded by grander houses and churches. That time of the morning, civilians and garrison alike were likely still at their breakfasts, which explained the faint haze of wood smoke that lay atop the town, drifting upwards and inland. If there was a palace or castle, he could not spot one right off, and he felt certain that there was no fortress near the waterfront to guard the harbour, though at the very top of the hills behind the last straggling town streets, there was a large stone structure with high walls that clung to the steep slope like a limpet or barnacle, with what looked like a fortified gate house at the end of a bare road that zigzagged up to it.

Could be bad if it has guns, Lewrie thought with a faint wince.

It was too far off to make out narrow arrow ports cut into the walls, and he could see no crenellations cut into the tops of the walls to make room for artillery. The place looked old, long abandoned, a relic of the days when boiling oil and large stones dropped on besiegers was in vogue. There were even narrow sheets of vines streaking the walls like green tears. Vandal, Goth, Norman, Spanish, or Turk? He didn't know, and could have cared less . . . unless there *were* guns up there, which could drop plunging fire onto his decks.

Instead, Lewrie looked more closely at the hills above the beaches, nearer the harbour entrance, trying to ascertain if French gunners had had time to erect stone redans to protect their guns . . . or if the enemy had had enough warning since his squadron's sails had hove in sight to light off furnaces for heated shot. In the haze from cookfires were there thicker skeins of smoke?

Time will tell, he told himself, lowering his telescope to look round once more. Aft and a bit off the larboard quarter, the column of transports was sidling seaward, hopefully out of harm's way, with *Vigilance* 'twixt them and the foe, and the most tempting target for the French gunners. Lt. Fletcher in charge of *Bristol Lass* had shaken out a reef in her fore course for a knot more speed to take shelter behind Lewrie's ship, just in case, and hands were aloft to do the same aboard the ships trailing *Bristol Lass* to maintain their one-cable separation.

When Lewrie looked forward, he could see down into the waist, open to the sky below the cross-deck boat tier beams, and realise that the loud noises of preparation for battle had ended, and that the upper gun-deck 18-pounders were all manned, the guns' tompions set aside, the guns standing run-in, with the gun-ports sealed, waiting orders to run out. Amidships, young powder monkeys were knelt with wood or leather carriers for cartridge bags, ready to serve up their charges for reloading, and amidships, the Marine boy drummer, and flautist, with a fiddler, were playing the lively tune, "The Jolly Thresher," which brought a smile to his lips.

What a fine, spirited crew I have, Lewrie thought with pride; *Just let us get through this morning without casualties, so we still have the same spirit by Noon, please Jesus!*

"The ship is at Quarters, sir," Lt. Farley reported from below on the quarterdeck.

"Very well, Mister Farley," Lewrie replied, turning grim. "How far off are we, Mister Wickersham?"

"Mile and a half, I make it, sir," the Sailing Master answered. "In eight to nine fathoms of water, so far. At the angle we're closing the shore, we'll be in about six fathoms when we're a mile off."

"That'll be close enough, sir," Lewrie told him. "And there are no surprises marked on your charts?"

"None 'til we get within four fathoms, sir," Wickersham assured him. "Old ship wrecks here and there."

"Very well," Lewrie said, nodding, then raised his telescope to take another long look at the hills where they had seen batteries. Those hills were three points off the starboard bows, slowly sliding more abeam when the guns in their narrow ports could fire without any risky angling of the truck carriages which might put too much of a strain on recoil tackle and breeching ropes.

The enemy had no restrictions. As Lewrie watched, thick blossoms of gunsmoke burst ashore, followed a second or two later by the distant *Crumps!* of their discharges, and Lewrie's stomach muscles tightened as he listened intently for the keen of approaching shot. There was no sound, but there were large splashes where roundshot hit the sea at least half a mile short, bounding up from First Graze to skip and create weaker, smaller splashes before the balls lost their momentum and left disturbed patches of foam where they sank.

"Count the guns!" Lewrie snapped, as the enemy reloaded.

"One mile offshore, sir," Mr. Wickersham cautioned.

"Thankee, Mister Wickersham," Lewrie said. "Mister Farley, you may open!"

"Aye, sir. All guns to aim for the right-hand battery," the First Officer told waiting Midshipmen. "We will fire by broadside."

Off they scampered to relay the order to the officers in charge of the gun-decks, who shouted the command to gun-captains and Quarter-Gunners, which delayed firing 'til truck carriages had been aligned, quoin blocks adjusted, and rough aim had been determined.

At last, word came to the quarterdeck that the guns were ready.

"On the up-roll, by broadside . . . fire!" Farley yelled.

Vigilance trembled to the titanic roars, and felt staggered and pushed seaward a foot or so by the force of recoil, shuddering to the weight of metal and wood truck carriages rolling back to the extent of the stout breeching ropes. The view of the shore was blotted completely out for a long minute before the dense fogbank of smoke blew away. Lewrie trotted aft to the flag lockers and taffrails to peer through its remnants.

There! Three, four, five, six spurts of powder smoke blossomed ashore from the right-hand battery as he watched, and this time there were moans of disturbed air rising in pitch as roundshot approached. Six tall feathers of spray leaped skyward within a cable of the ship, skipping up from First Graze and skipping to within one hundred yards before sinking.

A whole battery of six, Lewrie thought; *That means another full battery on the other hill, a lot more then we first thought. This may be a* very *warm morning! They've re-enforced since the first scout was made.*

"On the up-roll, by broadside . . . fire!" Farley shouted, and the world shook and howled once more.

Despite the smoke and the reduced view, Lewrie paced back forward to the corner of the poop deck where the starboard ladderway led down, remembering to take his time and look stern as a proper Captain ought. Over the roar of gun carriages being run out on the oak decks, there were distant *Crumps!* as the French guns replied. Among the drifting pall of smoke from *Vigilance*'s guns, feathers of spray leaped into life, even farther away from her sides.

"On the up-roll, by broadside . . . fire!" Farley yelled again.

All Lewrie could do was listen in such a cloud, cocking his head to one side. Three, four . . . and that was it? A long moment later, and there came the thuds of six more, as regular as a metronome.

Six from the further battery, but only four from the first? he puzzled; *Are we doin' some damage over there?*

"Check fire, Mister Farley!" he shouted down to the quarterdeck. "Let the smoke clear a bit so the gun-captains can adjust their aim!"

In the sudden, relative silence, Lewrie could even hear the mews of frightened seagulls as a swarm of them crossed *Vigilance*'s stern on their way to safety farther out to sea, and he watched them fly away for a moment before returning his attention landwards.

There! In the thinning haze of his ship's gunsmoke, six feathers of spray leaped to life, closer to her side this time, scattered like birdshot. One ball skipped from First Graze off the sea to the Second Graze, bounding along slow enough to almost be seen, before it slammed into the ship's timbers below the black, tarred gunwale and bounced off.

"Gabions or fascines, sir!" Lt. Farley shouted triumphantly.

"Is that even *English*?" Lewrie snapped back.

"The gun batteries, sir," Farley said, pointing with his telescope in one hand, "I got a good look at them, and they appear to be dug in, with a berm of earth in front of them, and bundles of tree branches and wicker baskets full of earth for protection! Fascines and gabions, sir! Little protection at all!"

Lewrie took a look for himself, now that most of the gunsmoke had blown clear, and made out fresh earth, horizontal wooden bundles, and fat baskets either side of the enemy artillery pieces, much like a crenallated wall . . . but a most insubstantial wall.

"Resume fire on the near battery, Mister Farley," Lewrie said, adding "and thankee for the explanation."

"Aye, sir! Pass word! On the up-roll, by broadside, fire!"

Vigilance rolled to starboard several degrees, then rolled back to decks-level, then a few degrees to larboard, then hung there, on the up-roll long enough for the jutting black iron guns to speak one more time, and jerk back in recoil, some now hot enough to leap from the decks a few inches and thud down with audible crashes. After a few more broadsides, barrels and carriages could leap almost a foot as they careened inboard, landing off-angle as the breeching ropes snubbed them, and threatening feet and legs of the men who served them!

Lewrie looked down into the waist where gunners were swabbing out with water-soaked rammers, and gun-captains laying their leather thumb stalls atop the vents to choke off any air that might ignite what powder and smouldering flannel cartridge bags remained from creating a smaller explosion that could shoot the rammer out the gun-port and snap the rammer man's arm like a twig.

They worked in bare feet for sure grip on the oak decks, those gun crewmen, with scarves round their heads to cover their ears, and the glim candle wax they used to save their hearing; bare chested, some of them, for early mornings in Autumn in the Mediterranean were hot. Ship's boys came forward with their containers, delivering the fresh cartridge bags to be rammed down snug. Two roundshot went in for double-shotting, then a damp oakum wadding.

Gun-captains pricked the cartridges with spikes down the vents, then drew the flintlock strikers to half-cock and primed their pans with fine-mealed powder from the flasks hung round their necks. Then, the men tailed on the run-out tackles, heaving their massive charges to thud against the port sills, carefully arranging the ropes of the run-out tackles and recoil tackles so they'd run smooth, and not take a man's foot off. Strikers were drawn to full cock, crews shied away, and gun-captains drew the trigger lines taut.

"On the up-roll, by broadside . . . fire!" And the guns leaped and stampeded back to be re-fed all over again, and it was like watching a robotic raree-show about the miracle of steam power and many moving parts, as regular as clockworks.

There was a thud as another French ball struck the hull, and this time, Lewrie clearly heard the whine-humming of a roundshot as it soared high overhead, right through the maze of rigging and sails, and passed far out to sea beyond.

Two, then six, Lewrie told himself as he counted the far-off *Crumps!* of enemy artillery; *We're hurtin' 'em! We're shootin' them t'pieces!*

"Sir!" Lt. Farley exclaimed, "I think we're drawing level with the western battery! Should we shift fire?"

Lewrie peered hard with his day-glass, eyes watering from the bitter gunsmoke, and, as the smoke thinned once more, saw that the ship had sailed beyond the first battery, which now lay two points abaft of abeam, and the one to the west was now coming up abeam.

"Check fire and shift aim, aye, Mister Farley!" Lewrie crowed. "I think we've hurt the first'un bad enough!"

He spared a glance at the eastern battery, delighting to see that protective gabions had been split and spilled, and that half of the openings between them no longer showed artillery pieces.

"Ready below? On the up-roll, by broadside . . . fire!" Farley yelled, his voice going raspy from the smoke and over-exertion. And twenty-six guns on both upper and lower decks roared almost as one.

One forlorn *Crump!* from one French battery, then five from the other, and more shot splashes near *Vigilance,* then the *Thonk!* of a hit on her timbers, once more bouncing off, for 12-pounder roundshot fired from a mile away could never make a real impression on solid British oak.

"On the up-roll . . . fire!"

On it went, several more broadsides, double-shotted, keened cross the waters to slam into the hillside, the protective gabions and fascines, carom off iron barrels with loud clangs, shatter wheels and dis-mount gun barrels, and now and then cut French gunners in half.

Even with candle wax crammed in his ears, Lewrie listened for return fire, leaning out over the bulwarks, trying to count the distant bellows from

French guns over the cries of officers below shouting the litany of "Run out your guns!" then "Prime your guns!"

He heard only four shots in reply, and they were no longer the metronomic steadiness of before, but stuttering; after two more broadsides from *Vigilance,* he could only hear three, then two.

"Targets are well abaft of abeam, sir!" Lt. Farley reported.

"Cease fire, Mister Farley," Lewrie called down to him. "I do believe we've done a good morning's work. Secure, swab out, and wash the barrels down."

"Aye, sir!" Farley replied, sounding pleased but weary.

"Mister Wickersham, alter course seaward," Lewrie ordered. "We will take position ahead of the transport column, and make a goodly offing."

"Straight up the Strait, sir?" Wickersham asked, making a lame joke of it. "Trail our colours to Reggio di Calabria once more?"

"Aye, and glower at 'em most fiercely as we do so!" Lewrie told him with a relieved laugh.

He left the poop deck, went to the starboard ladderway of the quarterdeck, and descended to the waist; his mouth was as dry as if he had been biting musket cartridges and getting gunpowder grit in his teeth. All round him, his sailors were securing the guns, cleaning them inside and out, removing flintlock strikers, inserting tompions in the muzzles, and running the carriages out to thump against the port sills, closed now, to bowse them securely.

They were as blown as racehorses after a long course, squatting on the truck carriages, or sprawling on deck, weary from their labours and the repetitive demands of loading, running out, and firing, their slop-trousers and loose shirts smutted with gunsmoke, but they were cheerful, joshing each other after a hard hour's work. Some queued up at the scuttlebutts to draw up a sip of water, and Lewrie joined one queue, telling the nearest men that they had all but silenced two entire French batteries, relating what he had seen from a better vantage post high above theirs.

When it was his turn, Lewrie drew up the long, thin, test-tube-like dipper and tipped it up to swish round his dry mouth, swallowing, and japing that he'd just taken a gram of gunpowder aboard.

"It'll be a quiet day, lads," Lewrie told them, "for we'll sail up north for one more scare for the French, then it's back to Milazzo."

"We gonna shoot up the bridge again, Cap'um sir?" a man asked.

"No, that's a dead'un," Lewrie told him. "We're going to look in at

Eufemia Lamezia one more time, the place we cruised past before, then home. Unless they've placed guns up there, we may not even have to shoot the place up. No drills this morning, and enjoy your rum issue, and a dinner with meat, it bein' a Tuesday."

With that, he returned to the quarterdeck and took his proper place at the windward corner, watching as the large main course, which had been drawn up to the yard against the risk of setting it afire by the blasts of their own guns, being lowered and filling with wind, feeling his ship begin to surge forward with more drive, creating a most welcome breeze to blow away the stink of powder smoke, and ease the day's warmth. Soon, once *Vigilance* was at the head of the column once more, and all ships outbound from the coast to deeper waters, he would go aft to his cabins, sluice the powder smuts and gritty feeling from his face and hands, get a tall mug of ginger beer, cool tea, or ale, and really stanch his thirst as he wrote up the account of the morning's action for his own log, Admiral Charlton, and Admiralty in far-off London.

Well, I'll write the first *draft, and Severance can polish it up and do the copies,* he told himself, feeling quite satisfied with the cruise so far; *And after that, I may even take a wee nap!*

BOOK FOUR

Maxime red effecta, viri; timor omnis abesto,
quad superest!

Mighty deeds have we wrought, my men; for
what remains, away with all fear!
                            —*AENEID*, BOOK XI, LINES 14–15
                            VIRGIL

CHAPTER TWENTY-NINE

$\mathcal{A}$nchored firmly, bow and stern, sir," Lt. Farley reported after some turns had been made round the capstans to equalise the scope of cable paid out. "Back atop our shoal of beef and pork bones," Farley added with a grin.

"Very well, sir," Lewrie said, appreciating the wee jest. In a way, it could be a complaint made by the people aboard a ship of the line that spent far too long in port, without sea time or action.

"Just about at the same place," the Sailing Master commented, after taking compass bearings on prominent features of the harbour at Milazzo, and referring to a handmade chart, marking off where those bearings crossed. "As you can see . . ."

He was interrupted by several arrivals at the base of one of the ladders to the quarterdeck; people looking for boats; the Bosun, so he could row round the ship and see to the squaring of the yards, and the tautness of both running and standing rigging; the Purser, Mr. Blundell, who wanted to go ashore for fresh provisions, and even had a list in hand; and Lt. Greenleaf.

"And why do you need a boat, sir?" Lewrie asked.

"Why, for the mail, sir!" Greenleaf exclaimed, pointing over the starboard bulwarks towards the Army encampment. "I just happened to notice that, once all ships were anchored, they hoisted the Have Mail signal by the beach."

"Go along with Mister Blundell and fetch the mail sack back," Lewrie told him, "He'll be busy with his shopping, I'm sure, so you can return whilst he's doing so."

"Might need more boats, to fetch our purchases aboard, sir," the Purser said. "Pasta, rice, fresh fruits, baked bread?" he ticked off on his fingers.

"Take a Mid with you, Mister Greenleaf," Lewrie said, "so the barge can shuttle back and forth as needed. And if you need another, Mister Blundell, have the Army signallers hoist Send Boats."

"Thank you, sir," Blundell said, doffing his hat. "Ehm, might there be anything you need that I could fetch off, sir?"

"Nothing 'til tomorrow, no, Mister Blundell," Lewrie said as he turned to go aft to his cabins.

Why does he always *make it sound as if I'm dealin' with a smuggler?* Lewrie asked himself; *A request for a barricoe of Chianti turns into a Midnight deal under the table, cheatin' the Customs!*

In his time aboard *Vigilance*, Lewrie had found that Mr. Blundell was a *reasonably* honest Purser, but his experiences with that sort in other ships made him think that *all* of them were "Nip Cheeses," fly and shifty folk who'd steal the coins from their dead mothers' eyes.

He took off his hat and hung it on a peg near the door, coming to an amused halt, for Dasher's doe rabbit, Harriet, was out of her wooden cage, dashing round the cabins in great leaps and hops, being chased by his cat, Chalky, who would leap, pounce, and corner it, eye to eye, nose to twitching nose, before they were off in another tail chase.

It was amusing 'til he crossed the cabin to his desk, finding fresh rabbit pellets on his carpets.

"Let's clean that up, straightaway," Lewrie said, sitting down to finish his report of the past days' actions.

"Aye, sir," Dasher said, "but they are havin' fun. Chalky an' Harriet are more playmates like. He only pats her with his claws in when he catches her."

"Scarin' the shit out of her," Lewrie wryly pointed out. "Pity that rabbits don't take to litter boxes."

He read over the parts of the report already written for a minute or so, then announced, "There'll be fresh vegetables comin' aboard for her. And mail from home."

"Newspapers, yea!" Dasher cried, for since his first day in the old HMS *Sapphire,* he had turned into a voracious reader. He did not read well or fast, and could make an eight-page newspaper last a whole week, but he was getting better at it.

Newspapers, huzzah! Lewrie thought, glancing aft to the larboard quarter gallery, where his supply of papers had dwindled; *If we don't get a fresh lot, I'll be usin' clam shells t'clean my bum!*

"Did ye hear, Mister Severance?" Dasher enthused. "There's mail comin'!"

"Glad to hear it, Dasher," Sub-Lt. Severance, Lewrie's clerk and aide said with a wee grin, though it would be his job to sort it all out for the wardroom, Midshipmen's cockpit, petty officers, then the rest of the hands, and see it distributed.

"Something wet, sir?" Deavers enquired.

"Cool tea?" Lewrie asked, hopefully.

"All but a swallow gone, sir," Deavers had to tell him. "But, we've plenty of ale."

"Ale will do," Lewrie said, returning to his reading. Pulling a fresh sheet of paper from his desk, and dipping his steel-nib pen in the inkwell, he began scribbling details of the last of their excursions, their appearance off Eufemia Lamezia.

After the sorting, Lewrie could almost rub his hands in glee and anticipation as he beheld a goodly pile of letters on his desk top. First off there was a thick letter, more like a packet, from Admiral Charlton. He broke the seal and spread it out, finding a hand-drawn chart of the port of Monasterace, with some depths jotted along the shore, idle guesses at the terrain behind the beaches, and not much else. Charlton congratulated him on his latest landings, and the damage done to the French convoy network and that bridge.

As you may see, though, since no Landings were envisioned at Monas-
terace, when the entire coast was attacked in the Spring, and its lack of
Importance at that time, there is little that I, or the ships of my Squadron,

*can offer you, now that the place has become of more Import, to the
Disturbance of French supply routes.*

Lewrie shrugged and heaved a small sigh of dis-appointment that there
would be little aid from that quarter; he would have to hope for fresher
intelligence from Mr. Quill and his minions.

*Anent your Relieving Lt. John Dickson of his ship, I Concur. You stand in
Lieu of the Authority that you would possess had Admiralty found it meet
to appoint you a Commodore of your Squadron, and had the perfect Right
to do so to improve the Effiency, and Morale, of all ships under you.*

    *From your description of this young man's abysmal Attitude towards
those under him, Officers, Petty and Etc., and his high-handed Treat-
ment and Dislike of his Common Seamen, had he been aboard a Ship in
my Command, I would have broken him for much the same Reasons that
forced you to act!*

Lewrie vowed that he would file this letter away for safekeeping; he had
a feeling that Lt. Dickson was the sort who had "interest" and patronage
from powerful people, and he'd need proof that he had not relieved him
for personal reasons!

*Do please keep me Apprised of your Intentions regarding Monasterace, for
it seems a grand place to strike and, as always, feel free to request any
additional Forces you might need from me to further your Success.*

    *Upon that head, I have had a continual Correspondence with Brig.
Gen. Caruthers, which has become Pestiferous, really, wondering how at
least one of his Regiments could sail with you sometime in the near
Future, the obtaining of suitable Transports, boarding nets, barges, and
Etc., and some means by which he could land some of his Artillery.*

"Schemin' bastard," Lewrie growled under his breath. "He just won't
quit 'til he's got Tarrant and the Ninety-Fourth, and takes over the whole
enterprise!"

He put Charlton's packet into a desk drawer and turned to more of his
mail. There was a letter from Capt. Middleton back in London, despair-
ing of supplying him any more transports, barges, or enough Navy crews
and junior officers to man them. Indeed, he warned, whilst Lewrie's ac-

counts of successful landings or bombardments went down well with Admiralty, there was a growing chorus of naysayers who decried the cost in *matériel*, in men, and the continued funding. Mentions had been made in the House of Commons as to whether Navy money could not be better spent, or whether the "experiment," as Middleton bracketed the word, was worth the candle! Middleton also wrote that a Brigadier of the Sicily garrison . . . un-named . . . had written his Member, who had read the letter in the Commons, suggesting that the enterprise should be *expanded*, with more transports, more troops, and a means of landing artillery to over-power *any* French force they met!

"Not just a *schemin'* bastard, but a *back-stabbin'* shit, too!" Lewrie fumed. "What do they want back home? More of it, or nothing? Mine arse on a band-box!"

There were some official letters from Admiralty, all of little importance, and then he could at last open his personal mail!

"Oh, my sweet, darling girl," Lewrie cooed as he opened one of Jessica's letters. She was having a *splendid* Season, a grand Summer! The weather had never been better, though in late season the Thames was beginning to smell a bit rank, but round Mayfair and the parks, it was barely noticeable, and the acres of flower gardens went a long way towards creating a delightful myriad of pleasant scents. She and his father, Sir Hugo, went riding in Hyde Park quite often, even if she had to use a proper lady's saddle, but they had also coached to his country estate at Anglesgreen several times where she could don breeches under her gowns and ride more confidently astride where no one could complain.

> *Alan dearest, when you return from the sea you will not recognise our back garden, which now has an octagonal gazebo set upon a raised wooden platform in the middle, with pea gravel pathways leading to it, round it, and to the stables & back gate. Half of the lawn I have turned to flower beds down each side and along the back, and so far (please God!) everything that we have planted has blossomed out most wondrously, especially the lavender!*

Half of one page of her long letter held a coloured pencil sketch of it, and it did look showy and pleasant.

Jessica assured him that everything, and everyone, under their roof was going well, and seemed pleased to be employed there, with no petty spats, though she did miss Yeovill's cooking. Oh, the cook she had hired when Alan had taken Yeovill back to sea was perfectly competent, especially at pastries and such, and when she had people over to dine, the fellow could produce a very acceptable repast.

Household expenses were well under control, and the "pin money" he'd set aside for her was more than adequate, with a decent sum left over at the end of each month. She'd had the swifts in to clean all the chimneys in preparation for Autumn, and had had a plasterer in to add some scrollwork in the front parlour high up near the crown mouldings, but he was not to fret over the cost, for she had done well with her painting, so far. She had done a portrait for £25, and had sold some more of her fanciful children's art through Ackermann's Repository in the Strand, and a new gallery in Old Bond Street; young farm animals she'd first sketched at Anglesgreen, frisky horses, children playing on the green commons in the village, along with the usual kittens and puppies, rabbits, and the rare wild deer that grazed in the woods up on the slopes above Sir Hugo's country house.

Alan, I must now make a Confession to you. The Harpsichord I purchased from Clotworthy Chute's emporium was not a reasonable £60, but an Hundred and Ten, and that was at a reduced Rate from what it really should have cost. I and Mr. Chute worked out a Payment Plan for so much for so many months, as a great Favour to his Friendship with you. At last, is is completely paid for, and when you see it and hear it, you will, I trust, understand why I simply had to have it. Its tones are most Melodic and Pleasing, and its Appearance, with such a Plethora of intricately inlaid filigrees is a Wonder to behold! When you return from the sea, I assure you that the Music to be made upon it will soothe your very Soul!

He wasn't sure whether to write and complain about her profligacy, kick Clotworthy's arse for bilking her, or praise her thrift and cleverness! At that steep price, he'd expect the damned thing to play itself!

Her father was doing well, though still in fret about the expedition that he couldn't afford to take part in. Obviously, finding evidence of Phoenicians, Romans, or the Knights Templars in America before Columbus would have to be done without him!

Her family, brothers and sisters and their offspring were all in health, as were the host of childhood friends and their husbands. The fellow in Law had made King's Bench; the man in Steam had gotten a contract for a cotton spinning mill; Heiliger the beer man was now shipping small beer to Deptford, Chatham, and Sheerness. Hard as he tried, Lewrie could not recall much of these gentlemen, for they'd been so many civilians with whom he had little in common to talk about.

Ah! Lewrie's dog, Bisquit, a former ship's mascot, was loving his back garden romps with Jessica's spaniel, Rembrandt, their walks in Hyde or Green Park, Jessica assured him, and Bully, the kitchen terrier, had turned out to be a superb ratter below stairs.

There were more letters from her to savour, and a pile from old naval friends, his father, and his former in-laws, the Chiswick brothers, Governour and Burgess, and Lewrie moved to the settee to sprawl for a long afternoon's perusal.

The Marine sentry outside the cabin door slammed his musket butt and boots on the deck, to announce a Midshipman Randolph, who entered with a folded over note.

"From Leftenant-Colonel Tarrant ashore, sir," he crisply said.

Lewrie took it and read it; an invitation to supper ashore at Tarrant's headquarters that evening. Mr. Quill had come from Messina, and would also dine with them. With fresh news about Monasterace!

"Aha!" Lewrie said, springing to his feet and going to his desk. "Do carry my reply to the Colonel, Mister Randolph," he said as he penned a quick response saying that he would indeed dine with him.

Tempting as the rest of his mail was, Lewrie opened the drawer that held Adm. Charlton's packet and pulled out the rough drawing to pore over once more. There was nothing for it; he would have to go to the chart space and compare the sketch to the printed charts. With any luck, Quill would have more to tell them, but in the meantime . . . he heaved a sigh, rolled up the sketch, fetched his mug of ale, and went out to the quarterdeck, calling for a lit candle to be fetched. The chart space would be dim and airless, and most likely much warmer than his cabins. He might even require a refill of ale.

CHAPTER THIRTY

*T*hey dined round half-past six in the early evening as the heat of a sweltering day had abated, beginning with cool white wine on the canvas-covered gallery in the front of Col. Tarrant's headquarters. Major Gittings was present, as was Mr. Quill, who looked perspired and uncomfortable in his usual black broadcloth wool suitings, but other than that he seemed cheerful enough. It might have been the weather, but Tarrant's hound, Dante, was much subdued, seemingly happy to sprawl in the shade by his master's chair without his usual rambunctiousness, near a shallow pan of freshwater from which he lapped now and again.

Supper was served indoors, a rather light repast of chicken and rice, followed by crisp grilled seafood and pasta in a white cream sauce, with various vegetable removes. They did not talk "business," not yet. That followed the Port, fruit, and local sweet bisquits. Finally, Col. Tarrant cleared his throat, tossed back his Port, and announced that Mr. Quill had some "trade" for them.

"It took some doing, sirs," Quill said with some pride in his voice, "but I finally prevailed upon *Don* Julio that the French were too strong in Melito di Porto Salvo, and we would not be raiding that place anytime soon, and that Monasterace was our choice for a raid. He relented, none too graciously, mind, and despatched some of his men to scout it out for us. If I may, sirs?"

He rose from the table, opened a canvas portfolio, and spread out a folded map on the table. Along with it was a sketch of the town and beaches, done from sea level as they would see it from the decks of their ships.

"As you can see, their work is quite thorough," Quill said as he tapped various points on the chart. "He sent that fellow 'Tonio, the one he publicly embarrassed, and kept the fee for himself, but 'Tonio did a good job, regardless. His cover was that he was smuggling good quality wine, so he could enter harbour and have a look-round of the area, drink and eat ashore in local establishments, and get to know some of the people, and what they think of the French, which is not much."

"Is there a garrison?" Major Gittings asked.

"Not so much a garrison as a detachment," Quill told him. "Only fourty or so men from their Commissariat to repair waggons that need work, and maintain a herd of draught animals, horses, mules, and such. From what 'Tonio gathered, and what he saw with his own eyes, is that the only armed troops are the escorts that pass through with every road convoy, fully loaded, or returning empty to Naples."

"How many convoys?" Tarrant asked, leaning over the table and the chart. "And what sort of escorts?"

"He was there three days before he sold off all his wine, and he reckoned that at least three west-bound convoys come through each day," Quill explained, referring to a sheaf of notes, "and another three come back from Reggio di Calabria empty. An hour or so before sunset, 'Tonio saw at least three stop and camp for the night, then get back on the road again a little before eight in the morning. As to escorts, it looks to be at least a troop of cavalry with each, Colonel.

"The French have set up a sort of system, sirs," Quill went on, a finger straying into the stylised marks that indicated the hills and mountains behind the coast. "From roughly here, there's the one road coming down to Monasterace, but up here, where 'Tonio and his men couldn't go, of course, there's a branch road that forks off the main one. Loaded convoys take the shorter route, though it is a rough path, whilst empty waggons take the longer way round, to make way for the ones full of supplies."

"Artillery?" Lewrie asked.

"None in the town that 'Tonio could see," Quill assured him with a faint grin, "and no guns passing through, either. Though, after you and your ship mauled the French so badly at Crotone, Catanzaro, and Melito, they may shift a battery there soon. By the by, Mr. Silvester got a letter to me, and said that the French have seemed to have given up on repairing or re-building that bridge above Pizzo, so these road convoys will be diverting through the mountains for some time to come!"

"A mauling, you say?" Major Gittings said, for he had not heard the details of *Vigilance*'s recent cruise yet and Lewrie had to fill him in, which made Gittings's eyes light up with humour.

"More Port, gentlemen?" Col. Tarrant asked with good cheer. "Or, might cool white wine suit? Seems a done deal, then, what? No guns in the vicinity, no garrison to speak of, and only random troops of cavalry to deal with. If we creep in when it's utterly dark, as we did at Bova Marina, we could destroy three or *four* convoys, *and* the replacement animals along with them."

"Burn the waggon and wheelwrights' shops, and take away their tools to dump in the sea, as well," Major Gittings contributed, "that the French would have to replace at great cost."

"There's no reason to even enter the town itself," Lewrie said, taking another long look at the handmade chart. "This long stretch of beach just east of it should suit us. Five fathoms of water for anchoring, about . . . a third of a mile off, is it?"

"Ehm, closer to half a mile, my notes say, sir," Quill informed him after a quick shuffle of papers. "West of the town, you could be within a third of a mile, but the beaches there are rockier, 'Tonio reported."

"Hmm," was Lewrie's comment to that. "The eastern beaches might be better for the transports, then, and I can place *Vigilance* closer to shore to the west to cover the troops, should there be any nasty surprises. This long ridge," he noted, tracing a finger along a rise behind the town, "any information on that?"

"'Tonio and his crew didn't go very far inland beyond the town, but he did make an observation that the ridge is rather low," Quill supplied. "Vineyards or olive groves, and some fruit orchards, with some thin woods? The paddocks for fresh horses and mules are laid out in front of it, along with huge piles of hay. Hundreds of the beasts, and all hungry, hah hah."

Lewrie turned his attention to the sea level drawing of the coast, and the ridge did appear to be low, compared to the hills just behind it, and none too steep, either.

"It ain't Locri or Siderno, thank God," Lewrie said with a wee laugh. "The French could've hidden an *army* behind those. Yes . . . I can anchor here, west of the town, and nought but the church steeple t'get in the way of my guns. I got very little from Admiral Charlton that's helpful, so . . . we'll go with what our local criminals have gleaned for us, right? Colonel Tarrant, would you be needing anything else from Charlton?"

"Hmm, don't see as how I would, sir," Tarrant said, shrugging. "He's no transports of his own, no barges, and none of his Marines are trained for this sort of work, so . . . unless you wish a frigate or a smaller warship to back you up, I don't think so, no."

"In that case, we've all we need, but fair weather," Lewrie concluded.

"The fewer to share the glory, hey?" Major Gittings said with a laugh. "I'll brief our company officers in the morning, after they've recovered."

"Hey?" Mr. Quill asked, perplexed. "Recovered? From what?"

"Stick your head outside and listen to them," Gittings urged. "There will be thick heads at breakfast, haw!"

Sure enough, even through the wooden walls of Colonel Tarrant's house, they could faintly hear snatches of song, load roars of merriment, and chanting to spur on contestants in some drinking games.

To shake off the rust from the sailors on all five ships, Lewrie ordered all those assigned to the rowing barges, those who would stand guard over them and the beach 'til the Army returned, ashore to drill at musketry, the bayonet, and their cutlasses.

In the tumult of armed men swarming over the bulwarks and going down the boarding nets aboard *Vigilance*, Lewrie stepped down from the quarterdeck to speak with his Commission officers.

"Ah, Mister Grace," Lewrie said, "do hand your accoutrements over to Mister Dickson. He'll be taking your place. And Mister Greenleaf? You'll stand in for Mister Rutland, who's busy with his other duties."

"Oh, sir!" Lt. Grace faintly objected. "Just when I've gotten good at it!"

"So long a naval career, so much still to learn," Lewrie cooed.

"I'll fetch my personal weapons, sir, and thankee!" Greenleaf exclaimed, filled with sudden eagerness. "Can't let Rutland have *all* the fun, now can we, sir?" he said, dashing off.

"Hah!" Grace japed as he took off his ammunition pouch, musket, and bayonet to give to Dickson, "Beg pardon, sir, but 'fun,' and Lieutenant Rutland, will *never* go together!"

"Oh, I don't know," Lewrie said, "I'm mortal-certain that I saw him smile, once."

"Thank you, sir," Lt. Dickson said in a formal manner.

"Captain Whitehead and our Marines'll most-like go inland on the Ninety-Fourth's flank," Lewrie explained, "so that'll leave you and Mister Greenleaf in charge of *all* our armed sailors ashore, Mister Dickson. The transports' parties will be under a Sub-Lieutenant or a Midshipman, and they'll be looking to you two for orders. In the past it's been little more than hold the beach, slouch about, and wait for the troops to come back to be rowed out, but one never can tell. You must hold your ground the best you're able, protect the boats at all costs, and fight back 'til the Ninety-Fourth or our Marines come to your rescue.

"Like horses, do you, Mister Dickson?" Lewrie asked him.

"Ehm, what, sir? Horses? Aye, as a matter of fact I do," the astonished officer rejoined.

"If you're attacked by cavalry escorts from the convoys, horses hate a bayonet or sword point to their mouths or noses," Lewrie cautioned him. "Keep 'em at a distance 'fore they bite your face off."

"I see, sir," Dickson hesitantly said, fearing that he was being twitted.

"It worked for me at the Battle of Blaauwberg when we re-took Cape Town from the Dutch," Lewrie told him, "though the Dutch horse had a very narrow front to attack us, up the spine of a *kop*. There will be infantry officers ashore to do the instructions today, so I expect that you and Greenleaf pay them close attention."

"I will, sir, and thank you, again," Dickson said, not sure if that "war story" was to be taken at full value.

"Off with you, then, lads!" Lewrie called out to one and all, "and we'll save your rum ration for you!"

Lt. Greenleaf came puffing up from the officers' wardroom below, in a clank of sword, two pair of pistols in his pockets and waist sash, a musket and bayonet in his hands, and a quickly assembled rucksack of edibles over one shoulder, with a full wood water canteen spanking his bottom as he and Dickson were the last ones over the rails, onto the nets, and down to the waiting barges.

Dickson settled in on the aftermost thwart of a barge, next to Midshipman Chenery at the tiller, looking up the side of the warship, and at

Captain Lewrie, who was leaning out over the bulwarks to watch the boats row ashore, and he didn't quite know what to think.

Losing command of *Coromandel* still rankled, and he could easily despise Lewrie for doing so, yet . . . once installed aboard *Vigilance*, as her junior-most officer, which also felt like an insult despite his date of commission being newer than Grace's, he had been either trusted to do his duties capably, or ignored, as if his come-down had never happened, and accepted into the wardroom society as just another new man. No one had twitted him or looked down on him since his arrival, as he'd expected, though he was certain that the questions about his abilities were there, but unspoken. Dickson was coming to feel almost comfortable in the wardroom, in their drinking games, their musical evenings in port, and in their banter over meals. Lt. Grace, whom he had been prepared to dismiss as a lower-class lout plucked from the Nore fisheries, had proven himself to be a most capable sea officer, even if his table manners were still a trifle clumsy, but Grace was a person whom Dickson was coming to *like*!

"Out oars, larboard," Midshipman Chenery called. "Shove off, bow man."

One thing was certain to Dickson, that he had done more exciting things than he ever had aboard other ships, since coming aboard *Vigilance*; more weapons drills, more live gunnery in action against French batteries, and now a chance to be second-in-command over the hundreds of armed sailors and the twenty-four barges that would land troops in a large-scale raid in a few days. There was even the prospect of face-to-face battle with the enemy, sword-to-sword!

Now, how could he continue to secretly sulk in the face of that?

CHAPTER THIRTY-ONE

*T*o achieve complete surprise, *Vigilance* led the squadron round Sicily once more, standing well clear of the Sou'eastern-most Cape of Passaro into the Ionian Sea. There was no timetable for when they hit Monasterace, no set day, and it was good that there wasn't, for once bound Easterly fourty miles or more off the Sicilian coast, weather decided to be un-cooperative.

The Autumn winds were fickle, breezing up in early morning, and fading away round mid-day, providing little relief from the glare of the sun that brought such oppressive heat, and the heat and the lack of wind was un-relenting 'til very late in the afternoons, leaving the sails slacking and then filling for hopeful moments, and all of the ships rolling and swan-ning cross seas hammered flat, and in those late afternoons, the almost cloudless skies would blossom with thunderheads and high-piled cumu-lus but never brought cooler winds or the promise of rain nearby. Darker storms would smear the horizons, forked with lightning and visible cur-tains of blessed rain, but not upon the five ships struggling East'rd, who were lucky to log five knots for most of the days. It was only round sun-downs when the winds increased to acceptable levels, rustling loose cloth-ing and drying perspiration in a form of relief. But, at sundown, sails were reduced so that all ships could keep station with each other in the dark, and five knots or so was the progress through the night.

Lewrie had thought to advance Eastward to 17 degrees East, and 38 degrees North before altering course to the Nor'west to close the coast off Monasterace a bit before Midnight, but, once attaining that point on the charts, the storms which had toyed with them over the horizons caught up with them, and it was wind and rain by buckets for two days, heaving large breaking surf on the landing beaches, making it impossible to do much more than stagger about under storm trys'ls and wait for the weather to subside.

"I'm beginnin' t'think that the gods of war are against us, Mister Farley," Lewrie sourly commented to his First Officer as they stood on the quarterdeck under a seething shower in their oiled foul weather coats and hats.

"I was just about to say, sir," Farley replied, craning his head upwards to look at the iron-bar streaming of the commissioning pendant. "Like Odysseus or Aeneas in the classic tales, denied their homes or a safe harbour by a vengeful bitch goddess."

Lewrie leaned far out over the windward bulwarks to look astern at the transports following *Vigilance*, the trailing ships almost lost behind brief curtains of rain, and all of them hobby-horsing in huge plunges that buried their bows, then lifted them up in clouds of sea spray. They were rolling, too, like the arm of a metronome.

"I wonder if any of our soldiers'll be able t'stand erect, does this keep up," Lewrie commented. "We've never kept 'em at sea this long, before. And nobody's usin' the 'heads,' 'less they can breathe seawater."

Lt. Farley joined him at the bulwarks to peer aft at the lead transport, *Bristol Lass*. "We've had a problem about that, too, sir," Farley said as he drew himself inboard. "The 'seats of ease' up forrud are underwater half the time, whether it's raining hard or not, and everyone below has been voiding their bowels or bladders into buckets. The Mids, Master at Arms, and the Ship's Corporals are keeping wary eyes out to prevent it, but there's only so much they can do. If it continues, I'll be presenting you with a *long* list of defaulters at Captain's Mast."

"Lord, flog half the crew?" Lewrie spat. "Right before we go ashore, or right after a successful raid? That'll do *wonders* for morale. But . . . we can't tolerate it."

"Unless we *allow* it for a time, sir," Farley suggested.

"Allow it?" Lewrie gawped.

"Set aside an area as temporary 'heads,' sir," Farley went on, "and assign a man from each eight-man mess as the bucket man for the day to carry the full ones up to be dumped over the lee side. Then, as soon as the weather clears, go back to the regular routine."

"Hmm, it might work," Lewrie said, scratching the stubble on his chin. "Arrange that, and pass word to the crew that it's a *very* temporary necessity. Aye, see to it, Mister Farley. And pray that the weather moderates before the ship reeks like a Dung Wharf scow."

"Very good, sir," Farley replied. "It's better than losing a man or two overboard whilst their trousers are down."

From the forecastle belfry Eight Bells chimed in quick pairs, to mark the end of one watch and the beginning of the Forenoon. Men off-watch came boiling up the ladderways from the lower gun and mess deck to relieve those who had been drenched during the Morning Watch. Lewrie noted that some sailors going off-watch removed their foul weather gear and handed them over to their replacements, prompting a thought that he must speak with the Purser about indenting for oiled coats and hats for all hands, though how long would it be for them to arrive from England in a supply packet was un-knowable.

"I'll be aft," Lewrie said as Lt. Farley was relieved by Lt. Greenleaf. "And if anybody sees the sun at the end of the Forenoon, summon me to witness *that* miracle."

It was dry in his cabins, thankfully, though dank, muggy, and humid. He stripped off his foul weather gear, and the towel that he had worn round his neck, now almost sopping wet. Rain had seeped onto his shirt collar and neck-stock, anyway, but none had trickled down his back. He asked Deavers for a dry towel, removed his stock and spread his collars, then patted down his hair, neck, face, and hands before he went to his desk. A fresh cup of hot coffee with sugar and goat's milk appeared without his asking as he spread out the hand-drawn map of the coast to study it one more time.

"We have some leaks in the overhead, sir," Deavers told him as he hung up the wet towel to dry out. "Just some wee drips, so far."

Lewrie raised his head to peer round his cabins, searching for them. He heard them: wee plops into buckets, metal pitchers, and the soup tureen from the dining coach sideboard. Chalky's ceramic water bowl had been moved to catch the drips, too, and the cat was sitting rapt, looking up to follow waterdrops, and trying to catch them with one paw, tail swishing the canvas deck chequer as if it was the finest sport.

"Can't pay the seams with hot tar in this weather," Lewrie said. "At least the cat's amused. Has anything vital gotten wet, yet?"

"No, sir," Deavers told him, "though I've put some sailcloth on your bed-cot, and the dining table just to be sure."

"We'll just have to cope," Lewrie said, returning to the map.

The operation looked straightforward enough; transports to the eastern beaches, *Vigilance* just a bit to the west of the town proper, and the Marines going in on Monasterace's outskirts; and the ship's guns able to cover the 94th's front, the town, and the far ridge at almost a mile's range. Any road convoys encamped for the night would be easy targets, too, as would the crowded horse and mule pens beyond.

Lewrie had envisioned a Midnight landing at first, but Colonel Tarrant and Major Gittings had worried that if the ship's guns had to be employed, they would be firing blind into utter darkness, and the immense stabbing flames from the muzzles would blind them further. It had been agreed that they needed to close the coast and anchor when it was still too dark for watchers ashore to spot them and sound an alarm, but Tarrant's soldiers would need a *touch* of dawn to be able to fire and reload. They had settled upon 5 A.M. as the best compromise.

How I'm t'get 'em ashore round then's the rub, Lewrie thought, as he leaned back in his chair and took a sip of his coffee; *wind and surf, sailin' in at what average speed? If there's no garrison, we could land any hour of the morning. Of course, the waggoners would see us long before and be gone by the time we drop anchors.*

It felt to him that his job was just becoming harder, more full of "ifs" that *couldn't* be planned for!

I just hope I'm bright enough t'pull this'un off! he thought.

The rain stopped just before sundown, though the winds still had to moderate, and the seas to subside. Overhead, the sky was a blank grey overcast, dull and unbroken. At least the "bucket brigade" from below could stop, and hot suppers could be boiled up in the galleys aboard all five ships. By the time Lewrie took a later supper of his own, a few stars could be identified in gaps in the clouds, and Lewrie could retire for the night, confident that the morning would bring a sky clear enough for sun sights at Noon, and improved conditions on the beaches to the north.

The evening air in the great-cabins was now cool and dank, with the upper halves of some sash windows in the transom opened for air, and Lewrie rolled into his bed-cot after snuffing the last candle in his shirt and slop-trousers, boots set near to hand atop one of his sea chests. He pulled a patterned quilt up to mid-chest and plumped up his pillows, yawning and stretching his whole body, even wriggling his stockinged toes.

Alter course round eight A.M. tomorrow, he promised himself; *Get our position fixed at Noon Sights, then I'll take* Vigilance *inshore 'til we sight the coast, then return to the squadron.*

There was a preparatory *Mrrf!* from below, then the thump of his cat landing atop the quilt by his left thigh, and Lewrie reached out to stroke Chalky's fur, prompting the cat to pad up to his face and press his nose against Lewrie's.

"Fifteen miles off, no closer, puss," Lewrie whispered in the dark, "then we'll stand off-and-on Monasterace 'til it's time t'sail in and anchor. Won't that be fun?"

Chalky flopped onto his side, to nestle against Lewrie's left chest, and to continued stroking, began to softly purr.

CHAPTER THIRTY-TWO

I'm a bloody cod's-head! Lewrie chid himself as *Vigilance* slowly stood shoreward; *My timing's off, and there's no help for it!*

Leadsmen in the foremast chains chanted the depths they found as his ship got within two miles of the coast, and Lewrie bent over the compass binnacle cabinet to hold his pocket watch in the light inside. He was off by at least half an hour or better, and to make things worse, the skies had cleared so completely that a setting moon still faintly illuminated all of his ships, turning their reduced sails into pale grey spectres. *Damn!* he thought; *twenty minutes to six!*

He put away his pocket watch and raised his telescope to peer beyond the foresails at the shore. There were lanthorns glowing along the water-front in Monasterace, some additional lights among the houses and taverns. On either end of the town, and behind it, he could see scattered campfires where teamsters and waggoners slept, where French escort troops drowsed, and by the glow of those fires he could espy a veritable sea of canvas-covered waggons.

No alert, please God, he prayed to himself; *Let 'em be asleep or dead drunk, just a little longer!*

"Steer half a point to larboard, Quartermasters," Lt. Farley directed the helmsmen, speaking in a conspiratorial whisper, as if a louder voice would carry shoreward. "We'll come to anchor just west of the town, in five fathoms," he explained to them.

Lewrie looked down into the ship's waist and was appalled to see the white of sailors' slop-trousers and the white pipe-clayed belts and cross-belts of the Marines. Everyone's slung rucksacks made from sailcloth were as plain as day, too. It was the time of false dawn, and it was just too bright! For a fearful moment, he considered a hasty recall of the whole affair, but . . . ! He raised his telescope one more time to look the town over, and there were so many waggons ashore, seemingly hundreds of them, enough to make up *four* typical convoys, and if he let the landing proceed, their loss, along with the livestock that drew them, *and* the replacement beasts, was just too tempting. It might cost the French supply system half its strength, take months for them to replace, and starve their forces in Calabria of everything!

Lewrie looked aloft at the sails that still drew wind, and at the commissioning pendant, which was curling lazily on the slight breeze, grumbling to himself the night-time lack of wind that had delayed the approach to the coast; something that could not be planned for. He peered again at the land, which was slowly coming closer and closer, and looked to the Sailing Master for an estimate of how far off it still was, but Mr. Wickersham and one of his Master's Mates were intent on their sextants and slates, in mid-determination.

"Eight fathom!" a leadsman called out, much too loud for Lewrie's taste. "Eight fathom t'this line!"

Two miles? Lewrie asked himself. He had pored over the charts so long that they were etched on his memory. The next soundings would be six fathoms, an irregular line of shoaling that paralleled the coast; he could close his eyes and see it plain as day.

"About two miles off yet, sir," Mr. Wickersham whispered.

"Thankee, Mister Wickersham," Lewrie said with a nod, heaving a deep sigh to calm himself. It was *so* damned light, already, and people ashore would be up and stirring, and one startled glance was all it took for the alarm to be raised; just one yawning fisherman on his way to the town docks, one French sentry shaking himself to keep his eyes open out beyond the warming fires at the edge of a clutch of waggons . . . !

"Seems quiet yonder, sir," Mr. Wickersham said.

"Let's pray it stays that way," Lewrie replied.

There was little talking or joshing from the sailors and the Marines gathered in the ship's waist. The loudest sounds were sprung from oak timbers and planking that worked against each other, the wee creaks and squeals of the sheaves in the myriad of pulley blocks, and the rustle of canvas overhead. The ship was moving so slowly that the waterfall rush of the sea down her flanks and under her bows was now a mere whisper.

"Six fathom deep!" the leadsman called out. "Six fathom t'this line!"

"Have them *pass* word," Lewrie snapped. "No damned shouting!"

"Aye, sir," Lt. Farley replied, and turned to speak to a Midshipman on the quarterdeck, who rushed forward to the forecastle.

The light wind, Lewrie thought, raising his telescope once more, peering at the beaches, which now seemed to loom close enough for the ships to run aground on them; *Light surf, no foaming rollers. Good!*

He lowered his telescope to grasp in both hands, fingers taut on the tubes, and closed his eyes to summon up the chart in his mind, wishing that he could dash into the chart space for one last, reassuring look. The coast shoaled gradually hereabouts, with no rocky outcrops marked, and no significant shipwrecks to stumble over. In Italian, the bottom was described as sand, mud, and large gravel, a decent holding ground. *Vigilance* drew seventeen and a half feet right aft, so five fathoms, thirty feet of water, was sufficient to her needs, but she could go into the four-fathom area with no risk to her bottom.

"Five fathoms, sir!" a Midshipman reported from the base of the ladderway in the waist. "The lead line shows five fathoms."

"Come about, sir?" Lt. Farley asked.

"No, hang on another minute," Lewrie suddenly decided, opening his eyes again, and stifling a gasp of alarm at how close the beaches looked.

"Four and a half fathoms, sir!" the Mid announced once word was passed aft.

"Round her up into the wind and be ready t'let go the bower!" Lewrie snapped. "Let go the kedge!"

Hands aloft, draped over the yards with their feet on the swaying foot ropes began taking in the tops'ls, and jibs and stays'ls began to slither down to the deck as the helm was put hard over to swing the ship's bows into the wind. Far aft, the kedge anchor splashed into the sea, its hawser rapidly paying out the hawse hole with a loud rumble. As the winds came more down the centreline of the ship, and what little way she still had fell away, the larboard bow anchor was let go, too.

"Haul the barges up and prepare to dis-embark!" Lewrie ordered, eager to get the boats away and clear of the gun-ports if the guns were needed at once. He looked to his right, down the coast, to see all four transports rounding up, too, bows to the wind with their fore tops'ls flat aback to the masts.

The kedge anchor bit into the bottom, snubbing the ship almost to a stop, and hands sprung to the capstan to begin tightening it so there would be roughly equal scope paid out to both anchors, at which point spring-lines would be set on the hawsers so the ship could be swung a few degrees about to create a greater arc of fire to take on targets ashore.

"Boats are alongside, sir!" a Midshipman reported after leaning far over the bulwarks.

"Away you go, Mister Greenleaf, Mister Whitehead!" Lewrie told the officers waiting in the waist, and, with a great eager shout, the armed sail-ors and Marines swung over the bulwarks and hammock stanchions onto the boarding nets to lower themselves into the waiting barges. It was light enough for Lewrie to see ant-like figures scrambling on the nets on the transports, too, a flood of red coats and blue jackets.

"Come on, get clear!" he muttered impatiently.

"I'd estimate that we are roughly a third of a mile from shore, sir," the Sailing Master announced. "A little closer than we had planned, but . . ." He gave a satisfied shrug.

"Good enough, Mister Wickersham," Lewrie said, distractedly, for the smoke from the convoy encampment's campfires was now joined by an host of smoke skeins rising from almost every chimney. Monasterace and its citizens were waking up and starting their breakfasts!

Two of *Vigilance*'s barges were clear of the ship, oars out but idling to be joined by the other pair, and Lewrie leaned out on the bulwarks, wait-ing to see the first barge crossing close under the up-thrust bow-sprit and jib-boom. There it was, at last, hands stroking hard at their oars! Half a minute later and the second rowed clear. Once a rough line-abreast was formed, Lt. Greenleaf swept an arm and pointed at the beach, and all four barges began to dash for the sands of the beach.

"Mister Farley, we can now open the ports and run out," Lewrie ordered with a great sigh of relief. "Pass word to Mister Grace that he is free to open upon anything threatening."

"Aye, sir," Farley replied, snapping fingers to summon that Mid to run below once more.

Lewrie turned to watch the twenty-four barges off the transports as they formed their own line-abreast on their way shoreward, a snaky and varying line depending on the speed and strength of the individual boat's oarsmen. Lewrie had been in Spanish Florida during the American Revolution, and had gotten a healthy distrust, and dislike, of snakes, fearful of the nights when they had camped rough. He'd seen more than his share of deadly rattlesnakes, too, and as he watched the transport barges go in, the word "sidewinder" sprang to mind, for that seemed to be the way the line-abreast weaved.

Two hundred yards . . . one hundred yards to go, and he tried to be stoic as the barges breasted the last glistening waves as they broke upon the beach, then oars were tossed vertically from the thole pins as the barges' bows slithered onto the sands, bow men springing out into shin-deep water to drag them onto firmer purchases. Lewrie could at last let his pent breath out. They were ashore!

He raised his telescope to watch Marine Captain Whitehead and his Lieutenants waving to form the ship's Marines into two ranks and smaller four-man sections to scout ahead as they left the beach and crossed the overwash barrows. Down the coast to the east of the town the 94th was advancing in skirmish order with the King's Colour and the Regimental Colour in the centre, gaily and brightly streaming.

"All they need is a brass band, sir," Lt. Farley commented, "or at least some fifers."

"Too noisy," Lewrie countered. "We don't wish to wake the French *too* early. Springs rigged on the cables?"

"Aye, sir," Farley told him.

"Deck, there!" a mainmast lookout shouted down. "Enemy sodjers in th' town! Comin' outta th' houses!"

"Oh, Christ!" Lewrie gawped, quickly raising his telescope to see for himself. "Pass word to Mister Grace. He is to take the *town* under fire, by broadside, and I don't care if he blows the bloody place to brick dust!"

There were dozens of men in blue coats and shakoes, white cross-belts stark in the pre-dawn light. They came rushing out of waterfront houses, stores, and warehouses by files, already dressed and booted, and under arms. More of them were emerging from the houses on the eastern edge of town, wee triangular company pennants flying in their haste to lead the soldiers onward.

"Mister Farley, have two nine-pounders fired to alert our shore parties, and hoist Number Ten . . . Enemy In Sight!" Lewrie snapped.

They were prepared for us, waitin' for us to get ashore, he thought; *By God, we've been* betrayed!

CHAPTER THIRTY-THREE

*W*hat the Devil?" Lt. Greenleaf exclaimed as two loud cannon shots erupted. He had just gotten his armed sailors settled in decent cover beyond the overwash barrows above the beach, where wind-sculpted and salt-stunted shrubbery stood chest high, and had taken a welcome sip of water from his canteen, and almost dropped it in alarm, turning to gawp at the ship. "Enemy In Sight?" he barked as the signal flag soared up the halliard.

Greenleaf stood fully erect to peer over the tangled shrubs at Captain Whitehead, who had turned to look behind him when the alert roared out. Whitehead heaved a great, exaggerated shrug to Greenleaf, then turned back to his Marines, ordering them to load and prime, then kneel to await whatever was coming. Pairs of scouts dashed out from either flank, suddenly moving warily and hunched over as if in dread of sharpshooters.

"Scouts are showing two shakoes, sir," the Regimental Sergeant-Major crisply reported to Colonel Tarrant, near the Colour party.

Two shakoes held aloft on the muzzles of the scouts' muskets meant that a large party of enemy had been spotted to their front.

"Which scout parties, Sar'n-Major?" Tarrant asked, pulling out a pocket telescope for his own look-see.

"Left flank and centre parties, sir," was the crisp reply.

"Both Light Companies to deploy to the left and front in chain order," Tarrant decided. "Scouts to retire, and the Line and Grenadier Companies to form line, there, in two ranks." He pointed with his telescope at a line of low old stone wall half-hidden in low shrubs.

Tarrant and the Sergeant-Major turned when they heard the two cannon shots from *Vigilance,* and saw the lone signal flag, wondering what it meant, for Enemy In Sight had not been displayed to them in the past, and it was not a part of the slim signals book that the Navy had shared with them.

"Enemy to our front, sir!" a runner shouted as he came dashing back from one of the Light Companies. "Enemy is infantry! Comin' from the waggon camps!"

He was quickly followed by a second runner, who shouted that the French were pouring out of buildings in the town, too, and Col. Tarrant could turn his head to see those, what looked to be at least half of a regiment, forming up in three-deep ranks from the town centre and the eastern edges.

"Some bastard's sold us out, Sar'n-Major," Tarrant spat as he trotted forward to stay in front of his rapidly advancing companies. "Take position along the wall, and be ready to hold fast, lads! We've a proper fight ahead! And we're going to *skin* the bastards!"

He hoped, anyway, though knowing that this morning would be a grim business. What else he might have said was swallowed by a stupendous roar as HMS *Vigilance* lit up in a full broadside, wreathing herself in a fogbank of powder smoke shot through with defiant jets of muzzle flashes. Down range of that titanic noise was nigh-deafening as upper deck 9-pounders, 18-pounders, and lower deck 24-pounders hurled iron roundshot at Monasterace and the French soldiers, that roundshot humming and skreeing through the air, rising in tone as it neared, followed by more crashes as the walls of houses, shops, and stores, and the trading warehouses facing the sea were blown apart, whole walls collapsing in vast clouds of plaster, wood laths, laid stone, and old mortar, smothering and crushing enemy soldiers too late off the mark to get outside and form up, and scything through French infantry.

"My word, sir!" the Sergeant-Major gasped.

"Indeed, Sar'n-Major," Tarrant said, feeling that not all was lost with Lewrie's guns backing him up. "Most impressive!"

"Shot, sir!" Lt. Farley exclaimed as he heard several cannon balls zoom past, high above the rigging. "They've artillery somewhere!"

"Well, of course they do, sir," Lewrie gravelled, "what's a good ambush without 'em? Up on that low ridge behind the town's my guess, among the orchards and olive groves, most-like. A well-laid plan they put together. 'Til we've fended off the enemy troops, though, we'll just have to take it."

"Deck there!" a lookout high above shouted down. "Enemy troops a'comin' from th' waggon camps left o' th' town!"

"An experienced Midshipman to the cross-trees, Mister Farley," Lewrie ordered, "someone who can make educated guesses as to their strength, and knows the difference 'tween infantry and cavalry. And do pass word to Mister Grace that he's to shift aim a bit to the left, for now, to keep 'em off the Marines and our landing party."

As Lewrie went up to the poop deck for a better view, _Vigilance_ thundered and shuddered as gun crews used crow-levers to raise the aft ends of the truck carriages to train their guns a bit to the left, as powder monkeys scampered up and down the ladderways to and from the powder magazines with fresh cartridge or to fetch more. Sailors tugged and grunted on the run-out tackles to sweat their heavy charges back to the port-sills for the next broadside.

"Prime!" Lt. Grace could be heard yelling through a brass speaking trumpet. "Cock you locks!" and older Midshipmen, standing in for officers, echoed his orders, 'til . . .

"By broadside . . . fire!"

Marine Captain Whitehead could now see the French infantry that inclined towards his position in the rough shrubbery, what looked to him to be at least two entire companies already in three-deep ranks, and taking mincing steps to their right to extend and form a front directly meant for his small party of Marines.

Whitehead heaved a grim sigh, pondering when he would order his men to fix bayonets, which would make reloading their Short India Pattern Tower muskets more awkward. He looked over his shoulder at the beach and the waiting boats, which suddenly looked so welcoming. The ship . . . so solid, so safe, and a grand shelter. Black iron muzzles were jerking into the gun-ports once more, and Whitehead drew a mental line from those muzzles to . . . where he *stood*?

"Everyone face down on the ground!" Whitehead roared suddenly. "Lie prone!" and he flung himself belly-down, wriggling frantically to get his canvas rucksack out from under his chest where it had swung on his way to the ground, hoping to get an inch or two lower.

God, so loud! A broadside experienced aboard ship was loud, but this was ear-splitting as the guns of all calibre went off as one, but to be on the receiving end, within a quarter-mile of it, featured the whiz, whoosh, keening of brutal iron passing mere yards above his head! He thought that the stiff stems of wild grass bent from the dragon's breath of disturbed air!

There were no explosive shells, just solid roundshot, but the earth under his chest heaved and shuddered, thrusting upwards, raising him an inch or so as the shot struck the ground and caromed upwards in great bounds. There were stone crashes as shot shattered the houses from which the French had come, and the fluttery whines of roundshot shards as balls struck something solid and broke into pieces, spraying mutilating bits of themselves in all directions.

And screams! Most welcome screams and death cries in French as roundshot went through those three-deep ranks like a game of bowls!

Capt. Whitehead dared raise his head from nuzzling the dirt and beheld a vast cloud of dust and dirt, as thick as a low-scudding cloud hundreds of yards beyond where his men sheltered, with up-flung clods of earth still pattering down from the massive divots that the shot had torn up. Through it he could see an entire street of the town in tumbled ruin, houses and such collapsed, and massive holes in their slate or terra-cotta tiles.

He dared stand up for a better view, and grinned wolfishly at the sight of those two infantry companies of French soldiers who had been reduced by a third or better, some of them staggering round like drunkards, others standing still and gape-jawed at the sudden ruin of their order, and the mangled bodies of their friends.

"Up, lads, back on your feet!" Whitehead ordered. "By sections, retire to the line of shrubs above the beach, and take positions to repel!"

Whitehead watched them rise and marvel, then step off with one rank guarding the rank that retired a few yards, then stop to guard the retreat of the first.

"Not a man hurt, by God!" he told himself, wondering just how long that would last when the French sorted themselves out.

"Jesus bloody Christ, that was close!" Lt. Greenleaf exclaimed once he stood up from his sudden protective crouch as the shot soared over. "That's our Vigilances, Dickson! They've their eyes in today!"

"Aye, masterful gunnery, sir," Lt. Dickson said in return, awed by being in front of a broadside. "Whew!"

"Whitehead's Marines are falling back to the edge of the beach barrow," Greenleaf said, looking all round. "I'll take half our men to stiffen their right. You take the other half and refuse the left. Just in case the damned Frogs try to bend round us to take the boats."

"Refuse?" Dickson asked, unfamiliar with the term, which was not in the Navy's terminology.

"Space 'em from the last Marine on the left end down to the water," Greenleaf explained. "I read it in a book. I was bored to tears, and the book helped pass the time. Go on with you, me lad."

Dickson looked round for some shelter for his half of the men, and there was almost none. Some could take position in the barrow and in the densely tangled maritime shrubbery that trailed down to bare sand, but from there was only sea grasses, thinly spaced. He felt the sudden need for shovels so he could entrench some of them halfway underground, but shovels and such were aboard *Vigilance,* and taking time to fetch them, *find* where they were stored on the orlop, would take too long, take men away to man the barge to row out . . . !

"Mister Bingley," Dickson called to the portly Midshipman who had conned one of the barges ashore, "assemble a boat crew. We need to shift one of the barges up to this end of the beach and run her ashore as far as she'll go, to form a barricade."

"A barricade, sir?" Bingley asked.

"Aye, Mister Bingley, a barricade," Dickson replied. "Something I read in a book."

"Take in on the kedge springline, Mister Farley," Lewrie ordered. "We need to shift fire on the French troops in front of the Ninety-Fourth before they get into musket range."

Farley raised his telescope for a look at the mass of blue-coat soldiers marching in good order from the waggons behind the right of Monasterace. "That may be iffy at the moment, sir," Farley pointed out. "There are at least two of their companies out in front of the main line, falling back slowly. We could hit them, instead. It's at least three-quarters of a mile range."

Lewrie took a look for himself. He made out two lines of ants in red and white pipe clay, spaced in what he took for chain order in four-man groups, well apart from the other groups, pouring a continual fire at long range from the man on the right, who retired to reload at the left end as the next fellow stepped forward and fired. Wee, silent puffs of powder smoke blossomed above and in front of them as they stoically retired a few yards after each man had taken a shot.

Opposing them were ants in blue coats and white trousers, set out in two-man teams; French Light Infantry moving carefully and slowly forward as the men of the 94th retired.

Voltigeurs, Lewrie suddenly recalled from his minor participation in the Battle of Vimeiro in Portugal some years back; *They call them "Vaulters," "Leapers," or "Grasshoppers."*

Lewrie realised that Lt. Farley was right; as good as his gunners were, as finely as his constant drills and live-fire training had honed them, at that range there would be mistakes, and at the moment it did look to be too close a thing to deprive Tarrant of a single soldier.

He looked for him, and found his white egret-plumed hat by the Colour party, pacing about just behind the rear ranks of his troops.

Christ, let the Frogs form column! Lewrie silently prayed; *If they form a huge block, it'd be the best target in the world for us!*

It appeared, though, that the French commander over yonder had determined that his line would be long enough, and deep enough, to lap round Col. Tarrant's flanks and his shorter line, even when the Light Companies at last fell back to either end of the line.

He *had* to do something, soon! He could not sit safely off the shore and watch the 94th, his Marines, his own sailors and all the sailors off the transports be gobbled up!

Lewrie turned his telescope to look at the large encampments of waggons and beasts, realising that they would never be able to get at them. Horses and mules were being led to the waggons and carts, backed into harnesses, and the outer-most convoy west of the town was already rattling off down the main coast road to carry their supplies to waiting French units.

Laughin' their fool heads off, Lewrie furiously thought.

He had been betrayed, he'd stumbled into a trap from which it didn't look as if he'd be able to escape without heavy casualties, and it hurt like Blazes! And all for nothing, not a single burning waggon or dead draught animal!

"Now, what the Devil are they doing over there?" Farley barked, jutting an arm to the beach west of town. "Are they coming back to the ship?"

Lewrie swung to look at that, too, and spotted one of the barges just shoving off, the last one to the left of the four. Oars thrashed to back-water as it worked itself off the sand and out to hobby-horse on the waves that rolled in, at least an hundred yards out.

"Greenleaf wouldn't allow that sort of cowardice!" Lewrie spat.

But no, the barge swung abeam the beach in deeper water, where the breaking waves surged in beneath it without breaking in surf, and rowed parallel for a while before turning to point at the sand once more, then dashed in, all oarsmen straining as hard and as quickly as they could to drive the barge back onto the sand far out to the left of the other three, and once the bows were aground, more men sprang to lay hold of it and drag it ashore 'til only the stern transom was in the water.

Now what was that about? Lewrie wondered, then turned his attention back to Col. Tarrant's predicament. The two Light Companies out skirmishing in front of his regiment were much closer to their own lines, now, and the French were advancing slowly, still in line.

"Not a broadside, Mister Farley!" Lewrie snapped. "Tell Grace he's to allow the gun-captains to fire as they bear, individually! Hurry! Tarrant needs the support!"

"Aye aye, sir!" Farley replied, turning to the harried Mid who had been scurrying below and back again to pass word once more.

"And I'll have the kedge spring hauled taut!" Lewrie snapped.

Colonel Tarrant could act as stoic as anyone, but the pretence was hard to maintain as he watched his Light Companies fall back from the French advance, yard by yard, and wounded men galled by the French fire stumbled back to the widely spaced bulks of their companies and beyond, to fall into the arms of soldiers along the low stone wall and dense shrubbery, crawl over, and be taken down to the beach to be ministered to by the Surgeon and his litter parties. Some of the four-man units out in front now consisted of only three, or two, still on their feet, and Tarrant could see the heart-breaking sight of men in British red coats and grey trousers sprawled, dead where they fell.

They had not taken many casualties, so far, and most hurts had been accidental, or wounds from which his men would recover after a spell in the airy hospital tent back near Milazzo, and some weeks on light duties. Tarrant was a soldier, had been since his twenties when his family had bought him a commission in another regiment, and he had served between the wars as it were, before transferring to the 94th in hopes of seeing real combat.

That had led him and the 94th to the Walcheren Campaign in Holland, and the rain, mud, sleet, and sickness that had decimated the unit, before being shipped as a skeleton battalion to Malta, and the onus of dull garrison duty.

Unlike most British officers, he had studied his chosen life, had read the manuals and accounts of how other officers had ordered their men about, had won their battles, and he'd read all the commentary written by men such as the late General Sir John Moore, about the need for reform in tactics, in morale, and the need for professionalism in the officer corps.

Now, he was about to use all that knowledge to fight a battle, fight his battalion to the best of his ability, but feared that, for all he'd learned, it might not be enough. He was out-numbered, and the French would *not* form a column that he *might* be able to wrap round from front and two sides and out-shoot them.

Vigilance's guns were firing, again, Tarrant noted, not in one of those crushing broadsides that had scythed away his initial foes, half-ruined the town of Monasterace, and set fires among the tightly packed houses. Individual cannon balls were moaning in the sky, and he was not sure what Lewrie and his sailors were firing at. It was possible that the French had disguised another regiment west of the town among the waggon camps, and those French soldiers were threatening the landing on the beaches to the west.

"Whoo, take 'at, 'Ole Trousers'!" a soldier in the front rank hooted, and men of his Line and Grenadier Companies gave out a cheer.

"Silence in the ranks!" Major Gittings shouted.

"Oh. Lovely," Tarrant said, grinning at last as he saw roundshot striking the ground in front of his skirmishers, among the enemy lines in their right flank. Gaps were being slashed into the three-deep ranks, and French soldiers were being shredded. They still came on at the urging of their officers, shuffling over to stay shoulder-to-shoulder with their mates, closing those gaps, but the roundshot still came moaning in, spurting clouds of earth and dust, creating fresh gaps which had to be filled by shaken men.

Tarrant judged that his Light Companies, with the four-man teams now joining their lines, were about two hundred yards in advance of his position along the low stone wall. The French *Voltigeurs* were about one hundred yards beyond, still scampering about in two-man teams, one man loading for the better shot, so that one could keep up a relatively rapid fire. His Light Companies were now firing by rank, the front rankers taking a shot in volley, then falling back behind their rear-rank men to load, whilst the rear rank stood ready to fire in their turn. At that rate, it would take them several minutes to take their places at either end of the main line. And they were in the way!

"Trumpeter, sound Retire!" Col. Tarrant shouted.

The crisp notes blared out and officers and men of the Light Companies turned to look behind them for a moment, then fired off their last volley, and turned about to trot away at the double-quick for either end of Tarrant's line.

"Now, Lewrie," he muttered, "I've given your guns room. Do your damnedest!"

CHAPTER THIRTY-FOUR

*C*ease fire, Mister Farley!" Lewrie yelled, as he saw Tarrant's advanced soldiers rushing back. "Tell Grace he's to broadside, now! Hurry! Tarrant's given us a clear field!"

Down the ladderways that Midshipman went once more, his tongue lolling out and panting, to pass word to the upper gun-deck and the lower gun-deck, and the guns fell silent for about a minute, long enough for the smoke to blow clear and give gun-captains time, and unclouded views, to take their aim.

"By broadside . . . fire!" the cry came at last, and the ship shuddered to her bones.

"Come on, come on, come on!" Lewrie impatiently groaned as his view of the action ashore was blotted out for a long minute. His ears were ringing, despite the candle wax he'd stuffed into them, and his eyes were watering from the acrid gunpowder fumes, but he needed to see!

At last, the smoke had hazed thin enough for him to raise his telescope and grin at the sight. His beloved guns had smashed into the centre of the French line of battle, not just its right flank, and there were great gaps opened where men had stood moments before, now mangled and flung back with limbs missing, their chests and bowels torn open from the front rank to the rearmost. There had been a gay French Tricolour flag waving, surrounded by boy drummers pattering away with their sticks, and they had disappeared! Some daring soul retrieved the flag and hoisted it erect, at last, and the French line began to shuffle towards the centre, shortening itself as enemy soldiers returned to shoulder-to-shoulder alignment.

"Now *that's* the way!" Col. Tarrant cheered as he watched the enemy line come to a stop to sort themselves out. The light troops in advance of their main line seemed to have forgotten what they were supposed to be doing, most of them turning to look back at the chaos. With the 94th's Light Company skirmishers retired, it *should* have been their turn to fall back and join the rest of their regiment for the main assault, but they seemed averse to entering that maelstrom of artillery fire. French bugles summoned them, but they obeyed slowly, at the walk instead of the trot.

Another broadside from *Vigilance* moaned in, roundshot fired at that range behaving like proper field artillery, scything through the re-formed ranks, but also striking a bit short to bound up and smash through, taking down more soldiers.

"That'll be the last of it, I imagine, Gittings," Tarrant said as the last clouds of dust and dirt subsided. "The French are now too close to us for Lewrie to risk it. We will open at seventy yards, in platoon fire."

"Cease fire, cease fire!" Lewrie was forced to order as the enemy got too near Tarrant's regiment. "Where's another place needin' support, Mister Farley?"

"I don't really see one, sir!" Farley shouted up to the poop deck where Lewrie stood. "There are some French infantry skulking just beyond our Marines, but we've shot them to pieces. There are more to the right of the town, where they were hidden, but they're decimated, too, and going over to join the regiment opposing the Ninety-Fourth. And, there's a sizable block of them along the top of that low ridge, but they aren't moving yet. Their reserves, not yet committed?" he opined.

"Deck, there!" a Midshipman posted in the mainmast cross-trees shouted down. "Cavalry! A squadron, leaving the ridge to the right of the town!"

Lewrie looked for them and found them, a mass of horsemen moving at the trot by fours, and he was tempted to take them under fire, but they were just too far away at the moment, half-masked by the fires set in the town, and looked to be bound for Tarrant's fight-to-come, as backup for that French regiment if Tarrant's men broke.

"Well, just Goddammit!" he gravelled, whooshing out a frustrated breath at his sudden impotence.

"'Ware, sir," Lt. Farley cried again, "it looks as if they're going for our Marines. But the enemy's too close for our fire."

"Mine arse on a . . . !" Lewrie spat, glowering angrily. He would have to be an idle spectator as the Marines . . . *his* Marines! . . . were attacked!

"Be ready, Greenleaf!" Capt. Whitehead called out as the French companies stirred their courage up to step over the bodies of their dead and wounded and begin their advance on his position. "The best sharpshooters . . . lie prone and snipe! Go for the officers and the sergeants with stripes on their sleeves!"

Not much real accuracy could be expected from a smoothbore musket, the Tower musket especially, but in training at the 94th's firing butts, some of his Marines had developed an eye for it. Now, those men threw themselves down to rest their weapons on their narrow-brimmed hats, cocked their firelocks, and waited for the French to come within range.

Bam! A single shot at about eighty yards took down an officer pacing ahead of his men with a sabre drawn and pointing the way. He put a hand to his chest and dropped. *Bam!* A grizzled older fellow with diagonal gold stripes on his sleeve dropped his musket as a ball shattered a thigh bone and swept him off his feet. A young Lieutenant who came dashing forward to replace his dead Captain gave out a loud shriek that the Marines could hear as his head exploded. A Corporal carrying his company pennant went down with a sudden red blossom of blood in the centre of his shirt and waist-coat, and several more were killed or badly wounded before they got within musket range.

"Front rank . . . fire!" Whitehead shouted, and over a dozen of the foe went down, but they were now halting and lifting their own muskets to level them. "Second rank, fire!" Whitehead shouted a tad louder, hoping to shake them and throw off their aim, but the French line was smothered with smoke as they pulled the triggers, and men to either side of White-head were thrown back or spun round.

"Steady, steady, reload and fire at will!" he roared, levelling his own musket.

"Kill the bastards, lads!" Lt. Greenleaf howled somewhere along the Marines' line, and armed sailors volleyed with the Marines. Out away from the centre, and the most powder smoke, Greenleaf could see about thirty or so Frenchmen rushing out to the left, and through the tangled shore scrub, as if to get to the beach and flank their position. " 'Ware, Dickson, mind your left!" Greenleaf shouted.

Dickson needed no warning; he could see the enemy soldiers as they tried to thrash through the dense scrub. He had his twenty men huddled behind the 29-foot barge, weapons ready, but wasn't sure when to fire, for he might only get off one volley before the French were upon them. Dammit, though, the French were too busy keeping their feet as they waded and stumbled through the shrub, their accoutrements getting hung up on every stout twig, and the sight was mightily tempting.

His heart was in his throat, his breath was rapid, and the hilt of his elegant sword felt slippery in his hand. It was Lt. Dickson's first exposure to real combat, and it wasn't even on the deck of a warship! It felt grossly unfair for him to play soldier on land. But he had to do something, the men were looking to him.

It took all he had to stand up and point his sword at the enemy.

"You men closest to the barge," he yelled, "give them a volley!"

Firelocks were drawn back to full cock; sailors squinted down the barrels of their muskets to take rough aim.

"Fire!" Dickson shouted.

Five or six French soldiers had managed to thrash their way to the sandy beach beyond the scrub, and they now spotted the British behind the barge, but they were swept away by that rough volley delivered at about forty yards' range. The ones still in the shrub got wide-eyed and tried to bring their muskets up to shoot back.

"The rest of you, shoot at the bastards in the shrub!" Dickson yelled, remembering that he had an expensive pair of Manton pistols in his coat pockets, and fumbled one out with his left hand.

More French soldiers were hit, knocked back by .75 calibre balls, but they only fell atop the shrub, bouncing as the springy underbrush held them and resisted being crushed.

"Front men, you're reloaded?" Dickson demanded, and got grunts and "Aye ayes" in response. "Front men, fire!"

More French soldiers went down, and the ones still unhurt began to turn about and retreat through the shrub, but making as little progress to the rear as they had when trying to attack.

"Come on, lads!" Dickson yelled, much encouraged. "Follow me! Fix your bayonets, pick up your cutlasses, and . . . repel boarders!"

It was the only thing he could think of as he left the shelter of the barge, ran round the bow, and sprinted towards the edge of the shrub, his Hessian boots twisting and turning at his ankles in the deep, soft sand of the upper beach. A Frenchman swung his musket his way, but Dickson brought up his pistol, cocked the lock with the back of his sword-hand wrist, and shot him in the chest, exulting that he had just killed someone, the first in his life.

His sailors began wading into the scrub themselves, having as difficult a passage as the enemy had had, howling and hurrahing with their bayoneted muskets out-thrust at the nearest fleeing Frenchmen, or slashing at their backs with cutlasses.

There had been thirty or so, Dickson estimated, now he had killed two, and his pistols were empty; five or six dead on the beach, ten or so draped over the scrub bushes, and the rest were fleeing as if mired in cold treacle. A smaller Ordinary Seaman at Dickson's side used a dead Frenchman as a springboard to leap ahead of everyone else and drove the point of his cutlass into a soldier's back, making him scream. Muskets went off and several more Frenchmen died at only ten yards' range, and there were some who were holding their muskets in the air, butt up, trying to surrender. The few who managed to escape the scrub scampered away as fast as they could run, but a volley from Lt. Greenleaf's party on the Marines' flank shot them down, too.

It was suddenly very quiet, but for the moans and whimpers of the wounded and dying. At the top of the overwash at last, Dickson could see that the French attack had been broken, and about an hundred or so French soldiers were milling about far out of musket shot, near the burning houses where they had hidden themselves before the attack was sprung. He saw Marine Captain Whitehead, now hatless, and Lieutenant Greenleaf, his hands and face blackened with gunpowder grit, in a brief conference, which he thought he should join.

"Good Christ," Capt. Whitehead rasped between gulps from his wood canteen. "For a minute there, I thought they'd have us all."

"Got most of their leaders, and they didn't have the will to stand and bear it," Greenleaf said. "Must've killed or wounded half of them," he added, sweeping an arm at the field beyond, where the bodies of French soldiers lay strewn in profusion, most grouped along the line where they had stopped and opened fire.

"I've lost nine dead, and six wounded," Whitehead grimly said. "You, Greenleaf? Dickson?"

"Half my lot," Greenleaf toted up. "Some damned good men."

"I, ehm . . . I don't know," Dickson had to confess, turning to look down to the beach. He saw Midshipman Bingley helping a wounded sailor to a seat on the bow of the barge, and counted at least seven of his men on the ground.

"Best go see," Whitehead told him.

"Good work, though," Greenleaf said, "breaking up that attack."

"Ship's flyin' a signal, sir," Able Seaman John Kitch pointed out, wetting a rag from his canteen to wipe his face.

"Ah, our ship's number, and . . . Recall," Greenleaf read aloud. "The Captain must mean for us to get back aboard before the French try again. Whitehead, I'll need half your Marines to help get that barge down there back in the water. Can the other half remain here and daunt the Frogs long enough for us to gather up the dead and the wounded?"

"Just the wounded," Whitehead said with a negative shake of his head. "We'll have to trust the French to bury our dead. But, we'll gather up our weapons and gear. The Captain will have to read their names without interment into the sea. Wish it was different, but . . . bloody Hell."

"Well, shit," Greenleaf spat. He looked far out beyond the town to witness yet another road convoy get under way, the waggon and the cart wheels, and an host of hooves, begin to raise a cloud of dust.

Untouched, and as safe as houses.

CHAPTER THIRTY-FIVE

*W*orking up their courage," Col. Tarrant said to Major Gittings as the surviving French drummers began a marching beat, and the men in those three-deep ranks, now shoulder-to-shoulder again and looking formidable, came on with their muskets held erect close to their left shoulders, bayonets fixed and glinting with dawn light. A shout rose from them, the *"Vive l'Empereur!"*

"After the mauling the guns gave them, I'm fair amazed that they are still *here*, sir!" Gittings tried to jape.

"Well, they are, unfortunately," Tarrant said with a wince of his face, "and now their blood is up. Does Lady Luck go against us, let me say that it had been a pleasure serving with you all these years, Gittings. I trust I'll see you later," he said, offering his hand which Gittings took and shook firmly.

"Later, sir," Gittings replied most formally and gravely before going down the long line of the 94th to take his proper place.

Down on the beach below the 94th, Lt. Fletcher off the *Bristol Lass*, and Lt. Rutland, now in command of *Coromandel* stood talking together apart from their armed sailors, peering up as the drums and the cries of the French infantry rang out.

They were both adventurous men, responsible men, who found it outside their natures to sit safe and snug aboard their ships when the bulk of their crews took risks ashore, trusting young Midshipmen and Sub-Lieutenants to look after them. Now, those senses of responsibility seemed to have landed them in a predicament.

"Too close, now, for *Vigilance* to continue firing," Fletcher said. "It's all up to Colonel Tarrant and his regiment."

"All on our own, aye," Lt. Rutland said, grimly nodding in his usual dour manner, "and from what his wounded related, he's out-numbered. Wish we could get our people back aboard, first."

"Can't just cut and run, and leave the Army stranded," Fletcher replied. "We'd never live it down. Might even be a courts-martial offence, unless Captain Lewrie orders it."

"Even then, though . . . his fault?" Rutland objected. "He's not that sort of poltroon. If I know anything about him, I'd wager he's trying to lash a raft together so he can come join us."

"Aye, he's a prime scraper, no error," Lt. Fletcher agreed.

They both turned their heads inland again as several men of the 94th known for their shooting skills began to snipe at the French as they came into extreme musket range.

"The French get through the Ninety-Fourth, we'll be fighting right at the surf line, with the remnants of Tarrant's soldiers at our elbows," Fletcher said.

"Oh, I don't know," Lt. Rutland slowly said, looking round the line of twenty-four barges drawn up on the sand, and the knots of seamen from each who were now gripping their muskets, or using whet stones from their rucksacks to put a keener edge on their cutlasses, determined to go game to the last. "You're in command, Fletcher, but let me make a suggestion."

"All ears," Fletcher tried to jape.

"Ten men to each barge makes two hundred and fourty armed men," Rutland told him. "We could wait down here to be swamped, but, do we each take half our lads and tack them onto each end of Tarrant's line, we might just make a difference. They wouldn't be so out-numbered."

"Make a fairer fight, aye," Fletcher said, nodding agreement with his jaw jutted forward in determination. "Better fight up there than wait to be slaughtered. You men!" he suddenly shouted in his best quarterdeck bawl.

"All from the first dozen boats, form up with Lieutenant Rutland. The rest from the other dozen, form on me! We came ashore ready for a fight, and we're going to join one! Come up, come up, and let's go kill some Frenchmen!"

Colonel Tarrant was gloomily studying the approaching French lines, worried that they still had the strength in numbers to wrap round his flanks, out beyond the limits of the low stone walls and the dense shrub when he heard a loud "Huzzah!" and had to turn about to look for the source. His jaw almost dropped open when he saw the packs of sailors coming up from the boats and the beach: scruffy and ill-dressed in slop-trousers and linen shirts, some sporting flat, tarred hats, others in stocking caps with long tassels, cutlasses in their belts, and muskets in their hands. Some wore waist-length blue coats with rows of brass buttons; here and there were Midshipmen with dirks at their sides, or waving curved hangers to urge their men on.

Tarrant had no idea if they could stand and fight like soldiers trained to the work, or break as faint-hearted as civilian militia hastily assembled, but that made no matter; he was welcome for them as the two equal-sized packs trotted to the ends of his line beyond his Light Companies and formed two ragged ranks.

"About eighty yards, do you think, Sar'n-Major?" Tarrant asked his experienced RSM.

"About that distance, sir, yes," The Sergeant-Major estimated, squinting his eyes and raising a thumb to measure against the height of the French in the front rank.

"Ninety-Fourth!" Tarrant bellowed. "By platoons . . . fire!"

The muskets of a third of the battalion erupted almost as one, creating that peculiar *Chuff!* as if they muffled each other's barks. Then the 94th did what the British Army did best, better than any army in the world, as the second third of the line levelled their muskets and took what aim they could to fire, followed by the last third of the line. And by the time they had fired, the first platoon on the right had reloaded and fired again to make a continual rolling hail of .75 calibre ball at the approaching foe, and no one was chanting *"Vive l'Empereur!"* anymore.

Col. Tarrant pressed himself between men in the front rank, up against the shrubs and the thigh-high stone wall to see better, and was heartened by what he saw, for the French commander, unsure if his men could do any damage at long musket shot, was still marching his soldiers into that galling fire, muskets still held erect on their left shoulders, and Frenchmen in his first rank were dying; not in great numbers yet, considering the range and the inaccuracy of the smoothbore muskets, but enough to make them shuffle sideways as they marched to shoulder up against their mates.

Tarrant heard the French drums cease over the roaring and the crackling twig noise made by his battalion's muskets. The French had come to a halt at about fifty yards' range, and their muskets were at high port as they cocked their locks at last and levelled.

"For what we are about to receive," Tarrant whispered, "may the Good Lord make us grateful." He winced as the French fired, hundreds of muzzle flashes, wee clouds of smoke from priming pans and barrels wreathing the enemy.

"Fire!" he heard someone shout over the roaring, and from each end of his line, additional volleys were fired; the Navy was in it at last, waiting for the range to come down to where mostly un-trained sailors could hope to score hits.

French .63 calibre lead balls spanged off the stone wall, and men of his battalion slumped away, some dead, some clawing and grasping at their wounds as they fell. Tarrant heard what sounded like a massive swarm of bees as French balls whipped past and a high *buzz! buzz! buzz!* They were firing high?

But his men were firing and loading steadily, platoon by platoon, joined now and then by crashing volleys from the Navy on both flanks, and it became a battle of attrition at short range, a matter of who could kill the enemy in greater numbers, first.

"Oh, bugger this," Lt. Rutland gravelled. "As thick as a full broadside!" he griped at the vast rising clouds of gunsmoke over both lines which made it harder for his sailors to shoot with any hope of hitting anything. He paced to the left end of his men, noting that the bulk of the French fire was directed at the centre of Tarrant's troops, not so much upon his half of the armed shore party. And he also noted that there was clearer air out to his left and ahead. He could see that his men, and probably Lt. Fletcher's men, had extended the line beyond the length of the enemy, and if he could get his men farther out to the left, and align them at right angles to the French line, his fire could be more effective, as effective as a stern rake on an enemy ship!

"Cease fire!" he roared in a voice that could carry from the quarter-deck to the forecastle in a gale. "Cease fire and reload. We are moving out beyond all this damned smoke! Everyone turn to your left! Now, staying in two files, follow me!"

He put himself at the head of the long two files and led them at a trot away from Tarrant's Light Company. Thirty yards out and they could all see the French line, blazing away almost blind as quickly as they could.

"Follow me, lads!" Lt. Rutland roared again, turning to his right to lead them inland 'til his sailors were looking at the end of the French line, on their right extreme flank, able to look down all three ranks. "Stop here, and turn to your right! Ready to *really* kill some frog-eating bastards? First rank, level! Fire!"

Rutland had gotten them within fifty yards' range before they opened fire. Some Frenchmen on the extreme flank spotted them and gave out warning shouts, but it was too late. The end of their line just crumpled as the first volley took at least twenty men down.

"Second rank . . . fire!" Rutland roared, and more French fell from all three densely packed ranks, and soldiers just beyond began to back away to try and form a second shorter front to refuse their flank, but they were still greatly out-numbered, and a third volley killed more of them and forced them to retreat.

"Ten paces forward!" Rutland ordered to shorten the range.

The French were bunching up, trying to re-form, officers waving swords to direct them, and screaming frantic orders. As they bunched up, though, they were under fire from the Light Company of the 94th, and men fell about as fast as they could be shoved into place.

Rutland's sailors were now firing from only fourty yards' range, and they could not miss such a dense block of men. The French were being whip-sawed, first from their flank, then from the main British line. A full quarter of their strength was now forming a new front at right angles to their main fighting line, but the left end of that line was being hammered by the 94th, and that end was being peeled away, casualty by casualty.

"Uh oh," Lt. Rutland said under his breath, realising that he'd rallied more Frenchmen than he had, ready to open fire on him and his sailors.

⚓

Not so far away, Col. Tarrant noted that the French fire had slackened appreciably, and that *something* was going on out on the left flank. His batsman, Corporal Carson, came panting back from the Light Company on that flank with a report.

"Those daft sailors are out on the enemy flank, sir, shooting them to pieces, and the French have turned hundreds of men their way."

"Good God!" Tarrant gasped, bending low to see under all of the smoke, spotted the armed sailors, the French reaction, and felt hope that this gruesome battle could turn his way.

"Ninety-Fourth!" he shouted. "Fix bayonets! Over the wall with you, and re-form ranks!"

The battalion's fire had to cease as his soldiers reloaded one last round, fixed bayonets, and began to crawl over the top of their wall. Col. Tarrant swung a leg over the wall, threaded his way to the front of the first rank, and drew his sword.

"Ninety-Fourth! Give them the bayonet! Charge!"

A wordless howl, a feral growl came from hundreds of throats as they held their muskets out-thrust from the waist and began to run forward, into enemy fire, with Col. Tarrant in the lead, waving his sword high to urge them on.

The French, in their haste to smother the British with fire, had been firing high and almost un-aimed for some time, slamming their musket butts on the ground to settle the powder charges and balls, firing blindly at a vast curtain of smoke.

Suddenly, out of that smoke pall, hundreds of men in red coats were running at them with bayonets fixed and muskets levelled to skewer them as they tried to reload.

Infantrymen dreaded the burst of spherical shell, the terror of bounding cannon balls that could take off a leg in a twinkling, and they dreaded the hammer blows of lead musket balls that could break bones, pierce lungs, and maim them for life. A quick death with no warning was preferred to the surgeon's saws.

But, what every soldier in any army feared most was the bayonet, and the French were no different. They wavered, groping for their own bayonets, for loading went faster with them sheathed at their sides, but it was too late for most to arm themselves equal to the hated *Anglais*, the *Biftecs*, the Devil *Goddamns*.

Men in the rear ranks just turned and ran for the rear in blind panic.

Some men with loaded muskets fired back, but the French and British lines had only been about fifty yards apart to begin with, and the 94th was on them before they could blink.

Men screamed, back-pedalling into their rear-rank mates, trying to fend off the bayonets with musket butts. More men screamed as they were thrust through their guts, and then it was a manic melee of swung musket butts smashing open French heads, men pinned to the ground with eight inches of steel in their bellies, jack-knifing their legs and arms upwards in Vees to fend off their deaths.

And the French regiment broke, fleeing in dis-organised swarms and trampling over their own officers in their panic-driven haste. A finely uniformed officer on a horse was trying to rally the clumped mass of the refused flank to face the sailors, but someone with his musket loaded shot him in the chest, tumbling him to the ground. That great mass of men, facing two directions at once, saw what was happening to the rest, and began to flee, as well, still being shot down by the sailors' line as they ran.

When the French ran beyond the reach of an extended bayonet, it was the 94th's turn to stop and pant for a second, then raise their loaded muskets and shoot more Frenchmen who were the last to break and run, the closest to them, and the easiest targets. They threw up their hands as bullets took them in the back, tripping and falling on their faces, and the field that led inland was littered with shakoes, fine French leather backpacks, muskets and cartridge boxes, canteens, and anything that could be discarded to let them run faster.

And littered with French dead.

"Loot!" someone in Rutland's lines shouted, and all of them gave out a cheer.

"Hold your places!" Rutland yelled, to little avail.

Sailors began to dash forward to pick over the mass of Frenchmen who had been piled up in windrows where they had tried to re-form and re-fuse the flank, whooping with joy as pockets were turned out, producing *cigarros,* pipes and tobacco pouches, coins, wee leather bottles of *ratafia* or brandy, many rosaries, and the rare pocket watch.

Sailors denied that deposit of potential wealth ran farther out in pursuit of the fleeing French to fall upon those who had been shot dead from behind. They didn't get far with that excursion, though, for HMS *Vigilance* was speaking, again, her guns firing in broadsides, and raising great gouts of earth at the panicked French regiment, and the cavalry squadron which had trotted down from the low ridge, and no one wished to be killed by their own artillery.

"Go on, run for your lives, you bastards!" Lt. Rutland yelled with hands cupped round his mouth, then ordered his greedy sailors to the rear before they got killed.

"Junior officers and Mids, keep order here," he gravelled, then began to walk over to speak with Colonel Tarrant, who was petting and calming the dead French officer's horse, cooing to it and taking hold of the loose reins to lead it in a small circle to take its mind off its fear.

"Colonel," Rutland said, touching the brim of his hat in salute.

"Ah, you're . . . Rutland, that's it," Tarrant said, brightening as he recalled him. "You were one of Lewrie's officers, I believe."

"Aye, sir," Rutland replied, "now in command of *Coromandel*. My men and I will be returning to the beach, and will be ready to carry your people off as soon as you wish to depart."

"Ah, yes," Tarrant said, stroking the horse's nose, "I suppose we've done all we could this morning. Not the result the French wished, is it?" he said, pointing to the field littered with blue-clad dead and moaning, begging wounded. "I and my men owe you a great debt of gratitude for your timely re-enforcement, *and* your inspired move out to their flank. My report shall give you great credit, as will the able assistance from Sir Alan's guns."

"Thank you for that, sir," Rutland said, chin tucked into his shirt collar, and reddening a bit to be praised.

"May take some time, our evacuation," Tarrant went on, thinking to saddle up and ride back to his battalion, but decided not, after seeing the blood that streaked the saddle; his white breeches were already soiled enough. "Wounded to care for, that sort of thing?"

"Aye, sir," Rutland said, turning his head to search for the fallen from his own men, and frowning in concern.

"We may not have burned a single waggon today, but I do think that we may call this engagement a victory, don't you?" Tarrant said with a wee grin as he let the horse go, gave it a slap on the rump, and watched it trot away towards the distant cavalry squadron.

"You could call it that, sir," Rutland agreed.

EPILOGUE

A light rain misted the anchorage near Milazzo, falling from the grey and featureless sky, and there were new leaks from the deck overhead plopping into wood or ceramic containers in Lewrie's great-cabins as he completed his report on the action at Monasterace, and a gloomy report it was. So many Marines killed in action, so many wounded and ashore in the Army surgery. Sailors and a few Mids lost, funerals read over at the starboard entry-port for those recovered to be interred in the deeps, and those they had been forced to leave where they fell.

Damage to the ship had to be noted, along with what repairs had been made after, and what it cost in lumber, Bosuns' stores, and paint, tar, and pitch, which must be replaced from the stores ship at Valletta on Malta.

Men and officers had to be praised, suitable for "Gazetting" in the London papers; Fletcher, Rutland, Greenleaf, Lt. John Dickson, and Marine Captain Whitehead, along with the brave doings of petty officers and individual seamen, as well as Midshipman Charles Chenery, who had ably assisted Lt. Greenleaf in repelling a French attack.

Then came the hopeful conclusions which did little to assuage his chagrin over being bested; so many French guns on the ridge silenced, so many hundreds of French dead and wounded in thwarting a well-planned and well-laid trap that should have utterly destroyed his landing force, all due to treachery and betrayal on *someone's* part that had informed the French not only of the where, but the how as well.

And Lewrie was mortal-certain as to who had betrayed them. It was all he could do to keep his simmering temper in check as he wrote that part.

I'll go shop for a gig, a rowboat, at Milazzo, he told himself; *I'll pay for it out of my own funds, no matter how scruffy it is. I'll not be left out of the next fight for the lack of a boat!*

He had never felt so frustrated and impotent in his life!

It only cheered him a little to write that Col. Tarrant of the 94th had sent him such praise for his gun support that had winnowed the French before the actual engagement, had finished driving them off after they had broken, and daunting every French attempt to move that cavalry squadron and attack his battalion whilst they were busy with retrieving their wounded, burying their dead, and carrying off their weapons before the evacuation, and making that return to the troop transports pacific and un-bothered.

Even if Tarrant had lost about 10 percent of his soldiers in the battle. When next they sallied forth on another raid, the troops would have much more elbow room in their below-deck berthing.

At last, with nothing more to say, he signed his name and set the last page atop the others, leaning back in his desk chair with a heavy sigh, tossing his pen on the desk top to roll about, which made Chalky perk up in hopes of a new play-toy.

Lewrie closed his eyes, feeling wearier than he could ever remember.

Gettin' older, I suppose, he told himself; *Old as the Admirals I've known. Poor bastards. Make a bold plan, then have t'sit back and only watch what happens? Might as well carry a penny whistle at my hip, not a sword, or a pistol! Ain't in my nature!*

"Mister Severance, my report is done," Lewrie said, sitting up erect. "Two fair copies, if you please. Cool ale, as much as he wants, Deavers. His is dry work."

"Aye, sir," his cabin steward said with a grin.

"Thank you, sir," Sub-Lt. Severance said.

The Marine sentry at his door banged his musket butt and his boots to bawl that Midshipman Chenery wished to see the Captain.

"Enter," Lewrie bade, standing up and arching his back.

"Beg pardons, Captain sir," Chenery said, "but there is a signal hoisted ashore. It reads . . . Captain Please Attend."

Lewrie made a face, thinking of how wet he was going to get.

"Very well, Mister Chenery," he said, "do hoist a reply, Will Attend. At least it ain't Captain Repair On Board!"

"Aye, sir," Chenery said with a wee laugh.

"Pass word for my boat crew to assemble, and see that a barge is led up alongside," Lewrie said, shrugging into his everyday coat. "How's your head?" Lewrie asked, pointing to the white bandages that swathed Chenery's head.

"Not too hurtful now, sir," Chenery sheepishly admitted. "It was only a bullet graze. By the time my hair grows back from where Mister Woodbury shaved me and sewed me up, I should be top form."

"Good," Lewrie said with a firm nod, "I mentioned you in my report, but an honourable scar goes down well. Except with your sister."

"Aye, sir," Chenery said, rolling his eyes. "I'll go fetch your boat, sir."

"My old hat and boat cloak, Dasher," Lewrie bade his servant. "And . . . one of my pocket pistols, Turnbow. Just in case the traitor dares show his face to cry innocence."

"Aye, sir!"

Lewrie trudged up the now well-worn path from the beachside pier to Col. Tarrant's headquarters and lodgings. Some attempts to spread sand and gravel to cut down on the mud looked to be an utter failure. He spotted Tarrant's huge shaggy hound, Dante standing on the front gallery under the canvas fly, up on all fours, looking eager to greet and his tail thrashing impishly. Lewrie was going to get muddy, and thank God it would only be his stuffy warm wool boat cloak, too thick and warm for such balmy Mediterranean weather.

He looked over at the small grove of sheltering trees, finding the sort of two-wheeled cart that Mr. Quill usually hired to fetch him out to the Army encampment, and another fine carriage drawn by a pair of sleek horses.

Well, damme! he thought, stunned; *That's Don Julio's coach! Is he here? I'll kill him, swear to God!* He swung his boat cloak back so he could reach into a coat pocket for the loaded single-barrelled gun, ready to draw.

"Don't even think about it!" he snapped at the dog in a black humour that Dante must have been able to sense, for he actually slunk to the far side of the front gallery.

Lewrie opened the door, and Tarrant's orderly, Corporal Carson was there in a trice to take his hat and cloak, and Lewrie walked into the room, where Col. Tarrant and Major Gittings, Mr. Quill, and two of *Don* Julio Caesare's criminal confederates, only one of whom Lewrie knew, the "'Tonio" that had done the scouting for them in the past, stood.

The other was a very lean, erect fellow with long black hair clubbed back at the nape of his neck, a pronounced Roman nose, and a startling pair of black eyes, dressed in burgundy "ditto" suitings over a gold silk old-style long waist-coat, filigreed with flowers.

"Ah, Sir Alan, welcome!" Col. Tarrant greeted him jovially. "Do partake in this excellent white wine, which has been iced, courtesy of our guest, *Signore* Lucca Massimo. Ice from Mount Etna, of all the wonders. *Signore* 'Tonio you know, of course," Tarrant said on. "It is my honour to introduce you to him. *Signore* Massimo, allow me to name to you Captain Sir Alan Lewrie, Baronet and Captain of HMS *Vigilance*."

'Tonio had to translate that since Massimo did not have a word of English, but his gaze was direct, his hand firm as they shook, and his voice was a mild *basso* as he said something in Italian.

"*Signore* Massimo is here to give us reassurances," Tarrant said.

"What sort?" Lewrie asked, his right hand still straying towards his right pocket.

"It seems that the man who betrayed your latest landing is now known, Sir Alan," Mr. Quill spoke up as Corporal Carson got Lewrie a chilled glass of wine. "Unfortunately, it was none other than *Don* Julio Caesare."

"I knew it!" Lewrie spat. "Felt it, rather! The bastard!"

Signore Massimo spouted off a long palaver in Italian, sounding apologetic, and 'Tonio translated for him.

Ten thousand French coins, in gold, though neither Massimo or 'Tonio knew the denomination, or what the French called them. It was just too tempting, and *Don* Julio had passed all that he knew of their plans to one of his *capos* in Reggio di Calabria, the same fellow whose artistic son had drawn the bridge at Pizzo for them. The *capo* had *not* been allowed to keep a single gold coin for his labours; all had been sent to *Don* Julio.

"It would seem that our ah, confederates are a tad more patriotic than *Don* Julio," Mr. Quill interjected. "Or, it was a matter of *Don* Julio's insatiable greed, and his failure to *share* over the years, that resulted in a, ehm . . . change of management, shall we say?"

"*Signore* Massimo assures us that he and his people will do anything possible from here on out to hurt the French any way they can," Col.

Tarrant said, "and help us in any way possible to make their lives as occupiers of all Italy as dangerous and uncomfortable as they can. There will be no more treachery, and we will be allies united to that end."

"Well . . ." Lewrie wheedled, feeling his indignation leave him like the rise of a covey of partridges, and disliking the sudden lack. Dammit, he came to rage like a mad man!

"So, from now on, *Signore* Massimo will be in charge," Mr. Quill said.

"And what of *Don* Julio?" Lewrie demanded.

Massimo said something in Italian, making wide hand gestures and sniggering a bit, and 'Tonio shrugged and translated.

"*Don* Lucca said that Julio Caesare sleeps with the fishes, now," 'Tonio said with an eye roll and a bigger shrug.

"Sleeps with the . . . ?" Lewrie spluttered. "What's that mean?"

"'Full fathom five our felon lies,'" Mr. Quill paraphrased from *The Tempest*, with a smirk, "'of lead his bones are made.'"

"Rope bindings, *Signore Capitano*," 'Tonio supplied, "an anchor at de feet? Somewhere-ah outta there-ah." He pointed seaward.

"Oh," Lewrie twigged. "Mean t'say I can't have the satisfaction of *shootin'* him?"

"No. *Signore*," 'Tonio said. "Too merciful."

"Oh, well . . . mine arse on a band-box," Lewrie said, deflating. "I s'pose that'll have t'do. Aye, I think I will have some of that iced wine. In celebration."

The gathering broke up soon after that, with *Signore* Massimo—*Don* Lucca now . . . making his last vows of co-operation, and the other fellow, 'Tonio, who now seemed to have risen in their organisation to a higher level, saw him out.

The air in Tarrant's lodgings was stuffy and humid from all of the rain, and Lewrie stepped out onto the front gallery to sip some more iced wine and give a relatively dry and mud-free hound a pet or two.

He watched as *Don* Lucca climbed into his carriage, which had been Julio Caesare's, and extend a hand from the lowered sash window in the door. 'Tonio was quick to bow over it and kiss the back of the hand, as if *Don* Lucca was the Archbishop of Canterbury.

Allies like these, Lewrie thought; *They'll be the death of us!*

⚓

Lt. John Dickson was snugger and drier in the wardroom of HMS *Vigilance*, sitting at ease in old buckled shoes instead of Hessian boots, his coat and waist-coat off, and his shirt sleeves rolled up, though he had not undone his neck-stock. By the light of two candles he was writing a letter home, pausing now and then to listen for Lt. Grace to rattle the dice as he and Lt. Greenleaf played backgammon, and Lt. Farley the First Officer mumbled under his breath to alter the ship's books to account for all the men who had been lost and put some other hands into tasks on the watch bills who might be able to replace them.

"Dickson, what do you know about Landsman Ryan?" Farley asked of a sudden. "He's in your division."

"Strength of an ox, but the wit of a flea," Dickson told him. "Best left on the foremast braces, the capstan, and lower deck-gun tackles." He smiled a bit, feeling pleased that the First Officer would value his opinion.

Dickson was writing another long letter home to his father and family, boasting a bit, and only slightly exaggerating his part in the derring-do of the battle ashore, tempering his account of his killing three Frenchmen with the requisite piety and regret that he secretly did not feel. But, it would go down well with the womenfolk.

When he shot his first foe, he had been amazed that he had not been shot himself, first, and the sound of his pistol going off, and the way it had jumped in his sweaty hand, had startled him almost to inaction. The second French soldier he had shot had been more deliberate, and at such close range that the man's dingy white waist-coat had been sooted with gunpowder. He'd had his hands up as if trying to surrender, and the terrified look on his face almost made Dickson titter with glee.

His third kill had been with his sword, and it had not really been necessary; the fellow had already been shot and had dropped his musket, bouncing on the springy scrub bushes as if attempting to get back on his feet, and Dickson had swung his keen-edged sword into the side of his neck, severing an artery, creating a flood of gore, gore that had a distinct coppery smell, and so *much* of it, that Dickson had found delightful. The man had clutched his neck and throat with both hands as if to stave off his death, knowing he was dying, looking Dickson right in the face with wide, terrified eyes, choking, gurgling, those eyes going dull and lifeless, and Dickson had felt like howling aloud with the immense joy of it, like an ancient barbarian. Though, he had been careful to not let the others see his elation.

Such exultant memories, Dickson thought as he paused with his quill pen an inch over the letter paper, almost as good as the moment of orgasm into a squirming, moaning girl!

He shook his head and returned to more important matters, such as his conclusions about this way of making war, which his patrons had requested. Frankly, he thought that this "experiment" in amphibious warfare had come a real cropper, and that Monasterace had been a complete failure which they had escaped by the width of a hair, and that the officer in command of the landing was lacking in forethought.

Does Admiralty and HM Govt. allow this to continue, the enterprise needs a new Approach. Now that it has suffered such Grievous Losses, and is in need of Replacements and Re-enforcement, it may be time for wiser Heads to prevail and declare it too Costly, and bring it to an End.

I will own that being reduced from command of Coromandel to 4th Ofcr. into Vigilance has given me some new Adventures, and a wee modicum of Renown, more so than command of an un-armed trooper, the Results of the Squadron's activities so far have been Niggling; a bridge brought down, road convoys burned and beasts slaughtered, some guns ashore silenced, and some casualties among the French garrisons along the Calabrian coast, all easily replaceable from the Emperor Napoleon's vast Reserves. I fear that Capt. Sir Alan Lewrie, Bt., settles too easily for Pence and Shillings, when he could be going after Guineas.

Do please relay my best Respects to those Gentlemen to whom I owe so much Favour and Advancement, in hopes that my humble Conclusions anent our Doings here in the Ionian Sea will be Useful to them.

Aye, Lewrie had taken him aboard with no seeing recriminations and had allowed him to see real action . . . had allowed him to learn how to kill with glee . . . but Dickson could not find it in his heart to ever forgive him the gross insult of taking his ship away from him and shaming him in the eyes of his former crew.

Sooner or later, this Lewrie would pay.